**Praise for Mary Jo Putney
and her unforgettable novels**

"A complex maze of a story twisted with passion, violence, and redemption. Ms. Putney just gets better and better."—Nora Roberts

"*Veils of Silk* is terrific. Haunting. Wonderful characterization and a true sense that something is really at stake. First-rate work."—Susan Elizabeth Phillips

"I have just read *Silk and Shadows*. 'Read' is perhaps the wrong word—'devoured' might be better. What a fabulous, fabulous book. Bravo!"—Mary Balogh

"A stunning novel of resplendent romance and glorious adventure."—*Romantic Times*

"Ms. Putney has a gift of nonstop sensitivity, wit, charm, and a sense of vitality for telling a wonderful love story."—*Affaire de Coeur*

Books by Mary Jo Putney

Bride Trilogy
The Wild Child
The China Bride
The Bartered Bride

Contemporary Romances
The Burning Point
The Spiral Path

Fallen Angel Series (in order)
Thunder and Roses (Nicholas)
Petals in the Storm (Rafe)
Dancing on the Wind (Lucien)
Angel Rogue (Robin)
Shattered Rainbows (Michael)
River of Fire (Kenneth)
One Perfect Rose (Stephen)

Silk Trilogy
Silk and Shadows
Silk and Secrets
Veils of Silk

Other Historicals
Uncommon Vows
Dearly Beloved
The Bargain
The Rake
Chistmas Revels (short story collection)

Regencies
The Diabolical Baron
Carousel of Hearts
Lady of Fortune

VEILS
OF
SILK

Mary Jo Putney

A SIGNET BOOK

SIGNET
Published by New American Library, a division of
Penguin Putnam Inc., 375 Hudson Street,
New York, New York 10014, U.S.A.
Penguin Books Ltd, 80 Strand,
London WC2R 0RL, England
Penguin Books Australia Ltd,
Ringwood, Victoria, Australia
Penguin Books Canada Ltd, 10 Alcorn Avenue,
Toronto, Ontario, Canada M4V 3B2
Penguin Books (N.Z.) Ltd, 182–190 Wairau Road,
Auckland 10, New Zealand

Penguin Books Ltd, Registered Offices:
Harmondsworth, Middlesex, England

Published by Signet, an imprint of New American Library,
a division of Penguin Putnam Inc. Previously published in an Onyx edition.

First Signet Printing, September 2002
10 9 8 7 6 5 4 3 2 1

To Mary Shea, with thanks for her unique contributions
to my writing career. And also, of course,
for being a friend.

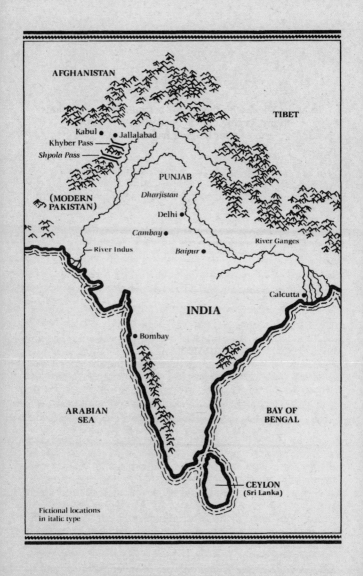

About India

INDIA IS ONE of the most complex and ancient societies in the world, and I was alarmed at the thought of the research that would be required to use it as the setting of *Veils of Silk*. However, since my hero, Ian Cameron, was an officer in the Indian Army, I crossed my fingers and plunged in.

Most Americans tend to think of colonial India as it was in the first half of the twentieth century. Yet that is only a small part of the story, for Britain's long involvement with the subcontinent went through many phases. It began on New Year's Eve in the year 1600, when Queen Elizabeth I signed a charter that gave the Honorable East India Company exclusive trading rights with the East Indies.

The Company was founded for purely commercial purposes, yet by the time of its demise two hundred and fifty years later, it had become the largest corporation the world has ever known. Not only did "John Company" have its own army and navy; it was responsible for almost one-fifth of the world's population.

After 1833, the Company no longer engaged in trade. Instead, it became a corporation that administered India on behalf of Great Britain. The Company and Her Majesty's government were so intertwined that royal troops served side by side with units of the much larger Indian Army. Incidentally, at this time British authority was referred to as the Sirkar; the term "Raj" did not come into use until much later.

Large portions of the subcontinent were never under direct British control. Over five hundred states, ranging from tiny to enormous, were ruled by native princes, a situation that continued right up until Independence in 1947. The princely states had varying degrees of independence, and in

1841 the strongest of them represented a real threat to British power.

The Sirkar had to be wary not only of powerful native princes and marauding frontier tribesmen, but also of Russia, for the tsars would have dearly loved to add India to the expanding Russian Empire. The covert conflict between Russian and British agents in Central Asia became known as "the Great Game," and it set the pattern for the twentieth century Cold War.

Until roughly the end of the first quarter of the nineteenth century, administrators and soldiers had close ties with natives and there was little of the appalling racism which blighted the later colonial period. In fact, since there were few European women in India, the Company encouraged its employees to take native wives or mistresses. Mixed blood was no great stigma, and many distinguished men, such as Prime Minister Lord Liverpool and Field Marshal Lord Roberts, had Indian ancestry.

A paradigm of the racial situation was the elite Indian Army cavalry unit known as Skinner's Horse. It was founded by James Skinner, the son of a British officer and a Rajput girl. By the end of the nineteenth century, James Skinner's mixed blood would have prevented him from serving in the regiment he had founded.

As transportation improved, more Europeans came out to India, and the influx of wives, missionaries, and moralists changed the atmosphere. British officers spent less time with their men, and the social lines hardened, contributing to the infamous Sepoy Mutiny of 1857. The Mutiny sounded the death knell for John Company, for afterward Parliament decided that India was too important to leave in the hands of a private corporation. The British government took over direct rule, including Company institutions such as the much-respected Indian Civil Service and the Indian Army.

A note about language. Most of the languages of Pakistan and northern India are closely related, and are derived from the Persian spoken by earlier invaders. A form of Urdu was the lingua franca of the Army, and Persian was spoken by the elite. Today, Hindi and Urdu are essentially the same language written in different scripts, and are sometimes referred to jointly as Hindustani.

Native princes, the First Afghan War, and early foreshadowings of issues that helped precipitate the Mutiny sixteen years later: for an author, the material was a positive embarrassment of riches. Though the romance of Ian and Laura is the heart of *Veils of Silk,* I have tried to also do justice to the story's fascinating setting. I hope you enjoy your imaginary trip to India as much as I enjoyed writing about it.

To everything there is a season,
And a time to every purpose under the heaven:
A time to be born, and a time to die;
A time to plant, and a time to pluck up that which is planted;
A time to kill, and a time to heal;
A time to break down, and a time to build up;
A time to weep, and a time to laugh;
A time to mourn, and a time to dance;
A time to cast away stones, and a time to gather stones
   together;
A time to embrace, and a time to refrain from embracing;
A time to get, and a time to lose;
A time to keep, and a time to cast away;
A time to rend, and a time to sew;
A time to keep silence, and a time to speak;
A time to love, and a time to hate;
A time of war,
And a time of peace.

Ecclesiastes 3:1–3:8

Prologue

❦   ❦   ❦

Bombay Harbor
September 1841

IAN CAMERON DIDN'T need his one good eye to recognize
Bombay; he could have identified India by scent alone. As
the schooner slowly edged into the harbor, he was assailed
by the aromas of spices and flowers and the faint, underlying odor of decay. He was equally assaulted by the vibrant
colors. The brilliant scarlets and golds were a shock after
the soft hues of the Arabian Sea.

The ship lurched in the trough of a wave and Ian caught
the railing with his left hand. The abrasive sights and sounds
of the docks made him yearn for the stillness of the Central
Asian desert that he had crossed after being rescued from
Bokhara. He had been so focused on bare survival that he
hadn't appreciated how the subtle tones of the desert had
gently reintroduced him to the land of the living.

During the weeks Ian had spent with his sister Juliet and
her husband, Ross, it had taken immense effort to maintain
his control, to make wry jokes and pretend that there was
nothing wrong with him that a little time and a few square
meals wouldn't cure. In spite of his best efforts, he doubted
that he had been entirely convincing. He had been inde-
cently grateful when the time came for him to return alone
to his regiment in India.

Absently Ian rubbed the black patch that covered his right
eye, then ran his fingers through his auburn hair. His head
ached, but less than usual. Perhaps that was because he was,
finally, in the land that had been home for most of his adult
life. During the last two years of hell he had wanted nothing
more than to return to India, and to his fiancée.

Georgina. Golden-haired, graceful Georgina, the most
sought-after English girl in northern India. Ian realized that
his heartbeat was quickening, as much with anxiety as with

anticipation. He forced himself to breathe deeply until the fear subsided. More than India, more than his friends in the regiment, he needed to see Georgina, to hold her in his arms again. Then he would be all right.

His knuckles whitened as his fingers clenched the teak railing. *Pray God he would be all right.*

Chapter 1

❦　❦　❦

Baipur Station
North Central India

NIGHTMARES AGAIN. LAURA awoke gasping and sat up in bed, one flailing hand striking the muslin mosquito curtain that surrounded her. Shaking, she buried her face in her hands.

As her fear eased, she wryly reproached herself for becoming so upset when her nightmares were such old friends. They had begun when she was six years old, when she had first witnessed the savagery that could exist between men and women.

Over time, new scenes had been added to her nightmares. The worst was the catastrophe that had destroyed her childhood, though the images were not limited to her years as Larissa Alexandrovna Karelian. In fact, the most humiliating event had taken place after she had become Laura Stephenson.

These days the nightmares were rare and usually occurred only when change was imminent. Unfortunately, the images had lost none of their vivid emotion. Fear, revulsion, and shame. Passion, disaster, death.

Wearily Laura brushed the tawny hair from her damp forehead. Most of the time she was a levelheaded woman of twenty-four, calm and collected to a fault. Yet in her nightmares she was always a frantic, terrified child, and no amount of maturity had changed that. She supposed she must content herself with being grateful that the bad dreams came only two or three times a year.

It seemed absurd to have nightmares when the change coming was one she welcomed. Tomorrow she and her stepfather would leave on a camping tour of the district, which was the most rewarding part of the yearly routine. Nonethe-

less, the prospect had woken her sleeping demons for one
of their periodic assaults.

The air had cooled to a comfortable temperature and on
the veranda the hanging wind bells tinkled faintly at a cat's-
paw of wind. Laura lifted the mosquito curtain and swung
her bare feet to the floor. Heedless of possible scorpions,
she crossed to the window, where she saw the first light of
dawn in the east. Good; that meant she didn't have to try to
go back to sleep again.

Like many Britons in India, she and her stepfather were
in the habit of taking early morning rides, before the heat
of the day took hold. Soon he would rise and they would
have tea and toast together. After their ride, he would attend
to his duties as district collector and she would see to the
myriad details necessary to close the house and prepare for
their journey. It would be a busy, predictable day.

But for a moment, before turning to light the lamp, Laura
savored the rippling notes of the wind bells and the other
rich sounds and scents of the night. As the breeze caressed
her face, the voluptuous darkness called to her. India's very
nature was passion, and sometimes—too often—she longed
to surrender to it. Unthinkingly she drew her hands down
her body, her palms shaping her breasts and hips as she felt
the warm pulse of flesh beneath the thin muslin shift.

Then, realizing what she was doing, she flushed and
turned away from the dangerous sensuality of the night.

Laura was in the cookhouse selecting supplies when her
father's bearer came to announce that the joint magistrate
was paying a call. She wrinkled her nose—the last thing a
woman packing for a trip needed was visitors—but said,
"Thank you, Padam. Tell Mr. Walford that I'll join him
directly."

She took the covered walkway that led from the cookhouse to the bungalow and went to her bedroom to check
her appearance. As expected after hours of bustling, she
looked as if she had been dragged through a bush backward,
with tendrils of light brown hair rioting in all directions
from the knot at the back of her head. That didn't bother
her much, but her clinging, perspiration-damped gown did,
for the last thing Emery Walford needed was provocation.
She called her maid and changed to a shapeless white muslin dress, then went to greet her guest.

Shaded by trellises covered with flowering vines, the veranda was the most pleasant part of the bungalow. As soon as Laura appeared, the magistrate stood, six feet of shy, handsome young man. "Good afternoon, Laura," he said. "I know you must be busy, but I wanted to say good-bye before you left." He swallowed, then said unimaginatively, "It's very hot today."

"But soon the cool weather will begin, for six glorious months." Laura gestured for him to sit down, choosing a wickerwork chair a safe distance away for herself. Even so, she was uncomfortably aware of his yearning. Ever since she was fourteen, men had desired Laura; even with her eyes closed, she could sense the hot, wordless pressure of male hunger.

Lord only knew why so many men wanted her, for she was no beauty and certainly offered them no encouragement; nonetheless, the desire was almost always there. Most men's admiration was gentlemanly and not a problem, but Emery's blatant longing was embarrassing. That was a pity, for she liked his intelligence and sweet earnestness; they would have been better friends if he did not so obviously lust after her.

As tea and *jelabi* cakes were served, the young magistrate said, "Wouldn't it be better to wait until the cool weather begins before starting the tour? The heat is so enervating."

"But camping is stimulating," she replied with a smile. "We've been looking forward to it for weeks. Father says that touring the district is the most important part of his job."

Eyes downcast, Emery stirred sugar into his tea. "I . . . we'll miss you and your father here at the station."

"We'll be back before you know it," she said briskly.

"Not until almost Christmas." He hesitated, as if trying to work himself up to say something important.

"With pig-sticking season coming, I'm sure you'll be busy," Laura said, craftily changing the subject. "Father said you've gotten a wonderful new horse from an Afghan trader?"

Emery brightened and began describing his new mount, a topic that saw them safely through the tea and cakes. Laura sipped and nodded at the appropriate places, but most of her attention was on the unwelcome knowledge that sooner or later, in spite of her attempts to keep him at bay, Emery

would offer marriage. There was nothing very complimen-
tary about such an offer, for at least half the British bache-
lors she had met in India had proposed to her; European
girls were so scarce that even the most horse-faced and
sharp-tongued received their share of proposals.

Still, though an offer seemed inevitable, she preferred to
postpone it as long as possible because her refusal would
create awkwardness. The handful of Britons in Baipur saw
a great deal of each other, and anything that caused tension
was to be avoided.

What was worse, she would be tempted to accept, for
Emery was amiable and very good-looking. More than once
she had caught herself thinking that he was not at all like
Edward, so perhaps it would be safe to marry him. It would
be a pleasure to have his strong arms around her, to feel his
lips and his hands . . .

Whenever her thoughts reached that point, speculation
was drowned by a wave of panic. The problem was not
Emery, but her, and marriage was out of the question.

Finishing her tea, she stood and offered her hand. "I
don't want to seem rude, Emery, but I must get back to
work. Otherwise we may find ourselves deep in the country
without tea, or quinine, or something equally essential."

"If you need anything, send me a message and I'll see
that it's sent immediately." The magistrate clung to her
hand, not wanting to release her. "Laura . . . there's something I must say."

Before he could say more, salvation appeared in the form
of Laura's stepfather. As Kenneth Stephenson climbed the
steps to the veranda, his perceptive gaze evaluated the tab-
leau and a glint of amusement appeared in his light blue
eyes. "Good day, Emery. You're just leaving?"

The young man flushed and released Laura's hand. "Yes.
I . . . I only stopped by to wish you both a good journey."
His longing gaze touched Laura for a moment, then he
turned away. "I'll look forward to your return."

As the young man collected his horse and rode away,
Laura ordered another tray of refreshments. "You came in
the nick of time, Father. I think Emery was about to declare
himself."

His voice serious, Kenneth Stephenson said, "You could
do much worse. He's a bit callow, but he'll make some girl
an excellent husband. He comes of a good family, he has

an easy disposition, and he's very good at his work. He'll go far."

"The farther the better," Laura said lightly. "I'd rather stay with you—you're much better company."

Her stepfather smiled a little wistfully. "You should find a husband and have a family of your own, Laura."

It was an old argument. "You're my family," she retorted. "You need me to take care of you and see that you eat properly."

He toyed with one of the crisp jelabis. "I won't always be with you, my dear."

Concerned at his tone, Laura studied her stepfather's face. It was easy to overlook the subtle changes in someone she saw every day. Now it was a shock to realize how thin he had become, how many lines there were in his sun-browned skin, and how his hair was now more gray than brown. He was older than most district officers, and living in India was arduous even for those who were young and strong. "You work too hard. Perhaps it's time for you to retire so we can go back to England."

"How do you really feel about India?" he asked. "I'd be content to spend the rest of my life here, but it's a hard life for a young woman. I sometimes wonder if you're just pretending to be happy so I won't feel guilty about bringing you here."

"You didn't 'bring' me—I insisted on coming with you, remember?" Laura gazed absently at the lush green countryside as she considered what to say. "I'm not sorry to live here. The land and people are fascinating, and I understand why you love them so. Yet even after five years, I find this country alien. I'll never understand it."

"One needn't understand to love," he said affectionately. "There's an intense Russian side of you that I'll never understand, but I don't love you any the less because of that."

"I'm not Russian—I'm a civilized Englishwoman." To prove it, she poured herself more tea and added a large dollop of milk. "I just happened to be born in Russia."

"And lived there until you were nine. No number of years in England will change that." Kenneth smiled. "When you look at me with those slanting gold eyes, you're the very image of your mother, and no one was more Russian than Tatyana."

"But I'm not like her," Laura said uneasily, "except on the outside."

He shook his head but didn't pursue the point. Catching Laura's gaze with his, he said, "If something happens to me, promise that you won't mourn too long, my dear, and that you'll seriously consider marriage."

Alarmed, Laura set down her teacup and stared at her stepfather. "This is a very strange conversation. Is there something you aren't telling me? Have you been feeling poorly?"

"No, nothing like that." He shrugged his shoulders. "It's just that a Brahmin priest once cast my horoscope and said that I'd die soon after my sixtieth birthday."

And his birthday had been the week before. Feeling as if an icy draft had touched her neck, she exclaimed, "That's nonsense, Father! How could a superstitious heathen know when you'll die?"

"Perhaps the priest was wrong. Then again, perhaps he was right. I've seen many things in India that are inexplicable in western terms," Kenneth said calmly. "I've also acquired some of the fatalism of the East, I think, for the thought of death doesn't bother me. I've taken stock of my life and on balance I'm satisfied with what I've done." He sighed. "But I worry about what will happen to you. I should have paid more attention to money matters, for I haven't much to leave you."

"You've given me everything that matters," she said in a low voice. "You needn't worry—I'll survive very well on my own."

"I know you can manage, but life is more than mere survival," he said gently. "It's also companionship, friendship, love. I worry that you'll choose to spend the rest of your life alone, and miss the chance to have so much more."

Laura bit her lip, unhappily aware that her stepfather had divined her aversion to marriage. It was not a subject she would discuss, even with him, for nothing would change her mind. Nonetheless, she was willing to fib if an untruth would give him peace of mind. "Life is uncertain, especially in India—you could outlive me by twenty years." She gave an exaggerated shudder. "But I promise that if something happens to you, I'll look for a husband. A woman needs a man, if only to kill all the really big bugs. You know how much I hate centipedes."

Kenneth chuckled, his expression easing. "When you marry, I'm sure you'll find other uses for a husband besides killing bugs. When you haven't got me to fuss over, you'll find that you enjoy the company of young men."

Perhaps she would, but she still wouldn't marry. Not ever.

Chapter 2

❦　❦　❦

Cambay Station
Northern India

IN A FEVER to return to his regiment, Ian Cameron spent
only two days in Bombay. After visiting his banker and a
tailor, he bought the best available horse, rifle, and revolver, then set off on the long ride to Cambay. He didn't
bother to send word ahead, for he would arrive almost as
soon as a message would.

He rode northeast through the vast green plains that swept
across India from the Arabian Sea to the Bay of Bengal, but
he found little pleasure in the familiar scenes of cheerful
people, gaudy temples, and patient water buffalo. During
the endless months of darkness in the Black Well of Bokhara, he had believed that if he were set free, if he could
once more stand in the sunlight, his life would return to
normal.

Instead, the darkness of prison seemed to have entered
his soul. Day and night—especially night—he was haunted
by fears that the darkness was on the verge of engulfing him.
Only Georgina could chase the shadows away, and the need
to see her drove him at the fastest pace his horse could
maintain. He had little interest in food or rest. In fact, he
preferred to avoid sleep because of his appalling dreams.
Usually the nightmares were of the Black Well, and he woke
up feeling suffocated and agonizingly alone.

Less often, he had mysterious, inexplicable dreams of
fire—of a raging holocaust that blazed across the land, destroying everything in its path. Then he awoke shaking with
anxiety, convinced that there was something he must do to
stop the fire, but he could never remember what.

On the whole, it was better not to sleep.

The road to the cantonment of the 46th Native Infantry
ran over a ridge. At the top he halted and stared hungrily at

the plain below. Nothing appeared to have changed in the two years he had been gone. In the distance troops were drilling on the *maidan,* the parade ground, their crisp marching and turns stirring up a cloud of dust that floated down the wind. Closer to hand, barracks, supply depots, and bungalows were laid out with military precision along a sprawling grid of roads.

Finally he allowed his gaze to go to Colonel Whitman's spacious bungalow. It was late afternoon, so Georgina should be home, dressing for dinner. If not—well, she wouldn't be far away. Within the next hour or two, she would be in his arms, and then the long nightmare would finally be over.

Impatiently he rode down into the bustling streets, where a scattering of soldiers and civilians were going about their usual business. Curious eyes followed his progress and once or twice he thought he heard his name spoken incredulously, but he didn't stop to talk. There would be time for that later.

When he reached his destination, he dismounted and tethered his horse, then took the bungalow steps two at a time. It would be more considerate to find a place to stay so he could clean up and send a message to inform Georgina of his arrival. But his mother always said that no one died of good news, and he didn't want to wait a moment longer than necessary to see his fiancée.

Ian's knock was answered by the colonel's bearer, Ahmed, who performed the functions of a butler. Unfazed by the visitor's travel-worn appearance, he said politely, "May I help you, sahib?"

"Don't you recognize me, Ahmed?" Ian said, removing his *topi,* the wide-brimmed pith hat that all Europeans wore to protect themselves from the blazing Indian sun.

The bearer's jaw dropped. "Major Cameron?"

"In the flesh. A little older and probably no wiser, but basically sound. Is Miss Georgina in?"

Ahmed said, "She is in the garden room, sahib, but . . ."

Ian cut off the rest of the bearer's sentence. "Don't announce me—I want to surprise her." Then he strode through the bungalow's main room, heart hammering at the knowledge that salvation was just a few feet away.

The garden room was an agreeably shaded section of the veranda that overlooked Mrs. Whitman's spectacular flower beds. And there, like the pot of gold at the end of the rainbow, was Georgina. She hadn't heard Ian's footsteps, so he paused in the doorway to savor the sight of her perched on the wicker sofa, intently working on her embroidery.

Over the months of his captivity her image had blurred in his mind; now he marveled that he could ever have forgotten her delicate features, the angle of her head, the way her bright ringlets shone like spun gold. In her flowing pink gown, she was sweet and clean and utterly feminine, everything he had longed for during the black months of imprisonment.

To see her was to feel that sanity was within his grasp. Softly he said, "Georgina?"

She looked up, then gasped and dropped her embroidery hoop. Her expression was more than surprised; it was horror-struck.

Her reaction made Ian painfully aware of what a sight he must present: bone-thin, dust-covered, wearing a too-loose uniform and a piratical black eye patch. He'd been a fool to come straight here; quite possibly Georgina didn't even recognize him. Striving for lightness, he said, "I admit that I look like a bandit, but surely I haven't changed out of recognition."

"Ian!" She started to rise, then swooned back onto the sofa.

Cursing himself for a thousand kinds of idiot, Ian went to the sofa and adjusted her crumpled figure so that she was lying comfortably with her feet a little higher than her head. She was perfumed and soft and round, exactly as a woman should be.

Her pale gold lashes fluttered open and she stared at him as he knelt beside her. "Ian." She raised an uncertain hand to his cheek. "Merciful heaven, it really is you."

He started to reply, then stopped, feeling as if he had just been stabbed in the stomach. The hand Georgina had raised was her left, and on the third finger she wore a gold band.

He caught her hand and stared at the ring. It was a wedding ring, it couldn't be anything else, and it was paired with a diamond engagement ring that was not the one he had given her.

His vision blurred, going black around the edges. He dropped her hand and stood up, still not quite believing. Then he realized that some of Georgina's roundness was a result of being in the middle months of pregnancy. In a grating voice that he didn't recognize as his own, he said, "I had hoped that absence would make the heart grow fonder, but obviously for you out of sight was out of mind. Is the lucky man anyone I know?"

"Gerry Phelps," she faltered, pressing a hand to her throat.

Of course. The Honorable Gerald Phelps, who had been Ian's friend and rival since they were cadets together at the military academy at Addiscombe, and who had been the most determined of Georgina's other suitors. Ian's face twisted. "I should have guessed. Gerry always wanted you. Why didn't you accept him in the first place instead of pretending to be in love with me?"

Her light voice breaking, Georgina cried, "I wasn't pretending, Ian, but they said you were dead! I cried for a week when the news came."

"Then dried your tears and married Gerry," Ian said bitterly. He glanced again at her swelling waist. "You certainly didn't waste much time in mourning."

She began to cry. Tears didn't diminish her beauty; Georgina had always been able to weep very prettily.

As Ian stared at his former fiancée, he felt something tearing deep inside him, ripping away the mask of normality that he had laboriously maintained ever since he was rescued. Fearing that if he stayed he might lay violent hands on Georgina, Ian spun on his heel and stalked out. She wailed his name as he left, but he didn't look back. After reclaiming his topi from Ahmed, he flung open the front door with a force that made the bungalow walls shake.

He found himself face to face with Gerald Phelps.

Gerry stopped in midstride, his expression a mixture of gladness and guilt. "My God, Ian, you really are alive! Someone told me you'd just ridden in, but I had trouble believing it. It's been so long." He started to raise his hand, as if to shake Ian's, then dropped it. "We all thought you were dead."

"So I have discovered." Ian considered smashing a fist into Gerry's handsome jaw; it might relieve some of his desperate fury. But if he gave in to violence, in his present mood he might do murder; Gerry had never been able to best him in a fight. "Congratulations on your marriage," he said viciously. "I don't know if the best man won, but isn't winning all that counts?"

Without waiting for a response, Ian pushed by the other man and swung onto his mount. Then he set off at the fastest speed the weary horse could manage.

Gerry Phelps watched him go, then went inside to find his wife. Georgina was leaning on the door frame of the garden room, hands knotted together, her face chalky. Gerry wanted to go to her and soothe the distress from her face. Even more, he wanted to hear her say that she was glad she had married him, but her distraught expression stopped him.

Husband and wife simply stared at each other, separated by more than the width of a room. Between them stood the ghost of a man who wasn't dead.

Ian was a quarter of a mile down the road before he realized that he had no idea where he was going. After pulling his horse to a stop, he sagged forward over its neck, no longer able to hold himself upright. The physical exhaustion he had been ignoring now pounded mind and body like the hammers of hell and his breath came in deep, ragged gasps. But far worse than his physical distress was the emotional pain, and a bitter piece of knowledge that he could neither accept nor deny.

Ever since he had been rescued, he had clung to the thought that Georgina would be his redemption; instead, he had found ashes. The darkness in his soul had finally broken free and even the blazing Asiatic sun wasn't enough to dissipate the black mists that swirled through him in waves of suffocating anguish.

Ian had just enough sanity left to know that he was falling to pieces, and he didn't have the faintest damned idea how to stop it. Like a wounded animal, he craved a burrow where he could suffer alone, but the club was too public, there were no hotels, and he would never be able to find a friend's home before he broke down in public.

Rapid hoofbeats sounded on the road behind and a voice shouted his name. Ian went rigid, wondering if Gerry Phelps was fool enough to come after him. The other horse galloped up on the right and was hauled to a sharp stop. Then a man's hand touched Ian's right wrist.

The fact that he was being accosted on his blind side snapped the last thread of Ian's self-restraint. As he twisted in the saddle, he swung his left fist in a wild, furious blow, wanting to strike and not caring who or where he hit.

The intruder wasn't Gerald Phelps. As his fist smashed into the other man's chest, Ian realized that he was assaulting his younger brother David, who wore the uniform of a captain in the 46th Native Infantry.

David managed to stay in his saddle, though only just. For an endless moment, the two men stared at each other. Then a wry smile crossed David's tanned face. "I haven't forgotten that I owe you ten pounds, Ian, but you don't have to beat it out of me. I would have paid long since if you hadn't gone and gotten yourself killed in Turkestan."

Ian said helplessly, "Christ, David, what are you doing here? When I left India, you were in the Bengal Engineers."

"Calcutta was dull so I exchanged to the 46th three months after you left for Bokhara. I thought life in the north would be more exciting." With fierceness that belied his casual words, David reached out and gripped Ian's hand. The third of the four Cameron offspring, David had the steadiest disposition and the greatest share of common sense. He was also one of the few people whose company Ian might be able to endure at the moment.

Releasing Ian's hand, David said, "What the devil happened to you in Bokhara?"

Ian shook his head, incapable of answering.

David frowned as he studied his older brother's drawn face. "Where are you staying?"

"Nowhere. I just got back." Ian's voice cracked for a moment. "I went directly to Colonel Whitman's."

There was a moment's silence. Then David said flatly, "I see. Come with me. My bungalow is nearby. The man who shares it is away for a couple of months, so there's plenty of room."

Mutely Ian turned his horse and rode after his brother. Just a few minutes more. He could manage that long. Just a few minutes more.

Chapter 3

❦ ❦ ❦

CONFUSED, IAN ROLLED over and blinked dazedly when he awoke. Then he remembered. Cambay. The disastrous meeting with Georgina. Finally, thank God, David. When they reached the bungalow, his brother had suggested that Ian rest and guided him to one of the bedrooms. Ian hadn't even bothered to undress before sprawling facedown on the bed. Within seconds he had fallen into exhausted unconsciousness.

Slanting rays of ruddy late-afternoon sunshine sifted through the shutters, but what day was it? Perhaps he had slept for a full twenty-four hours, as when he had arrived at Juliet's fortress after the wild flight across the Kara-Kum Desert. On both occasions, his rest had been more like coma than sleep.

He was still groggy with fatigue but doubted that he would sleep anymore, for the black mists still tormented him. Gravely he considered the image. Mists sounded too benign; the shadows were more like snarling black dogs that circled around him, obscuring his mind, snapping and slavering as they waited for the kill. Like wolves, perhaps?

Deciding that it would have been wiser to stick with mists, he got shakily to his feet and walked to the washstand. The mirror over the basin showed a filthy, bewhiskered visage that was enough to frighten anyone. Certainly it had frightened Georgina. Mouth tight, he turned away and opened the door to the bungalow's main room. David sat at the desk, writing a letter.

Ian asked, "How long was I asleep?"

His brother looked up. "Less than two hours. I didn't expect to see you until tomorrow morning."

No wonder Ian didn't feel rested.

David continued, "How about a bath? Then we can dine and you can tell me what's happened during the last two years."

The suggestion was a good one, for after shaving, bathing, and changing to fresh clothing, Ian felt as close to human as he was likely to get. By mutual agreement, neither of the brothers asked questions until they had eaten. Or rather, until David had eaten; Ian consumed only a few mouthfuls, then used his fork to push the remaining food around his plate.

When David finished, he signaled for the table to be cleared. "Care for some brandy?"

Ian considered the decanter. "I think I will, though it's probably a mistake—after two years in Islamic countries where there was no alcohol, a drink might put me flat on my back."

David filled two glasses and pushed one down the gleaming table. "Apart from exchanging to the 46th, not much has happened to me in the last couple of years. But how did you escape from Bokhara? It was reported that you were imprisoned shortly after arriving in the city, then executed about a year later."

Ian shrugged. "The report was half right—I was imprisoned but not executed—not quite. After a year and a half in the filthiest hole imaginable, I was rescued by Juliet and her long-lost husband. We escaped to Persia, and here I am."

David's brandy glass halted in midair halfway to his mouth. Incredulous, he said, "Our sister Juliet? And Ross Carlisle?"

After Ian had sketched in the details, David gave a soft whistle of amazement. "You were damned lucky."

"Indeed." Ian selected a mango and began carving it into slivers with the razor-sharp Persian dagger his sister had given him. "I remind myself of that all the time."

"So Juliet and Ross are together again," David said thoughtfully. "Why the devil did she run off in the first place? I never understood that. I know that Juliet has more than her share of Cameron impulsiveness, but leaving Ross after six months of marriage seemed like pure insanity."

"I don't know why she left—she didn't confide in me. But Ross is satisfied with her explanation. That's all that counts." Ian halted for a moment as he remembered the vivid closeness he had seen between his sister and her husband. He was happy for them, but the memory made his own situation seem all the bleaker. Disgusted with his self-pity, he continued, "They'll be arriving back in England soon. Not only has Juliet turned into an adoring and more-or-less dutiful wife, she is well on her way to providing Ross with an heir."

David grinned. "Trust Juliet not to waste any time."

"Georgina didn't either."

His brother's expression sobered. "Don't judge her too harshly, Ian. When the news came that you'd been executed—and it was a convincing report, not just a vague rumor—Georgina was badly broken up. Because I was your brother, she spent hours talking about you whenever we met."

"Then she turned around and married the next man in line."

"She's the sort of female who needs a man."

Ian swallowed his first mouthful of brandy. As he had expected, it hit with the impact of a blow. He welcomed the effect; with luck, it would soon render him unconscious. "Chivalrous of you to defend her, but with all due respect, I'm not interested in being fair-minded just now."

David's brows drew together. He was fond of Georgina and didn't blame her for believing that her fiancé was dead. But she *had* married Phelps very quickly . . . and her haste had created the very devil of a situation for Ian. "If it's any comfort," he said at last, "you were widely and honestly mourned by everyone in Cambay, from Colonel Whitman to the lowliest sweeper."

"No, I can't say that it's much comfort," Ian said dryly as he reduced the mango to a pile of juicy pulp and reddish rind.

David studied his guest uneasily. He had grown up idolizing his older brother, utterly confident that Ian's endless strength and good nature were equal to anything. It was Ian who had taught David how to ride like a Bedouin, how to defend himself against larger boys, and how to sneak out of the house when they were supposed to be asleep.

But the man who had returned from Bokhara was almost a stranger. His thin face all harsh planes and angles, Ian looked much older than his thirty-two years. He hadn't once laughed, and his rare smile was a meaningless twist of the lips. Uncertainly David said, "Will you exchange to another regiment? I imagine that seeing Georgina and Gerry together all the time would be . . . difficult.''

''An understatement.'' Ian stabbed a slice of mango with the tip of his knife and studied the juicy flesh as he considered the question. Abruptly he flipped the fruit to the plate uneaten. ''I'm going to resign my commission. I have no idea what I'll do instead, but I've had enough of fighting Indians and playing the Great Game against the Russians. To hell with it all. Her Majesty's bloody empire will have to stand or fall without me.''

The bitterness of his words momentarily silenced David. Then he realized that there was a piece of family news that was relevant to Ian's future. ''Fortunate that you want to leave the army, because you're needed back in Scotland.''

''Whatever for?'' Ian asked, unimpressed. He pushed the plate of mango fragments away and drank more brandy.

''You're now the laird of Falkirk.''

Ian's face went rigid. ''How can that be?''

David sighed. ''About a year ago, there was an accident. Uncle Andrew and both his sons were drowned on the loch. They were fishing when one of those vicious squalls blew up.''

Ian shoved violently away from the table. ''Bloody hell, all three of them killed at once? That's damnable.''

As he paced across the room, his first reaction was shock and grief, and it took time to grasp what the news meant to him personally. Falkirk was the Cameron family seat, but Ian's late father had been Andrew's younger brother, and Ian had never imagined that he might inherit the estate and title. He had been raised to make his own way in the world, yet now, through a senseless tragedy, he was Lord Falkirk.

Realizing something else, he stopped pacing and looked narrowly at his brother. ''With me reported dead, you were next in line to inherit.''

''Yes and no.'' David leaned back in his chair. ''Of course the lawyers notified me, but in the same post there was a letter from Mother ordering me not to start thinking I was Lord Falkirk, because you were still alive.''

For a moment Ian's mood eased. ''Did I mention that it was Mother who found Ross in Constantinople and bullied him into going to Bokhara?''

''I'm not surprised to hear it. She was determined to make the lawyers wait the full seven years before declaring you dead." David grinned. "She's gotten much more forceful over the years. Widowhood seems to suit her."

Ian rubbed at his aching temple. "How much do you mind not inheriting Falkirk? In spite of Mother, you must have begun to think of it as yours."

"Oh, I wouldn't have minded being Lord Falkirk, drafty castle and all," David admitted a little wistfully. "But I'd rather have you alive. Besides, I'm not ready to leave India yet. I'll earn my own piece of Scotland in my own time."

At least his brother didn't hate him for having survived. Ian resumed his pacing, finally coming to a halt by a window. As he stared out at the dark velvet night, he tested the idea of returning to the land of his birth. As a diplomat, Ian's father had spent most of his life abroad, so Falkirk had been his children's British home. Ian had lived there as a small child, spent his school holidays exploring the wild hills and swimming in the beautiful, treacherous sea loch.

Scotland, the land of his fathers, cool and green, as familiar as his own bones. In his present state of turbulence, the idea of Falkirk shimmered like a distant beacon on a stormy night. Losing Georgina had left a huge hole in the middle of his spirit, but Falkirk could fill some of that emptiness. It gave him a place to go, and a reason to make the effort.

He turned and leaned against the window frame, arms folded across his chest. "I guess I'll be going back to Scotland."

"I hope you'll stay a few days before you start back," David said. "Lord knows when I'll see you again. It will be years before I'll be able to visit home."

Having decided to leave India, Ian would have liked nothing better than to do so immediately, but that was impossible. "Before I leave, I've an errand to perform in Baipur. When I'm done, I'll stop in Cambay on the way back to Bombay."

"What kind of errand?"

Ian thought of darkness and cold and despair, and the man who in worldly terms had been an enemy, but who had become as close as Ian's own shadow. "For a year I shared my cell with a Russian colonel, until he was executed. He kept a journal in a small Bible, and I promised that if possible, I'd send it to his closest relative, his niece. As of three or four years ago, the girl lived at Baipur. Since I'm this

close, I'll take the journal in person rather than send it
through official channels.''

David's brows rose. "What on earth is a Russian girl
doing living at an Indian district station?''

Ian cast his mind back to what Pyotr had said. During the
monotonous months, they had learned much about each other's lives. "The child's mother was the colonel's younger
sister, Tatyana, and her father was a Russian cavalry officer.
After Tatyana's first husband died, she went to a Swiss spa
to bury her grief. There she met a Company administrator
called Kenneth Stephenson, who was on his way home to
teach at the Company training college at Haileybury. They
married and lived at Haileybury until Tatyana died five or
six years ago."

"The Company must have loved having a Russian at the
heart of their training college," David said, amused.

"According to Pyotr, his sister wasn't the least political,
but she could charm any man in creation. At any rate, after
she died, Stephenson asked to be assigned to India again.
He was made district collector in Baipur, and his stepdaughter came out with him. Pyotr hadn't had any contact with
his niece for some time, but there's a good chance she's still
in Baipur.''

"The political agent in Cambay will know," David said.
"What's the girl's name, and how old is she?''

"Larissa Alexandrovna Karelian, but Pyotr always called
her 'his little Lara,' '' Ian replied, rolling the "r's" on his
tongue. "He said she'd been an early baby and Larissa Alexandrovna seemed too long a name for such a tiny mite,
so she became Lara. Since Pyotr had no children of his
own, his niece was special to him.'' Ian thought again. "I
don't know how old the girl is, but from the way Pyotr
talked, she must be thirteen or fourteen. Old enough to have
the journal, and to know how her uncle died.''

To himself, Ian admitted that it would be simpler if the
girl were no longer within reach. Then he could send the
journal, with a brief explanation, to a Russian embassy. But
he owed Pyotr too much to take the easy way out, so he
must visit the child himself.

Hesitantly David said, "Do you have a headache? You
keep rubbing your forehead.''

Ian's hand dropped. "I've had headaches ever since I lost
the eye, but they've been diminishing. Maybe they'll stop

altogether some day.'' Suddenly David's unspoken sympathy was more than Ian could bear, and he felt a crashing need to be alone. "If you'll excuse me, I'm ready to call it a night."

He walked to the table and finished the last of his brandy, then withdrew to his room with more speed than courtesy. There he stripped off his outer clothing and lay down on the bed clad only in a pair of lightweight drawers. But in spite of fatigue and brandy, sleep eluded him.

He had always assumed he would spend his life in the army, had never considered leaving until he heard himself say that he was going to resign his commission. Yet as soon as the words came out of his mouth, he had known he had no choice. Once the military life had suited him as water suited a fish, but no more.

Above his head, the huge fan called a *punkah* turned lazily, sending cooler air over his heated body. Outside on the veranda, a servant called a *punkah wallah* pulled the rope that caused the fan to rotate. Eventually the servant decided it was time for bed, and the long, fabric-covered blades of the punkah creaked to a halt, leaving the inside of the bungalow silent.

As the air went still, the yellow flame of the oil lamp lengthened. Ian found himself watching as if mesmerized. He had deliberately left the lamp lighted, for in Bokhara he had developed a distaste for darkness.

His lips tightened to a bloodless line. It was time, past time, to be honest. What he felt about darkness was nothing as mild as distaste; it was surging, irrational terror.

Nor was darkness the only fear he had acquired in prison. As his bare chest rose and fell in agitation, he forced himself to face the ugly facts he had been trying to deny since his rescue.

He was afraid of being alone, yet he found it difficult to endure the company of other people.

He was terrified of being confined against his will.

He was afraid to sleep because he feared his dreams.

He was a coward, a man sworn to honor's code who had betrayed himself more profoundly than anyone else could ever have betrayed him.

He was not the man who went to Bokhara, but a dry, broken husk who would never be the same again.

He feared death. Infinitely worse, he feared life.

One by one, he mentally ticked off his weaknesses, studying each one until it settled in his mind and made itself at home. But bitter as those truths were, they were not as painful as the final, brutal fact that he had desperately refused to accept. Even in the privacy of his own mind, it was almost impossible to say the words to himself, but finally he did.

He was impotent.

As Ian's nails dug crescent-shaped grooves in his palms, he rolled the syllables around in his mind. Impotent. A eunuch. Half a man. Never again would he know the basic human satisfactions of passion and physical closeness, never would he have a wife or child.

The knowledge seared like white-hot iron. There might be men of naturally monkish disposition who would scarcely notice the loss of their sexuality, but he was not one of them.

Looking back, he knew exactly when the damage had been done; during the worst of the beatings administered by the prison guards, he had been kicked savagely, and repeatedly, in the genitals. After that day he had never felt desire again.

At the time he had barely noticed, for hunger and despair had already extinguished passion. The question of whether he had been rendered a eunuch seemed academic, for women were no more than a distant memory and he had expected to die in Bokhara.

But he had survived, and the question of his virility became relevant again. When freedom and decent food didn't restore him, he had refused to believe that he might have suffered permanent damage. Instead, he convinced himself that being reunited with his fiancée would make him whole. Georgina would arouse him, for her ripe curves had enticed him from the first time they met.

When she had accepted his proposal, he had been impatient to teach her the pleasures of the flesh, for during their stolen moments of privacy she had proved to be an apt pupil. But because she was only nineteen, her parents had insisted on a long engagement. That was one reason he had been willing to go to Bokhara, for he had found it difficult to wait.

Throughout the years in Central Asia, his fiancée had occupied his thoughts, even after desire was no more than a memory. She became a symbol of everything he had loved and lost.

After his rescue, he had made his way back to Georgina in search of healing. Yet when he saw her, he felt not a single flicker of desire, even before he had discovered that she was married. Though she was as attractive as ever, sexually he might as well have been dead.

For a desperate moment he considered visiting the beautiful Indian girl who had been his mistress until he had fallen in love with Georgina. Leela was no inhibited English maid but a skilled courtesan, and their relationship had been passionate and mutually satisfying. Yet when he thought of her now, his body did not respond in the slightest. Not a twitch, not a tremor, even when he recalled precisely what they had done together.

He had a brief, horrifying vision of visiting Leela and failing utterly to perform. She was kind and would not laugh at what he had become; instead, she would pity him, which would be far worse.

Nor would he deceive himself with the hope that he was suffering from a temporary condition that would eventually heal, for he had had enough of self-delusion. It had been over three months since his escape from prison. But though his overall physical condition was much better, there had been no change in his sexual nature, not the slightest hint of improvement. The time had come to accept that the worst had happened, and that a vital part of his life was gone forever.

After working his way through to the final bleak conclusion, Ian released his breath in a ragged sigh. He had had quite enough merciless honesty for one night; what he craved now was cowardly surcease. He rolled to his feet, lifted the lamp, and returned to the darkened drawing room, where he found the brandy decanter in a cabinet. Recklessly he filled a glass almost to the brim and dropped into the nearest wicker armchair.

He was taking a deep swallow when the door to David's bedroom opened and his brother wandered in, half-dressed and blinking sleepily. In the last three years, David had developed an impressive set of muscles; just as well that he hadn't retaliated when Ian had hit him.

It occurred to Ian that since he would leave no heirs, it was likely that David or a son of his would eventually inherit Falkirk. Finding some comfort in that thought, Ian tilted the glass toward his brother in an informal salute. "Sorry to have woken you, but I decided that I need to get seriously drunk."

David raised one hand to cover a yawn. "No matter. I'm a light sleeper."

Not as light as Ian, who could not remember when he had last had a normal night's sleep. More to himself than to his brother, he said, "I've been very lucky. Miraculously saved from durance vile, inheriting a title and a comfortable fortune." His voice broke. "That being the case, why the hell am I so miserable?"

David regarded him with grave blue eyes. "Having just lost the woman you love, I think you're entitled to be miserable."

Ian let his head fall back against the chair as he pondered his brother's words. Did he love Georgina? Two years earlier he had certainly believed himself in love. He and Georgina had been perfectly matched, she had made him laugh, and he had wanted to bed her. He had also enjoyed winning her away from all her other suitors. She hadn't been a deep thinker, but then, neither had he. Perhaps that had been love; now, he really didn't know what he felt about her, beyond a lacerating sense of loss.

He gulped another mouthful of brandy. "Georgina was wise to accept Gerry," he said dispassionately, "for the Ian Cameron she wanted to marry died in Bokhara."

If she had still been single, she might have felt honor-bound to wed Ian, for a colonel's daughter knew her duty. But of course he could not have married her once he recognized his incapacity. Finishing the first glass of brandy, Ian leaned over and poured another, spilling some because it was hard to judge distances with only one eye.

David crossed to the cabinet and lifted the decanter. "Mind if I join you in getting drunk?"

Ian's fingers tightened around his glass. "As a matter of fact, I do mind. I'd really rather be alone."

David's face became expressionless. "Very well." He started to leave, then swung back. "I know you're hurting, Ian, the pain radiates from you like heat from an oven. But in the nature of things, eventually you'll feel better—there are other women in the world, and I think you'll enjoy being the laird of Falkirk. Meanwhile . . . ," he groped for an oblique way to express his fear, "don't do anything foolish, will you?"

Jarred to find that David had sensed what he had not acknowledged even to himself, Ian said, "Don't worry. I'm a coward, but not that much of one." His lips curved into the mockery of a smile. "Besides, I haven't the right to throw away what Juliet and Ross risked their own lives to preserve."

After studying his face, David nodded, satisfied, then went back to his bedroom, leaving Ian with the solitude he both craved and feared. Wearily he tucked the decanter in the crook of his arm, then picked up his brandy glass and lamp and retreated to his room. There, with workmanlike efficiency, he set out to drink himself into a stupor as quickly as possible.

Before he could achieve his goal, a wave of violent nausea surged through him. Desperate for fresh air, he stumbled outside, barely making it across the veranda and into the garden before his outraged body purged itself of the brandy. Head spinning and gut churning, he fell on his knees by an oleander bush and retched until his stomach was empty.

Too weak to stand, he buried his sweat-slick face in his hands, shaking and chilled in spite of the night's warmth. He hadn't expected brandy to be a long-term solution, but he had thought it would give a few hours of desperately needed oblivion. But apparently even that was to be denied him. His suffocating misery was the worst he had ever known, a pain of the mind more agonizing than any of the body.

As Ian's hammering heart slowed to normal, he faced one last ominous truth: he couldn't go on this way. He had told David that he wouldn't do anything foolish and he meant it, for he had caused his family enough grief.

But the world was a dangerous place for a man who found life excruciating. In spite of his best intentions, he was doomed unless he found something—or someone—to take his mind off his own despair.

Chapter 4

❦ ❦ ❦

THE BRITISH ADMINISTRATION building was the largest ed-
ifice in Baipur, with a Union Jack hanging limply from a
pole in front and a crowd of the inevitable petitioners and
gawkers lolling about the veranda. All watched with interest
as Ian dismounted. One stepped forward to take his horse
while another went inside to announce that an unknown Englishman had arrived.

By the time Ian reached the top of the steps, a sturdily
built Briton of middle years had come out to greet him.
"Good afternoon. I'm George McKittrick, senior judge
here." He offered a hand and a smile. "What brings you to
Baipur?"

Ian had discarded his uniform along with his commission
and had not yet gotten used to identifying himself as Lord
Falkirk, so he said tersely, "My name's Ian Cameron, and
I'm looking for Kenneth Stephenson. Is he here now?"

McKittrick led the way inside. "Sorry, but he's touring
the eastern part of the district. Won't be back for weeks."

So the hunt wasn't over yet. "My business is actually
with his stepdaughter, Larissa, or perhaps she's called
Lara," Ian said. "Do you know if she's with him?"

McKittrick's brows drew together. "Lara? He has a
daughter, Laura. I suppose she could be his stepdaughter,
though neither of them ever said as much. And yes, she
went with him."

Thinking that the girl must have anglicized her name, Ian
said, "Can you give me a map of the district, and Stephenson's schedule of stops?"

"Of course." McKittrick gave an order to a native clerk,
then turned back to Ian. "It's getting late in the day. Will

you do my wife and me the honor of spending the night with us?''

India was sometimes called the land of the open door because of the unfailing hospitality that a Briton met wherever he went. However, though Ian had regained enough control to present a fairly normal face to the world, doing so was difficult, and he didn't feel up to being civil to a tableful of strangers. "Sorry—I won't be stopping. I need to find the Stephensons as soon as possible, and there are a couple of hours of daylight left."

The judge's face fell. "A pity. My wife will be disappointed—it isn't often we see a new face in Baipur."

Ian felt a twinge of guilt. A small station like this would have only four or five British officials and a few other family members, so if Ian stayed, his visit would be the social high point of the month. However, guilt was not enough to change his mind. He said vaguely, "If I come back this way, I'll gladly take you up on your offer, but today I really must continue on."

McKittrick asked no more questions, and within fifteen minutes Ian was on his way again. That night he camped in the countryside, as he had every night since leaving Cambay. If Stephenson was holding to his schedule, Ian should find him within a day or so. Then Ian could present the Bible to Lara, give the necessary explanations, and be off the next morning.

He knew that there was no real need for haste, but once he had decided to return to Scotland, he had become feverishly impatient to be on his way. With insight that he would not have had before his imprisonment, he recognized that he had replaced his obsession with Georgina with a fixation about going home. Not the healthiest state of mind, he thought with black humor, but at least obsession helped him maintain his grasp on sanity.

When they reached the fork in the dusty road, Laura reined in her horse. "I'll turn here, Father. If I go into the village with you, I'll get caught up in the official welcome, and it will be hours before I can get away."

Kenneth Stephenson halted his own mount. "You really aren't needed to help set up the camp—the servants will do a fine job."

"True," she admitted, "but supervising their work gives

me a good excuse to avoid sitting through all the flowery
speeches, which will inevitably be followed by recitations
of all the grievances that have accumulated over the last
year.''

He grinned. "It will take at least three days to deal with
all of the questions about whose buffalo wandered into
whose field, and whose head got broken over it.''

"But you'll settle them all to everyone's satisfaction.''
Laura's brows drew together as she studied her stepfather's
face. Under the shadow of his topi, his skin was pale and
his expression drawn. "Don't stay too long. You look
tired.''

"A little,'' he admitted. "I'll come back early and take
a nap before dinner.'' He made a clucking noise to his horse
and turned down the right-hand path.

Laura took the left fork, which led to the campsite. When
her father finished in Nanda, they would head north, then
work their way west again. Progress was leisurely, for touring was a vital part of a district officer's responsibilities.
While in theory a collector like Kenneth was primarily concerned with land taxation, in practice he was also magistrate, engineer, and even physician to the people of his
district. Most of all, he was the physical expression of the
Sirkar, the British government.

The campsite was in a forest clearing, and the towering
trees that surrounded it gave welcome shade. As expected,
all was in order, with bullock carts unpacked, a dozen tents
erected, and a cooking fire lit. On the far right side of the
clearing, the tethered pack animals grazed peacefully on the
lush grass.

After dismounting and handing her horse over to a groom,
Laura entered her tent. Camping was an odd mixture of
discomfort and luxury, and she was always amused to see
framed watercolors of Britain hanging on the canvas walls,
and to feel her feet sink into a thick Indian carpet.

With a sigh, she removed her topi and pushed sweaty hair
off her forehead, hoping that the cool weather would arrive
soon. After washing the dust from her face and neck, she
went from her tent to her stepfather's. When she stepped
inside, she chuckled. Not only were his furnishings correctly placed, but the book of essays he had been reading
the night before had been replaced at precisely the same

angle on the table. He was quite right; her supervision
wasn't needed.

Even so, Laura checked everything in the camp carefully,
chatting with the cook and other servants as she ensured
that all was in order. Keeping Up Standards was the first
rule drilled into Englishwomen when they arrived in India,
and it included everything from dressing for dinner to un-
flinching courage in the face of mortal danger. Though
Laura doubted that what she wore had much effect on the
prestige of the British Empire, she dutifully did her part.

As he had promised, Kenneth Stephenson returned before
sundown. "I'll be going hunting tomorrow," he said as he
dismounted. "The headman told me there's a man-eating
tiger in the area. Two villagers have been killed in the last
fortnight."

Laura gave the dense trees an alarmed glance. "Perhaps
we should have camped by Nanda rather than out here."

Kenneth chuckled. "Even a man-eater won't attack a
camp this size. But don't wander off into the forest to gather
flowers, and tell the servants to be careful as well."

Laura frowned as she studied her stepfather's face. He
looked distinctly unwell. "Have you forgotten to take your
quinine? You look like you're sickening with fever."

He grimaced. "You're probably right. I'll take a couple
of tablets and a nap and be fine by dinner."

Laura's gaze followed him as he went to his tent, but she
was not unduly concerned. Fever was a way of life for Europeans in India, and most people ignored it unless they
had a particularly bad attack.

As she went to her own tent to bathe and change, a great
cat roared in the forest. Laura paused to listen, wondering
if it was a tiger or a lion. A lion, she decided.

The cat roared again as Laura ducked under her tent flap.
She shivered, feeling a vague sense of foreboding. In India,
danger was never far away, and she sensed that tonight it
was drawing close. Determinedly she shook the feeling
away. Tonight was just a night like any other.

Laura had dressed and was about to have her maid pin up
her hair when the bearer, Padam, summoned her. His voice
agitated, he called through the canvas, "Miss Laura, come
quickly. Stephenson Sahib is ill."

Her earlier foreboding returned. Ignoring her loose hair, Laura brushed by her maid and ducked out the door of the tent. The sun had set and it was full dark as she hastened across the clearing, Padam right behind her.

A lamp was lit inside the tent, and the canvas glowed with mellow light, but as soon as Laura stepped inside she was struck by the stench of illness. Her stepfather was sprawled on his bed, and even through the mosquito netting Laura saw that his face was grayish white and his breathing rapid and shallow.

Laura's heart accelerated with terror. India had diseases that could kill in a matter of hours; one could lunch with a healthy man, then learn that he had died before dinner. Struggling to control her fear, she went to her stepfather's bedside. As she laid a hand on his forehead, his lids flickered open. It took a moment for his eyes to focus on her, but when they did, he murmured in a voice of eerie calmness, "You'll have to be strong, Laura. My time . . . has come."

"Papa, no!" she cried out, reverting to her childhood name for him. Alarmed by the hysteria she heard in her own voice, she swept aside the mosquito netting and perched on the edge of the bed, then lifted his wrist to feel for his pulse. The beat was fast and thready, as fragile as a songbird's.

He managed a faint smile. "Try not to be . . . too upset, Laura. I always said . . . that I wanted to die in India."

Fiercely she said, "You'll die here someday, but not yet."

His feeble headshake denied her words. "I think it's cholera, my dear." He drew a long, shuddering breath. "Remember that you promised . . . not to choose aloneness. And . . . don't mourn for too long." His eyes closed again.

Cholera was a messy, undignified disease, and the variety that Kenneth had contracted progressed with unbelievable swiftness. The only treatment Laura could offer was laudanum for the pain, and fluids to counter the dehydration caused by vomiting and diarrhea. Padam and her stepfather's valet, Mahendar, helped with the nursing, but their stricken expressions showed that they had already given up on their master.

In spite of Laura's furious attempt to save her stepfather through sheer will, his life inexorably ebbed away. She felt a curious duality; in one sense the moments dragged with agonizing slowness, yet at the same time they raced past, spilling away like the sands of an hourglass.

Kenneth spoke only once more. As his stepdaughter sponged his forehead, he whispered, "Laura."

"Yes, Papa?" She bent over to hear his words.

Her unbound hair tumbled across his wrist, and he touched the tawny strands with shaking fingers. "You and Tatyana . . . were the best thing that ever happened to me." He drew a labored breath, and then his expression brightened, the marks of pain disappearing. Once again his lips formed the syllables, "Tatyana," as if in greeting. Then his eyes closed.

Laura sank to her knees beside the cot, clenching his hand between hers. Bending her head, she wept uncontrollably for the man who had been loving father, kind teacher, and beloved friend.

When she lifted her head again, he was gone.

It was nearly midnight when Ian finally reached the village of Nanda. There he was given instructions and a village youth to guide him to Kenneth Stephenson's camp. After passing through a series of moonlit fields, they came to the edge of a dense forest that spread as far as the eye could see.

The young guide stopped and pointed into the woods. "Follow this track and you will come to Stephenson Sahib's camp. I would go with you but panthers hunt the paths at night."

Ian didn't blame the boy; he wasn't keen on going through the forest alone himself, though the risk of wild beasts bothered him less than leaving the moonlit fields. However, he had learned that it was possible to bear darkness when he was in the open air, so he thanked the guide, then set his teeth and urged his tired horse into the forest. Very soon, his mission would be accomplished, and he could start for home.

Laura was given no time to mourn. She was still kneeling by her stepfather's bed when Padam said, "Miss Laura, the tiger is near. We can hear it growling in the forest, hunting for prey."

For Laura, past and present had melded together, and the anguish she felt for Kenneth's death rekindled the shock and grief she had experienced when she lost her first father. Once more she was nine and alone and terrified, and it took time for Padam's voice to bring her back to the present. She wished he would go away. What did a tiger matter compared to the death of the only person in the world whom she had loved?

Urgently Padam said, "Stephenson Sahib's spirit has departed, miss. It is time to be concerned with the living. All in the camp are in danger. Something must be done."

Dully Laura realized that her stepfather's death meant she was in charge of two dozen people. The knowledge helped steady her grief-stricken mind; even so, she fumbled for words, though she had been speaking Urdu daily for years. "Build more fires around the edge of the camp. That will keep the tiger away."

"There isn't enough fuel, memsahib, and gathering more would be dangerous," the bearer explained patiently. "A man-eater is usually an old tiger, perhaps injured, always unpredictable. You must be ready with the guns if it decides to attack."

Guns? Laura opened her mouth to protest that her marksmanship was nonexistent. Kenneth had tried to teach her to shoot. She had managed to learn how to load and fire several kinds of weapons, but she had found the lessons so upsetting that her stepfather had discontinued them.

Still, no one else would do better, for her minimal experience was more than any of the servants had. It was her responsibility to set aside her grief, even though she loathed and feared guns. She closed her mouth and got to her feet. With bitter humor, she recognized that she was about to Keep Up Standards with a vengeance.

Kenneth had not been an avid hunter, but firearms were a necessary part of life in India. He had brought three weapons on tour: a pistol, a double-barreled shotgun, and a powerful rifle for big game. Her father's valet, Mahendar, brought out the guns, and one by one she loaded them with clumsy fingers. After showing Mahendar and Padam how to cock and aim, she put the pistol and rifle in their charge. The shotgun she kept herself, since she thought it would be the best weapon for frightening off a tiger.

Laura led the way outside and gave orders for a second fire to be built fifty feet from the main cooking fire. There was enough fuel for two fires, and she thought that if the servants slept between them, they would feel safer.

Though she dutifully went through the motions of securing the camp, she doubted that there was any real danger. Tigers seldom attacked humans, and even a man-eater was more likely to drag a solitary laborer from a field than to invade a busy camp. Still, tigers invoked panic far out of proportion to the risk, and Laura owed it to her servants to deal with their anxiety.

She managed to keep her voice calm and her step steady, but inside she quivered with grief and fear. She had always refused to consider what she would do if her stepfather died; in India, where disease was swift and lethal, she had been as likely to die as he was. But now he was gone and her life would change utterly. She had lost not just her family, but her home and financial security. She wanted to collapse on the ground and wail like a child.

When the fires were steady and the servants had begun to settle down, Laura beckoned to the three grooms. "Come, we must move the animals closer. They are in more danger than we are."

The men exchanged uneasy glances. "Don't worry, I'll guard you." Laura tried to sound cool and confident. "Padam, stay here with the pistol. Mahendar, bring the rifle and come with me."

Laura made a show of cocking the shotgun, then led the way through the cluster of tents. Behind her the youngest groom carried a torch. Their shadows swayed wildly as the small group walked to the edge of the clearing where the horses and bullocks were tethered. The animals were nervous and hard to handle, and the grooms had their hands full soothing their charges so the beasts could be led to a safer spot near the center of the camp.

Laura took the rifle from Mahendar so that he could help the other men. Then she chose a position between the line of animals and the forest and waited, shotgun in hand, the rifle lying ready at her feet. Again she reminded herself that no animal was likely to attack the camp, but this close to the forest it was harder to maintain her calm.

The tropical night pulsed with life, mysterious and dangerous. Shifting shadows looked like crouching beasts that vanished when she looked directly at them. In the distance jackals howled, and once the distinctive cough of a panther

sounded from a spot that was shockingly near. She jumped
and tightened her grip on the shotgun, but there was nothing
to be seen in the teasing shadows. After wiping sweaty palms
on her skirt, Laura raised the barrel of her weapon again
and trained it at the forest darkness.

When trouble came, it was fast and incoherent. Two feline roars shattered the silence, so close that she half expected to feel claws sink into her flesh. A shrill whinny
sounded behind her, and she glanced back to see a pony
rear and jerk its reins free from the groom who was trying
to calm it. Eyes rolling, the pony bolted, setting off a chorus
of frightened bellows and whinnies from the other animals.
The youngest groom shouted, "The tiger comes!" and
pointed at the forest beyond Laura.

As Laura spun around, she heard rustling in the undergrowth. In sudden panic she fired one barrel of the shotgun
at the sound. She had forgotten to brace herself for the re-
coil, and the gun jerked, sending the shot high as the stock
kicked bruisingly into her shoulder. Acrid smoke stung her
eyes and her deafened ears rang, but she gripped her gun
more tightly and discharged the second barrel, this time
aiming lower.

Irrationally convinced that an enraged tiger was about to
burst out of the forest, she dropped the shotgun and grabbed
the rifle that lay on the grassy turf by her feet. The weapon
had the power to fell an elephant; as her finger curled around
the trigger, she prayed that if the tiger attacked, her aim
would be good enough to stop it.

Imprisonment had sharpened Ian's senses, and he smelled
and heard Stephenson's camp long before he saw it. But as
he drew close enough to identify individual noises and
odors, he pulled his horse to a stop so he could listen more
closely.

Something was wrong. It was past midnight and the camp
should be quiet, but instead it was wide awake. More than
that, he detected the subtle aroma of fear, a scent as un-
mistakable as it was indescribable.

He frowned. This was a safe, settled part of India, and it
was unlikely that bandits would have attacked. Still, he had
been a soldier for too many years to ride heedlessly into an
unknown situation. He dismounted and led his horse away
from the path, moving silently over the soft leaf mold.

As he neared the campsite, he heard sharp human voices speaking Urdu and the grunts and whickers of agitated animals. He tethered his horse, then cautiously approached the perimeter of the camp, his holstered revolver ready to hand.

The boundary where forest met clearing was marked by thick undergrowth, which provided convenient cover. Stopping behind a large bush, he peered into the clearing. A churning group of men and bullocks blocked his view of the tents, but the layout confirmed that this was the camp of a British official.

His gaze went to the single guttering torch, which illuminated a youth who was trying to coax a nervous pony toward the tents. Other shadowy human shapes were moving about, but before Ian could study them, all hell broke loose. Two feline roars, one bass and one tenor, sounded from the shrubbery to his right. As the blood-chilling sounds split the night air, the pony whinnied shrilly and broke free, bullocks began bellowing, and someone shrieked that the tiger was coming.

Startled by the racket, the jungle cats bolted away through the undergrowth, passing less than a dozen feet from Ian. An instant later a shotgun blasted after them. As pellets shredded leaves and slammed into tree trunks around him, he cursed and dived to the ground, rolling to get out of the field of fire.

The gun thundered again, and this time the shot came closer. Ian crouched behind a tree and studied the darkened clearing. The torch had been dropped or burned out, and all he could see were horses and bullocks rearing and tugging at their tethers, their solid forms silhouetted against the campfires. The only man he could discern was less than twenty feet away, and a flicker of light along the barrel showed that the damned fool was raising a rifle and aiming it directly at Ian.

Apparently the gunman was trying to protect the camp from some imagined danger, and Ian had wandered into the middle by accident. Under the circumstances retreat would be the better part of wisdom, but he had always preferred offense to defense. He was also royally irritated at being shot at. That being the case, no sooner had Ian seen the movement of the rifle than he broke from cover and dashed toward the gunman, keeping low.

After two swift steps, he launched himself in a flat dive.

His shoulder caught the man squarely and they both crashed to the ground, with Ian landing on top. As they fell, he wrestled the rifle away, the weapon discharging deafeningly into the air.

The skirmish was over almost before it began. Only then, as Ian used one arm to pin his opponent to the grassy turf, did he discover that the slim form beneath him belonged not to a gun*man* but a gun*woman*.

"Bloody hell!" he swore as he hastily rolled away. The clearing was too dark to distinguish details, but clearly the woman was European, with a pale face and a cascade of light-colored hair. Judging by her lush curves, she was too old to be Pyotr's niece Lara; perhaps Stephenson had re-married and this was his second wife. Speaking in English, Ian said, "Sorry to have knocked you down. Are you all right?"

"You're English," she said stupidly as she raised herself to a sitting position.

"Scottish, actually." He sat back on his heels. "I do hope that you don't intend to revive the old English custom of using Scots for target practice."

"I . . . I thought you were a tiger," she faltered.

"You should have looked more closely," he said dryly. "I lack two more feet, a tail, and quite a lot of stripes." Glancing up, he saw that several natives had been drawn by her scream, but when they heard English speech, they stopped a dozen feet away.

Ian stood and grasped her hand, easily lifting her to her feet. "Thank God you're a dreadful shot." He released her fingers, which were icy cold. "Why were you blasting away? No tiger would attack a camp this size."

"Th . . . there's a man-eater in the neighborhood," she said in a husky, uneven voice. "We were shifting the ani-mals away from the forest when one of the men thought he saw a tiger. I heard roaring and something moved in the undergrowth, so I fired."

"Having had a front row seat, my best guess is that a curious panther and a caracal were investigating the camp," Ian said. "Their paths crossed, so they tried to outroar each other. When you started shooting, they wisely took off."

"A caracal?" she repeated.

Beginning to wonder if the woman was drunk or dim-witted, Ian said impatiently, "Surely you've heard of caracals. They're rather like overgrown house cats with long tufted ears." He handed her rifle back. "The next time you use this, remember that the first law of hunting is never to shoot at something you can't see clearly. You didn't manage to kill anyone, but next time you might not be so lucky."

"I'm s . . . sorry," she said, her voice on the verge of tears.

Embarrassed by her reaction, Ian said, "No harm done." Glancing around, he found that apparently every Indian in the camp had come to watch, but there were no other Europeans; not the collector, and not young Lara. "Where's Kenneth Stephenson? I need to talk to him."

"You . . . you can't." Her voice broke.

Trying to control his irritation, Ian said, "This is his camp, isn't it?"

"M . . . my father's dead." She bent her head and ran distracted fingers through her wild hair. "He . . . he died of cholera. A few minutes ago. Perhaps an hour."

"Dear God," Ian said softly, feeling like a clumsy idiot. No wonder the young woman was disoriented; with her father barely dead, it was amazing that she could string a coherent sentence together. She had even attempted to defend the camp against possible danger, and while the results had been incompetent, he gave her full marks for gallantry. "You're Laura Stephenson?"

She nodded, swaying a little.

Ian stepped forward to take her trembling arm. "You need to lie down."

Head bent, she made a small choked sound, and her weight sagged against him. As he slid his arm around her waist to hold her upright, he said, "Incidentally, my name is Ian Cameron."

Head still bent and face obscured by hair, she said, "Wh . . . why are you here?"

"My business can wait till tomorrow." Switching to Urdu, Ian said to the ring of servants, "Which of you is Miss Stephenson's maid?"

A graceful young woman stepped forward. "I am, sahib."

"Take your mistress to her tent and put her to bed. If there's laudanum, give her some so she'll sleep."

The girl glanced uneasily at the circling forest. Correctly

interpeting her disquiet, Ian said, ''Don't worry, I guarantee you'll be safe for the rest of the night.''

The maid responded to the authority in his voice and came forward to lead her dazed mistress away. Ian had rallied soldiers in the midst of ambush, so it wasn't difficult to restore the confidence of a camp of demoralized servants.

But as he gave orders, collected Stephenson's guns, reloaded, and retrieved his weary horse, he wondered what the devil had become of little Larissa Alexandrovna Karelian.

Chapter 5

❦ ❦ ❦

INSTEAD OF SLEEP, the laudanum sent Laura into a black paralysis laced by nightmare images of her stepfather. He stood before her with his familiar warm smile, but when she tried to touch him, he receded away, vanishing into the swirling darkness that had already claimed her mother and first father.

In fifteen years of nightmares, Laura had never succeeded in preventing her parents from leaving, yet it was not in her nature to stop trying. Surely if she said the right words, did the right thing, she could persuade Kenneth to stay. Yet time and again she failed. It occurred to her that perhaps she could follow him into the darkness. With immense effort, she forced her numb limbs to move and ran after his retreating figure, desperately calling, ''Papa!'' as she clawed through the barriers that came between them.

Then, with miraculous suddenness, she ran smack into her stepfather's solid frame. His arms went around her and finally she was safe. Weeping with joy, she clung to him. ''Papa,'' she whispered, burrowing into his embrace. ''Papa, I had such a horrible nightmare. I dreamed that you died.''

A deep, unfamiliar voice penetrated the mists that surrounded her. ''Miss Stephenson . . . Laura, wake up.''

Dazedly she raised her head and found that it was not her stepfather holding her, but a stranger, a lean, harsh-faced man with a black patch over one eye. He would have been frightening if it weren't for the kindness in his voice. ''You were sleepwalking,''. he said softly. ''Are you awake now?''

Uncertainly she pushed away from the stranger's embrace and looked around. The dream barrier she had fought her way past must have been the tent flap, for she was now outdoors, standing barefoot a dozen feet from the smaller fire. Fifty feet away, by the larger fire, she saw the sleeping forms of the servants, and drowsy bullocks and horses were scattered about.

Piece by piece, her memory of the previous night returned, from her stepfather's death until the arrival of this capable stranger. Cameron, he had said his name was. Ian Cameron. Her gaze returned to the gaunt planes of his face. "So it wasn't a nightmare—my father really is gone."

"I'm afraid so. Come and have some tea. I just brewed another pot." He guided Laura to a folded blanket that had been laid by the fire. After she sat down, he poured a mug of tea, sugared it heavily, and pressed it into her hands. She drank automatically, scarcely noticing the scalding heat. In the east, the sky had a rosy tint. Soon this dreadful night would be over.

By the time she had drained the mug her haziness had cleared. It occurred to her that she should be embarrassed at sitting cross-legged in front of a total stranger, wearing only a light nightdress. Yet she was not uncomfortable, probably because Ian Cameron was so matter-of-fact about the situation. Holding the mug out, she said, "Sorry to be such a nuisance."

He leaned over with the pot and poured her more tea. "Actually, you're holding up remarkably well. Most women would be having strong hysterics in these circumstances."

As she sipped the second mug, she examined her companion. Last night he had been terrifying when he exploded out of the darkness and overpowered her, and even now the eyepatch gave him a piratical air. Yet his stern features were well-formed, and in the glow of the fire his hair was burnished auburn. It was a surprisingly warm color for a man who had the wary, fine-strung alertness of a predator. Seeing the rifle that lay near his hand, she said, "You've been awake all night guarding the camp?"

He nodded. "I doubt it was necessary, but I knew people would rest better if there was a lookout."

Thinking that he carried himself like a soldier, she asked, "Are you in the army?"

He gave her a sharp glance. "I used to be a major in the 46th Native Infantry."

His expression did not encourage further questions, so she returned to drinking her tea. Her companion might have

resigned his commission, but mentally she started thinking
of him as Major Cameron; he was too forceful to think of
as plain Mr. Cameron.

It was now light enough to distinguish colors, and the
forest had become an arena of competitive bird choirs. The
servants began stirring at the other fire, and soon the clearing filled with the scent of baking *chapatis,* an unleavened
bread that was cooked on a griddle.

Ian took advantage of his companion's distraction to study
her appearance, since the night before he had been unable
to determine much except that she was a bit above average
height. Now the dawn light revealed that her eyes were an
unusual shade of clear light amber, almost the same color
as her long straight hair. Though Laura did not have Georgina's vivid, cream-and-gold prettiness, her features were
strong, and she had a contained quality that hinted at mysteries. It was an intriguing face, the sort one remembered
long after mere prettiness was forgotten.

His gaze drifted lower. Though she showed an unfeminine lack of fussiness about the unconventional circumstances, the figure revealed by her nightdress was very
feminine indeed.

He sighed, thinking that it was further proof of his incapacity that he could be so objective about a very attractive
girl. He had never been a womanizer who tried to bed every
female he met, but he had always had a masculine awareness of the women around him. He had not appreciated how
much pleasure that awareness lent to life until it was gone.

His gaze returned to his companion's still profile. She was
indeed bearing up well, but it was apparent that paralyzing
grief lay just beneath her calm surface. Regretting that he
must increase her misery, he said, "Miss Stephenson, I'm
afraid there are some decisions that only you can make."

She looked directly at him. "What decisions?"

He was intrigued to see that her amber eyes had an Oriental slant that was as attractive as it was exotic. "Do you
want to take your father's body back to Baipur?" He hesitated before adding, "The weather is hot, and the trip will
take days by bullock cart."

As she understood what he was hinting at, her face tightened. "My father can be buried here. He loved all of India—it doesn't matter whether he rests in Nanda or Baipur."
She ran distracted fingers through her hair, tangling it even

further. "I must send a man to the village to inform the headman of my father's death, and to ask about a burial site."

"I've already done that," Ian said. "I imagine the headman himself will arrive soon to talk with you."

The soft-footed cook came and set down a tray that held a platter of fresh chapatis and a bowl of dal, a mixture of spiced lentils. When Laura stared blankly at the tray, Ian said, "You'd better eat something. It's going to be a difficult day."

Obediently she picked up a chapati, tore off a piece, and used the fragment to scoop up a mouthful of dal. After she had chewed and swallowed it, she said, vaguely surprised, "I'm hungry. I think I haven't eaten since yesterday morning."

Eventually Laura ate twice as much as Ian, though that was no great feat, given the state of his appetite. When they had finished, she said, "Your business with my father—is it something I can help you with? I . . . I know you must be eager to be on your way again."

"I'm in no particular hurry," he said mildly. "If you wish, I can escort you back to Baipur."

She blinked and looked away. "I would like that," she said in a low voice. "If you're sure you don't mind."

"I'm sure." Though she would not have asked him to stay, Ian could see that she was grateful for the support of a countryman. Rather to his surprise, he realized that he actively wanted to assist her. He would have helped any woman in distress, but Laura Stephenson aroused his protective instincts. More than that, he felt a sense of affinity with her, even though the source of her pain was very different from his own.

After composing herself, she said, "You still haven't told me why you came all the way to Nanda to find my father."

"Actually, my primary goal was not your father," Ian said. "I'm looking for a Russian girl named Larissa Alexandrovna Karelian. I was told she was Kenneth Stephenson's stepdaughter. Do you have a stepsister by that name?"

Her expression immediately became shuttered. "I am Larissa Alexandrovna, or I once was. What do you want of me?"

Startled, Ian exclaimed, "You're Lara?"

Her dark brows arched. "Indeed. Why is that surprising?"

Ian shook his head, feeling a fool for having missed the obvious. "I'm sorry, I had it firmly in mind that Lara was a girl of thirteen or fourteen. I didn't expect a grown woman." If he hadn't assumed she was English, he would have known immediately, for she had Pyotr's high, dramatic Slavic cheekbones. Those slanted amber eyes attested to the centuries when Russia had been harried by the Golden Hordes of Central Asia. The inevitable mixing of the races had given rise to a Russian proverb Pyotr had sometimes used: "Scratch a Russian and you'll find a Tartar." His niece was living proof of his words, for clearly her ancestors had included Mongol warriors; the expression she wore at that moment would do credit to Genghis Khan in a mistrustful mood.

With more than a hint of hostility, she said, "I've been Laura Stephenson since I was ten. No one calls me Lara now."

"But your uncle did."

"My uncle?" Her hostility vanished and her face went suddenly pale. "You know my Uncle Pyotr?"

"I'm afraid I'm the bearer of more bad news," Ian said gravely. "Colonel Kushutkin died in Bokhara last year."

She closed her eyes and a spasm of grief crossed her face. "I was afraid something had happened to him," she said sorrowfully. "It had been so long since his last letter, and even longer since I saw him in person. I was only thirteen during his last visit to England."

Ian nodded, enlightened. "That must be why he talked of you as a much younger girl—it was the image he carried in his mind."

Her hands clenched convulsively. "My mother always said Pyotr's taste for adventure would lead to death in some wild, distant place."

"It did," Ian said, "but not before he had seen and done things most men only dream of. He told me once that only a poor-spirited coward would want to die in his own bed."

"How did you know him?"

"We were prisoners together in the Black Well of Bokhara." Ian's throat tightened. He hated speaking of what had happened there, but Lara had a right to know. "There are many Russian slaves in Bokhara, and the Foreign Office was worried that they would provide an excuse for the tsar to invade and annex the khanate. I was sent to Bokhara to ask the amir to release the slaves, which would remove a source of provocation. Unfortunately, I made the mistake of going to Kokand first, and the amir decided that meant I was a spy. He threw me into the Black Well, where Pyotr had been imprisoned for six months. We shared the cell for a year. In the end, he saved my life.''

Laura gave Ian a searching look. "How?"

"The amir finally decided to execute me. When the guards came, I was feverish, out of my head. Pyotr Andreyovich insisted on going in my place." Ian stared into the fire, remembering. In the last moments before he was taken away, Pyotr had tried to tell Ian something, speaking with frantic urgency, but Ian was so delirious that he had understood only that his friend was going to die. He remembered nothing else. Ever since, he had had the frustrating sense that he had missed something vital, yet no matter how much he tried, he couldn't recall what. "Pyotr said that a quick execution was better than staying in the Black Well and dying slowly of the lung condition he had."

Her brows drew together. "Why did the guards accept him in your place?"

"Probably it never occurred to them that anyone would choose to be executed before his time," Ian replied. "It helped that Pyotr and I were about the same height, both skinny as scarecrows, and with beards covering most of our faces. His hair was darker than mine, but we were so filthy that the differences weren't obvious—especially not to men who thought that all *ferengis,* all Europeans, looked much the same."

Tears glinted in Laura's eyes. "So because you were younger and more likely to survive, Pyotr gave you a chance at life."

Yes, and it had been an excruciatingly difficult gift to accept. But that was not something that Pyotr's niece needed to know. "I heard later that your uncle died with great bravery. He stood straight and crossed himself, saying that he died a Christian. Then he commended his soul to God."

"Strange," she murmured. "I didn't know he was religious."

"Perhaps he wasn't earlier, but prison has a way of reducing life to its essentials." Ian had envied Pyotr his faith, which had grown through the months until it became a beacon that warmed them both. Then Pyotr had died, and the light had died with him.

Visibly bracing herself, she asked, "How was he executed?"

More and more, Ian admired her. India polarized European women, making them either frail or strong. Laura was not frail. "Pyotr was beheaded," Ian replied. "It's unpleasant to think of, but quick and relatively painless. The amir considered himself humane when he changed from hanging to beheading."

"Forgive me if I'm not impressed by the amir's kindness," she said dryly. "But at least you managed to survive. Did the British government arrange for your release from prison?"

"Hardly. They were quite willing to assume that I was dead," Ian said, not quite able to conceal his bitterness. "My sister and her husband came to Bokhara and rescued me from that damned hole by sheer bluster."

Laura's eyes rounded. "Your *sister*?"

"Juliet is rather remarkable. If you like, I'll tell you the whole story later, but now I want to carry out Pyotr's last request." Ian leaned over to his baggage and extracted a small rectangular package, then handed it to Laura. "He asked me to see that you got this if I ever had the chance. Since I knew where your stepfather was stationed, I decided to deliver it in person."

She unwrapped the waterproof covering to find a small Russian Bible. The volume was a work of art, with a cover of tooled leather and a hand-painted frontispiece that depicted the Virgin and Child in the distinctive style of the Orthodox Church. But the greatest value lay in the fact that every available inch of blank paper was covered with penciled words written in Russian.

"It's Pyotr's prison journal," the major said. "He wanted you to have it."

She thumbed through the Bible, aching inside at the knowledge that her only uncle had written these words, and now he was dead. "Have you read what he wrote?"

Cameron shook his head. "I learned some spoken Russian from Pyotr, mostly curse words, but I don't read or write the language at all. Can you decipher it?"

She stopped on a middle page and studied the Cyrillic

script, which was so small as to be almost illegible. "My Russian is still fluent and I'm familiar with Uncle Pyotr's hand since he wrote me regularly, but this is almost like a code. He seems to have used abbreviations and left out words to save space." Brow furrowed, she slowly translated, "I think this says 'God be thanked, company has arrived. An Englishman, more's the pity, but better than nothing.' " She smiled, then bit her lower lip. "I'm sorry. I'm sure he didn't mean it as an insult."

"You needn't apologize for Pyotr. I was equally unenthralled at finding myself sharing quarters with a Russian officer. But in time I realized that I could not have asked for a better companion in adversity."

She sighed. "You knew him far better than I did. To me, Pyotr was a magical figure, not quite real. He would swoop in every few years bearing gifts and telling tales. I remember one story about a great bear that traveled the ice fields of the north searching for the Pole Star. Instead, he found a princess named Lara. The next day, Pyotr was gone again." Remembering, she ran her palm over the gilded leather, wishing she could draw out the essence of her uncle. "Thank you for bringing me this. It helps a little to have something of his."

The Scots burr in Cameron's voice became more pronounced. "I'm sorry he isn't here in person. If he hadn't sacrificed himself, perhaps he would be. Juliet and Ross would not have left Pyotr in prison if they had found him alive instead of me."

Hearing the guilt and regret, Laura said, "But you told me Pyotr was very ill. He always had weak lungs, so he probably would not have survived the extra time in prison."

"There's no way to be sure of that," Ian said tightly. "Neither he nor I were physicians. He might have been strong enough to last another six months."

The pain in the major's voice made Laura feel a fleeting sense of kinship with him. Pyotr and Kenneth might be beyond grief now, but their survivors would be suffering for a long time. "You mustn't blame yourself for living," she said gently. "If you hadn't, I might never have known what happened to my uncle, nor had this to remember him by." It didn't go far enough, but she was too drained to manage more. "I'd better get dressed. As you said, it's going to be a difficult day."

* * *

For Laura, the hours passed with the distorted, heightened reality of a dream. By the time she had dressed in her one dark gown, the headman of Nanda had arrived. After praising Kenneth's justice and wisdom, the headman offered a burial site on a hill overlooking the small local river. Two "untouchable" women came from the village to help Laura prepare her stepfather's body for burial. She was grateful for the women's sympathy and experienced help, and was unsurprised to learn that they had come at Major Cameron's request. His aid was nothing if not practical.

In a hot climate, burials took place as soon as possible, and all too soon it was time to take Kenneth Stephenson to his final resting spot. His wrapped body was carried on a bamboo bed borne by eight men. In a Hindu family the pallbearers would be close relatives, but these were a mixture of Kenneth's most senior servants and volunteers from the village.

Laura walked behind her stepfather's bier. Major Cameron was beside her, silent but quick to help when her steps faltered. Behind them followed the whole population of the village, the women wailing with grief at the loss of the man who had been not only the face of the British Sirkar, but their friend.

The grave had already been dug and a sturdy wooden cross planted at the head. It was a peaceful place, shaded by a jacaranda tree and cooled by the breeze from the river. In spring, the air would be fragrant with blossoms. Laura watched numbly, her only goal to get through the burial without breaking down in public. This was one occasion when she might have discarded British calm for tempestuous Russian emotion, but over the years control had become second nature to her.

With no clergyman or prepared service, there was an awkward moment of silence after the interment. Smoothly, before the interval grew too long, Major Cameron began to recite in English, "The Lord is my shepherd, I shall not want . . ."

Laura blinked back stinging tears, grateful that Cameron had chosen a psalm that Kenneth had loved rather than the somber burial service.

After ending, "and I shall dwell in the house of the Lord forever," Cameron added, "By a man's works we shall know him. Though I did not have the privilege of knowing Kenneth Stephenson in life, the love and honor shown today by those he served is the highest tribute a man can receive. May he rest in peace.''

The major repeated everything he had said in Urdu, the villagers nodding in approval. After the grave had been filled in, people pressed forward to lay garlands of marigolds on the earthen mound, many of the women openly weeping. As the major had observed, Kenneth Stephenson had been much loved.

But no one would miss him as much as Laura. As she walked stiffly back to camp, she had never felt so alone in her life.

Chapter 6

❦ ❦ ❦

AFTER THE FUNERAL, Laura went straight to her tent, for only there could she allow herself to cry. Tears racked her as afternoon faded and night fell. She was shamed by the knowledge that she wept not only for her stepfather, but also from sorrow for the empty life that lay ahead of her. It was unlikely that she would ever again be so close to another person.

Eventually her tears dried from sheer exhaustion. She managed to sleep for a few hours, only to wake again in the still hour before dawn. This time there was no disorientation; she knew exactly where she was and what had happened. Nothing would bring her stepfather back; it was time to face the rest of her life. Getting to her feet, she located by touch the robe and slippers that her maid always left by the bed.

Outside the air was pleasantly cool. The forest never slept, and she paused in the door of her tent to take stock. The scene was rather like the morning before, with the servants sleeping around the larger fire. In the distance a hyena howled.

Much closer was Major Cameron, who sat cleaning a shotgun by the nearer fire. His figure was silhouetted against the light, giving an impression of dark, whipcord power. He was very unlike the civil service administrators Laura knew. Even the other army officers she had met could not match his air of taut, finely honed menace. She should have been wary, yet instead she was drawn to him, and not only because he had been kind to her. Something about the man made her feel safe, even though he was not a safe man.

Hearing her movement, his head came up sharply. Laura held still until he identified her. "Don't you ever sleep,

Major?'' she asked as she approached the fire and sat in a camp chair.

"Nowhere near enough. But since I'm insomniac anyhow, I might as well make use of it." He fixed a rag in the split end of the cleaning rod. "This gun should have been cleaned after being fired the night before last, but with so much going on, it got overlooked." As he lifted the barrel of the disassembled weapon, he added, "And call me Ian— I'm not a major anymore."

"I thought that military titles followed a man around for the rest of his life." Laura saw that the shotgun was Kenneth's. She was glad the major had thought of it; her stepfather had always been meticulous in caring for equipment.

"The army is behind me," Ian said tersely. "I've no desire to be defined by it for the rest of my life."

Laura must have still been a bit sleepy, or she never would have asked, "Why did you resign?"

He raised his head and gave her a hard glance that made her sorry she had asked, but before she could withdraw the question, he said tersely, "I'd had enough of the army."

Wanting to smooth over the awkward moment, she said, "Thank you for . . . taking care of so many things. The funeral, the guns, everything. I don't know what I would have done without you."

He began rubbing the pieces of the firing mechanism with an oiled rag. In the ruddy firelight, his face was a dramatic collection of shadows and sharp planes, both fascinating and disquieting. "One way or another, you would have managed."

"I suppose. But you made everything much easier." She gazed into the fire. "Strange how quickly things can change. A day and a half ago I had a life and a family. Now they're both gone. I'll find something to fill in the empty spaces, but I have no idea what. The idea is a bit frightening."

Ian frowned as he held the gun barrel to the fire, peering through it to check for cleanliness. "You've no family at all?"

"Pyotr Andreyovich was the last. I suppose there are some distant cousins in Russia, but none that I remember. My first father was an only child, so there are no near relations on that side. My mother had two older brothers, but one, Sergei, died fighting Napoleon before I was born, and Uncle Pyotr never married. So now there is just me."

"What about Stephenson's family? They may not be blood relations, but you've been one of them for years."

Laura's mouth hardened. "They didn't really approve of his marriage to a wild Russian. My mother was too dramatic and unconventional for them—like a peacock among pigeons. She and I were tolerated for my stepfather's sake, but never welcomed."

Ian began to reassemble the shotgun. "It's hard to imagine having no relatives. I don't see mine very often, but knowing that they exist is a kind of anchor in the world."

"Be grateful they're an anchor, not a millstone."

"I've some of both sorts." He gave a faint smile that softened his features. "Do you have plans for the future, Miss Stephenson? Or haven't you had time to think about that?"

"If I'm to call you Ian, you must call me Laura." She smiled wryly. "I've only known you for a day, but it seems much longer."

"You don't like the name Lara? Pyotr always called you that, and the name suits you. It's unusual."

"I'd really prefer Laura. I'm used to it, and besides, there's nothing unusual about me," she said uneasily. "I'm a thoroughly unremarkable female. As for plans . . . I really don't know. My father left me a bit of income, enough for me to survive, but not much more, so I suppose I'll go to a city and look for employment. I'd make a decent teacher or governess, and the work would save me from boredom. After running my father's household for years, I'm used to being busy."

"That sort of menial job would be burdensome for a woman used to being independent." He hesitated a moment. "I know it's none of my business, but marriage and family are what most women want. It's to your credit that you chose to make a home for your stepfather, but now he's gone. India must be full of men who would be honored if you would accept them. In return, you would have comfort, family, and the security of being loved."

He sounded just like her stepfather. Laura recalled that she had told Kenneth that she would look for a husband if he died. She dismissed the promise; she had given it only for his peace of mind. Wanting to avoid the topic of marriage, she said, "I don't know if I'll stay in India. I might return to England."

He reassembled the shotgun, the barrel locking into place with a decisive snap. "Then you won't want a husband whose career will keep him here. But for a woman as attractive as you, there will be eager suitors wherever you go."

Though the words were a compliment, his manner was so detached as to be downright irritating. He might say she was attractive, but he certainly didn't act as if he believed his own words. Tartly she said, "To be honest, I really don't wish to tie myself to a husband. I've gotten along without one perfectly well for twenty-four years and I don't see the need to marry now. I'm quite capable of taking care of myself."

He gave her an appraising glance. "You sound like a woman who has been pestered on this subject before. My apologies."

He saw more with one eye than most people saw with two. Hastily Laura said, "Are we leaving for Baipur in the morning? I was so distracted yesterday that I didn't make any preparations, but there's no reason to stay here any longer."

He lifted her father's rifle and began to break it down for cleaning. "Unfortunately there's still the man-eater. With your father gone, the responsibility for killing it has devolved on me—this afternoon the headman asked if I'd have a go at it."

"I'd forgotten about the tiger," she admitted. "Tracking the man-eater could take days or weeks."

"I'm afraid so," he said apologetically. "You might prefer to return to Baipur with your servants rather than wait for me to escort you. While I won't stay here indefinitely, I should try for at least a fortnight before giving up."

Laura hesitated, feeling that the decision of whether to stay or go back alone was beyond her. "I'll wait and see. Perhaps you'll shoot the beast on your first attempt."

"That could happen. The villagers have been diligent, wanting everything ready for when your father came. They've built a *machan*, a platform, at a water hole that the tiger visits regularly." He used the cleaning rod to push an oiled rag down the rifle's barrel, scrubbing up and down to remove all the corrosive grains of black powder. "The moon will be almost full tonight, so they'll stake out a kid as bait. If the tiger cooperates, it might be all over by tomorrow."

"I assume you've hunted tigers before."

"Yes, though it's been five years." He began rubbing the rifle's hammer with the oiled rag, his expression distant. "The last time was when my brother-in-law visited and I took him hunting in the hill country north of Cambay. We spent several days stalking a tiger before cornering it in a rocky gorge. Ross was in the best position for a shot, so I waited for him to take it. But he didn't fire, even when the tiger whirled and charged right at him. Ross went down, and I was sure he'd been killed—scared the devil out of me. I took a wild shot at the tiger and missed, then went to Ross, expecting to find him in bloody pieces. Instead, he was fine. He had deliberately dropped to the ground to let the tiger bolt by him and escape."

Ian's voice took on a tinge of self-mockery. "I was so relieved that he was all right that naturally I lost my temper and started roaring furiously at him, telling him how many kinds of an idiot he was. Ross patiently waited me out— he's the most reasonable man I know, it's his only fault— then said that he had decided that the tiger skin looked better on the original owner than it would on his wall. Besides, what kind of sport was it when he had a rifle and the tiger didn't?"

Laura chuckled. "He may have a point."

"So I realized after I calmed down. A tiger is a magnificent animal—perhaps it's jealousy that makes men want to hunt them down. But as Ross said, the odds are stacked heavily in the man's favor, which isn't really very good sport. After his visit, I lost my enthusiasm for trophy hunting. I've concentrated on animals that could be eaten ever since."

"Speaking of eating, when tigers develop a taste for human flesh, they definitely have the advantage over unarmed villagers," Laura observed.

"Too true. That's why I'm going after this one. It's already killed at least a dozen people in Nanda and the neighboring villages. This morning I'm going to scout the area of the water hole. In the afternoon I'll go to the machan so I'll be in position when dusk falls." Almost casually, he added, "Care to join me for that?"

"On the machan?" she asked, startled.

He nodded. "To avoid disturbing the wildlife we'd have

to walk, but the pond is less than three miles from the village."

Laura considered. Today Kenneth's belongings must be sorted, the bedclothes burned as a guard against possible infection, some of his possessions distributed to chosen servants and others packed to be taken back to Baipur. But none of that would take long, and when she was done, time would hang heavy on her hands. "I'd like to go. I've never been on a tiger hunt."

"This won't be a colorful one with elephants and beaters," he warned, "but it will be quite safe, and might be interesting. Of course, it could also be deadly dull if the tiger doesn't put in an appearance."

She watched intently as he began reassembling the rifle. He had a physical grace, a quality of being wholly in command of his body, that intrigued her. How would those deft hands feel if they touched her?

Her face colored when she realized the direction of her thoughts; a decent young Englishwoman would never have such fantasies. Of course, she was neither decent nor English. How fortunate that Ian Cameron was uninterested in her, because he was the sort of man who could make female judgment fly straight out the window. In proof of which, Laura found herself saying, "Please forgive me if the question is horribly impertinent, but has losing an eye made shooting more difficult?"

His thick brows rose sardonically. "Wondering if I'll be able to prevent you from being eaten?"

"Of course not." She blushed again. "You did say it would be safe in the machan. And surely a tender young kid would be tastier than an old spinster."

"I'm not fool enough to answer a comment like that." Again he gave a fleeting smile that was too soon over. "Actually, my shooting is better than ever. It made sense when I thought about it, because a marksman closes his off eye when aiming. Having only one eye simplifies the process, and it seems to increase my concentration on the target. Of course, it's fortunate that I'm left-handed. If I shot right-handed, losing my right eye probably would have ruined my marksmanship."

"How interesting that there is a positive benefit," she said, intrigued. "What are the other effects of losing an eye?"

"Well, people stare more." He touched the eyepatch. "Asiatics have an almost mystical respect for vision—to lose an eye is to be incomplete and quite possibly wicked. Some of the natives make signs against the evil eye behind my back."

"I didn't know that," she said in a small voice. "I'm sorry, it was rude of me to ask."

"I'd rather be asked outright than have people try to avoid looking me in the face," he said. "I lost the eye as a result of a beating in prison and it was painful and a nuisance, to say the least. However, I was so grateful not to lose the other eye that I didn't spend much time cursing fate."

He fingered the eyepatch again. "I'm still adjusting to the differences. Oddly enough, though I haven't as wide a field of vision, the range has increased from what it was at first." He thought a moment more. "I had constant headaches at first, but they're decreasing. It is hard to judge depth and distance—sometimes I find myself pawing the ground like a pony because I can't tell if there's a step in front of me. And don't ask me to pour a drink unless you're feeling adventurous about the results. Still, it's getting easier all the time."

"There's at least one other benefit that you might not appreciate," Laura said lightly. "You look *very* dashing with an eyepatch. When you go into society, you'll have to fight off romantic young ladies."

His lighter mood vanished as if it had never existed. "I sincerely hope not." He got to his feet and lifted the shotgun and rifle. "Where do you want me to put these? Now that they're yours, you should probably keep them in your tent."

Though Laura accepted his change of topic, his dismissal of her comment didn't change her opinion: like it or not, the former major was fated to attract female admiration. How fortunate that Laura knew that marriage was not for her, or she might have been tempted to throw out some lures.

Ian spent a productive day acquainting himself with the water hole and the surrounding forest under the direction of Punwa, a taciturn woodsman from the village. It wasn't until they separated and Ian began walking from Nanda to the camp that it occurred to him that he felt better than he had in a long, long time. The demanding events of the last day and a half seemed to have temporarily freed him from the dark wheel of his own misery. He was still not his old self, for the shadows of melancholy had merely retreated a short distance, not vanished. Nonetheless, for the first time he could believe that a day would come when life would again be more pleasure than pain.

The hours he had spent in the forest had been healing. He had always loved nature, whether it was the desert, the jungle, or the beloved hills and coast of Scotland. Though not in most ways a patient man, he was capable of spending hours waiting for birds and animals to reveal themselves. But there had been little time to enjoy the natural world since his escape from Bokhara. He had spent the previous months in convalescence and travel, and there had been no opportunity to simply be still.

No, that wasn't true. There had been opportunity, but he had been incapable of enjoying anything.

Ian was skirting a pond outside Nanda when a dozen wild peafowl fluttered up. The metallic blues and greens of the males shimmered with impossible beauty. No wonder they occupied an important place in Hindu myth and legend; if India had a national bird, it was the peacock.

But dignity vanished when the creatures began to drink. Tails tilted whimsically to the sky when they bobbed forward to dip their beaks in the water, then dropped when the birds straightened up to swallow. The flock teetered back and forth like a collection of feathered seesaws. As Ian continued on his way, he found himself smiling. There hadn't been many smiles in his life lately.

Laura made him smile. As he resumed walking to the camp, he realized that she was the principal reason for his improved mood. He had talked more freely to her in the last day than to anyone since Pyotr had died. Perhaps it was because she was Pyotr's niece; Ian was intrigued by occasional gestures and turns of phrase that reminded him of her uncle. She also had some of Pyotr's character, for even in the depths of grief she was capable of humor and compassion.

Yet he suspected that the underlying reason he felt comfortable with Laura was because she, too, was suffering. Since his escape from Bokhara, Ian had learned the harsh truth behind the old proverb that misery loved company.

The only occasion when he had felt close to another person had been the night when his sister had wept on his shoulder, convinced that her marriage was over. Juliet's pain had drawn him out of himself to try to comfort her. He had even given some advice that, Juliet later informed him, had made it possible for her to heal the breach with her husband.

It had been much harder to be with her and Ross when they were radiantly happy. In fact, it was difficult for him to bear the company of anyone who was normal. But Laura's presence was soothing, for her pain and vulnerability were similar to his own.

He hoped that she decided to wait for him to accompany her back to Baipur. The journey would delay his departure for Scotland for several more weeks, but that was of no real importance. He wanted to assure himself that she was back among friends before he said good-bye.

Idly he wondered why she was so set against marriage; she did not have the manner of a woman who despised men. The most likely explanation was that she had suffered a broken heart. If so, perhaps she would be willing to accept a husband when she recovered. He hoped so; he disapproved of such a waste of womanly warmth and charm. Beyond that, he felt a responsibility for Pyotr's niece; he didn't like thinking of her living the gray life of a governess in another woman's house.

But it wouldn't come to that. Ian might be less than a man physically, but there was nothing wrong with his judgment. Laura was the sort of woman who would always attract men eager to love and protect her. She, at least, would not need to spend the rest of her life alone.

Chapter 7

❦ ❦ ❦

LAURA HAD DRESSED in her custom-made riding clothing for the trek to the machan. After the major inspected her tan divided skirt and high boots, he gave a nod of approval. "A practical outfit. A pity more Englishwomen don't do the same."

"The divided skirt was my father's suggestion," she explained as she hooked a canteen to her belt and donned her topi. "So much time is spent on horseback in India that he thought it would be better if I rode astride except on the most formal social occasions, which means hardly ever. And he flatly forbade me to wear a corset in the hot weather. He claimed that corsets were responsible for the fact that so many Anglo-Indian women are in delicate health—they can't breathe."

"He sounds like a man of rare good sense. I'm sorry I didn't have a chance to meet him."

Laura was sorry, too. The thought produced one of the waves of disabling sorrow that swept through her several times a day. She fell in beside Ian and they began their hike to the water hole. The path wound among the village fields, then through light forest interspersed with grassy meadows. The sunshine and lovely countryside lifted her spirits. Though she would never stop missing her stepfather, neither would she allow herself to be drowned by despair.

As she had observed earlier, Ian saw more with one eye than most people did with two. As they walked he wordlessly drew her attention to things she would otherwise not have noticed. In fact, his awareness of their surroundings was a product of all his senses, not only sight. It was he who heard the almost inaudible wingbeats of a brilliantly colored sunbird that hovered like a hummingbird by a flow-

ering shrub. Later he pushed aside some grasses to reveal a
cluster of white flowers. The blossoms looked unremarkable, but when he picked a sprig and handed it to Laura,
she found that they had a sweetly haunting fragrance.

Not all of his discoveries were so innocuous. After twenty
minutes of walking, he halted and threw up one hand to
block Laura's progress while he studied the forest to the
left. Then he beckoned her into a protected spot among the
arching aerial roots of a banyan tree, directing her gaze
toward a tree about a hundred yards away. Obediently she
shaded her eyes with one hand and peered upward, wondering what she was supposed to see.

Her jaw dropped when she recognized the creature loung-
ing among the dappled shadows. It was a leopard. The great
cat's spots were near-perfect camouflage as it sprawled lazily along a branch, paws and tail drooping with the bone-
less ease of a child's rag toy.

When the rasping voice of a leopard sounded right next
to Laura, she nearly jumped out of her skin. She gave a
strangled gasp and whipped her head around, fearing to find
that a leopard had dropped onto her companion. Instead, to
her amazement, she discovered that Ian was the one making
the sounds. Bemused, she glanced back at the real leopard,
wondering how it would react.

Slumber disturbed, the cat's head shot up and its ears
cocked forward. After a moment of intense listening, it
flowed silently down the tree trunk and vanished in the
grass.

Nervously Laura watched the rippling stalks that indicated that the panther was coming to investigate what it
clearly thought was a rival. She didn't believe that Ian would
allow either of them to be eaten—but apart from cocking
the hammer of his rifle, he seemed remarkably unconcerned
by the fact that a dangerous predator was stalking them.

After a taut minute had passed, the leopard emerged from
the high grass a dozen feet away from Laura and Ian. Whiskers twitching and body low, it hesitated and swung its head
back and forth, sniffing curiously as it tried to locate its
fellow.

When its gaze reached Ian and Laura, the furry face took
on an expression of near-human shock. The leopard's reaction was so comical that Laura almost laughed aloud. The

beast looked like a vicar enraged by the discovery of a frog in the baptismal font.

Hackles rising, the cat spat furiously at the man who had the impudence to speak like a leopard. Then the beast whirled and bounded away with fluid, heartstopping grace. In the blink of an eye, it was gone.

Laura discovered that she was holding her breath, so she exhaled shakily. "What was that all about?"

Ian gave her the closest thing to a real smile that she had seen yet. "I thought you might be interested in seeing a leopard. Lovely creature, wasn't he?"

"Yes, but I prefer cats that aren't large enough to eat me," she said with asperity.

"We were in no danger. Look how he ran away when he saw that we were humans."

Laura arched her brows. "Are you going to try to convince me that leopards never attack humans?"

"No," he said as they resumed their progress. "But killing humans is an aberration. Men talk about the law of the jungle, but animals seldom kill except for food." A hard edge entered his voice. "Humankind could learn a great deal from them."

Ahead a flock of green bee-eaters whirled away, disturbed by the approaching humans. Laura looked not at the birds but at her companion, and at the slight smile on his face as his gaze followed them upward.

"Did you know that if you sit and watch for an hour almost anywhere in India, you can usually count a hundred species of birds?" he said. "I used to make a game of it. Once I counted one hundred seventy-three breeds in an hour."

Laura felt a rush of sympathy so intense that it threatened to choke her. What had it been like for a man with such love of the outdoors to be locked in a dank, filthy hole without sunshine or flowers or birdsongs? It must have been hell in the truest sense of the word. Swallowing the lump in her throat, she said, "Why didn't you go into the forest service instead of the army? You know more about the Indian countryside than anyone I know."

"I probably would have been wiser to do that, but to an energetic eighteen-year-old, civilian duty sounds dull." He gave her an ironic glance. "I was mad keen to go into the army and defend the empire from the heathen. The young

lack a proper respect for life." He checked the angle of the
sun. "Time to stop loitering. The woodsman, Punwa, will
be waiting for us."

Another ten minutes of walking brought them to their
destination. The machan was a crude platform a dozen feet
above the ground, built in a tree that gave a clear view of
the water hole. The builders had placed it downwind so that
human scent would not disturb the animals that came to
drink.

Ian linked his hands together to provide a foothold for
Laura, and she scrambled up to the platform. He himself
waited on the ground until Punwa arrived with the kid that
was to be used as bait. After the small creature was tethered
and the woodsman had left, Ian swung easily up to join
Laura. "The man-eater is an old male with a bad paw and
a distinctive limp. Punwa says that a young tigress sometimes comes here as well, but she has never attacked a human. So if a tiger shows up and I don't shoot, it will be
because it's the wrong one."

"Won't she eat the kid?"

"Probably. We'll have to hope that the right tiger comes.
Even if he doesn't, we'll have plenty of company." He settled down with his back against the tree trunk, rifle and
ammunition convenient to his left hand. "It's interesting.
Since all animals need water, they usually observe a water
hole truce. Creatures that are enemies elsewhere will ignore
each other when they're drinking."

After that, neither of them spoke. Though it never would
have occurred to Laura to choose to spend a night watching
a pond, she found the ever-changing cavalcade fascinating.
A suspicious, quick-eyed jackal trotted up to the far side of
the pond and lapped its water at the same time that several
of the graceful spotted deer called chital were drinking near
the kid. As the jackal left, a troop of exuberant rhesus monkeys romped up, acting much like a human family pick-
nicking in the country. They were soon followed by a
chattering flock of parakeets, the noisiest of the pond's visitors. Some of the visitors showed mild curiosity in the kid,
but none disturbed it.

Yet interesting as the parade was, Laura found herself
distracted by Ian's closeness. The machan had room for two
people, but only just, and their shoulders almost touched.
Her senses heightened until she was conscious of his

slightest movement. While her gaze might be on the dive of a little blue kingfisher, all head and beak, her skin prickled with awareness of her companion's breathing, and the warmth of his body.

For eight years she had tried to forget the magic of a man's touch, but Ian was making a shambles of her resolutions. She wanted to reach out and embrace him, bury her face against his throat and taste the salt of his skin.

Her reaction fueled her worst suspicions about her nature. If her companion had shown the least interest in her—if his fingers had brushed her hand, or if he had smiled into her eyes—she would have melted like wax in the Indian sun.

Thank heaven Ian was oblivious to her overheated imagination. As Laura ruthlessly suppressed her longings, she swore that she would not allow herself to get into such an intimate situation again. Though the major was indifferent to her modest charms, another man might not have been.

Dusk fell rapidly, and it was nearly full dark when a tiger emerged languidly from the underbrush. In the bright moonlight, its stripes shone pale gold. Laura had never seen a tiger in the wild, and she caught her breath, awed by its dangerous beauty.

Even that tiny sound caused the massive striped head to swing toward the machan. She held utterly still until the tiger resumed its stroll. Ian silently raised his rifle, but held his fire. Laura wondered how he could identify the correct tiger at night, then remembered that he had said that the man-eater had a bad paw. This beast had no limp, so it must be the innocent tigress rather than the rogue they sought.

Catching the predator's scent, the kid gave a thin bleat of fear. Instantly the cat dropped into a stalking position and slunk toward the staked animal, tail switching and hindquarters quivering with anticipation. Laura bit her lip to prevent herself from asking Ian to shoot into the air to drive the tigress away. Doing so might save the kid at the price of alerting the man-eater, if it was near.

The kid backed to the end of its tether and bleated again, its terrified cry sending a chill down Laura's spine. The sound also affected the tigress, for she abruptly abandoned her stalk. Majestic as a queen, she walked up to the kid, lowered her head, and sniffed. Briefly the large beast and the small stood nose to nose. Then the tigress gave the kid a friendly swipe with her huge tongue, using a force that staggered the little animal.

Peace having been made, the tigress moved to the water and drank, then disappeared into the night. Laura released her breath. The water hole truce had held, or perhaps the tigress's maternal instincts had been roused by the kid's vulnerability.

Laura glanced at Ian in time to see his head turn toward her. Neither spoke, and she could not see his face in the shadows, but words were not needed to know that they shared the same sense of wonder over what they had seen. For a moment she felt as close to him emotionally as she was physically.

After the tigress, traffic slowed down and eventually Laura began to feel drowsy. She was trying to suppress a yawn when Ian took off his jacket, folded it into a crude pillow, and gestured for her to lie down. By shifting his position a little, he created enough space so that she could rest.

Gratefully she accepted his unspoken suggestion. After unpinning her hair, she curled up on her side, the improvised pillow under her head. Laura had always been aware of the fact that every person had a subtle, individual scent, and Ian's jacket carried his. It made her feel safe, so safe. . . .

She was floating in the dreamy space between waking and sleeping when the insight emerged. The reason she felt so safe with Ian was because he didn't desire her. Most men did, and she was always uncomfortably aware of their yearning. But the feeling that she got from the major was very like what she had felt from her stepfather: kindness and protection.

Because she was so accustomed to generating male desire, she had been disconcerted when Ian was not attracted to her. But the present situation was better; if he did not desire her, it was safe for them to be friends.

It was a delicious thought to carry into sleep.

Ian kept watch through the night, but the man-eater did not come. Nonetheless, his vigil was not unpleasant. The grasses on the far side of the water hole rippled like pale silk in the moonlight, and the soft sound of Laura's breathing was as soothing as gentle music. He liked having her close. He tried to imagine that it was Georgina sleeping beside him, hair loose and one hand curled against his thigh, but he couldn't quite bring the picture into focus. Georgina might dance all night, but she would never stay quietly in the forest.

At dawn Laura woke and sat up, moving carefully so she wouldn't fall off the machan. A shaft of sunlight slanted through the leaves and struck the hair that tumbled luxuriously about her shoulders, turning it to glowing bronze. Her slanted eyes were the same shade, and Ian once more thought of a cat—a sleek, pretty puss who dined on cream and slept on silk.

"I have an interesting assortment of sore muscles." She yawned and stretched her arms. "But I assume that the maneater didn't oblige us."

"I'm afraid not," he replied. "I warned you that it might be a dull night."

To his regret, she tied her hair back with a ribbon as she continued, "Still, I'm glad I came. It was quite an education. And the kid must be grateful that there was no more excitement. A second tiger might not have been as charitable as the first."

Ian handed her one of the chapatis he had brought. After they'd eaten and each had a drink from Laura's canteen, he descended from the machan, then helped his companion down. Her waist was slim and supple under his hands, and he enjoyed touching her even without the undercurrent of sexuality that would have been there before Bokhara. If only . . .

He swore at himself; thinking about what might have been was a sure path to despair. He untethered the kid and they began the trek back to Nanda. By the time they reached the fields outside the village, the morning sun had loosened muscles stiffened by a night in the machan.

They were walking along a broad grassy track that divided the field on the left from the forest when Ian raised a hand to shade his eye and squinted into the distance. "There's Punwa now, coming to learn what luck we had. Would you mind waiting here for a few minutes? I need to return the kid and also make arrangements with Punwa to go hunting later this morning. If the tiger won't come to us, we'll have to go to the tiger."

Laura gave him a quizzical look. "I know that you said you don't sleep much, but surely you must sometimes?"

"Not if I can help it," he said, his voice hardening. Kid in tow, he set off toward Punwa. Laura knit her brows as she watched him go. Even when he was in a more relaxed mood, the major reminded her of a tautly drawn bowstring; if he didn't learn to rest, someday he would shatter.

She turned toward the nearby field, where women and children were already working. Recognizing many of them from previous tours, Laura waved. The nearest was a young wife named Kunthi. Laura called a greeting to her and received a shy smile in return. The girl gestured toward a child who was picking wildflowers at the edge of the field. "Remember my Narwa, memsahib? He is not so little now."

"What a big boy he has become," Laura called back. "I would not have known him."

His attention caught by the conversation, Narwa gave Laura a sunny smile and began walking toward her, clutching flowers in both pudgy hands. Since he wasn't much above two years old, his legs were bowed and his course erratic. Laura smiled and perched on the trunk of a fallen tree, guessing that he would prefer to reach her under his own power.

Between one heartbeat and the next, the scene changed from pastoral peace to horror. Catching movement out of the corner of her eye, Laura glanced casually to her right—and froze with shock when she saw a tiger slinking out of the forest, belly tight to the ground in a predator's stalk. This was no startled leopard or maternal tigress but the man-eater himself, a quarter ton of muscle, teeth, and claws. And the object of his hunt was Narwa, who, oblivious to danger, was bringing Laura his bouquet.

Hoping that her voice might frighten the tiger off, she jumped to her feet and shouted, *"Ian!"*

But instead of fleeing, the beast accelerated, bounding out of the grass with long strides that covered the ground rapidly in spite of the limp in his left forepaw.

His charge brought him into view of the field workers, who began screaming. Kunthi was closest. With an anguished shriek she began racing toward her son, though she was too far away to reach him before the tiger did.

Hearing his mother's voice, Narwa turned and saw the gold-and-black menace thundering down on him. He whimpered but made no attempt to flee.

Driven by pure instinct, Laura bolted across the open ground, her stomach twisting as she calculated distances and angles. Narwa was about twenty yards from Laura, the tiger perhaps sixty yards beyond and closing fast. Ian was so far away that it would be a difficult shot even if he had heard the shouts and turned around. Worse, if he fired from his present position, he would risk hitting the child or Laura. Only Laura had a chance to make a difference.

By the time she reached Narwa, the tiger was so close that she could see the blazing gold lights of its eyes. It was bunching its muscles for the final spring when she pulled off her topi and threw it at the beast with a furious snap of her wrist.

By sheer luck, the hard shell of the topi banged into the tiger's left eye. As it faltered, hissing with rage, Laura bent and scooped the child into her arms without stopping.

Time seemed to slow down and every sensation was magnified. Narwa was a solid, wiggling weight, and the scented blossoms clutched in his hand tickled her neck. In the distance, the women in the field wailed their despair.

While Laura got a firm grip on Narwa, she pivoted to her right, hoping the heavy tiger would be further slowed by having to change direction. Then she sprinted toward the tree trunk, which would give some protection if she could get behind it. She had once been told by an experienced hunter that if a tiger missed its first rush, it was slow to recover and attack again; surprisingly often its quarry escaped. But the hunter had been talking about tigers who stalked fleet-footed deer, not a woman burdened by a frightened, kicking child.

Behind Laura the tiger's snarl rose to a vicious pitch, but she dared not take the time to look back. The tree trunk was only two strides away. If they could reach it . . .

Before she could complete the thought, she was struck in the side with a brutal force that knocked her clear off her feet. She landed on her back, Narwa still clutched in her arms, and looked up into the horrifying face of the tiger. It roared, a deep sound that frightened her to her marrow and revealed dagger-long fangs that could bring down a buffalo.

Tigers usually killed with teeth rather than claws, but the massive paw swinging toward Laura looked lethal enough to finish off both her and the child. She began to roll, cradling Narwa in her arms. If she was on top when the tiger struck, perhaps the boy would escape harm. Laura found it bizarre to know that in a moment she would be dead. She had never imagined such a lurid ending to her life. Perhaps she should be thinking about the state of her soul, but her last thought was a hope that Papa would be waiting for her, and Tatyana. . . .

The boom of a rifle shattered the air, followed seconds later by another shot. The tiger roared again, this time with pain. Laura looked up to see it rear into the air, the terrifying bulk blocking the sun as the beast twisted and lashed out helplessly with its forepaws. Then, with a hair-curling howl, it collapsed to the earth, legs still thrashing.

Before one of the flailing, lethally clawed paws could hit Laura or the child, Kunthi reached them. She was a small woman, but with superhuman strength she seized Laura beneath the shoulders and dragged her clear of the tiger's death throes. When Laura and the child were both safe, Kunthi pulled Narwa into her own embrace, weeping and rocking back and forth as she cradled her son, who was bellowing with outrage.

Too numb and breathless to move, Laura was still sprawled on the ground among Narwa's crushed flowers when Ian arrived on the scene, having covered the distance in an amazingly short time. He dropped to his knees beside her. "Laura, are you hurt?" he asked urgently. He laid down his rifle, then raised her to a sitting position, one arm around her shoulders.

"I don't know," she whispered, having trouble finding the breath to speak. "Its paw struck my right side."

After examining her side and hip, he whistled softly. "You were incredibly lucky—your canteen must have taken the force of the blow. It was torn off and is lying over by the tiger. Good God, the claws shredded the lower edge of your skirt. I don't see blood, though. Do you feel pain anywhere?"

Laura made a gingerly assessment. Her ribs were sore, but the metal canteen seemed to have prevented any serious injury. "Just bruises, I think." She smiled unsteadily. "Papa gave me that canteen. He said it might save my life, but I don't think this is quite what he had in mind."

"Perhaps he was watching over you this morning." Ian shook his head. "When the tiger knocked you down, I thought you were done for. If it had connected solidly . . ."

By this time, half the village had gathered around and everyone was chattering excitedly. One of the last to come was Narwa's gray-faced young father, who pushed through the crowd and embraced his wife and child. More calmly, Punwa examined the dead tiger. Glancing up, he said, "Fine shooting, Cameron Sahib. Both bullets through the heart."

With Ian's help, Laura managed to get to her feet, then shuddered as she stared down at the tiger. The beast was enormous, at least ten feet long from its nose to the tip of its tail. If it had been just a fraction faster, she would be dead now, and probably Narwa with her.

She began to shake and Ian's arm went around her. In spite of the sun's heat, she felt chilled and was grateful for the warmth of his lean body. "How did you manage to shoot twice so quickly?" she asked. "The shots were only a few seconds apart."

"My rifle is a breechloader," he explained. "It can be fired much faster than a conventional muzzleloader, especially when one is terrified out of one's wits."

"It was certainly a more effective weapon than my topi."

"Perhaps, but throwing the topi was the difference between escape and disaster. It was quick thinking on your part." His arm tightened around her, and when he spoke again, there was cold anger in his voice. "Look at the tiger's left paw, the crippled one. That's the scar of a bullet. A hunter wounded the beast, then didn't track it down to finish the job. The stupid fool was probably responsible for turning this tiger into a man-eater."

"If the Hindus are right, justice will catch up with him in another life," Laura said with brittle humor. "Perhaps he'll come back as a mouse and be eaten by a cat."

Ian's expression lightened. "I sincerely hope so."

The village headman came over. "You are shaken, memsahib. Would you like a ride back to your camp in a bullock cart?"

Knowing how jarring a bullock cart was, Laura shook her head. "I would rather walk. It will relax me."

Since Ian said he didn't need another tigerskin, the headman promised that the pelt would be sent to Baipur after it was tanned. From there, it would be forwarded to whatever new home Laura chose. She thought that she would enjoy walking on this particular beast.

Finally they resumed their interrupted walk to the camp. Laura felt steadier, but she was still glad to take Ian's arm.

When they were out of sight of the village, he said, "If you ever come back to Nanda, you may find that the villagers have set up a small shrine to the tiger lady."

"They might turn me into a minor deity?" she said, bemused.

"Such things have happened before—some Punjabis have established a cult in honor of a British political officer." An amused glint in his eye, he added, "I think you'd make a decent deity. How many women would take on a tiger before breakfast?"

She shuddered as an image of looming fangs flashed through her mind. "I still can't believe that I did what I did."

"Diving into the path of a man-eater is not a rational action, but under life or death circumstances, one often reacts from pure instinct. It's like being in battle."

"Then thank heaven I'm not a soldier!"

He looked into her face, his gaze warm. Then, to her surprise, he bent over and kissed her lightly on the forehead. "It's a privilege to know you, Larissa Alexandrovna."

The touch of his lips was fleeting, but for some reason Laura's knees weakened again. Perhaps it was Ian's use of her true Russian name that made the moment special. But as they continued along the path, she realized ruefully that she would seriously consider challenging another tiger if it meant that he would look at her like that again.

Chapter 8

❦ ❦ ❦

I DON'T KNOW how Ian manages to maintain his spirits, but thank God for his laughter and good nature. We talk of almost everything, except politics, and learn much from each other. I now remember to call him a Scot, not an Englishman, and he uses my patronymic, as a decent Russian would. Can harmony between our two hostile, suspicious empires be far behind?

Laura smiled at Pyotr's ironic comment. Every night she read some of his journal before going to sleep. Her progress was slow, partly because it took time to translate her uncle's sparse, cramped words, more because she found the effort as emotionally draining as it was rewarding. The last time she had seen Pyotr she had been little more than a child, and his letters over the years had mostly been witty accounts of his travels. But through his journal she was coming to know him as a man, and that made her mourn his passing even more.

At the beginning, as her uncle told about his unexpected imprisonment and gradual loss of hope, his entries had been terse and infrequent. The pace picked up and the tone became lighter after Ian had been put in the Black Well. It was obvious that their companionship had been a vital support for both men.

She was learning as much about the major as about Pyotr. When first imprisoned, Ian had been able to laugh at adversity, and his physical and emotional strength had helped keep her uncle alive. But as the months dragged on, he had lost the ability to laugh. She hoped that someday he would find it again.

But she would never know if Ian Cameron would recover

from his experiences, for tomorrow they would arrive back in Baipur. The day after, he would be gone from her life.

She sighed and decided that it was time to get to sleep. Turning to the next page of the Bible, she started to tuck in her bookmark. Then she stopped, her brows drawing together. Most of the entries were written in the margins in tiny, precise script, but this page had several lines sprawled across the printed text. There was something frenzied about the lettering. Moreover, the words were written in the almost illegible scrawl that marked Pyotr's handwriting toward the end of the journal, when his health had deteriorated.

It took time to puzzle out the words, and at the end she was still unsure if she had translated correctly. Her best guess was, *"May God have mercy on my soul, for in my cruel arrogance I set a fire that may destroy India. I pray that the Lord in His infinite wisdom will send a rain to quench it."*

She wondered if she should ask Ian if he knew what her uncle had meant by his ominous words. Then she shrugged and set the volume down. There was no point in bothering Ian with something that was probably a product of fever and depression. She doused the lantern, settled into her pillows, and drew the sheet up to her shoulders.

The week-long journey had been blessedly uneventful compared to the turbulent days in Nanda. The bullock carts kept the party to a slow pace, and as they ambled through the lush countryside, Ian had proved to be an agreeable traveling companion. Though he had no interest in Laura as a woman, he seemed to enjoy her company. Most of the time they rode side by side. Ian talked little, but when he did, his comments were always to the point and often amusing in a dry, acid-edged fashion.

When Laura needed it, he was also capable of quiet compassion. One night after they had made camp, she climbed alone to the top of a nearby hill to admire a spectacular sunset. As the sun dropped below the horizon in a flare of scarlet and gold, a wave of paralyzing grief engulfed her.

Never again would she share such sights with her stepfather. For Laura, beauty was diminished if it wasn't shared, and the pain of loss sent silent tears down her cheeks. She wept not just for Kenneth, but for Uncle Pyotr, for her splendid, outrageous mother, and for her first father, whose death was so painful that even now her mind refused to contemplate it.

Then a large hand wrapped around hers, the firm clasp drawing her back from despair. She knew that it was Ian without looking, and was profoundly grateful both for his company and for his stillness. As the color faded from the sky, he gave her his handkerchief, then escorted her back to the camp. Neither of them spoke of the incident; there was no need.

Just as Ian had an uncanny ability to sense Laura's moods, she was equally aware of his. Under his controlled facade he was full of darkness, and often he withdrew into some unreachable mental zone. She worried about how little he ate and slept. Evenings they talked until weariness sent Laura to bed, but Ian was always awake when she retired and when she rose the next morning. It was hard to see how he kept body and soul together.

Perhaps his insomnia was contagious, for she was also finding it difficult to sleep. She rolled over and punched the pillow with irritation. Though Ian did not find her attractive, the reverse was not true. As the days passed, her interest in him was increasing to near-infatuation. Not only did she crave his company, but the slightest accidental contact between them left her longing for more.

She despised her weakness. Knowing that there was a very real danger that she might do something that would embarrass them both horribly, she tried to keep her distance from him. She mounted and dismounted without his aid, became expert at passing cups without touching fingers, and no longer took his arm when they went exploring on foot. Luckily Ian didn't seem to notice that her behavior had changed; she would have been humiliated if he suspected how much she was attracted to him.

She knew that some of her interest was a result of simple proximity, for her low carnal nature made her susceptible to men. But Ian himself was the real problem; his combination of kindness and mystery acted on her like catnip on a tabby. She wanted to help him become the man he had been before suffering an ordeal that she could only dimly comprehend; she wanted to see him laugh, as Uncle Pyotr had seen him laugh.

In a burst of vulgarity, she faced the dangerous truth: she
wanted him to bed her.

She spent a moment contemplating his image in her
mind's eye. He wasn't precisely handsome, for that was a
description better suited to tame men who belonged in
drawing rooms. Though she was sure that Ian could hold
his own in formal society, he had a larger-than-life quality
that belonged more to the world of heroic adventures. If a
princess needed rescuing or a dragon needed slaying, she
couldn't think of a better man for the task. Though she was
no princess, he had done an admirable job with the tiger.
She watched him whenever possible, admiring his strength,
the smooth, controlled quality of his movements . . .

She found herself flushing. There really was far too much
of her mother in her. Sighing, she rolled over again, trying
to convince herself that she was grateful that her association
with Ian would soon be over. When he was gone, she would
become a well-behaved Englishwoman again. If she tended
her infatuation carefully, it might save her from making a
fool of herself over another man for years to come.

The thought was not much comfort.

Nonetheless, tired from a day of riding, she finally dozed
off, only to have her slumber disturbed by a choking sound
outside her tent. She came awake instantly, thinking it might
be a leopard. The noise was repeated, and she realized that
it came from a human throat. After donning her robe and
slippers, she went outside to investigate.

There she discovered that the sounds emanated from the
tent next to hers, which Ian was using because rain had
driven him from his preferred spot under the open sky. Seeing that there was a light inside, Laura scratched on the
canvas door panel. "Ian, are you all right?"

There was no answer, so she set maidenly modesty aside,
opened the flap, and ducked into the tent. The dim light
showed Ian sprawled on the cot, his face haggard, his torso
bare and shining with sweat. She was bemused to see that
even in bed he wore his black leather eyepatch.

His condition was terrifyingly reminiscent of her stepfather's last illness. Swiftly she crossed the tent and put one
hand on his forehead, but his temperature was normal. Ian
flinched from her touch and his eye opened. For an instant,
she saw a frantic light in the blue depths. Then he recognized her and instantly shuttered his expression.

"I heard strange sounds and thought you might be ill, especially since the lamp was lit," Laura explained soothingly. Removing her hand, she added, "You don't seem feverish."

The skin over his cheekbones tightened. "I'm not. It was nothing, just a bad dream. Endless dark, suffocation, dread, pain, cowardice. And fire. Mustn't forget fire." He shuddered. "All the usual things." His gaze went to the oil lamp on the table. "Spending several months in total darkness increased my affection for light. That's why I sleep with a lamp or candle when I'm indoors."

Laura guessed that Ian was still shaken by his nightmare, or he would not have said so much. Briefly she wondered at the coincidence of his mentioning fire, since she had just read that strange entry in Pyotr's journal. Perhaps later she would talk to Ian about that. Then she set the thought aside; far more important was Ian's state of mind right now.

Perching on the edge of his cot, she took hold of his wrist. His whole body vibrated with tension, and, as she expected, his pulse was hammering. "Care to tell me more? I'm something of an expert on bad dreams."

He exhaled raggedly. "In prison I welcomed sleep, for it was the only way of escape. I dreamed of my childhood in Scotland and Persia, of my family, my friends. The hard part was waking to reality, which was more beastly than any nightmare could be, particularly after Pyotr Andreyovich was taken." He ran shaky fingers through his hair, which sweat had darkened from auburn to chestnut. "Ironic. Now that I'm free, I dream of captivity. Of death and decay and betrayal . . ." His voice trailed off.

"I see why you prefer not to sleep," Laura said briskly. "But the nightmares will abate in time."

He gave her a sardonic glance. "Have yours? You did say that you are an expert on bad dreams."

She hesitated, unable to give him glib reassurances. "I don't have them very often now."

"I suppose that's something to look forward to," he murmured, unimpressed. His gaze narrowed. "What haunts your nights, Larissa Alexandrovna?"

She drew in a sharp breath, for his use of the patronymic hit uncomfortably close to the Russian setting of her nightmares. "Nothing very interesting," she said evasively. "Just some of the less pleasant memories of my childhood."

Ian accepted that. They might be friends, but that didn't mean they were close enough to share nightmares.

Changing the subject, he said, "It belatedly occurs to me that an unmarried girl should not be sitting on a man's bed. Not unless social custom has liberalized considerably in the last couple of years."

Laura became uncomfortably aware of the impropriety of their situation. Her glance fell to Ian's bare chest, with its mat of dark hair and taut, well-defined muscles, then darted away. She sensed no carnal thoughts from him, but suddenly her own emotions were scalding. Hands clenching nervously, she got to her feet. "I imagine that London is as rigid as ever, but one of the wonderful things about being in the Indian countryside is that the rules are more relaxed here. Propriety can take a back seat to common sense. You're not going to assault me just because we're alone in your tent, and I'm not going to have an attack of vapors just because your shirt is off."

"Very true." His mouth twisted with surprising bitterness. "You're perfectly safe with me."

She knew that—and she resented the fact as much as she was grateful for it. Keeping her voice gentle, she said, "Try to get some sleep. You look tired."

He shook his head. "I'll get up now—I've had enough dreaming for one night."

She nodded and crossed the tent, but before she could raise the flap, he said, "Tomorrow we'll reach Baipur. I just want to say . . . thank you for being someone whose company I can bear."

Laura gave him the ghost of a smile. "I must thank you, too, for doing so much for someone who was a stranger to you. You've been a godsend this last week." Her smile deepened. "Not to mention the fact that you saved me from becoming tiffin for a tiger."

She turned and was about to leave, but his voice stopped her again. "If I write, would you answer?" he said uncertainly. "I—I'll want to know that you're all right."

Her fingers tightened on the folds of canvas. "Of course I would. I'd like to hear from you." Then she slipped out into the night.

Notice of Kenneth's death had been sent ahead, so when they arrived in Baipur the small British community immediately drew Laura into its warm embrace—literally so in the case of Emily McKittrick, the judge's wife. After a long hug, Emily suggested that Laura stay with her and her husband rather than be alone in the Stephensons' bungalow. Laura refused. As she explained to Emily, she had a great deal of packing to do and decisions to make, so she might as well get on with it.

Another, unmentioned, factor was that Ian would be spending the night at the McKittricks' before heading west to Bombay. Being under the same roof with him would prolong the pain of separation and increase the risk that Laura would do something foolish. Better to make the break now.

She said a quick, formal good-bye to Ian, for they had made their true farewell the night before. Then she went to the bungalow she had shared with her stepfather. Greeting the servants who had been left behind and directing the unpacking kept Laura busy for the rest of the day.

It was an emotional afternoon, for every object in the bungalow had associations with her stepfather: the Indian chess set that they had used; his favorite upholstered chair, which had taken on the contour of his body; the rose bushes that she had carefully nurtured in a hostile climate because he had loved the blossoms; the books they had discussed. There was no end to the memories. Soon Laura stopped trying to suppress her tears and just let them flow, changing to fresh handkerchiefs as needed. The more she wept, the sooner she would heal.

The only member of the British community who had not been available to offer his condolences earlier was Emery Walford, who had been visiting an outlying village. He remedied his earlier absence by calling on Laura as soon as he returned to Baipur.

Glad of an interruption, she went to the drawing room and greeted him warmly.

Clasping her hand, he said, "You have my deepest sympathy, Laura. Your father will be greatly missed."

His sincerity almost brought on fresh tears, but she managed a smile instead. "He told me once that there might be cleverer men in the world, but none more honorable than his colleagues in the civil service. He knew that the future would be secure in hands like yours. He thought highly of your work, you know."

"I'm honored. Your father was a model of the kind of

official I want to be—wise, kind, and honest to the back-
bone.'' When Emery's eyes adjusted to the indoor light, he
said with quick concern, ''You've been crying. Is there anything I can do?''

She shook her head. ''Thank you, Emery, but I imagine
I'll be crying on and off for some time to come. Everywhere
I look, there are memories of him.'' To alleviate his worried
expression, she said lightly, ''I must look a fright. Weeping
elegantly is one of those ladylike skills I've never acquired.''

''You look beautiful,'' he said intensely. ''You always
do.''

''You flatter me,'' she said, touched. Knowing that he
would want to be of assistance, she continued, ''Later, after
I've decided what I'm going to do, perhaps you can help me
arrange for shipping the things I want to keep.''

''Of course.'' After a long pause, Emery said, ''Laura,
I know that it's inappropriate to speak of this when your
father has only just died, but I'm concerned for your future.'' He swallowed hard. ''You must know how I feel
about you. I intended to wait until I was promoted, but now
your father's death has left you alone in the world.'' He took
a step closer. ''Give me the right to support you, Laura. I
love you, and I want you to be my wife.''

Her stomach knotted with sudden anxiety as she recognized the hot pressure of desire emanating from Emery. She
should have seen this coming, but she had been so absorbed
by thoughts of her stepfather that the proposal caught her
off balance. As she groped for a kind refusal, he stepped
forward and put his hands on her shoulders, then bent and
gave her a tentative kiss.

For an instant Laura responded, her lips moving against
his. He was young and strong and his ardor enfolded her
like a goosedown comforter. How lovely it would be if she
dared marry, if she had a husband who would hold her like
this, who would care for her as she would care for him. . . .

Her momentary yielding was all the encouragement Emery needed. His arms came hard around her. As his kiss
became more demanding, Laura was jolted back to reality.
She could never marry, not this handsome young man, not
anyone. She tried to pull away, but Emery was too absorbed
in sensation to notice that her response had changed. Sharply

she turned her face away from his. "Please, Emery, let me go."

Instead of complying, he pulled her tighter. "I've loved you ever since I met you, Laura," he whispered. "You're everything I've ever dreamed of finding in a woman. Beautiful, kind, understanding . . ."

Laura began to struggle in earnest, but Emery's sporting pursuits had given him muscles that she couldn't match. She gasped, "Emery, stop this!"

She shoved against his chest and drew her breath so that she could call the servants. Before she could, the front door opened. Then a familiar deep voice swore, "Damnation!"

An instant later Ian wrenched Emery away from Laura. Expression savage, he spun the younger man around and struck him with devastating power, first in the jaw, then in the stomach. Emery made a strangled sound as he crashed into the wicker sofa, then pitched to the floor.

Ian hauled the magistrate to his feet and was preparing to hit him again when Laura cried out, "No, Ian, don't hurt him!"

For a moment she feared that Ian hadn't heard and that in his fury he might kill Emery. Barely in time he checked his next blow. Instead of striking, he shoved the younger man back so that he sprawled across the sofa. "You despicable young swine," he snapped, "How dare you assault Miss Stephenson! I should stake you out as tiger bait."

"It was mostly a misunderstanding, Ian," Laura said unsteadily. "Emery proposed, and I guess I didn't make it clear enough that I wasn't interested."

Emery sat up, arms folded over his injured stomach, his face ashen. "I'm sorry, Laura," he gasped. "I didn't mean to frighten you, but I was overcome by the force of my feelings." He lifted his gaze to Ian. "You have every right to chastise me, sir, for my conduct was unpardonable."

"Yes, it was," Ian agreed caustically. "Infatuation is no excuse for assault."

Laura intervened again. Emery had given her a few bad moments, but his feelings were genuine and his intentions honorable. She knelt by the sofa. "You've paid me a great compliment, Emery, but I can't marry you. I should have said so sooner, but I didn't want to jeopardize our friendship."

"Can you forgive the insult I offered you?" he asked, his expression wretched.

"It was not meant as an insult, so no forgiveness is needed." She stood, sorry that he was hurting. Though his love for her might be rooted in the fact that she was the only eligible European female in the district, she would not demean his feelings by saying that. "We'll forget what happened today. I won't speak of it, and neither will Major Cameron."

With a feeble attempt at humor, Emery said, "My stomach won't forget in a hurry. You have a punch like a mule, Major Cameron." After a pause, he stammered, "Thank you for stopping me. For as long as I live, I'll never forgive myself for frightening Miss Stephenson."

"Let's not have an orgy of guilt," Ian said dryly. "Just don't do it again with another girl."

With what dignity he could muster, Emery left the bungalow.

As soon as he was gone, Ian moved toward Laura, concern on his face. "Are you all right?"

"I'm fine." Though she longed to go into his arms for comfort, in her present state, she didn't dare. Sinking onto the sofa, she buried her face in her hands. Dear God, how could she have enjoyed the embrace of a man she didn't love, especially when she had spent the last week mooning over Ian Cameron? She really was shameless.

When she had regained her control, she lifted her head again. "That was my fault. I've always been able to keep Emery from being difficult, but today I was careless."

His brows raised. "Don't blame yourself. That young idiot was the one who was out of line."

She smiled humorlessly. "Yes, but they say that men are more prey to their passions. It's a woman's responsibility not to say or do anything that might be misinterpreted."

"You're hard on your own sex, but that is neither here nor there." He looked down into her face, frowning. "I'd come to say good-bye, but perhaps it will be better if I return tomorrow, when you've had time to recover from your experience. If you take an early morning ride, may I join you?"

Surprised, she said, "Aren't you leaving in the morning?"

"There's no need to go first thing." He was watching her

with a strange intensity that was a little unnerving. Laura turned away, thinking that he only wanted to assure himself that she had recovered from the scene with Emery.

After settling what time he should come for her, Laura resumed her work with an inward sigh. Earlier in the day she had wisely decided not to prolong their parting, yet here she was, willing to do just that. Where men were concerned, she really had no willpower to speak of.

Chapter 9

❦   ❦   ❦

IAN'S EMOTIONS WERE churning as he rode away from
Laura's bungalow. Deliberately he chose a route leading
away from the town, for he was not ready to return to the
McKittricks' bungalow. He needed time to think.

Part of his turmoil was simple fury at the way Laura had
been mauled by her overeager suitor. He could not remember the last time he had been so angry; it was fortunate that
Laura stopped him before he broke the young fool's neck.

Even more disturbing than anger was the notion that
struck Ian after Emery had left. It was an idea so outrageous
that it shamed him, yet it was irresistibly appealing and
made a bizarre sort of sense.

Laura had made it clear that she didn't wish to marry.
Based on what he had seen, her resolution was almost certainly rooted in a distaste for physical contact with men. He
had not realized that when he first met her, for she had been
relaxed and accepting with him. But she had also been in a
state of shock because of her father's death, and that had
affected her usual behavior. At least, that was what Ian now
deduced, for she had withdrawn physically as she regained
her normal equilibrium.

She had not withdrawn mentally; on the journey to Baipur, she had been the best of companions, willing to talk
when he was, but entirely comfortable with long silences.
Yet she did not like being touched, for she avoided even the
most casual of contacts. She had tried to make her withdrawal unobtrusive, but he had noticed immediately.

He noticed everything about her.

The revulsion she had shown while trying to escape young
Emery confirmed Ian's theory. Laura hadn't feared her
suitor. She must be fond of him or she wouldn't have been

so tolerant of his misdeed. Yet she had hated his embrace, even though he was a good-looking and decent young man.

Perhaps her distaste for physical intimacy was a result of some youthful trauma at male hands, or perhaps she was just born that way; some women were. But whatever the reason, obviously she wanted to avoid the earthier side of life.

Laura wouldn't make a wife, and he couldn't make a husband. He gave a twisted smile. Clearly they were made for each other.

Since facing the fact that he was a eunuch, he had seen himself as flawed, inadequate. Yet virility was only a small part of gender. Many men abstained from sexual relations, some for religious reasons, some for practical reasons or lack of opportunity, others from choice.

What was the measure of a man?

Ian had always enjoyed women in ways that were quite nonsexual; his favorite childhood playmate had been his sister. He had always assumed he would marry, for he wanted children and a wife who was a companion as well as a bedmate. As soon as his income had grown to the point where marriage was practical, he had started looking. He had wasted no time in proposing when he met the right girl.

Now the life of marriage and children he had envisioned was forever out of his reach. Yet marriage was more than sex; it was also a source of companionship and an economic partnership. He was still quite capable of providing for a woman, of protecting and cherishing her. And love itself existed in many forms, most of which had nothing to do with physical passion.

By sheer chance, he had found a woman who might welcome a husband who would make no sexual demands, but who could provide support, friendship, and the possibility of love.

His mouth tightened. It would be easy to find out if Laura was willing to consider what he still had to offer.

All he had to do was lay bare his soul.

The next morning, Laura prepared her hair with special care, donned her most flattering riding costume, and had the cook pack a basket with cakes and a jug of hot tea. She was ready and waiting when Ian arrived for their ride.

He greeted her warmly but seemed preoccupied. There

was little conversation as they rode into the rolling hills. Laura didn't mind; it was enough just to be with him. There seemed a special brightness in the morning air, and she tried to memorize it, along with every other aspect of the ride. In the future, she would use her imagination to come back to this place, to this special time. Even lonely old spinsters were allowed to dream.

A half hour's ride brought them to a tiny abandoned shrine. It was a peaceful place, with vines curling over the ancient stones and playful monkeys swooping through the trees that surrounded the flower-strewn clearing. The shrine itself was simply a free-standing wall covered with weathered bas-relief sculptures. The central image was of a jolly, elephant-headed being who improbably rode on a rat.

Laura slid from her horse and tethered it. "I thought this would be a good place to stop for refreshments. I've never seen any people here, but sometimes offerings are left."

Ian dismounted and secured his horse, then nodded toward the bas relief. "That's because it's a shrine to Ganesha, the happy god, who removes obstacles from the paths of mortals. Who wouldn't want to invoke prosperity and good fortune?"

Laura regarded the image thoughtfully. The elephant head contained wise, human eyes. Though she had visited the shrine many times, she had known nothing about the resident godling. She reached into her basket for one of the small cakes and laid it in front of Ganesha. "Who indeed?"

Ian gave a faint smile before beginning to prowl around the small clearing. "Have you decided what you will do now?"

"I think I'll go back to England." She perched on a convenient rock. "There's much I love about India, but I'm tired of heat, tired of disease, tired of being surrounded by an alien culture that I'll never fully understand. My income would support me better here, but I want to go home."

"I'm concerned for you, Laura." Ian stopped his restless pacing and turned to her. "I owe your uncle my life. Since he is gone and you have no other family, perhaps I can fulfill my obligation to him by making sure that you are well provided for."

She looked at him in surprise. "You owe me nothing, Ian. You brought me Pyotr's journal and helped me through a very difficult time, so I think the accounts are even." She poured a cup of tea. "I shall manage very well on my own. Besides, it would hardly be proper for you to support me."

"It would be quite proper under certain conditions." He took a deep breath. "Before I say more about that, there's something I must ask you."

Puzzled by his seriousness, she said, "Of course."

"You have said that you don't wish to marry, ever. Forgive me for being intrusive, but is it because you . . ." He paused to search for words before saying carefully, "you wish to avoid the . . . the physical side of marriage?"

Laura felt the blood drain from her face. Dear God, she knew he was perceptive, but how had he guessed that? Stiffly she said, "That is really none of your business, Major Cameron."

He raised one hand. "Please, bear with me. I know the question is an unforgivable impertinence, but I have a good reason for asking. I started in the wrong place by talking about finances. I should have begun by explaining why your feelings about marriage are important to me. I'll do that now." He halted, strain visible in his face. "But first, I'd like your word that you won't tell anyone what I'm going to reveal."

Laura stared, unable to guess where this strange conversation was going. "Unless you're going to confess to a crime, you have my promise."

He turned away, his broad shoulders rigid under his dark coat. "While I was in prison, I was severely injured during a beating. I am . . . no longer capable of marital relations."

She gasped, horrified at the revelation, and at what it was costing him to tell her about it. "Are you sure?"

"Months have passed since my escape and there has been no improvement," he said flatly. "I'm not the man I was, and I've accepted that I never will be again."

Tears stung her eyes. No wonder she had never felt the least trace of desire emanating from him. All of the time she had been quietly lusting after him, he had been trapped in his own solitary hell. "I'm so sorry," she whispered.

He swung around to face her. "I didn't tell you because I wanted your pity," he said harshly. "I told you because I want to marry you. In order to properly evaluate my proposal, you must know the truth about me."

If Laura had been prone to swooning, she would have done so. Instead she lifted the teacup she still held and took a gulp. Then another. Feebly she said, "You want to marry me?"

"Yes. Am I right that you would refuse me if I was capable of . . . normal marital relations?"

"You're right, I would certainly not accept such a proposal." Her brows drew together. "Are you suggesting that we contract a marriage of convenience—that we would go our own separate ways, but I would have the protection of your name?"

"No, I mean a real marriage in every way but one." His smile had a bitter edge. "There are some who would say that physical intimacy is the purpose and bedrock of marriage, and perhaps they are right. But marriage is more than the procreation of children—it's also companionship, support, and shelter against the world. There are many marriages where husband and wife cease to share a bed, but the bonds of matrimony still hold. I care for you a great deal, Laura, and you seem to enjoy my company. I hope—I pray—that that might be a solid foundation for marriage."

She swallowed hard, too confused to know how she felt about his proposal. "Is what you're suggesting even legal?"

"Nonconsummation is grounds for annulling a marriage," he admitted, "but whose business is it what we do—or don't do—in the privacy of our own bedchamber?"

"It may be no one else's business." She finished her tea and carefully set the cup down. "But it doesn't seem quite right somehow."

"It would be different from most marriages," he agreed. "Yet different doesn't automatically mean wrong."

"That's true." She considered, her brows drawing together. "A marriage such as you're suggesting might be . . . possible."

His expression eased. "I'm glad you're not refusing out of hand. At the same time, I don't want you to accept unless you fully understand what you would be giving up. At its best, physical love is perhaps the closest mortals can come to heaven."

Laura grimaced as the indelible memory of her parents' violence flickered through her mind. "I wouldn't know about that, but I do know that passion can also be beastly and destructive. I want no part of it."

"You must be very sure of that," he warned, "for if you marry me, you'll lose the opportunity to change your mind.

It might be unjust of me, but I don't think I would be a complaisant husband if you decided to take a lover."

"Blunt words, Major," she said coolly. "Give me credit for knowing my own mind. Or are you trying to undermine your case?"

"I'm trying to be honest, for a marriage between us will have no chance without honesty." He crossed the clearing and knelt on one knee before her. His gaze searching, he said, "It's too soon to talk of love, Laura, but I hope you'll give my proposal serious thought. We are uniquely suited to each other, for you wish to avoid physical intimacy and I am incapable of it. If we care enough about each other to take the chance, perhaps we can build something deeply rewarding between us."

She could see in his face how much he did care. Afraid of what he might read in her own expression, she got to her feet and slipped away from him, drifting across the clearing.

Ironic that Ian thought she disliked physical intimacy when her real fear was that she would like it too much. The shattering of her family had taught her the appalling dangers of passion. Later, her one brief experience with carnal love had proved that she carried the same destructive seeds in her own nature. Only by refusing to let herself be drawn into passion's snare could she be sure of avoiding disaster.

Yet it wasn't important that Ian was wrong about why she had decided not to marry. What did matter was that he was proposing a marriage that did not contain the one element that terrified her. Here was a chance to have companionship, security, someone to love—things she had thought forever out of her reach. And if she accepted him, she could fulfill her promise to her stepfather to find a husband while being true to her private vow to shun unruly lust. Her stepfather would have approved of Ian, for the two men were alike in many ways. Steady. Kind. Safe.

But the fact that such a marriage was possible did not mean that it would be devoid of difficulties. Laura's pacing had brought her to the stone wall, so she turned and regarded Ian in silence. He had not moved, and he watched her with the same stillness he would have exhibited if she were a wild creature that he was trying to lure to his hand.

Ruefully she recognized that the analogy was uncomfortably correct. She already desired Ian, and surely desire

would increase in the proximity of marriage. She could bear
that in return for the pleasure of his company; nonetheless,
marrying him would be a leap into the unknown.

Yet how could she refuse a man she was already half in
love with? As he had said, they were uniquely suited to each
other. And she wanted him; dear God, how she wanted him.

Fiercely she reined in her emotions. Her rational side
wanted more information before making such a momentous
decision. Or perhaps her mind sought reasons to justify what
her heart cried out for. "I know even less of your future
plans than you know of mine, Ian. Where would we live?
What will you do now that you're no longer in the army?"

"While I was in Bokhara, I inherited my uncle's estate
on the Scottish coast, not far from Edinburgh. Managing
that will keep me busy and provide a very decent income.
You won't want for anything, and you'll have a respected
position in society." After a moment, he added, "For what
it's worth, there's a title. I'm the fourteenth Baron Falkirk."

"So you're a lord, and you aren't happy about it," she
said thoughtfully. "Why not?"

His features hardened. "I inherited because three men
died. I can't be happy about that, even though I've had my
fill of the army and I've always loved Falkirk. Inheriting it
is like a poisoned apple, lovely to contemplate, but bitter
within. That's why I haven't started using the title—I haven't
yet come to terms with what it means."

"The deaths are a great tragedy, but you're not responsible," she said reasonably. "Since someone had to inherit,
what is wrong with the fact that it was you? I'm sure that
wherever your uncle is now, he's pleased that the family
patrimony has gone to someone who will cherish it."

After a pause, he said, "You're right, of course. One of
the things I like about you is your admirable common
sense."

"If I had common sense," she said tartly, "I would not
be considering your proposal."

"Then I must hope that sometimes you'll have sense, and
other times you'll have none at all." He sighed. "As I said
earlier, I want to be honest with you, Laura. I can provide
for you in a material sense, but I've changed for the worse
in more ways than one. Though I used to have an amiable
disposition, I've been living in a black fog for months. On
a bad day it takes every shred of will I have just to get out

of bed, and the good days aren't much better. Sometimes I feel like a dried husk that will blow away in the next strong wind.''

He paused to consider, then shook his head. "That's not a very good description, but I don't know a better one. Lately—since I met you—the good days have outnumbered the bad, but I'll still probably be a moody and difficult husband.''

She considered his words calmly, her slanted golden eyes thoughtful, then said simply, "Melancholia.''

Startled, he said, "I've never been melancholic.''

"You were never imprisoned and tortured before, either,'' she pointed out. "Melancholia is not uncommon, you know. My father's father suffered from terrible spells of it. He would stay in bed for days on end. When he did get up, he drifted about like a body searching for its lost soul. But always the darkness passed, and then no one could match his high spirits. In your case, the melancholy was surely brought on by your experiences. When it lifts, you may never suffer from it again.''

She nibbled on her lower lip reflectively. "If you were never despondent in the past, melancholy would hit you all the harder for being unfamiliar. My grandfather said that his first bad spell was the worst, because he feared it would never end. In time, it became easier for him to weather the moods.''

Ian thought about that. Both Juliet and David had counseled patience, saying that things would improve. Laura went one step further; by matter-of-factly naming his condition, she had made it easier to understand. Perhaps he wasn't uniquely cursed.

Melancholia. In his pre-Bokhara days, he had never quite believed in it, for his own temperament was naturally buoyant. He'd vaguely assumed that people who claimed to be suffering from melancholia were simply self-indulgent. With a little effort and self-respect, they would be perfectly fine. But if what Ian had been experiencing was melancholia, in the future he would have a great deal more sympathy with those who were afflicted. "I hope you're right. But if you are and I improve much in the future, I might become very different from the man you would be marrying.''

"Everyone changes with time, Ian. I like you very well the way you are—if you learn to laugh again, I think I would

like you even better. So much for melancholia.'' She made
a dismissive gesture with her hand. ''Are you an agreeable
man?''

Startled by her abrupt change of direction, he said cautiously, ''Probably not. How do you define agreeable?''

''In the literal sense of being willing to accommodate the
wishes of others,'' she explained. ''My mother once said
that the most comfortable marriages are between two people
who are both easygoing, who do not always insist on having
their own way. When two such people *do* disagree about
what to do, the one who cares most about the result will get
his or her way, and the other accepts it good-naturedly.''

Intrigued, he said, ''Your mother sounds like a wise
woman. But what if there is a difference of opinion and both
parties care greatly about how the issue is decided?''

''Then they fight,'' she said, eyes twinkling. ''But I am
an agreeable person—most of the time—and you seem to be
also. I don't think we would fight often.''

Ian thought of his own parents. His father had always had
to have his own way, in matters great and small, and his
mother had always submitted meekly. Ian had not been surprised when his sister rejected meekness in favor of rebellion. ''I suppose I'm agreeable in the sense you mean, if
not always in other ways.''

''Very good.'' She cocked her head to one side. ''Do you
have any other dark secrets to reveal?''

''One more, and this may be the worst,'' he said with
wry humor. ''The lords of Falkirk were border bandits for
centuries, so the family seat is built for defense, not comfort. It's one of those frightful medieval castles with twelve-
foot thick walls, smoking chimneys, and ancient weapons
lurking in dark corners.''

''Ghosts?'' she asked hopefully.

''Three or four, but they're a harmless lot. Far worse are
the drafts. When the wind blows from the North Sea, it
would freeze the ears off a stone elephant.''

''You should not say such a thing in front of our friend
Ganesha,'' she said with mock reproval. ''And don't think
you can frighten a Russian with tales of cold. Compared to
St. Petersburg, your Falkirk will seem like Calcutta. We
Russkis are very good at creating warmth in a frozen land.''

Though her words were teasing, they were also absolutely
true, for Laura had already created warmth in Ian's frozen

heart. "I think I've covered the worst of my dark secrets," he said. "Do you have any to confess?"

Her levity faded and she glanced away, her absent gaze falling on the bas relief next to her. "I haven't your ability to be honest about things that are deeply painful, Ian. That isn't a dark secret, but it certainly is a flaw in my character."

"If that's your worst failing, I'll be a lucky man." He smiled a little. "I suppose the only thing that would make me withdraw my proposal is if you have a husband stashed somewhere. Do you?"

She shook her head. "Nary a husband to my name."

Knowing that he shouldn't rush her but unable to bear the suspense, he said, "Are you ready to make a decision, or will you need more time?"

Laura reached out and rubbed Ganesha's round, jolly belly with her palm. Ganesha, the happy god, who removed obstacles from the paths of mortals. "Laura Stephenson is a calm, rational Englishwoman who thinks that what you are proposing is mad," she said slowly. "But Larissa Alexandrovna is a demented Russian, and she says I should grab this opportunity with both hands, for I'll never have another like it."

Hope welling in his heart, he rose to his feet and walked toward her. "Then by all means remember that you are Russian."

Laura turned from Ganesha to look at him. "What was your father's Christian name?"

"The same as your father's—Alexander." He stopped directly in front of her, close enough to touch but restraining the impulse to do so. The last thing he wanted was to alarm her now.

She took a deep breath. "Very well, Ivan Alexandrovich, I accept." Reaching out, she grasped both his hands in hers. "And I hope to heaven that we don't both live to regret this!"

"I won't," he said with absolute conviction. "And I swear I'll do my best to see that you don't, either."

"Ah, well, nothing ventured, nothing gained," she said jauntily. "And what do I have to lose but my sanity and peace of mind?" Her icy hands tightened on his and her voice dropped. "I'm terrified, Ian, but I'm also delighted."

With a gratitude too profound for words, Ian raised her

hands and kissed them gently, first the left, then the right. In Cambay, he had realized that he must find something to care about if he wanted to survive. Now, in this golden-eyed girl, he had found his reason to go on living.

Chapter 10

❦ ❦ ❦

As THEY RODE back to Baipur, Ian said, "Unless you object, I'd like to get married as soon as possible. Within a fortnight, if the legalities can be completed and there's a Christian clergyman available."

Laura drew in her breath. "It seems so sudden. An hour ago I was a dedicated spinster and now I'm planning my wedding." Her brow furrowed as she thought. "But it does make sense to marry soon. There's an English missionary who comes to Baipur, and he should arrive within the next week. I'll have finished settling my affairs here so we can be off the day after the ceremony."

His gaze slanted over to her. For the first time, she realized that Ian always rode with her to his left, the side of his good eye, so that he could see her easily. "Do you prefer to travel fast and light or slow and comfortable?" he asked.

She grinned. "What if I tell you that I can't stir without twenty bullock carts and forty servants?"

"If that's what Lady Falkirk wants," he said stoically.

"Goodness, you really are agreeable," she said, impressed. "But I prefer riding on horseback with few or no servants. Traveling in state makes me impatient, though Papa and I had to do it because of his position. My maid is a native of Baipur and is to marry soon herself, so she won't want to come with me. I can manage alone until we reach Bombay."

He regarded her quizzically. "You really won't miss having an army of servants?"

"Not in the least." She wrinkled her nose. "I know we must have large households to uphold British prestige, and it does provide work for people who need it, but having so many servants is as much nuisance as luxury. Often it would be easier to do the job myself rather than wait for someone of the right caste to be summoned. Once a dead bird lay in the garden for half a day before the right sort of untouchable could be brought in to remove it. It seemed very peculiar, because I was new in India and hadn't learned that none of the higher cast Hindus could touch a dead body without being defiled."

He gave an understanding nod. "As a junior officer, I found it bizarre that a soldier who would risk his life for me without a second thought would refuse to accept water from my canteen. Still, the Hindu rules about cleanliness are healthy."

"My father used to say that all the customs that seem incomprehensible to a European evolved to meet valid social needs," Laura said. "However, to return to the subject of our journey to Bombay, it will be simpler and faster if we travel without an entourage."

"Then we will," Ian said. "Incidentally, we must go through Cambay, though it's out of the way. I told my brother I'd spend a few days with him before going home."

"You've a brother in India?"

"Yes, David's an officer in my old regiment." Ian made a wry face. "My earlier stay in Cambay was so brief that I didn't see any of my old friends. Frankly, I'd just as soon not have to face them all and answer the same questions over and over, but I did promise my brother."

"Then of course we'll go to Cambay," she said warmly. "Tell me about David, and about the rest of your family."

He smiled a little. "You want to find out about them while there's still time to change your mind?"

She chuckled. "Actually, since I have so few relatives of my own, I quite like the idea of marrying some."

With her encouragement, Ian spoke of his family and his childhood for the rest of the journey back to Baipur. It was the longest Laura had ever heard him talk. His mood was lighter and more relaxed now that she'd agreed to marry him. It was nice to feel that she had made a difference.

Listening, she began to develop a picture of Ian's early life. Raised abroad, he had a wider perspective than most Britons. His father, who had been knighted for his diplomatic services, had apparently been brilliant and difficult, while his mother sounded sweet but overwhelmed by all of the strong personalities in her family. As the oldest child, Ian had early developed the habit of looking out for others; becoming an army officer had been a natural progression.

She thought she'd like his two younger brothers, but his sister sounded alarming. Ian finished describing Juliet just as they reached the stables behind the Stephenson bungalow. As they dismounted, Laura said, "Let's see if I've gotten this right. Your sister is a redheaded Amazon who can outride most men, shoot the whiskers off a mountain goat, then put on an evening gown and reduce every man in sight to languishing sighs?"

He smiled. "That's not quite what I said."

"She sounds terrifying," Laura said gloomily as she handed her reins to the groom.

"Actually, I think you'll get along with her very well. Better than . . ." He stopped abruptly.

"Better than whom?" She took his arm, thinking that the era of keeping her distance was over, and good riddance.

After a pause, Ian said, "Better than most women would. You both have unconventional streaks. While it's more obvious in her case, I think you'll understand each other very well."

"I'm not at all unconventional," Laura protested. "I'm one of the most unremarkable of women."

As they entered the bungalow, he turned that too-perceptive gaze on her. "That's not true. You really are something of an original. I wonder why it bothers you to admit it."

He'd been honest with her; she owed him honesty in return. With some difficulty, she said, "When I came to England, I didn't enjoy being a strange little Russian. At school, the other girls laughed at my accent and my peculiar slanty eyes. I couldn't change my eyes, but I did my best to become as much like everyone else as possible. I was much happier not being singled out."

"You can be a strange little Russian with me," Ian said. "I like that aspect of you. And I think your eyes are beautiful."

As his gaze met hers, Laura felt a glow of warmth that started in her heart and gradually spread until it encompassed her whole being. Her stepfather had loved her, but Ian was the first person to say that he actually liked the Russian side of her. Perhaps that was why the Larissa Alexandrovna who still lived inside Laura Stephenson had instantly wanted to accept him.

To be grateful for his injury was unthinkable; if Laura could wave a wand to restore him, she would have done it in an instant, even though it would mean that they couldn't marry. But she couldn't change Ian any more than he could bring the late Lord Falkirk back to life. That being the case, she took her own advice and rejoiced in the fate that had brought them together.

For the next week, Laura was so busy that she had little time to grieve for her stepfather. The other Britons in Baipur accepted her betrothal with pleasure. Emily McKittrick observed that Ian was a bit overserious, but she had no doubt that he would make a splendid husband. Even Emery Walford sent Laura a short, awkward note wishing her happiness. Then he set off on a district tour of his own, so he needn't attend the wedding.

The Reverend James was notified and the wedding scheduled for the next week. Aided by the other two British women at the station, Laura spent the intervening time at the dreary task of dismantling the life she had lived in Baipur. Ian arranged for the transportation of the items Laura wanted to keep. Her trunks would be carted to Benares, floated down the Ganges on a barge, then shipped to Edinburgh from Calcutta. Even the tiger skin would be forwarded when it arrived from Nanda.

Before Laura was quite ready for it, her wedding day arrived. Emily McKittrick, who had only sons, had entered into the preparations with enthusiasm, acting as unofficial mother-of-the-bride, organizing details, and expressing occasional regrets that the wedding would be such a small one.

With the help of her maid and Emily, Laura donned her best day dress, a high-necked ivory-colored gown with lace trim and swooping bell-shaped sleeves. Small white rosebuds from her garden were twined through her hair, and she carried a bouquet of brilliantly colored Indian blossoms. Both Laura's attendants assured her that she was as beautiful as a bride could be, a compliment that she took with a large dose of salt. What she did know was that she was as nervous as a bride was supposed to be.

Judge McKittrick had offered to give Laura away. As he

led her down the aisle of the small Christian chapel, her heart was hammering so loudly that she was sure the spectators must hear it. As panic threatened to overwhelm her, Laura fiercely reminded herself that this marriage would be essentially different from that of her parents. She was not like her mother, nor was Ian like her father. She and Ian were levelheaded adults, and together they would build a safe, sane relationship.

But her unpersuaded heart banged even harder when she saw Ian waiting at the altar, tall and dark-coated and stern. What on earth was she doing? In many ways, he was still a stranger. In fact, she only had his word for the fact that he was incapable of marital relations. What if she was the victim of a diabolical plan to lure her into matrimony?

For a moment Laura was on the verge of bolting. Her fingers curled into Judge McKittrick's arm like claws. Amusement in his voice, the judge bent his head and whispered, "Buck up, my girl. Every bride panics on her wedding day. My darling Emily fainted at the altar, though she claims it was because of the heat. Don't worry, you're getting yourself a fine man here."

As Laura realized that she was suffering from wedding-day hysteria, her mood swung from terror to a wild desire to giggle. Absurd to imagine that Ian would scheme to lure her into marriage; she wasn't interesting enough to warrant such extreme measures. Besides, her own perceptions had confirmed the truth of what he had revealed to her.

She was struggling to keep her face straight when the judge handed her into the keeping of her future husband. Glancing up, she saw that Ian's expression was strained. He must be as nervous as she. All perfectly normal, since marriage was one of life's most important steps. But Ian was her ally, not her enemy, and she wanted to be with him. Reaching out, she clasped his hand and together they turned to face the minister.

"Dearly beloved . . ."

As Reverend James intoned the familiar words, her tension eased. The only difficult moment was when the minister said, "First, it was ordained for the procreation of children . . ."

Laura involuntarily flinched. She had been to her share of weddings, but never consciously noted that phrase. She almost glanced up into Ian's face, and only her knowledge that doing so would be unpardonably cruel gave her the control to keep her gaze forward. She and Ian might not be able to procreate, but the same service had just said that marriage was a holy estate not to be undertaken only to satisfy men's carnal's lust. At least they were getting half of it right.

Then she was taking her vows. "I, Larissa Alexandrovna . . ." Not only was it her legal name, but Ian's acceptance of her heritage had made her want to marry under the name with which she had been christened.

It was Ian's turn next, and his faint Scots burr was more pronounced than usual. Then he slid the ring onto her finger. It was exactly what Laura had requested: a plain gold band, with no embellishment but their initials and the date etched inside.

Ian's deep voice was steady as he said, ". . . with my body I thee worship . . . ," though his fingers tightened on hers. Laura felt another complicated pang. She had never recognized quite how earthy the wedding service was

"Those whom God hath joined together, let no man put asunder." Laura felt a shiver of guilt when she heard the admonition. She would not be entering this marriage if she hadn't known that she could leave if she wanted to, but such a thought was dreadfully out of place on her wedding day.

Finally it was time for her new husband to kiss his bride. Ian's lips were firm and pleasant. As they touched hers, Laura realized with a small shock that they had never kissed before. Warmth flowed between them, easing her doubts. This might be a marriage like no other, but, by God, it was going to work. She would make sure of that.

With a sigh, Ian stretched out in the deep tub of hot water. After two years of living in filth, he never tired of bathing. And the relaxation the bath offered came none too soon, for if the week between engagement and marriage had been a strain, the wedding day had been even worse. Too many jolly congratulations, too many heartfelt good wishes, too many knowing smiles. Just plain too many people; the weight of their interest and concern had been overwhelming. The peace Ian had found traveling from Nanda in Laura's company had vanished almost as soon as they became engaged. More than once he had been tempted to suggest that they marry by the old Scottish custom of jumping over a sword. Then they could set off for Bombay immediately.

But even though his nerves had stretched to near snapping point, for Laura's sake he had endured it. Every woman deserved a wedding day where she was the center of attention, and he would not deprive her of that. And it had been worth it, for she had been a luminous bride, her hand trembling, but her golden eyes glowing and her soft voice steady.

She had stayed close all day and her presence had enabled him to endure the wedding breakfast even though he was suffering from his worst headache in weeks. Finally the festivities were over and they had been driven in style to this luxurious pavilion where they were to spend their wedding night. The pavilion was owned by the wealthiest merchant in Baipur, who had given Laura the use of it in honor of his friend Kenneth Stephenson.

Ian and Laura had arrived at the pavilion just as the sun was setting among streamers of fiery light. Situated on the edge of a mirror-smooth little lake, it was an extremely romantic spot to spend a wedding night. Soft-footed servants had provided a supper, of which Ian had eaten nothing. Then the newlyweds had been ushered off to separate bathing rooms. Ian's was fit for a maharajah, with a giant marble tub sunken in the floor and endless hot water. Laura's would be equally sumptuous.

Wanting nothing more than to be alone, Ian had immediately dismissed the servants. Then he had stripped off his clothing and lowered himself into the bath. He used none of the scented oils—he was too much a Scot to want to smell like a nosegay—but the hot water was wonderful. He didn't emerge until the bath began to cool, and by that time most of his headache was gone.

After drying himself, he donned the embroidered blue robe that had been provided. The folds fell around him as gently as a whisper; Indians had nothing to learn about sensuality.

Returning to the bedroom to await his new wife, he checked that the bedside lamp had enough oil to burn until morning, then went to a window and looked out at the lake. Lotus plants floated on the dark water, their pale blossoms closed for the night. He felt like a lotus himself, suspended between past and future, darkness and light, despair and hope. And the key to light, hope, and the future was Laura.

He had thought that she would be a long time in her bath, but she came sooner than he had expected. Turning at the sound of her footsteps, he watched her enter the room, his heart giving an odd lurch as she paused. Her tawny hair had been brushed into a waterfall of polished bronze that spilled halfway to her waist, and she looked soft and heart-stoppingly lovely. She wore a long, European-style night-gown made of layers of translucent white silk that drifted around her like a cloud and revealed that her figure was even lusher than he had realized.

It was exactly the sort of garment a girl was supposed to wear on her wedding night, designed to arouse both desire and tenderness. He thought, for the thousandth time, of what he was depriving her. But it was too late for regrets; he could only hope that she was right in saying that she knew her own mind.

She smiled shyly. "What happens now?"

He tried to speak and couldn't. After clearing his throat, he tried again. "I'd like to hold you. Just hold you. If you don't object. Or we can talk."

He would not have been surprised if she had politely declined, for he was still unsure how far her dislike of touching went. Uneasily he realized that they hadn't even discussed the basic issue of whether they would share a bed or he should make up a separate pallet for himself.

Laura answered his question without a word, crossing the cool marble floor and walking straight into his arms. She smelled of jasmine and was soft, so soft. Ian drew her close with exquisite care, resting his chin on the top of her head as his hands slowly stroked down the graceful curves of her back. He whispered, "I thought that I would never hold a woman again."

She nestled closer. "You can hold me whenever you want."

Ian's tension dissolved like mist in the morning sun. He was physically aware of Laura in a way that he had never been with a mistress, for in the past passion had overpowered subtler perceptions. Freed of the rude urgency of desire, he could savor the texture of fine-spun hair falling across the back of his hand, and the velvety feel of her nape; the warmth of her breasts compressed against him, the greater warmth of her loins; the arc of her ribs, the slight depression of her spine, the gentle flare of her hips. Lightly he kissed her hair, awed by the rediscovery of what a wondrous creature a woman was.

Feeling immensely protective, he bent over and lifted Laura in his arms. "Time to put you to bed. You must be tired."

After a quick inhalation, she relaxed in his grasp. "Not so tired that I couldn't walk, but this is a nice way to travel."

He carried her to the canopied bed and pushed aside the mosquito curtain, then laid her on the cotton-filled mattress. Gently brushing the tawny hair from her cheek, he said, "Shall I join you, or would you prefer for me to make up a separate bed?"

"I would like very much for you to join me." She caught his hand and drew him down beside her. "You said we should have a real marriage in all ways but one, and I'm sure that includes sharing a bed."

"Yes, but insomniacs aren't very restful bed companions." He pulled a light cover over them. "You're allowed to change your mind if I toss and turn so much that I ruin your sleep."

"I'll worry about that if it happens." She rolled onto her side and pressed the soft length of her body against him, one arm going across his chest as naturally as if she had lain with him a thousand times before.

He was touched by her willingness to accept her new situation. He had expected her to be much warier about physical closeness. "Pyotr Andreyovich claimed that in spite of the reputation Russians have for being tempestuous, there's a vast patience, a willingness to accept, at the center of the nation's character. You have that."

"Perhaps." She gave a delicate yawn, covering her mouth with one hand. "Or it could be English patience. Actually, I'm not sure there is any such thing as national character."

"Perhaps not." He smiled a little as she dozed off, trusting as a kitten. Though it was not how he would once have imagined spending his wedding night, it was more than he had dreamed possible just a fortnight before.

But it wasn't enough. Dear God, it wasn't enough. His contentment vanished as he studied his wife's elegant profile. For the first time, he realized just how much of passion was mental. Though he was incapable of physical desire, his mind and emotions ached to possess her, to penetrate her, body and spirit, to make her his own in the most primal of ways. In doing so, he would also be opening himself so that her healing warmth could flow into the darkest corners of his soul.

But he was trapped by the limitations of his body. There was no solace in the knowledge that he and Laura would not be together if he were unimpaired; the bitter rage that rolled over him had nothing to do with reason.

In the wake of fury came black, suffocating despair, a melancholy so profound that he feared it would scald the woman lying in his arms. He disengaged from her embrace with trembling hands, praying that she wouldn't wake.

Then, desperate for fresh air, he made his way to the window again. His entire being was saturated with agony, a pain so different from physical suffering that it defied description. Outside the dark waters beckoned, a drowning pool of peace and surcease. And yet, he thought with a trace of bitter humor, even if he had the strength to will his own destruction, he was too damned good a swimmer to drown in a pint-sized pond. He would fail, just as he had failed at everything that gave life meaning.

Shivering with anguish, he folded his arms around his midriff and leaned against the window frame, too drained to support his own weight. He had wanted Laura to be his salvation. Instead, in his selfishness, he would drag her down into the depths of his own mortal despair.

And that was the most agonizing thought of all.

Laura awoke and reached sleepily across the smooth sheets, wanting to touch her new husband, but Ian was not there. Suddenly alert, she sat up and looked about. By the light of the bedside lamp, she saw that he was at the window. He might only have wanted a breath of fresh air, but she didn't believe that, for his bowed figure radiated unimaginable bleakness.

He had warned her of his dark moods, and she sensed that now he was in a more desolate place than any she could imagine. She stared helplessly at his back, unsure whether it would be better to go to him, or to leave him alone. If he rejected her comfort, it would not only be horribly painful, but it would make it harder for her to reach out to him in the future.

Her indecision was brief. Quite simply, Laura was incapable of watching someone suffer without trying to help.

Silently she slipped from the bed and crossed the cool floor. Ian didn't hear her footsteps. When she drew near, she saw that he was in a trancelike state, his face rigid and his fixed gaze unseeing.

She slipped her arm around his waist and leaned against him. At first his chilled body was stiff as a statue. Then his taut muscles flexed. For a brief, ghastly moment, Laura thought he was going to break away from her.

Instead his arms circled her with rib-bruising force, and he buried his face in her hair. He was shuddering like a man who had been running for his life and had finally reached the end of his endurance.

Acting from instinct, she caressed him, rubbing his back, smoothing his auburn hair. "Ah, *doushenka,* my soul," she murmured, using the tenderest of Russian endearments. "It's always darkest before the dawn, isn't it? The demons of despair don't want to lose you to the light, so they are fighting for your spirit. But they won't win, for I want you more."

Her words shattered his last threads of control and he began shaking with the dark, rasping sobs of a man who had never learned to cry. Perilously near weeping herself, Laura rocked him in her arms, praying that his tears would be healing, like the lancing of an infected wound.

After the storm had passed and he was still again, she whispered, "Come, my dear. You need rest," and led him back to the bed. His movements were brittle, as if a misstep would cause him to break, but he came without protest.

When they were back under the light blanket, she pulled him into her arms so that his head was pillowed on her breast. At first he clung to her like a drowning man clutching a branch, but slowly his terrible tension ebbed and his body softened.

For Laura, it was enough to know that the worst of his misery was past, but to her surprise, in time his breathing took on the slow, steady rhythm of sleep. Perhaps tonight his frayed spirit would finally begin to rest. And tomorrow, God willing, would be a better day.

Chapter 11

❦ ❦ ❦

THE NEXT MORNING, Laura woke as soon as Ian moved. Opening her eyes, she found that the slanting rays of the early sun were filling the room with a honey-golden glow. The two of them lay face to face about a foot apart, her right hand interlaced with his left. To her relief, her husband's expression was composed. The demons had retreated back to the shadows.

"I'm sorry about last night," he said quietly. "I thought I'd come to terms with what I am now, but apparently that is something that must be done more than once."

"I'm afraid so," she said ruefully. "Though I know my stepfather is dead, a dozen times a day I find myself thinking 'I must tell Papa that' before I remember that he's gone. It hurts over and over—but a little less each time." Her fingers tightened on his. "You have also experienced a great loss, so it's hardly surprising that it continues to hurt."

"I sincerely hope that next time it hurts less," he said dryly. "There are better ways to spend a wedding night than holding together the shattered pieces of an old crock."

She gave a slow, teasing smile, glad that he could joke about what had happened. "You're not that old."

"But a crock?" He smiled with real amusement and propped his head up with one hand. "You're a saucy baggage."

There was powerful intimacy in sharing a bed, and it emboldened her. "And you," she said softly, "are a man who asks too much of himself. Uncle Pyotr said in his journal that you were born to be a hero—'the sort of man who can inspire other men, who can risk his life in battle with courage and flair.' But while you would have met death with valor, surviving an endless, pointless ordeal requires a different kind of strength. Perhaps you can't forgive yourself for not being as good at enduring as you were at risking your life.''

Ian's expression became unreadable, but he did not pull away. ''Did Pyotr say all that?''

''The gist of it. I'm extrapolating some.''

''He was perceptive.'' Ian raised their joined hands and lightly kissed her knuckles. ''If you can understand that and still look me in the face, I'm a very lucky man.''

His words sparked an idea, and daringly she reached out to the cord that held his eyepatch in place. ''I really would like to look you in the face, Ian.''

He became very still but didn't stop her. Laura didn't know quite what to expect, and what she found under the patch was something of an anticlimax: just a closed lid curving over a surface that was sunken a bit more than a normal eye. ''I'm rather disappointed,'' she said lightly. ''I'd begun to think of the eyepatch as Bluebeard's closet.'' She leaned forward and kissed him at the corner of the closed eye.

''Not Bluebeard's closet, but the mark of Cain,'' he said harshly.

When Laura looked at him with alarm, his expression smoothed over. ''I'm just being melodramatic. That's Scottish national character, for those who believe in such things.'' Before she could question his comment, he sat up and propped some pillows behind his back. As he replaced the eyepatch, he said, ''What was your first father like? You've never spoken of him.''

Disconcerted, Laura rolled onto her back and frowned at the canopy of the bed. Ian laid his hand on her wrist. ''I'm sorry—it looks like this is a subject you would rather avoid.''

''No, it's all right,'' she said softly. Though she had always avoided speaking of her Russian father because the memories were too painful, on this sunny first morning of marriage she found that some of the sting had gone away. ''He was the very image of a dashing, romantic cavalry officer—tall and handsome and reckless. He seemed larger than life, though I suppose most fathers seem that way to small children.

''He had also something of his own father's melancholic temperament. When he was in a good mood, he was the fondest, most exciting father in the world. Other times he was moody and a little frightening, so I took care to stay out of his way.'' She thought a moment. ''Strange. When my father died, he was about the age you are now. Much too young a man to die.''

''No age is too young to die,'' Ian said. ''What happened to him?''

Ignoring the question as if Ian hadn't spoken, Laura said, ''I remember one winter when he took me riding in the country. He held me in front of his saddle and we flew over the snow, making wild jumps over ditches and fences. It was wonderful, like riding the north wind. I felt completely safe because I was with my father, but my mother was furious with him for risking my life, though she was just as reckless a rider herself. In fact, that's how she died—a fall when she tried to take a fence that any reasonable person would have refused.''

''A great pity that she didn't take more care.''

Laura sighed. ''Yes, but it was the way Tatyana would have chosen to go. She was still beautiful, still able to bewitch every man who looked at her. She would have hated being defeated by age. In fact, for her, riding carefully would have seemed like a small-spirited surrender to the inevitable.''

''Like my sister, your mother sounds a bit overpowering.''

''You would have adored her,'' Laura said with conviction. ''Everyone did, even women who disapproved of her. Apart from the fact that my mother was not melancholic, my parents were very much alike—beautiful and headstrong and passionate. They had wild fights and equally wild reconciliations.

''Once, to apologize for some failing, my father filled the drawing room and bedroom with flowers, even though it was winter and must have cost a fortune. Another time my mother lost her temper and threw every cosmetic and bottle of perfume she owned at him. He just laughed and dodged the missiles. Said she had a terrible aim and that the bedroom was going to smell like a whorehouse. I was lurking in a corner and made the mistake of asking what a whorehouse was. Tatyana rang for my nurse to take me away, so I didn't learn what my father meant until years later.'' Laura's mouth hardened as she remembered the scarlet rouge splashed across the wall, for the memory immediately triggered one that was infinitely uglier.

Ian lightly touched her hand. "Such parents make for colorful stories, but it must have been a somewhat alarming existence for a child."

"It was." Laura gave a wry smile. "It's hard to believe that two peacocks like my parents produced a wren like me."

"You're not a wren," Ian said affectionately. "More like a swan who has the wrongheaded notion that she's a goose."

His tone warmed Laura right down to her toes. "More like an owl than either. In fact, Kenneth called me his little owl sometimes. It's strange, but temperamentally I'm far more his child than that of my natural parents."

"Your first father sounds very different from your second."

Laura grinned. "That's because my mother had me choose her second husband."

Ian's brows lifted. "Really?"

Laura built up her own pillows so that she could lounge against them as Ian was doing. "Well, after Tatyana consulted me about my preference, she accepted Kenneth, who was my choice." She glanced at her husband and saw that the loose robe he wore had fallen open over his chest. She had a powerful desire to touch him, to brush her fingers across the dark auburn hair, to pull aside the robe so she could explore further . . .

Hastily she turned her gaze away. "After . . . when my first father was gone, my mother decided that she needed to get away from St. Petersburg, so she took me to a spa in Switzerland. I think she decided that it was the best way to find a new husband. Not only was she short of money, but she was the sort of woman who had to have a man in her life."

"From your tone, you don't quite approve of the haste with which she remarried," Ian said shrewdly. "Yet for most women, marriage is the preferred choice. Few have the courage to voluntarily face the world alone, as you were willing to do."

His comment made Laura wonder if some of her own stubborn determination to stay a spinster had been a result of distaste for the speed with which Tatyana had sought another husband. She filed the thought for later consideration. "There was no danger of her being alone for long. Men always surrounded her like bees around a jampot, and the Swiss spa was no exception. Some only wanted affairs and those she dismissed immediately. But it didn't take her long to acquire several serious suitors."

"How did Kenneth Stephenson manage to enter the race? He doesn't seem to have been the sort to spend his time lolling about a fashionable spa."

"It was pure chance that brought him there," Laura replied. "He was returning to England to teach at the Company training college at Haileybury. The friend he was traveling with had had health problems in India and wanted to visit the spa, so they did. Kenneth told me once that as soon as he saw Tatyana, he knew that he wanted to marry her. He was fifteen years older than she and not at all dashing, but he was very determined once he made up his mind."

"When did you mother solicit your opinion?"

"One day over ices she calmly asked if there were any of her suitors I would prefer for a father," Laura smiled reminiscently. "One was an enormously rich Italian count, another an equally wealthy Swiss banker. There was a French silk merchant and a Prussian general. Looking back, I realize that Kenneth had the least money of the whole crew."

She chuckled. "I did rather well out of the competition, because several of the suitors were clever enough to try to buy my favor. The Italian count gave me an exquisite doll, then suggested I play elsewhere with it. The banker always brought the most incredible sweets, the Frenchman supplied me with ribbons, the general arranged for me to ride a pony, and so forth. But Kenneth was the only one who really talked to me. When Tatyana introduced us, he went down on one knee so our eyes were level, then said that he was very pleased to meet me, Larissa Alexandrovna, as if he really *was* pleased. And he didn't only talk—he listened. When my mother asked for my preference, I didn't hesitate. The next day she told me that she was to marry Mr. Stephenson and we were going to live in England."

"Were they happy together, the peacock and the owl?"

Laura nodded. "Oddly enough, they were. I think my mother had had enough of high romance and melodrama. She told me once that a woman should marry for friendship and stability." Tatyana had gone on to say, with a twist of bitterness, that passion was as treacherous as shifting sand.

"It was wise of her to ask you for your choice," Ian said reflectively. "A child was most likely to look beyond the exterior trappings to the essence of the man. Kenneth Stephenson might not have been the best choice in worldly terms, but he was surely the best available stepfather for you."

Laura repressed a slight shiver. "The mere thought of having a different man as stepfather gives me the chills. But I wasn't the only one to benefit. Perhaps Tatyana didn't love Kenneth at first, but she did later. Much as she enjoyed flirting, she never looked seriously at another man."

She glanced at Ian. "Now you know everything interesting about me, Lord Falkirk."

"I doubt it, Larissa Alexandrovna Karelian Stephenson Cameron, Baroness Falkirk," he said with a smile. "But I think this is enough pillow talk for today. We need to get up, breakfast, and be on our way."

Laura nodded and climbed out of the bed, then languidly stretched her arms over her head, arching her back to loosen her muscles. She felt wonderful; the emotional highs and lows of the last day must have been good for her.

As she straightened, she saw that Ian was watching her with an odd, strained expression. As she gave him a puzzled glance, he drew her into his embrace. "Thank you for marrying me, Laura." Then he kissed her.

She loved the feeling of his lips on hers, and the warm, tingly sensation that spread through her. What marvelous, sensitive things mouths were. And the rest of him felt quite wonderful, too. When he lifted his head away, she said rather breathlessly, "Thank you for coming up with the idea, then talking me into it."

He smiled, then turned away. "I'll dress in the bathroom."

Her gaze followed him as he collected his clothing, then walked out of the bedroom. Thoughtful of Ian to leave. She had enjoyed sleeping with her new husband, but she still felt shy about disrobing in front of him. Perhaps in time she would feel less self-conscious.

As she summoned the young maid who had been assigned to her, Laura reflected on how well everything was working out. Though she had been frightened by Ian's despairing mood the night before, the aftermath had brought them closer. As Ian had said, it was not the typical wedding night—but it was not a bad beginning for a marriage based on friendship.

12th January 1840. We made the mistake of talking politics and ever since the atmosphere has been horribly strained. Ian and I are both killingly polite, when in truth each of us would give our immortal soul to be free of the other's company for even an hour. Bloody English warmonger.

Laura smiled wryly and rested the journal on her knees. Uncle Pyotr always referred to Ian as English on the occasions when the two men were at odds. She tried to imagine what it would be like to be confined day and night with another person, to never have an instant's privacy. Even she and her stepfather might have gotten occasionally tired of each other's company. It must have been far worse for two strong-minded military men who came from hostile nations.

She glanced up and saw that Ian had taken the three horses down to the stream to drink. It was their fourth day on the road, and they were taking a lunch break. At least, Laura had eaten. As usual, Ian had consumed scarcely enough to nourish one of the little striped palm sqirrels.

They had fallen into a comfortable travel routine, moving at a pace that covered a fair amount of ground without being too tiring. Laura knew that Ian would be going much faster if he were alone, but he was always considerate of her comfort. His quiet solicitude made her feel cherished; in return, she pampered him in small ways that he seemed to enjoy.

Every night so far they had stayed at government-operated *dak* bungalows, which were austere but adequate. An odd sort of honeymoon, perhaps, but she was perfectly content. The pleasure of having Ian next to her more than compensated for the mild inconvenience of sleeping in a lamplit room. Unfortunately, he still wasn't sleeping a full night. Often he quietly rose and went for fresh air. But he always came back, and there had been no repetition of his wedding night breakdown.

While Ian stretched his legs and took care of the horses, Laura read more of Pyotr's journal.

15th January 1840. Ian and I almost came to blows this morning. The most ridiculous thing. I said he was giving me

*too much of the food, he said I was hallucinating, and we
had the most tremendous row, with insults in at least five
languages. Quite the wrong reason to fight—prisoners are
supposed to accuse each other of taking too much of the
food, not too little. But I know Ian has been giving me a
larger share. I suppose he's afraid I'll die on him if he
doesn't feed me up. Impertinent cub. But he's probably right.*

*17th January 1840. We were arguing over breakfast—or
rather, I was trying to argue and Ian was ignoring me—
when the world went berserk. No solidity anywhere, dust
and pebbles raining down from the walls. Holy Mother, if
you can't trust the earth, what can you trust? I was sure
the stones were about to fall and crush us—one of the worst
moments of my misspent life.*

*Don't know quite how it happened, but when the quake
ended, Ian and I were kneeling in the middle of the cell with
our arms clutched around each other, me bellowing prayers
in Russian and Ian swearing in English. Such great brave
officers. I felt like an idiot, but Ian sat back on his heels
and began to laugh, and then I had to do the same. After
that it isn't possible to be angry with each other anymore.*

Laura smiled a bit mistily. The self-deprecating humor in
Pyotr's journal couldn't disguise the terror of the earthquake, or the complicated, ever-strengthening bonds between the two men.

She glanced up to see Ian approaching. "Time to go,
Lady Falkirk." As she rose, he added, "What were you
smiling about?"

"I just read about an earthquake, when you both thought
the walls were collapsing," she explained as she packed the
Bible in her saddlebags. "Pyotr described how it resolved
a period of strained relations between you."

"I don't recall that the incident did either Pyotr Andreyovich or me much credit," Ian said dryly, "but it's true
that after that, we never again had problems getting along."

"Actually, I thought it was a rather sweet story." Accepting Ian's aid, she mounted her horse, then grinned down
at him. "But do you know what most impressed Pyotr with
the nobility of your character?"

Ian swung into his own saddle. "What was that?"

"The fact that you gave him the pouch of tobacco and

clay pipe that you had on you when you were imprisoned.
Pyotr was rapturous in his praises of your generosity."

Ian shrugged. "I seldom smoked and it was obvious that
he would enjoy the tobacco more than I. He made it last for
months. Of course, he could only use the pipe when there
was a friendly guard who would light it for him."

"Giving it may have been a small thing for you, but it
meant a great deal to him," she said as they set their horses
in motion, the pack animal ambling along behind Ian.

Changing the subject, Ian said, "You need some practice
shooting—this evening, if it's not too late when we stop.
You probably won't be attacked by a tiger again, but you
really ought to be better prepared than you were at Nanda."

Laura made a face. "I don't like guns."

"This has nothing to do with liking them—it's a simple
safety precaution."

"But it really isn't necessary," she argued. "Within a
few weeks we'll be on our way back to Britain."

"Which means that there are several more weeks here in
India," he said patiently. "Granted, we're unlikely to run
into trouble, but you never can tell when you'll need to use
a weapon. If something happens and you have to defend
yourself, you should do it competently."

She gave him an unenthusiastic glance. "If I had been
more competent, your head might have ended up mounted
on the wall above someone's fireplace."

He smiled. "My first lesson will be on how to recognize
a suitable target."

She sighed. Her husband had the expression men always
wore when they were telling you what to do for your own
good. However, she was good at evasive maneuvers; surely
she could avoid a shooting lesson for the time it would take
them to get to Bombay. She looked around for something
interesting enough to justify a change of topic.

Ian had chosen this remote, seldom-traveled road because
of the spectacular scenery. At the moment they were in a
narrow, forested valley flanked by towering stone bluffs.
Laura's idle gaze followed the path of a kite, a common
Indian bird of prey. As it approached the base of one of the
cliffs, she expected it to sheer off, but instead it abruptly
vanished. "That's odd," she said. "A kite flew right into
that cliff."

Ian's gaze followed her pointing finger. "Perhaps there's a cave there," he suggested.

"Could we stop and explore?" Laura asked hopefully.

After a short pause, he said, "If you like. It shouldn't be hard to get up there." He turned his horse from the road and began working his way through the light undergrowth, the packhorse behind and Laura bringing up the rear.

A few minutes later they were at the foot of the cliff. Laura scanned the sheer face, then pointed. "The kite vanished over there, in the clump of boulders below the darker rock."

After they had ridden the last few hundred yards, Ian swung from his horse and tethered it. Face set, he said, "If you keep an eye on the horses, I'll see what I can find."

Laura bit her lip as an unwelcome thought struck her. "We can skip this, Ian. Having spent a couple of years in a prison, you probably don't share my enthusiasm for caves."

"For God's sake, Laura, I'm not so incapacitated that I can't make myself enter a cave," he snapped.

It was the first time Ian had been short-tempered with her, and Laura guessed that his anger confirmed exactly how difficult it would be for him to go underground. Yet though she could understand, his words still stung.

Her reaction must have shown, for Ian's voice softened. "I'm sorry—I shouldn't have barked at you. You're quite right—caves used to interest me, but now I loathe them. But it's better to face fear than run away from it."

"You really are hard on yourself, aren't you?"

"Scottish Calvinists usually are." Expression harsh, he spent a moment staring at the tumbled boulders. He seemed to be drawing in on himself, marshaling his strength. She guessed that his ability to make himself do what must be done had kept him alive.

He set off on his search and was lost from sight. A few minutes later the kite erupted into the air with an indignant shriek, the limp body of some small creature in its claws. Ian called out, "The kite has shown the way. There's a cave, all right, and it might be sizable. At least, the entrance is large enough for a person to enter." He emerged from between the rocks. "Of course if a man can enter, so can bats, leopards, hyenas, snakes, and so forth."

Laura made a face. "Wouldn't there be signs of that?"

"There are no signs of larger beasts—the snakes and bats I can't vouch for. Just a moment while I get a couple of lanterns." He went to the packhorse and rummaged through their store of camping equipment. Because of Ian's dislike of sleeping in the dark, they were well supplied with lamps and oil.

Laura was disconcerted when he pulled his revolver from his holster and offered it to her, butt first. "Remember how I just said that you never can tell when you might need a weapon? It's wise to be armed when going into an unknown cave that might be inhabited by hungry or angry animals."

"Even when you're just a few feet away?"

"Even when I'm just a few feet away," he repeated. "Danger can come from nowhere in an instant, and there is no substitute for being prepared."

She put her hands behind her back and stared at the revolver with acute dislike. "If you insist I go armed, give me the shotgun. That doesn't require much aiming and a face full of buckshot should discourage even a hyena."

"Fair enough, if you don't mind carrying the extra weight." He loaded the shotgun and handed it to Laura.

Carrying the weapon gingerly in her left hand, she followed Ian through the rocks to the cave entrance, which was about a yard across and almost six feet high. There was a small open space in front of the dark cleft, but all around were massive boulders. "It's interesting how well hidden the entrance is," she said. "Unless one is exactly in this spot, it's invisible. If I hadn't seen that kite, we'd never had known there was anything here."

"Interesting indeed," Ian murmured, a thoughtful expression on his face. "I wonder if it is entirely an accident." Without further comment, he ducked his head and disappeared into the passage. A minute later, he gave a soft whistle of astonishment, the sound echoing from the walls of a substantial chamber.

Eagerly Laura followed, shotgun in her left hand and lamp in her right. The entryway was a dozen feet long and curved to the left with a surprising amount of uniformity. The bend blocked natural light, and when she emerged into the chamber the only illumination was from their lanterns. But that was enough to reveal a sight that made her gasp in blank astonishment.

It wasn't a cave that they had found. It was a temple.

Chapter 12

❦ ❦ ❦

ENTHRALLED, LAURA TURNED in a slow circle. The chamber was perhaps twenty feet wide and twice as long, with a ceiling that arched well over their heads. A double row of pillars carved into lacy filigree ran the length of the temple. The far end was shadowy, but she could make out the contours of a statue that was larger than life size. Every inch of the walls was covered with paintings that showed vivid color even in the lamplight. "Magnificent," she breathed. "How old do you think this is?"

"A thousand years? Two thousand? Your guess is as good as mine. Probably hasn't been used in centuries, but it certainly is in splendid condition." Lamp lifted high, Ian began walking the length of the chamber. "This might have been a natural cave to begin with, but a huge amount of work went into expanding the space and smoothing the walls."

"Do you think we'll find a fabulous ruby in the navel of a solid gold statue?"

"I doubt it. The really wealthy temples are famous places of pilgrimage, while this shrine must have been used by a fairly small group of people. Used, then abandoned, but not before the worshippers concealed the entrance. At least that's my guess." Ian studied the painting of a man wrestling with a serpent. "Even if there were valuables here, I wouldn't touch them. Bad luck to steal from a temple, even an abandoned one."

"You're right, of course," she said repentantly. "But this is still a wonderful adventure. Do you recognize what deity the temple is dedicated to?"

Ian raised his lamp and gestured toward the statue, which depicted a majestic being who danced within a ring of fire.

"Siva in his aspect of Nataraja, the Lord of the Dance. He symbolizes the endless cycle of life—creation, preservation, destruction, then rebirth."

Laura stared at the image, fascinated. Limbs supple and face serene, the four-armed god stood perfectly balanced on one foot, his other leg eternally poised for the next step of the dance. Even without Ian's explanation, she would have found the sight deeply affecting. The temple and statue were more than beautiful; they also inspired the reverent awe that Laura associated with Christian churches.

As she began walking toward the statue, she discovered a doorway tucked behind one of the pillars on her right. Curious, she stepped through and found herself in a much smaller chapel. Instead of more paintings, the walls were entirely covered with carving. Groups of human figures were interspersed with bands of abstract design to create a dazzling richness of form.

It took a moment for Laura to see beyond the general effect to the details, but when she did, shock ran through her like a lightning bolt. Her shotgun dropped from nerveless fingers, hitting the stone floor with a metallic clatter. Barely managing to hang onto the lamp, she gasped, "Merciful heaven!"

For the exquisitely carved figures were engaged in what were usually called lewd acts. In the wavering lamplight, they appeared to writhe as if they were alive, and their actions left nothing—absolutely nothing—to the imagination.

Hearing the fall of the shotgun, Ian called sharply, "Laura, is something wrong?"

She tried to answer but no sound came out of her choked throat. A moment later Ian whipped through the door of the chapel, revolver in hand. Then he stopped dead, his gaze going from Laura to the walls, then back again. "Damnation."

Laura swallowed hard and turned to him. "D . . . do people really behave like that?" She gestured toward one group of figures.

"I've never heard of a real man who could stand on his head while making love to three women simultaneously," Ian said dryly. He uncocked his revolver and holstered it, then came over and put his arm around Laura's shoulders. "Are you feeling faint? You look white as a sheet."

She hid her face against him, feeling hot and humiliated

and a little dizzy. But the figures drew her mesmerized gaze again. "Are . . . are male organs really that large?"

He followed her gaze. "Definitely exaggerated," he said with even more dryness. "Come on—I'd better get you outside before you faint."

With Ian's firm hand on her arm, Laura made her way out to the small open area in front of the cave. The blaze of sunshine blinded her and she swayed unsteadily.

Ian caught her arms and lowered her into the shade of a boulder. "Put your head down," he said, kneeling beside her.

Laura bent forward and buried her face in her hands. The dizziness receded, but closing her eyes did not eliminate the vivid images from her mind. One couple had particularly caught her attention. They stood upright, the man supporting the woman as she wrapped her legs around his. Their naked loins were pressed together, and his hand rested on her round buttock. Utterly obscene, of course—yet their faces had shown such joy.

But there was no joy in Laura. The experience proved that she was as depraved as she had always suspected, for blood throbbed hotly in secret places of her body for which she had no name. Grimly she fought the shameful, pleasurable sensations, until she was able to raise her gaze and say with creditable calm, "I'm fine. Sorry to act like such a ninny."

"You're entitled to be shocked," he said with a faint smile. "One wouldn't find anything like that in an Anglican church in a village in upper Surrey."

She gave an unsteady chuckle. "Or in any Christian church. Why do Indians put such things in their sacred places?"

"I'm no theologian, but I think it's fair to say that westerners try to rise above the limitations of the body, to deny the needs of the flesh and become as close to pure spirit as possible," Ian said, expression reflective. "But many Hindus celebrate the body, believing that erotic energies are one way of seeking the divine—the joining of male and female is a symbol of the union of man and God. It's very different from the western religious tradition, but makes sense within its own terms."

Laura nodded slowly. "The carvings were exquisite, and there was a . . . a sweetness about them, a sense of peace.

Though I still can't imagine them in Surrey." Her brows
drew together. "But I find some Hindu practices, like burning widows, utterly bizarre. Do they also make sense in
their own terms?"

Ian shrugged. "I don't pretend to fully understand Hindu
customs. But I've observed a pervasive sense of spirituality
in Indian life that is stronger than anything I've seen in
Europe."

"How did you come to learn so much about Indian religion?"

"I made a conscious study of it. As an officer, I had to
command troops of all the major Indian religious groups,
and I don't think it's possible to lead men well without understanding what they believe in, and what they value."

"Are all British army officers like you?"

"The good ones are. Unfortunately, there are some who
look upon all natives as ignorant blackamoors." Ian
frowned. "When I was a griffin, fresh off the boat, an old
major told me that things were better in the old days. Officers and men spent more time together, which led to better
understanding. But more and more, the British are withdrawing into private enclaves. The major predicted that if
things don't change, the Sirkar will live to regret it. Indians
will loyally serve men they respect, but they have too much
pride to let fools treat them as inferiors."

"The major may have had a point," Laura admitted. "But
then, old men always think things were better when they
were young. The Company puts a great deal of thought into
training administrators—making sure they speak the languages, know the law and customs. That's why my father
spent years teaching in Haileybury. And don't army officers
have to pass language exams before they can command
native troops?"

"True, but language is only the beginning of understanding." Ian smiled reminiscently. "When I took the examination for Persian, they thought I'd cheated because I didn't
make any errors. I was almost thrown out of Addiscombe
before I could explain that I'd lived in Persia as a boy." He
got to his feet and picked up one of the lanterns. "I'll go
retrieve your shotgun. Do you want to go with me so you
can see more of the temple?"

Laura shook her head. "I think I've had enough adventure for one day." And the Lord of the Dance was an image she would never forget; she had no need to see him again.

She leaned back against the boulder and fanned herself with her topi while her husband was gone. The mere thought of her response to the erotic sculptures made her face hot. If she had any refinement at all, she would have swooned instead of staring. And how could she have been so lost to propriety as to ask Ian about the size of male organs? Thank heaven he was unshockable.

She should have known that the size was exaggerated, for she had seen other statues of naked males, in both Italy and India. The reproductive organs had always been much smaller than what was depicted in the temple. She was grateful that her stepfather had thought it more important to show her great art than to shield her from improper sights. A pity that her wits had been so disordered that she had blurted out her embarrassing question.

Before she could berate herself further, Ian returned. As he helped Laura to her feet, he said, "Shall we report the location of the temple to the authorities?"

She regarded him thoughtfully. "You wouldn't ask that unless you didn't want to report it."

"The temple has kept its mystery for centuries," he said obliquely. "It seems a pity to betray it to the modern world. But you're the one who found it, so it's your decision."

Laura bit her lip as she gazed back toward the temple. Even though she was within a dozen feet, the entrance was invisible. Remembering the sense of holiness inside, she said, "Without priests and worshipers, this temple might turn into nothing more than a sight for curiosity seekers. Let's leave it to its peace. If the Lord of the Dance wishes to be rediscovered, he'll lead someone else here."

As they made their way back to their horses, Laura smiled wryly to herself. While she could accept that erotic sculptures might be spiritual symbols, there had been nothing at all spiritual about her reaction. Still, the experience had been—educational, even if the sculptor had exaggerated.

In deference to the shock Laura had experienced in the temple, Ian dropped the subject of rifle practice for the rest of that day. The next morning, however, she seemed fully recovered, so as they were finishing lunch he said, "This is a perfect time for a bit of target practice." He got to his feet and offered his wife a hand up. "Half an hour a day and you'll be a sharpshooter in no time."

Ignoring his hand, Laura drew up her knees and linked her arms around them, her golden eyes narrowed like a suspicious cat. "I'm impressed at your natural caution, but I truly can't see why it's necessary for me to learn how to shoot well."

"I'm not naturally cautious, and that lack very nearly got me killed more than once during my first year in India," he said dryly. "Remember, this is definitely not Surrey. As your husband I'm responsible for your safety. Though I'll do my best to protect you, there is no substitute for having some capability to protect yourself."

Her eyes narrowed still further, and calculation showed in their depths. At length she said, "If you're responsible for my safety, as your wife I'm responsible for your health. I'll do my best with a rifle if you'll promise to eat more."

Taken aback, Ian said, "I eat as much as I want. Why should I force-feed myself?"

Uncoiling with feline grace, Laura got to her feet. "Because you're too thin and you don't eat enough to keep a marmot alive." She poked a none-too-gentle finger into his ribs. "Judging by the looseness of your clothing, you used to have a little flesh on your bones instead of looking like a scarecrow. Your appearance does me no credit. People will think either that I'm a terrible housekeeper, or that marriage is making you waste away from sheer misery."

"If you think I'm thin now, you should have seen me when I was just out of prison," he said with some irritation. "I'm in perfectly good health."

Dropping her teasing manner, Laura said earnestly, "Ian, if my grandfather was any guide, lack of appetite is another effect of melancholia. At the beginning of one of his spells he would stop eating, and I'm convinced that being half starved made his melancholy worse. If you feed yourself decently, your body will be grateful, which might help leaven your black moods."

Ian curbed his irritation and considered Laura's theory. It was quite true that he was eating far less than he used to, for food was one of many things that he no longer enjoyed. Perhaps his wife was right and better nourishment might contribute to greater well-being. "Very well, it's a bargain.

I'll eat more and you'll work on improving your marksmanship."

Laura knelt and picked up a chapati, covered it with the last of the curried rice mixture they had had for lunch, then rolled it up and gave it to Ian. "Here's the rest of your meal. Now where do you want to give me my first lesson?"

"There's a good spot just off the road. Shade from the sun and a large earth bluff to absorb stray bullets." He bit into the chapati unenthusiastically. "Do you want to use my rifle, which is a breechloader, or your father's muzzle-loader?"

"My father's, since I'm familiar with it."

Ian collected both rifles and ammunition, then led the way to the spot he had chosen, still munching on the chapati. Straw would have tasted equally exciting, but he supposed it wouldn't hurt him to eat more. After swallowing the last bite, he said, "Do I really look that dreadful?"

A gleam of amusement showed in his wife's eyes. "For a scarecrow, you're fairly attractive." She slipped her hand into the crook of his arm. "Put on a couple of stone more weight and you'll be devastating."

He smiled, then pulled a piece of paper from his pocket because they had reached the impromptu shooting range. After impaling the paper on a stubby branch that projected from a dead tree, he stepped off twenty paces. "If you hit the paper on your first try, this lesson will be over before it starts."

Lips tight, she wiped her palms on her skirt. Then she took the rifle from Ian, loaded it with clumsy hands, and cocked the hammer. Under his appraising gaze, she raised the gun and fired, the sharp crack of sound echoing through the woods and sending a squawking crowd of alarmed birds into the air.

As Ian watched the shot go wild, he was glad that he'd found such a large earthen backstop; anything smaller and the bullet might have missed the bluff and gone into the forest. Seeing Laura shoot, it wasn't surprising that she couldn't hit anything, but he was unperturbed. What mattered was that she had begun to try. "Very good. Now reload and take firing position again, but don't shoot yet. I want to show you some points of technique."

As she obeyed, he saw how pale her face was, but with

grim determination she reloaded, then raised the rifle and sighted along it. The barrel wavered back and forth.

Ian stepped directly behind Laura and put his arms around her so that his hands were over hers. He guided her aim, trying to demonstrate by example. "Easy now—try to relax. You're strung so tightly that you can't hold the rifle steady."

Her death grip on the weapon eased some, but Ian frowned when he realized that within the circle of his arms, her whole body was trembling. Keeping his voice low and soothing, he continued, "We're in no hurry, so take your time aiming." He let go of the rifle and stepped away from Laura. "You closed both eyes when you shot before, so this time try to keep them open. Do you have the paper in your sights?"

As she nodded, the rifle swayed to one side. Ian said, "Don't shoot until you're ready. When you pull the trigger, don't jerk it but squeeze it v-e-r-y slowly so that the barrel won't move and spoil your aim."

It was vain advice. Her whole body spasmed when she shot, and again the bullet went into the bluff. Without looking at Ian, Laura rammed in another charge and tried again, with no better result. If anything, it was worse. After another futile attempt, Ian said, "Perhaps the rifle is too heavy for you." He unholstered his revolver. "Try this—it's much lighter. When you're comfortable with a handgun, you can try the rifle again."

Laura swung around with such fury in her eyes that if the rifle had been loaded, Ian would not have been surprised if she had fired it at him. Instead, she hurled her weapon to the ground. "I'm not touching that filthy thing," she snapped. "You can bully me into shooting a rifle, but there's no way in hell you can make me fire a pistol!"

Her reaction was so intense that Ian rocked back on his heels. "Laura, what's wrong?" He kept his voice even, trying to conceal how disturbed he was. "This is far more than a ladylike distaste for weapons. Why do handguns bother you so much?"

Hissing like the furious cat she resembled, she said, "If you'd seen your father's brains spattered across a wall, you'd hate pistols, too."

"Dear God!" Ian breathed, suddenly guessing what lay behind her reaction. "Did your father commit suicide?"

"Yes," she said starkly. Her anger was draining away,

leaving her pale as ashes. "And I was the one who found him."

The shock she had shown in the temple was nothing compared to the devastation in her face now. Ian jammed his revolver into its holster, then wrapped his arms around his wife, trying to physically shield her from the anguish of her past. As he rocked her back and forth, she began to cry as if she would never stop. She felt as small and fragile as a fawn.

In a low, furious voice, Ian swore, "Damnation, how could he do such a thing? How could any man shoot himself when his own child was nearby and might find him? How *could* he?" If Laura's father had not put himself beyond human justice, Ian would have gladly wrung the man's neck with his bare hands. To hell with dashing and romantic; no wonder Tatyana and Laura had both loved Kenneth Stephenson for his kind, steady nature.

Though his words had not been meant for her, Laura responded by raising her head and looking at him in confusion. "You're angry with my father for shooting himself?"

"You're damned right I am." Feeling helpless, he brushed at the tears that glimmered on her cheeks, wishing that he could do more. "And you should be, too. I don't care how mad or sad or melancholic your father was—to do something like that to his family was unforgivable. Especially to do that to a child. If he found life absolutely unbearable, he could have found a better way to kill himself, one where no one would ever suspect."

Laura's brows drew together. "It sounds like you've given some thought to the etiquette of suicide."

"I have," he said tersely. "That makes me qualified to say that it's unforgivable for a man to subject his loved ones to what you and your mother suffered."

Laura was silent as various emotions chased across her face. Finally she said with a note of wonder, "I *am* angry with my father." Blindly she balled her hand into a fist and slammed it into Ian's shoulder. "What he did to Mama and me was despicable." She struck him again, crying out, "It wasn't my fault. *It wasn't my fault!*"

She had a very decent right hook. Ian caught her fist before she could use it again. "Of course it wasn't your fault," he said quietly. "For God's sake, why didn't you tell me before? I would never have asked you to touch a gun if I'd known.''

''I've never spoken of it to anyone, not even Kenneth, though my mother must have told him.'' She closed her eyes for a moment, and her face showed the fierce effort she was making to control her emotions. More calmly, she continued, ''It was midafternoon, a Saturday just before Easter. My parents had a huge fight, and Mama went storming out.'' She wiped her eyes with the back of her left hand. ''Later I heard a shot from my father's study and raced downstairs. At first I was afraid to open the door. When I finally did . . .'' Her voice broke. ''He . . . he was so handsome. But since then, I can't think of him without also remembering what he looked like that day. I began screaming. I didn't stop for two days.''

''Is this why your mother decided to leave St. Petersburg?''

Laura nodded. ''She wanted to get us both away. St. Petersburg had too many memories. She was right, too. Going to another country gave us other things to think about.'' For the first time she noticed that Ian was holding her fist. ''Lord, Ian, I'm sorry,'' she said ruefully. ''I hit you?''

''Nothing to signify.'' He let go of her hand. ''Shall we resume our journey? From now until we're on a British ship heading home, I'll make sure that I'm no more than six feet away from you at any time, so you won't ever have to defend yourself.''

Her eyes flashed. ''No! The lesson isn't over yet.'' She picked up her discarded rifle and began to reload.

Not quite believing what he saw, Ian said, ''Are you sure you want to do this?''

Face set, she replied, ''I'm going to hit that damned target if I have to keep trying all night.'' She raised the rifle and fired. She didn't hit the paper, but this time she kept her eyes open and pulled the trigger more smoothly.

Again Laura reloaded and aimed. Eyes straight ahead, she said softly, ''If I didn't love him so much, I wouldn't have hated him so much for what he did.'' The gun blazed. This time bark chipped from the tree trunk six inches from the target.

Ian stood by, silent except for an occasional terse suggestion. Laura wielded the rifle with a fierce concentration that told him as much about the woman he had married as she had revealed by her anguished tears.

The session seemed to last an eternity. Finally one of her shots struck the target dead center. The paper spun into the air, then drifted to the ground, a hole clearly visible in the middle. Drained but satisfied, Laura slung the rifle over her shoulder and turned to Ian. Hands on hips, she said, "Tomorrow the revolver."

He gave her a slow smile. "Has anyone ever mentioned what a formidable woman you are?"

"I am a Russian," she said with self-mocking humor, as if that fact were sufficient explanation.

Perhaps it was.

When they reached the dak bungalow that night, Laura went to bed as soon as they had eaten. She was exhausted, though not so far gone that she couldn't appreciate the fact that Ian upheld his end of the bargain by eating far more than usual at dinner.

At first she slept deeply, but later the old nightmare returned. The beginning was exactly the same. She was Lara, six years old and frightened by her parents' incomprehensible wildness. Then, as hysteria mounted, the dream abruptly shifted three years later in time. Once again she stood in front of the study, terrified to enter but knowing that she had no choice. Her small hand reached up to the cold brass knob and turned. The heavy door swung open with a screech, revealing her father's shattered body sprawled across his blood-drenched desk.

Then the dream began to take a new course. For the first time, terror burned away in a rush of fury that scoured her like flame. The familiar scene shimmered and changed. To her amazement, her father sat up, miraculously whole, and looked at her. Then he stood, walked over, and knelt beside her, taking her hands in his. "I'm sorry, Larishka," he whispered, his handsome face haunted. "Forgive me."

Laura began to cry, real tears that ran down her face and woke her up, confused and disoriented. Then Ian's arms came around her, as solid and reliable as the earth itself. She clung to him, weeping against his chest.

When her tears had abated, Ian said quietly, "The old Russian nightmare that you mentioned once?"

"Yes, but this time it was different." Skipping over the

early part of the dream, she described the scene in her father's study, and how it had changed from all of the other times she had experienced it.

When she finished speaking, Ian said thoughtfully, "For fifteen years you were caught in that moment of horror. Perhaps your anger has set you free, so that now you can remember the best of your father as well as the worst." His hands stroked her back, smoothing away the tension. "I wouldn't be surprised if you never have that dream again."

"If so, I won't miss it!" she said fervently. Then, rueful, she added, "I seem to have spent most of the last two days crying on your shoulder. If I'm not careful, you may dissolve."

"It's hard to dissolve a scarecrow," he said, amusement in his voice. "Besides, there's a certain rough equality here. Think of how tedious it would be if one of us was sane and healthy while the other one wasn't. As it is, we're perfectly suited."

Though the words were delivered lightly, Laura realized that they were quite true. Like called to like; the fact that she and Ian were both troubled might be why they were so understanding of each other. With an uneven chuckle, she settled into his arms. "I know that there's always supposed to be a silver lining, but you must have looked hard for that one."

"I did have to dig a bit." He massaged her temples with sensitive fingertips. "Think you can go back to sleep now?"

"I think so. I feel as if I've just set down a boulder I've been carrying for years." Yet though Laura was relaxed, and even content, it was a long time before she slept again.

The fury and hatred she had denied for fifteen years had lost some of their power now that she had faced them, and it was possible to think of her father with kindness. More that that, with love. Yes, he had been wickedly wrong to kill himself as he did, but he and Tatyana had been victim of their natures, torn by forces that raged beyond control. It wasn't difficult for Laura to understand her parents. After all, hadn't she inherited their dangerous capacity for wildness? At least her father's devastating example had demonstrated the dangers of passion. For that, at least, she supposed she should be grateful.

When she finally slept, she had a new dream. In its way, it was as alarming as her Russian nightmare, though it was far more enjoyable. She was in the chapel of the hidden temple, where men and women celebrated the many forms of union.

But this time Laura was one of the lithe-bodied women who gave herself with such abandon, and the man whose strong body joined with hers was Ian. The sensual pleasure that she feared and craved surged through her. It was a rage of irresistible rapture, both beautiful and terrible, and it bound her, body and soul, to the man in her arms.

Once more she woke with tears in her eyes, and this time she did not fall asleep again.

Chapter 13

❀ ❀ ❀

AS THEIR HORSES began the descent to Cambay, Laura scanned the streets and buildings that spread into the distance. "The cantonment is enormous. Of course, even a small military station is large by the standards of civil administrators. Were you always posted here?"

"No, for the first nine years the 46th was stationed in Ferozepore, on the edge of the Punjab. I was delighted, of course." Ian's smile was sardonic. "There were plenty of opportunities for action, and at nineteen I was mad keen for a taste of glory."

"I gather that war didn't live up to your expectations?"

Ian was silent for so long that Laura thought that he wouldn't reply. The closer they had gotten to Cambay, the quieter he had become.

But as they finished descending from the hills and rode onto the plain, he said, "War is incredibly ugly and often pointless, and it brings out both the best and the worst of human nature. With life and death the stakes, war is the ultimate game, the supreme test of courage and honor. That's why it never goes out of fashion. Once my illusions wore off I found no joy in battle—yet I can't bring myself to regret having experienced it."

It was a brief, piercing glimpse into a world that had been inhabited not only by Ian, but by Laura's father and uncles. Unsure what she expected to learn, she said, "Would you have given the same answer three years ago?"

"Three years ago, my simple mind was never disturbed by deep thought or ambivalance," he said. Pointing to a road on the left, he continued, "We turn here. That's my brother's bungalow under the trees."

It was a spacious, pleasant-looking place. "Will we be

staying long?'' she asked. "I wouldn't mind sleeping in the same bed for several nights in a row."

"Three days should be enough to take care of the basic social obligations," Ian said tersely.

Laura was uneasy about the visit herself, for she was about to meet the first member of Ian's family. Though he had assured her that the Camerons would love her, Laura was uncomfortably aware that a peer of the realm could have made a much better match than one with an orphaned, Anglo-Russian female of unremarkable face and nonexistent fortune. Of course Ian's injury had made it impossible for him to marry in the usual way, but no one would know that. His friends and family would think that Laura was an odd choice, possibly a designing female who had tricked Ian into marriage.

Sharply she told herself to stop worrying about what other people might think of her. They were married, and she didn't regret it. She didn't think Ian did, either.

They reined in their horses in front of the bungalow. Ian dismounted and went to assist Laura down. Before he reached her, the front door swung open and a young man in a scarlet-coated uniform bounded down the steps. "Ian! Glad to see that you've made it back. Did you have a successful trip?"

Though the newcomer had darker hair and a more compact build, Laura had no trouble identifying him as Ian's brother, for there was a strong facial resemblance. However, the grin on David's face was uncomplicated, quite different from Ian's guarded expressions.

"Very successful, David," Ian said, shaking his brother's hand with obvious pleasure. "Not only did I find Pyotr's niece, but I married her. Let me introduce you to my wife, Laura."

From her horseback vantage point, she saw that David's reaction was pure shock. "But . . ." Whatever he started to say was tamped down immediately. With a warm smile, he crossed to Laura's horse and offered his hand to help her down. "It's a pleasure to meet you, Laura. Welcome to Clan Cameron."

As she dismounted, she said, "I know this is rather sudden."

"With attractive females in such short supply, romance is often sudden in India." David scanned her with open

approval. "Leave it to an experienced campaigner like Ian
to act swiftly when he discovered that you weren't the
schoolgirl he expected." He nodded to a groom who had
come for the horses, then ushered his guests to the house.
"Come inside and have something cool to drink. You must
be parched after riding all day in this heat."

As the three of them mounted the steps to the bungalow,
David said, "I'd better warn you straight off, Ian. Everyone
in the regiment regretted missing you on your earlier visit
to Cambay, so the officers' mess decided that when you
returned, they would give a grand ball in your honor. This
way everyone will have a chance to say hello."

Ian grimaced. "I know the regiment loves an excuse to
celebrate, but is a ball really necessary?"

"Yes," David said, sounding more like an older brother
than the younger. As he opened the door for Laura, he
added, "Having a wife to present makes it doubly necessary."

They entered the main room of the bungalow. As David
gave orders for lemonade to be served, Ian asked Laura,
"Will you mind having to face a mass of strangers?"

His taut expression made it clear how much he disliked
the prospect of being guest of honor at a large gathering.
Wanting to remove some of the tenseness from his face, she
said reassuringly, "I'm delighted at the chance to meet your
friends." She frowned as a thought struck her. "But I really
haven't anything suitable to wear to a ball."

"One of the local tailors is said to be a wizard with ladies' clothing, and he could make you a gown in a couple
of days," David said. "I'll ask him to call on you tomorrow."

"Then we should be able to manage." Ian's voice was
neutral, but he still looked strained. Laura hoped that the
next few days didn't undo the progress he had made.

*15th March. Beware the Ides indeed. For the last fort-
night, I've been wholly undone by fever. It's so cold and
damp in this filthy cell. Would have died, I think, if Ian
hadn't held me in his arms when I was shivering, rubbed
my hands and feet, and generally acted like a blanket. We
are reduced to the most basic kind of animal warmth, like
a litter of puppies.*

* * *

It took time for Laura to decipher the entry, for Pyotr's handwriting was so feeble as to be almost illegible. It was her first morning in Cambay and David had taken Ian off for the day. Ian had wanted to stay with Laura so that she wouldn't have to face the inevitable callers alone. Though she would have liked to have him with her, she thought the brothers should have some time together, so she had shooed her husband off. Now she was taking advantage of the quiet to begin transcribing her uncle's journal into English.

The next entry was clearer, though not much.

22nd March. Ironic that I have come from the vastness of the Russian sky to this evil little cell unfit to lodge a donkey. I would have said once that such confinement would make me mad. Perhaps it has—or perhaps, here, I have found wisdom.

The Great Game—that is what Ian calls the silent struggle that Russia and Britain are waging across the steppes of Central Asia, what we call the tournament of shadows. I've always told myself that I was devoting my life to helping the Motherland defend her borders, but perhaps my young friend is right and I have spent my life on a game between two empires who squabble like children—a superior kind of chess for the bloodthirsty and power-mad. I loved the suspense, the danger, the knowledge that I was a hidden force whose plans could upset empires, perhaps change the course of history.

Yet now it sometimes seems that the real purpose of my life has been to bring me to the Black Well, where there are no more games to occupy my childish mind. For the first time I am forced to face my own soul. Not for nothing are prisons associated with growth of the spirit, for the wall between physical and ethereal grows ever thinner. I despise this place, and when death comes to set me free I shall be ready. Yet here I have found a friend closer than any I have known since my older brother died fighting Napoleon. Thirty years it has been since Sergei died—thirty years. In the heady delights of the Game, I had forgotten what it was like to have a friend.

Laura laid down her pen and stared at the words that she had laboriously copied into the blank journal David had supplied. Tears stung her eyes, an ache for both her uncle and her husband. Yet there was also gladness, for in the midst of adversity, Pyotr had found something infinitely precious.

She was about to start on the next entry when David's bearer, Bhawar, entered the sitting room and bowed. "Lady Falkirk, Mrs. Colonel Baskin is calling. Will you see her?"

"Of course. Please show her in." Laura closed the Bible. Though Ian had warned her that regimental wives would come to look her over, she hadn't expected visitors quite so soon. She supposed that it was inevitable that the first would be a colonel's lady. The status of army wives was linked to that of their husbands, so one of the highest-ranking ladies of the station would consider it her duty to inspect any new females.

As Laura rose to her feet, a handsome, chestnut-haired woman in her late thirties swept in. "Good day, Lady Falkirk. I'm Blanche Baskin. Let me be the first to welcome you to Cambay."

Laura glanced at the bearer. "Please bring us tea, Bhawar."

As Mrs. Baskin sat down, she said admiringly, "You speak Urdu very well. An unusual skill for a white woman."

"Among civil service families, it's a point of pride to speak to the natives in their own language." Laura took a seat by her visitor. "Also, there were so few Britons where I lived that not speaking Urdu would have meant a very silent life."

The other woman gave an elaborate shudder. "Thank God army stations are large enough so that one can have at least the semblance of a social life. A woman needn't speak any Urdu at all, though a dozen or so phrases are useful." Her shrewd gaze ran over Laura, openly appraising. "I heard that you're Russian, but you speak like an Englishwoman."

Briefly Laura considered snubbing the woman's curiosity, but she didn't want Ian's friends to pity him for marrying a shrew. "I was born in Russia, but I lived in England from the age of ten," she explained. "My stepfather was in the Indian Civil Service. After teaching at Haileybury for some years, he took another post in India. That's where Ian and I met."

After more scrutiny, Mrs. Baskin gave a nod of satisfaction. "You'll do very nicely for Ian."

"Good of you to approve. I'll be sure to tell my husband," Laura said, unable to repress the acid in her voice. The tea arrived and she poured cups for each of them.

As she accepted her tea, the colonel's wife gave an engaging smile. "You're wishing me to the devil, aren't you, Lady Falkirk? But there is worse to come, for every woman at this station is perishing to meet you. Ian was considered quite a prize even before he inherited the title, and his returning from the dead is such a dramatic tale. Now there are wails of regret that you got him before any of the belles of Cambay had a proper crack. By the way, if you haven't heard yet, the ball will be held at the club two nights from now."

Exasperated that everyone seemed to know more than she did, Laura murmured, "You are well informed."

"Not as well informed as I'd like to be." The other woman leaned forward, head cocked to one side. "Tell me, Lady Falkirk, what is Ian like in bed? I freely admit that I did my best to get him there, but he was quite a stickler about not sleeping with the wives of other officers."

Laura gasped, shocked speechless at the question. She could feel her face turning a hot, mortified red.

Mrs. Baskin sat back in her chair. "Now I've embarrassed you," she said contritely. "You have so much the look of a sensible, worldly woman that for a moment I forgot that you're still a newlywed on your honeymoon."

"I am certainly not worldly enough to be unshocked when married women discuss their affairs," Laura said stiffly.

The other woman's elegant eyebrows rose. "You disapprove. But why should I be a model of wifely virtue when my husband keeps a dear little black mistress in a house less than half a mile from my own?" Bitterness entered her voice. "He brought me to this beastly country where three of my children died before their first birthday, and the two who survived were shipped back to English schools when they were scarcely out of the nursery. I think I'm entitled to what consolations I can find."

In a few words, Mrs. Baskin had laid bare her life, and Laura felt a stab of uncomfortable sympathy. "I'm sorry."

"Don't waste your time feeling sorry for me. Just be grateful that you're on your way home." Having revealed as much as she was going to, Mrs. Baskin got to her feet. "If you can survive me, child, you can survive the rest of the hens. I really do wish you and Ian well. He's one of the more decent men I know, and your blushes have answered my question about his amatory skills.'' She inclined her head. ''I shall see you at the ball.'' Then she swept from the room, chin high.

Laura was left in a daze. If Mrs. Baskin was an example of Cambay society, no wonder Ian had been reluctant to participate. But other women called during the day, and they all seemed normal enough, though admittedly curious about Ian's wife.

Toward the end of the afternoon, the *derzi* that David had summoned came and measured Laura for her ball gown. Then she thumbed through his motley assortment of fashion plates. Wanting Ian to be proud of her, she selected a gown that was more stylish than her usual conservative garb. It was hard to choose among the derzi's fabric swatches, for he had some gorgeous materials. Eventually she settled on a luscious blue silk that shimmered with subtle peacock highlights.

It had been a full day, but it turned out that there was one last visitor in store. Bhawar came and announced, ''There is a female who wishes to speak to Falkirk Sahib. When told he was from home, she asked to speak to the sahib's wife.''

''Send her in.'' To Laura's surprise, the visitor was a young Indian woman with a child in her arms. Dressed in a threadbare but neat crimson sari, she was very lovely.

The young woman set her child down, then pressed her hands together and bowed her head over them in the traditional Indian greeting. *''Namaste.* I am Leela. You are the wife of Major Cameron Sahib?'' She spoke English, and spoke it rather well.

Laura returned the greeting. ''Namaste, Leela. I am Mrs. Cameron. Is there something I can help you with? If you prefer to speak to my husband, he will be home soon. You may wait, or call again after dinner.''

Leela debated for a moment, then shook her head and gestured at the little boy who clung to the skirt of her sari. ''My son would be restless waiting. Please, lady, will you ask Cameron Sahib to call on me? It is most important that I speak to him.''

Laura glanced at the boy, then froze, her stomach twisting. The child was perhaps a year and a half old, and he was Eurasion, with a complexion several shades lighter than that of his mother. Laura stared at the boy's face, looking for a resemblance to Ian. Well-cut features, a strong jaw—it was quite possible that the boy had a Scottish father.

Lips stiff, Laura said, "I shall give my husband the message. Does he know where you live?"

"Tell him that I am in the same place. He will know. Thank you, lady. Please, do not forget. My need is great." Then Leela bowed, hoisted her son in her arms, and left.

Laura was in the shadowed sitting room, curled up in a chair with her arms folded, when her husband returned a little later.

"It's dark in here." Ian struck a match and lit one of the lamps. "Dinner won't be for a couple of hours. David went to spend some time with his company. Though he got excused from duty for today and tomorrow, he doesn't like to neglect his men."

After hanging his topi by the door, Ian came and kissed Laura on the forehead. "You look tired. Were you overwhelmed by army wives? I should have overruled David and stayed with you."

Laura surveyed her husband. His time with his brother must have been rewarding, for he looked relaxed again. "The parade of visitors started with Mrs. Baskin," she said flatly, "who wanted to know what you were like in bed."

Ian stepped back as if she'd slapped him. "Sorry you had to face that," he said after regaining his composure. "Even for Blanche Baskin, it's an unusually crude remark. Blanche isn't really a bad sort, though shocking people is her greatest pleasure in life. After her, other visitors must have seemed like models of propriety."

"Quite. Especially the Indian woman who was here a few minutes ago. Leela, her name was. I gather that she's an old and dear friend of yours." Laura's eyes narrowed. "She had a little boy with her, perhaps eighteen months old, and half European if I'm any judge. Leela asked that you call on her. I gather that it's a matter of some urgency. She said that she still lives in the same place, and that you would know where."

As Laura spoke, the atmosphere between them solidified, twanging with tension. "I see." Ian's face was as opaque as granite. "I'll call on her now. Her cottage isn't far."

"Very thoughtful of you," Laura said, making no attempt to keep the edge from her tone.

Ian picked up his topi. "Laura . . . ," he said hesitantly, then stopped, as if not sure what to say next.

"Don't waste time here. I'm sure that Leela is anxiously awaiting your visit." Laura got to her feet and stalked to their bedroom, closing the door with elaborate care.

With her husband was safely out of earshot, she lifted a pillow from the chair and hurled it across the room, where it knocked a startled lizard from the wall. Ian might have been a stickler about not committing adultery with army wives, but little Leela was proof that he was a man, with a man's needs. At least, Laura thought savagely, he had been. Given what had happened to him in prison, she didn't have to worry about him bedding his old mistress during his evening's visit.

Shock at the wickedness of her thought extinguished Laura's anger, leaving only hurt behind. She pushed aside the mosquito netting and curled up on the bed, reminding herself that even if Leela had been Ian's mistress, it had been long before he had met Laura. But reason did nothing to assuage her sense of betrayal.

When she had agreed to marry Ian, she had anticipated that there would be problems that she couldn't imagine. Now one had surfaced. Shaking, she hugged one of the pillows to her stomach. It was deeply disturbing to learn that having a limited marriage did not make her immune to jealousy.

When Ian returned from Leela's bungalow, he was braced for Laura's wrath, but she was sitting quietly at the desk in their bedroom, transcribing from Pyotr's Bible to her own journal. She had bathed and changed and looked serenely lovely in the lamplight. He wondered how long that would last; she had seemed ready to chop him into crocodile bait when he left.

She glanced up when he entered the room, her expression unreadable. "Is . . . everything under control?"

"Yes." He took off his coat and removed his cravat. "In case you're wondering, the boy isn't mine."

After a long silence, Laura said, "I assume that you're at least a little sorry that he isn't."

Ian's stomach muscles clenched at how accurately she had divined his ambivalence. He had been disconcerted to hear about Leela's visit, but he had also felt a sudden, furtive hope that he might have an unplanned child to compensate for the ones he would not have in the future. "A little," he admitted warily, "even though it would have been a great complication."

His wife took his answer in stride. "But Leela *was* your mistress, wasn't she? Or was that my fevered imagination?"

Ian sighed and turned a straight chair around so that he could straddle it, crossing his arms on the back. "She was, for about two years. I ended the arrangement amicably a couple of months before going to Bokhara. There was a remote chance that she had been with child by me but didn't know before I left. When I saw her tonight, though, she was quite definite that the child isn't mine. He's only fifteen months—not old enough."

"Then who is the boy's father?"

"A good friend of mine, an officer named Jock Coburn. After I ended things with Leela, he made an arrangement with her."

"Is she in difficult straits because he has abandoned her?"

"Jock would not have neglected his own child and its mother." Ian ran his fingers through his hair. "Unfortunately, he died—I didn't know till Leela told me tonight. He drowned when moving his company across a river during the monsoons. That was before the baby was born and he hadn't yet made arrangements for Leela's support. After his death, she lived on her savings. I'd given her a bit of a nest egg and Jock had been generous. But now she's destitute and she doesn't want to be a kept woman anymore."

Laura nodded. "I imagine it's a rather insecure existence. Leela came to you hoping for financial aid?"

"Yes—she didn't know who else to turn to. She's not from Cambay, so she has no family near, and what she has elsewhere is very poor. That's why she was sold in the first place."

"Sold?" Laura said sharply.

He grimaced. "I'm afraid so. At least she was fortunate in her master, an elderly merchant who treated her well. After he died, she went into business for herself. Now that she has a child, though, she wants a different kind of life."

Laura's eyes narrowed, and Ian wondered if her temper

was building toward an explosion. But she said only, "What are you going to do for her?"

"What makes you think I didn't turn down her request?"

"You would never deny help to someone for whom you felt responsible," Laura said expressionlessly. "Nor would I think better of you if you did."

Once again his wife was perceptive. Ian said, "I'll arrange an annuity for Leela. It won't cost much to keep her in comfort. I'll also pay school fees. With a decent education, the boy should be able to find a good position in the government."

"That seems very fair."

There was an uneasy silence, broken when a bell rang in the distance. Laura said, "Does that mean dinner is ready?"

"In about ten minutes. I'd better change."

Laura stood and went to the door so he would have the bedroom to himself, but before leaving she said, "Why did Leela ask to see me? The matter could have been handled without my knowing. Was she trying to make trouble?"

"She's not a troublemaker. I think, quite simply, that she was curious and wanted to see my wife." Ian gave a wry smile. "Leela complimented me on my taste, by the way—said you were a fine lady. Since she knew that Jock was the boy's father, I think it didn't occur to her that you might draw a different conclusion."

Laura's glance was ironic, but she didn't dispute the point. Her hand was on the doorknob when Ian decided to take advantage of her improved mood. "Why were you so angry earlier? I never claimed to have lived a life of unimpeachable virtue."

"There's a difference between knowing something in the abstract and being faced with it in the particular, especially when 'the particular' is beautiful and has a baby in tow," Laura said dryly. "I suppose the incident made me realize how little I know about your earlier life. I'm sorry I was unreasonable, but I'm not really a reasonable woman. I merely pretend well." She gave him a fleeting smile, then slipped from the room.

Ian watched her go with a frown. On the whole, he had gotten off easily. Most wives would have weeping hysterics if confronted by a husband's former mistress. Nonetheless, the incident had created a chill between them. He had a nagging feeling that he hadn't heard the last of the matter.

* * *

After a leisurely dinner with David, Ian and Laura retired and went right to bed. At first Laura lay on the far edge of the mattress. Ian guessed that she was still unhappy about Leela. He hoped that she wouldn't make a habit of staying away; he rested much better with his wife in his arms.

Fortunately, night eradicated the barriers that had been erected during the day. Ian woke later to find that Laura had inched over and wrapped herself around him like a vine. To his bemusement, this was not one of the close-but-nonsexual embraces they usually shared, for one of his wife's hands had come to rest on his genitals. With only a thin layer of fabric between them, the warmth of her palm was very pleasant, though nothing like what he would have felt if he had been unimpaired.

He felt a violent spasm of bitterness at the unfairness of fate, but swiftly he brought it under control. Bitterness was old news. Carefully he moved her hand to his chest.

There was a certain black humor in the situation. Awake, Laura might be a virgin and frightened of physical passion, but in her sleep she was staking him out as her territory with unerring wifely possessiveness. In a way, her gesture was rather endearing. He was certainly hers; quite apart from their marriage vows, he wasn't much good to any other woman.

Bitterness again. It dissipated when a more cheerful thought struck him. Since Laura had been the one to breach the tacit physical limits between them, he was entitled to bend the rules a bit himself. Gently he laid a hand on her breast. It was deliciously soft and full, even more so than he had guessed. She had packed away the elaborate silk negligee of her wedding night and was wearing a simple muslin nightgown instead. He could feel the pebbled texture of her nipple through the light fabric when he stroked it with the ball of his thumb.

As her nipple hardened, he sighed and removed his hand, not wanting to waken her. Without words Laura had made it clear that touching with sexual overtones was off-limits. He wondered if they would ever know the casual physical ease that was usual between lovers—simple things like not worrying where hands were when they embraced, and undressing in front of each other. He would like to see her naked, even though he was incapable of taking full advantage of that state. But because he didn't want to pressure Laura into anything that would make her uncomfortable, they might never become relaxed with each other. Some women married and bore children without once letting their husbands catch a glimpse of bare flesh.

Nonetheless, before settling to sleep again, Ian caressed her other breast. There was bittersweet pleasure in feeling the lovely curves.

At least bittersweet was an improvement over bitter.

Chapter 14

❧ ❧ ❧

THE YOUNG SERVANT made a last adjustment to one of Laura's ringlets. "There, memsahib," she said cheerfully. "You look very fine."

Being a bachelor establishment, David's bungalow was not well supplied with mirrors, so Laura had to cross the room to see how she looked in a small glass that was better suited for shaving than a lady's toilette. The maid, Premula, had done a fine job of styling her hair. Laura complimented the girl, then stood on tiptoe to see how her ball gown looked.

When she saw her image, she inhaled with wonder. She had never owned such an elegant garment in her life, and the shimmering blue silk was spectacular. A little too spectacular—she hadn't realized that the lace-edged neckline would be so low.

Uneasily she looked down at herself. An embarrassing amount of bare flesh was showing, but the basic problem was less the style of the dress than the way she was built. Now that it was too late, she remembered why she had always chosen more conservative styles. Her natural figure tended toward the hourglass shape that men fancied, and her tight-laced corset and gown emphasized it to an absurd degree.

Nervously Laura touched the elaborate ringlets. "You really think I look all right?"

"You shall be the toast of the ball, memsahib," Premula said reassuringly. "Now, if you have no more need of me, I must go to my own lady." The maid bowed and left. She had been sent by Blanche Baskin, with a note saying that Blanche didn't expect a gentleman's house to have a decent lady's maid. It was a generous gesture. Perhaps Ian was right that the colonel's wife wasn't a bad sort in spite of her appalling frankness.

Laura frowned as she thought of her husband. During their three days in Cambay, she'd scarcely seen him alone. Though the affair of Leela was closed, there was still a certain tension between them. Or perhaps the problem was that they were surrounded by people and it was taking all of Ian's energy to cope with the strain. Laura would be glad when they resumed their journey in another day and a half.

The bedroom door opened and Laura turned to see Ian enter. Her eyes widened. "Oh, my," she breathed. "There's something about a man in uniform."

Ian smiled a little at her expression. "Does a uniform make that much difference on a scarecrow?"

"You look," she said honestly, "absolutely magnificent."

Though Ian was no longer an officer, David had convinced him that full-dress uniform should be worn for a regimental ball in his honor. It was also the easiest choice, since all of Ian's possessions had been given to David after his presumed death. Not having any other formal evening wear, Ian had agreed to the uniform, though without enthusiasm.

Laura was glad that he had, for in his scarlet-coated, black-faced and gold-laced regimentals, Ian was a sight to turn any woman's head. She guessed that the derzi had taken in the seams, because the coat did an impeccable job of displaying her husband's broad shoulders and narrow waist. He was still too thin, but in a splendidly lean and pantherish way, and his eyepatch added exactly the right dashing accent.

"You look rather magnificent yourself," he said, his expression warm with admiration. He handed her a velvet-covered jewelry box. "This is for you, since I didn't give you a wedding present. You might want to wear these tonight."

No woman was immune to the allure of jewels, and Laura opened the box eagerly. Then her mouth dropped open and once more she said feebly, "Oh, my."

Resting on the white silk lining was a gorgeous sapphire necklace and matching earrings.

"You said you were wearing blue, so I thought these stones would go well. Allow me?" Ian lifted the necklace and fastened it around her throat. "Someday I'll give you topazes, to match your eyes."

Laura turned to look at herself in the mirror, then inhaled sharply. The gems shimmered with blue fire, fit for a princess. For a moment she saw not herself but Tatyana, garbed in silk and sapphires for an imperial ball. The memory sent goosefeet running down Laura's spine. She swallowed hard. "I don't think I ever realized quite how much I resemble my mother."

Ian rested his hands lightly on her shoulders. "If so, she was a very beautiful woman."

"She was, though I don't look *that* much like her." Laura turned and kissed her husband. "Thank you, Ian. This is the most splendid gift I've ever received." She replaced her simple gold earbobs with the sapphire earrings, which dangled halfway to her shoulders and flashed with cool light at every movement of her head. "Now I can outface any catty female in India."

He smiled and offered his arm. Together they went into the sitting room, where David waited. He also looked remarkably handsome in uniform, though not quite as impressive as Ian. Give him a few more years and a few more lines in his face, and perhaps he could come close to matching his older brother.

David's eyes widened when he saw his sister-in-law. "Good heavens, Laura, you are absolutely stunning."

She blushed a little, because her ability to sense male desire confirmed just how sincere his admiration was. But David's regard didn't worry her, for he was the sort of man for whom it would be literally unthinkable to make an improper advance to his brother's wife.

In fact, Laura realized with rising delight, at tonight's ball she could be gay and giddy without worrying about the consequences. With Ian as her husband, she was safe from the unwanted attentions of other men for the first time in her life.

She took David's arm with her free hand. "Shall we go? With two such handsome escorts, I'll be the most envied woman in Cambay. And I'm going to have a *wonderful* time tonight."

As they left, Ian wished dourly that he was equally sure of how the evening would go.

* * *

The Cambay Club had originally been founded as a center
for sporting activities, but over time it had become the focus
of social activity for the entire British community. It occupied a lofty two-story building surrounded by gardens, with
one whole wing given over to a ballroom. Waltz music
wafted through the warm night air as they went up the front
steps to the veranda.

As they entered the club, David said, "Ian, you'll be
swamped with people all night. Shall I take Laura in charge?
I can perform introductions, fend off lovestruck subalterns,
procure refreshments, and generally look out for her."

Ian glanced at his wife. "If you don't mind, Laura, that
would simplify matters. I don't want to neglect you, but I
do have two years of social obligations to take care of tonight."

"Fine," Laura said agreeably. "David will take good
care of me." She stood on her toes and gave her husband a
quick kiss. Under her breath, she said, "This will soon be
over, *doushenka*. Meanwhile, try to enjoy the occasion. You
have a lot of friends who care a great deal about you."

There was strain in his face, but he managed a wry smile.
"You see too much, *Larishka*."

She chuckled at hearing one of the pet names that Russians were so fond of using. Then they entered the ballroom
and there was no more time for private conversation. Brilliant with lamps and tropical flowers, the ballroom was said
to be the grandest in northern India. The company was
equally grand, with women decked in colorful evening
gowns and men in equally colorful uniforms from all of the
regiments stationed at Cambay.

As guests of honor, Ian and Laura were immediately surrounded. For a while there was an informal receiving line, with
people greeting Ian and then being presented to Laura. It
was a blur of names and faces, except for Blanche Baskin,
who wore a gown so low that she risked pneumonia even in
India. After brushing aside Laura's thanks for the loan of
Premula, she floated away in the company of three men.

During the rush, David stood beside Laura and told her
what she should know about the people she was meeting.
When the press finally thinned, he said, "Care to dance? A
waltz will seem restful by comparison."

Laura accepted her brother-in-law's offer with pleasure.

"I hope I also have the chance to dance with Ian tonight. Do you know, he and I have never danced together?"

As they stepped onto the floor, David said, "The disadvantage of a whirlwind courtship. However, I'm sure the lack will be remedied tonight."

Laura's dancing was no more than adequate, but David turned out to be excellent. As they whirled across the floor, he said, "I want to thank you, Laura."

"For what?" she said, puzzled.

"For marrying Ian. When he first returned, he seemed on the edge of a breakdown. I was worried about him." David's pensive gaze went across the room to where his older brother stood in the center of a knot of people. "But he seems like a different man now. While he still has some way to go, I know that he'll be all right. I suspect that much of the credit should go to you."

"Some, perhaps," Laura said. "But Ian has been as good for me as I have been for him. When we met, my stepfather had just died and I was in dire need of a shoulder to cry on."

David smiled. "Isn't that what marriage is supposed to be—two people caring about and helping each other?"

"I don't know yet," she confessed. "I've only been married a fortnight. When I can speak with authority, I'll let you know."

David chuckled and spun her into one last flourish as the music ended. Again Laura sensed strong feeling emanating from her brother-in-law. He really did find her attractive—and the feeling was mutual—but what mattered was that he had accepted her into the family without question. If the rest of the Camerons were even half as nice, she would have no problems.

The waltz over, David said, "I see at least six men coming this way to plead for dances. There are never enough women here, much less attractive ones, so if you wish, you'll be able to dance holes into your slippers."

She glanced up at him with a laugh. "Then introduce me first to the ones who are least likely to step on my toes."

David did exactly as requested. As Laura smiled and stepped into the next dance with a cavalry captain, she knew that she had been correct in thinking that she would have a splendid time this evening. She hoped Ian was doing as well.

* * *

After half a dozen dances, Laura excused herself to go to
the ladies' retiring room so she could catch her breath. The
luxurious chamber had a large mirror which revealed that
her hair was living a wild, free life of its own, and that her
gown was even more daring than she had thought. It was
too late to do anything about her décolletage, but she tidied
her hair, then sponged her face with cool water. After drying it with a lavender-scented towel, Laura subsided onto a
wicker sofa and began wielding her lace fan. For the moment the lounge was empty of guests, and she reveled in
the quiet.

The door opened and she glanced up to see a petite blond
girl enter. The newcomer was stunning, with bright golden
hair and porcelain features that perfectly fulfilled the fashionable ideal of beauty.

The girl halted and placed one hand on the back of a
chair, her fingertips biting into the wicker. "I'm Mrs. Gerald Phelps," she said in a faltering voice. "I know that we
haven't been introduced, Lady Falkirk, but I must talk with
you."

Laura noted that the girl was pregnant, and from her pal-
lor, she seemed on the verge of fainting. Concerned, Laura
said, "Are you feeling unwell? Should I call someone?"

The blond girl perched nervously on the edge of the chair
and delved into her reticule. "I'm well enough. I want to
speak because I . . . I have something I must give you."

"Oh, dear." Laura's hands flew up to check her sapphire
earrings. "Have I been shedding bits and pieces?"

"This has nothing to do with tonight. You see, before my
marriage I was Georgina Whitman." She said the name as
if it was all the explanation required. Finding what she
wanted in her reticule, she handed the small object to Laura.

Laura blinked with surprise when she found herself holding a very handsome diamond ring.

Speaking quickly, Georgina said, "I know I should have
given the ring directly to Ian, but the one time I saw him
after he came back, I was too stunned to think of it. Then
he was gone, and since he returned to Cambay, there has
been no opportunity. I suppose I could have contrived one,
but it would have been . . . awkward. Even more awkward
than speaking to you." Her fingers twined together. "After
Ian was reported dead, I tried to give the ring to David, but
he was sure that Ian would have wanted me to keep it, so I

did. But of course Ian's survival changed everything, so the ring must be returned.''

Numbly Laura gazed at the ring. A sizable center diamond was surrounded by a circle of tiny brilliants. It was most impressive; India was known for fine gems, like the sapphires around Laura's own throat. She raised her gaze to Georgina. So Ian had wanted to marry this golden creature, who came from his world, was lovelier than Laura would ever be, and had enough honor to do something she found very difficult.

Laura would have preferred to be able to hate Georgina, but she couldn't. In a handful of words the younger woman had sketched a betrothal, Ian's presumed death, another marriage, and, by implication, a hideous shock when Ian had returned from the grave. Hardly surprising that the girl was distressed.

Obviously Georgina assumed that Laura knew about the broken engagement, and Laura would rather have her nails torn out with red-hot pincers than admit her ignorance. Trying to keep her voice even, she said, ''That's very generous of you, Mrs. Phelps, but are you sure you don't want to keep the ring? Given the unusual circumstances, Ian didn't expect you to return it.''

''Oh, no, no, I couldn't possibly keep it. My husband . . .'' Georgina stopped and swallowed hard.

''Ian's return must have been very upsetting for you,'' Laura said sympathetically. She glanced at Georgina's waistline. ''I hope your health hasn't been affected?''

Georgina put her hand on her stomach. ''Oh, my health is fine, or at least, normal for a woman in my condition. The only problem is . . . the shock . . . since Ian came back we haven't . . . my husband won't . . . I don't know how . . .'' Her agonized words came to a complete halt, and she flushed and looked away.

Yes, Ian's return had caused trouble. Laura felt reluctant compassion for the girl. On the other hand, she wanted to murder Ian. Slowly.

Part of her wanted to pitch the ring out the nearest window, but it was too valuable for such cavalier treatment, so for safety's sake Laura unwillingly slipped it on her right hand. ''I'm sure that things will sort themselves out in time, Mrs. Phelps,'' she said gently. Her speech was interrupted when several women entered the lounge, which was fortunate because Laura had no idea what to say next. Getting to her feet, she bid a polite farewell to Georgina, whose color was better now that she had discharged her duty.

But Georgina's peace of mind had come at Laura's expense. As Laura returned to the ball, she wondered with deep, smoldering fury how many other surprises her husband had in store for her.

A bright-eyed young subaltern said, "Sir, do you think we'll be sending troops to Central Asia soon? We need to secure Bokhara and the other khanates before the Russians do."

Ian sighed. Another fire-breathing disciple of the "forward" policy, which preached that continuous expansion was necessary to protect existing British territories. "I have no idea what the government's policy is, but having been to Central Asia I can testify that the mountains and deserts make the khanates almost impossible to invade. The Russians have mounted several expeditions under conditions more favorable than we can manage, and they've met disaster every time."

"But now that Afghanistan is under our control," the subaltern replied, respectful but undeterred, "we have a perfect base for launching operations deeper into Asia."

"Afghanistan is not under British control," Ian said dryly. "Replacing a capable, popular ruler like Dost Mohammed with a weak, despised puppet of our own was one of the stupidest things the British government ever did. If we didn't have several regiments in Kabul to back him up, Shah Shuja would be off the throne in a fortnight. In fact, the Afghanis might revolt and attack our garrison at any time. They don't like our heavy-handed brand of statesmanship, and I can't say as I blame them."

A colonel frowned. "For a British officer to say that is damned near treason, Falkirk."

"I am no longer an officer," Ian retorted, "so I feel no obligation to disguise my real opinions. The British are on thin ice in Afghanistan, and it could break at any time."

The subaltern said, "But they're just a bunch of savages. They can't match trained British troops."

"Probably not in a pitched battle," Ian agreed, "but I know those 'savages' rather well, and they are some of the finest warriors in the world. Not only are they fearless, but they are fighting on their own ground. I wouldn't want them at my back if I were launching an attack on Khiva or Bokhara.''

An uneasy silence fell on the group, broken when a new arrival said, ''How did you manage to escape from Bokhara, Falkirk? Is it true that your little sister brought in two camels' worth of gold and ransomed you?''

The story of his escape was one that Ian had repeated often, but at least it had no political implications. As he recounted the facts for the dozenth time, he thought that it was a miracle that he was still civil and coherent after two hours of being caught in a cannon barrage of voices and faces. But there were old friends present whom he was genuinely glad to see, so the evening wasn't quite as difficult as he'd expected.

What *was* difficult was watching Laura's triumph, for there wasn't a man at the ball who wasn't entranced by her. When Ian first saw her dancing with David, a surge of visceral, possessive anger swept through him. For the first time in over two decades, Ian had wanted to strangle his younger brother. David was obviously half in love with Laura already, and unlike Ian, he was whole and sane.

Even during an attack of irrationality, Ian knew that David could be trusted to behave himself, but the same couldn't be said of others. It appeared as if every officer in Cambay wanted to dance with Laura, and she was obliging them all. Laughing and drinking champagne that had been chilled in ice from the Himalayas, his wife was a bewitching temptress. She had the kind of sensual allure that drew men like bees to honey even if a woman was plain as a fencepost—and Laura was no fencepost.

Though he had never thought of himself as a jealous man, his anger increased whenever he caught a glimpse of his wife. He had never been troubled by Georgina's flirting, but then he had been whole, calmly sure of his ability to satisfy his woman. Now he was infuriated by the way other men were openly admiring Laura's luscious figure and tumbling bronze hair. And they were normal men who could give her what he couldn't.

As the evening advanced, again and again Ian's brooding gaze went to his wife. He wanted to sweep her away from her admirers and teach her the lessons in sensuality that her awakened body was wordlessly asking for. He knew that he could satisfy her, for he had not lost the skills of hands and mouth, or his understanding of what pleased a woman. But he was afraid to try, for limited lovemaking contained the potential for catastrophe. Once Laura had tasted the forbidden fruit of passion, she might develop an appetite that would lead her to the bed of a man who could teach her the final lesson.

Ian's fraying control finally snapped when he realized that his wife had left the ballroom. Half convinced that she had gone out into the balmy night with one of her admirers, Ian broke away from the group that still surrounded him. "Excuse me, but I'd like a dance with my wife before the night is over."

He began to work his way toward the doors that led onto the veranda. He was passing a small knot of cavalry officers when one said, "Leave it to Ian Cameron to go to a backwater like Baipur and find the most beddable female in India."

Ian spun about. "And what is that supposed to mean?" he said, his tone menacing.

The young officers blinked back at him, startled and uneasy. Two were acquaintances of his, the others strangers. One ventured, "Entirely a compliment, sir. Lovely girl. Very gracious. Every inch a lady."

Another chimed in, "We all envy you."

At least that was more polite than referring to her as "beddable." Realizing that he was in danger of making a complete idiot of himself, Ian nodded curtly and continued his hunt for his errant wife. As he searched the crowd, he saw that she had reappeared on the edge of the dance floor.

Before she could brighten the next slavering fool's evening, Ian stalked over to her. Sourly he noted how the shimmering blue gown clung to her lush curves and made every breath she drew an exercise in provocation. "Shall we go out for some fresh air, madame?" he said, taking hold of her elbow. "The club gardens are very fine, and there's a small boating lake as well."

She gazed up at him, her topaz eyes narrow and glittering. "What a splendid idea."

Ignoring people who wanted to talk to him, Ian guided them outdoors and onto one of the walks that threaded through the verdant greenery. As they moved away from the sounds of revelry, he said in a voice pitched low so that no one would hear, "You certainly seem to be enjoying your-self."

"Isn't that the point of a ball?" From the tautness on Ian's face, Laura guessed that he was having a difficult evening. She probably shouldn't raise the subject of Georgina, but her anger proved stronger than her compunctions. Voice edged, she began, "I was having a wonderful time—until a few minutes ago."

Before she could elaborate, he said harshly, "A pity that you must suffer the company of your husband when there are so many more amusing men present, but I could no longer stand still and watch the vulgar display you were making of yourself."

"The vulgar display I was making?" she said, so astonished she forgot her own anger. "What on earth do you mean?"

"I mean that I am surprised and not pleased to find that my modest bride has such a talent for acting like a trollop," he said through gritted teeth. "You were flirting and dancing with every man in four regiments. In fact, you weren't just dancing—you were all but offering yourself on a platter."

After a speechless moment, she retorted, "I was dancing with your friends in plain sight of half of Cambay! If that's acting like a trollop, I must plead guilty. I thought men wanted their wives to be a credit to them. Would you rather I wore sackcloth and was rude to everyone you know?"

Using unnecessary force, he batted aside a branch of spice-scented blossoms that overhung the path. "Sackcloth would be preferable to a gown that barely covers you and is in danger of falling off at any moment!"

Outraged, she said, "Half the women here are wearing gowns that are cut lower!"

"But none of them have your figure," he said grimly.

She glanced down at herself in disbelief. "This is the body God gave me, and I really don't see anything unusual about it."

"You have a figure like one of the women in a Hindu erotic sculpture, and the way you were flaunting it, every man at the ball couldn't help but notice." They reached the little lake and Ian steered them to the right along the path that followed the bank. "Is this your first visit to the gardens? It appeared as if every man at the ball was doing his best to get you into the shrubbery, and surely one or two of them were successful.''

"What is that supposed to mean?" she said, her voice dangerous.

"It means," he said tightly, "that I wonder just how far you have disgraced me."

"How dare you speak to me like this?" Laura tried to pull her arm away, but his grip was too strong. "*I* have behaved with perfect propriety, but ever since arriving at Cambay, I've been told more about your rakish past than I ever wanted to know."

"Trying to change the subject?" he said furiously. "That's a classic way of drawing attention away from one's own lapses."

Laura wrenched herself from his grasp, so enraged that the intensity of her anger frightened her. The distant voice of reason said that she should get away from Ian before one of them said something unforgivable, but he was between her and the club. She spun on her heel and stalked out to the end of the low dock that jutted into the lake, her hands clenched into fists.

Ian followed her and caught her arm again, turning her to face him. "Have you nothing to say for yourself?"

"I certainly do!" She raised her right hand and the diamond ring flashed in the moonlight. "Recognize this, Lord Falkirk? Your former fiancée returned it to me."

As Ian stared at the ring, taken aback, Laura said with lethal precision, "I've now met your former mistress, your former fiancée, plus a genuine trollop who expressed regret that she never managed to seduce you. Though for all I know, Mrs. Baskin was successful but wanted to spare my feelings." When he didn't reply, she said acidly, "If you wanted a harem, you should have stayed in Bokhara and turned Muslim."

An expression of unspeakable pain crossed his face and his grip tightened bruisingly on her arm. For a horrible instant she feared that he was going to hit her, but he mastered himself. "That is all in the past," he said, voice shaking. "Your misbehavior is in the present. I thought I was marrying a lady."

"I'm not a lady—I'm a Russian trollop, remember?" She knocked his hand away from her arm. "I was wrong, too— *I* thought my husband was a reasonable man, but clearly I was wrong. Dear God, it was a mistake to marry you against my better judgment!''

Her words cut the air like a dagger. There was a long, suffocated silence before Ian said in a voice strained to breaking point, ''As you know, if you want to end the marriage, you have grounds for annulment.''

With horror, Laura saw how close to disaster the argument had brought them. Yes, she could get an annulment, if she revealed what Ian had told her after asking her to swear secrecy—but when she saw the devastation on his face, she knew that she could never do that to him. Never. ''You're not getting rid of me that easily,'' she snapped. ''I don't want an annulment—I want to murder you, which isn't at all the same thing.''

In a spontaneous gesture swifter than thought, Laura raised her hands, planted them in the middle of Ian's broad chest, and shoved him off the dock into the lake.

Chapter 15

❦ ❦ ❦

LAURA'S ACTION CAUGHT Ian off-guard and he pitched backward into the lake with an enormous splash. As he plummeted below the surface, the water cleared his head as nothing else could have. My God, how could he have said such things to his wife?

The water was surprisingly deep. Slowed by the tangled waterweed and the weight of his uniform and boots, it took time for him to kick his way to the surface. He emerged sputtering for breath. Above him, Laura knelt on the dock, her blue gown spilling unheeded around her as she peered frantically into the dark water. "Ian, are you all right?"

"I'm fine, thanks," he said as he treaded water. "Sometimes a dunking is the only way to deal with a pigheaded Scot."

Seeing that he was uninjured, she relaxed back on her haunches. "That will teach you to insult a Russian, laddie," she said, eyes narrowing. "We neither forgive nor forget."

With her slanting gold eyes and purring voice, Laura looked so outrageously catlike that Ian half expected to see a lashing tail. He began to laugh with a bone-deep mirth that bubbled from a part of his soul that he thought had died. "Lord, what a dangerous little witch you are," he gasped. "It may be a mistake to teach you how to use a gun."

"I can't believe that I pushed you in," she said in a mortified voice. "I've never done anything like that in my life. But you made me so *angry*."

"I was rather angry myself, and with less reason than you had." He raised his hand to Laura and she automatically grasped it with the vague idea of helping him from the water. Instead, with a jerk of his wrist, Ian yanked her head-first into the lake.

Laura's brief, horrified shriek was cut off when she plunged into the water. For a ghastly moment she flailed beneath the surface, constrained by her corset, dragged down by her saturated petticoats, and desperate for air.

Before panic could take hold, a strong arm caught her around the waist and swept her up until her head was above water. She wrapped herself around Ian like ivy, too thankful for his support to castigate him for his treachery. When she had coughed up the water she had swallowed, she said, "You wretch! I can't swim."

"That will teach you to push your husband into the water," he said in a dulcet tone. "A grave insult to my lordly dignity."

Laura began to laugh, which set Ian off again. As they clung together, convulsed with amusement, she felt a warmth in her heart that spread through her whole body. Dear heaven, it was good to hear him laugh. She looked into his face, where the indomitable eyepatch was still in place, and saw that he looked a decade younger and so handsome that her heart twisted. This was how he once had been and, God willing, would be again.

When his mirth had subsided, he said, "Swimming is something else I'll have to teach you, since you're going to be living on a sea loch." He kept one hand on the dock and the other arm securely around her waist. "I'm sorry for all the beastly things I said, Laura. I've never been prone to jealousy in the past, but seeing you with so many other men who wanted you, and who can give you what I can't . . ." Amusement gone, his voice trailed off.

"I really can't understand why men think sex is so almighty important," she said with exasperation. "Trust me to know my own mind, Ian. I've said it before and I'll say it again—I don't want physical passion." Remembering what he had said about her coquettishness, she went on, "I've always been able to feel when men desired me—it's an uncomfortable pressure that's as obvious as heat from a fire. I learned early to maintain my distance so that my behavior could never be misinterpreted. If I seemed flirtatious to-night, it's because for the first time in my life I could relax without worrying about unexpected consequences. As your wife, I felt safe."

She felt him wince. "From everyone except me," he muttered. "Lord, I insult you and you give me a tribute that is downright humbling. If you wanted to punish me, you've managed it nicely."

"I don't want to punish you—I just want you to trust me in the future." She looked earnestly into his face. "I swear before God that I would never betray you, Ian. In fact, isn't that exactly what marriage means? I'm not going to break my vows for the dubious pleasures of adultery. Not now, and not ever."

"Thank you," he said quietly. He kissed her on the forehead, his lips gliding along a film of water. "I'm sorry you've had to face the only two women in India who have mattered to me. I wouldn't describe my past as particularly rakish, and I will take no responsibility for anything Blanche Baskin might say. I suppose I should have told you about Georgina. Yet there was never a time when it seemed appropriate to say, 'By the way, I was engaged to another woman, but that's ancient history now.' "

"Is it ancient history, Ian?" she asked softly. "Yes, Georgina married someone else, but that doesn't mean that you're not still in love with her. She's far more beautiful than I, and rather admirable. Up until a fortnight before you met me, you thought you were going to marry her."

"The man who loved Georgina Whitman died in Bokhara," he said painfully, "and perhaps the ability to love died with him."

Knowing that his loss was also hers, Laura swallowed and tucked her head against his throat, feeling the beating of his pulse beneath his moist skin. "Didn't you still love Georgina when you returned to Cambay?"

His arm tightened around her ribs. "While I was in the Black Well, I clung to the thought of Georgina as if she were a talisman, hoping that if and when I saw her again, everything in my broken life would magically become whole. That being the case, I won't deny that it was one hell of a shock to return and find that she'd married one of my best friends."

He gave a shuddering sigh. "But when I finally saw Georgina, there was no magical mending of what was broken. Even if she had still been single, I couldn't have married her as I am now, yet she might have felt honor bound not to end the engagement. That would have created a ghastly mess—far better that matters turned out as they have. Gerry always loved Georgina, and they're well suited.''

He kissed Laura again, this time on the lips. A shimmer of droplets fell from his hair to her cheek in a teasing caress. ''Actually, you're the only loser by what happened, because now you're stuck with me, against your better judgment.''

''I only remember that I went against my better judgment when I'm furious.'' She gave a rueful laugh. ''I still have trouble believing that I shoved you into the lake. I'm afraid that Larissa Alexandrovna took over for a moment.''

''I hope she doesn't do that too often,'' he said with amusement. ''The water is much colder in Scotland.''

Laura kicked her feet lazily in the water, enjoying the unaccustomed weightlessness of floating, and the way their bodies drifted intimately together. ''Has it occurred to you that we're in the lake while a ball in your honor is going on without you?''

''I do believe you're right,'' he said in a wondering voice. ''Though by this point in the ball, guests of honor no longer matter. People are making merry for its own sake.''

He shifted his hold from Laura's waist to under her arms. She inhaled sharply as his hand brushed her left breast, leaving slow fire in its wake. Not noticing her reaction, Ian let go of the dock and swam on his side toward the shore, effortlessly holding Laura's head above water. She relaxed and enjoyed the feel of his powerful muscles rippling against her.

A dozen strokes brought them to water shallow enough to stand. Ian scooped Laura into his arms and carried her up onto the bank as sheets of water cascaded from her saturated gown. After he set her on her feet, she did a quick check of her jewelry and was glad to find that earrings, necklace, and rings were all still in place. Apart from that, however, she was a wreck. Her sodden skirts and petticoats weighed a ton, and her slippers and fan were gone, presumably to the bottom of the lake.

Ian matter-of-factly lifted a swath of her heavy skirts and wrung the fabric until a cascade of water spilled onto the grass. Then he took a step and did the same to the next section of material. His practical actions produced a wholly unexpected side-effect wherever he touched her. The brush of his fingers against her calf as he gathered the heavy silk— the heel of his hand skimming down her abdomen when he released the compressed fabric—the back of his wrist against her knee—every contact ignited more of that teasing fire that Laura had experienced in the lake. She stood breathless and still as a statue while silent flames pulsed through her.

She felt bereft when Ian finished and began wringing out his scarlet coat. What on earth was happening to her? First fury, and then fire. As she ran stiff fingers through the havoc of her hair to comb out the worst of the tangles, she uttered a sharp mental order for Larissa to go away and leave Laura alone.

When she had regained command of herself, she wriggled the engagement ring from her right hand and handed it to her husband. "Here, this is yours. And don't you *dare* ask me if I want it."

Ian smiled wryly. "That wouldn't be very tactful, would it?"

As he tucked the ring into a pocket, Laura said hesitantly, "Perhaps you should tell Georgina what you told me tonight, about how you think it's better that the two of you didn't marry. She's miserable. I think your return from the dead has driven a wedge between her and her husband that will be very hard to heal. It would probably help if you made her feel less guilty. Unless, of course, you prefer that she and her husband continue to suffer."

From Ian's silence, she feared that she had gone too far, but at length he said, "No, I don't want that. I was too busy thinking of my own problems to consider how my return affected Georgina's marriage. I'll call on her tomorrow and see if I can do something to mitigate the damage I've caused."

"That's very honorable of you."

His mouth made a quick, bitter twist. "Not honor but the illusion of honor." His expression smoothed out and he put his arm around Laura's shoulders. As they walked squashily toward the club, he said, "I'd rather not drip my way across the ballroom. Let's sneak around the building and find a servant to call a carriage and let David know that we've left."

As they cut across an expanse of moonlit grass surrounded by flowering shrubs, Laura glanced over toward the ballroom. The bright notes of a waltz shimmered through the air, twining with the rich scent of blossoms. "I never did dance with you,'' she said wistfully. "I guess I'll have to wait until Scotland now.''

Ian glanced down at her, then chuckled. "No need to do that.'' He stepped back and made a low bow. "Lady Falkirk, may I have the pleasure of this waltz?''

After a surprised moment, she gave a slow smile and offered him her hand. "Oh, yes, my lord.''

He drew her into his arms and they began to waltz, making slow circles through the moonlight. Though Ian must not have danced since going to Bokhara, he moved with the sureness and grace of a natural athlete. Laura tilted her head back and gave herself up to the music as she had with no one else that night. She enjoyed the strength of Ian's hand on her waist, the firm clasp of his fingers on hers, the knowledge that their bodies moved only inches apart. Though the future might bring a thousand nights of dancing, she knew she would never forget the magic of this first enchanted waltz, performed by the light of the silvery moon with the grass soft beneath her stockinged feet.

As the music ended, Ian said softly, "I told you how I felt about Georgina, but not how I feel about you. I care a great deal for you, Laura, and you suit me far better than Georgina would. A pity that you're getting the battered, patched version of me, a lot less useful and amusing than the old one.

She smiled dreamily. "I'm not sorry, because if you weren't battered and patched, we never would have married.''

He smiled back, then bent his head and kissed her. Though his words were far short of a declaration of love, his embrace made up for the deficiency. Perhaps it was Ian's rediscovery of laughter that added a new dimension to his kissing. Laura closed her eyes and reveled in the flowing warmth that started deep inside and rendered her languid with delight. She slid her arms around his neck and pressed against him, feeling the trickle of moisture as damp clothing molded between them.

She didn't want Ian to release her. When he did, she opened her eyes to see him regarding her with a dark, enigmatic gaze. Her warm glow cooled as she realized that tonight had changed things between them in ways she did not yet understand.

Before her self-questioning could go any further, David's familiar voice broke the intense silence. "There you are—I was beginning to wonder if a leopard got you.'' He gave a low whistle as he got close enough to see them clearly. ''Lord, you both look like drowned kittens. I know you've always headed for water with the passion of an otter, Ian, but in the middle of a ball?''

Ian laughed and stepped away from Laura. ''It wasn't a leopard that threatened but a crocodile. After a fierce underwater battle, the beast was vanquished.''

On hearing the laughter, David's face lit up, as delighted as Laura earlier. But he didn't comment, merely took a closer look at his sister-in-law, his eyes widening. ''Laura doesn't look like any kitten I've ever seen.''

''If you don't stop staring at my wife like a tiger eyeing a choice tidbit,'' Ian said pleasantly, ''I'll break your arm.''

Laura looked down at herself guiltily. If her silk gown had been daring before, soaked it was downright indecent.

David chuckled. ''I doubt that you could—I've grown quite a bit since the last time you tried—but let's not bother to find out.'' He removed his scarlet jacket. ''Better put this on, Laura. You don't want to catch a chill.''

As Ian took the garment, David continued, his voice amused, ''It's a waste of breath telling any normal man not to gape at Laura—in her current water sprite mode, even a Hindu *sadhu* who has renounced all fleshly concerns would sit up and take notice.''

When David casually referred to ''normal'' men, Laura felt a faint hesitation in Ian's movements as he draped the jacket around her shoulders, but his voice was even when he said, ''Please give my thanks to the colonel and his wife and explain why I can't do it in person. It's been a memorable evening.''

Which was, Laura decided as they made their watery way around the club, an understatement.

It wasn't until later that night, when Laura was comfortably curled up against Ian and almost asleep, that she was struck by a frightening realization that shocked her back to wakefulness. Earlier she had been so absorbed in the events of the evening—first socializing, then anger, then laughter and dancing—that she had not fully recognized the dangers of her behavior.

Now she was horrified to realize that she, who had always cultivated calmness, had succumbed to rage and jealousy.

Though pushing Ian into the water had not endangered him, her action had been only a hair's breadth away from uncontrolled violence. What was happening to her? She had believed that abstaining from physical passion would save her from the lethal excesses of her nature. But twice now, when Ian gave her the shooting lesson and tonight when she became infuriated about his former fiancée, she had utterly lost control. Obviously the passions of the heart were as volatile and hazardous as those of the body.

She slid her arm around her sleeping husband, her face tightening. She could see only two possibilities: learn to control herself better, or leave Ian, for both of their sakes. And that was really no choice at all, because she could no longer imagine life without him.

2nd May. A landmark day! I saw the sun again, and blinked like a mole at the brightness. Ian and I were removed from the Well, then separated. I was taken to the office of the prison warden, where a chamberlain and two mullahs waited. They promised me royal favor, a position as military advisor, a residence of my own, and a young wife "as graceful as a doe." In order to obtain these delights, all I need do is admit to spying for the tsar, convert to Islam, and swear fealty to Amir Nasrullah. Conversion would be the work of a moment: I need only say "There is no God but the one God, and Muhammed is his prophet," and I will be free. Not to mention clean, warm, and well-fed.

I won't pretend that I didn't waver. Once I would have seized the offer with the hope of later escape, thinking that it didn't matter what religion I professed. But it does matter, if not to God, then to me. I'm dying; of course all men are, but in my case, I know the time is marked in weeks or months, not years.

And, by blessed St. Cyril, when the time comes I want to die knowing that I have not denied the faith I was raised in, the church my ancestors bled and died for. I want to go to an Orthodox heaven with gilded onion domes and incense and samovars, not a Muslim paradise filled with houris who regrow their virginity every night. I've never understood the charm of that—virgins take everything so seriously. Give me a woman who knows what she's doing, not that I could do anything with her in my present state, but I wouldn't mind

*having a pretty lady on my lap, where I could pat her knee
and think of better days.*

*I wonder what heaven is like, if it exists? I like to think
of it as a great city with different quarters for every faith,
but all within visiting distance of each other. While I may
not want to reside in the Islamic heaven, I'd certainly want
to be able to call on my Muslin friends and smoke a pipe
or two. I expect that the paradise of the Roman Church
will be right next to that of the Eastern Church, so there
can be jolly joint festivals on the great saints' days. The
Lutherans will have their own quarter—a cold and virtu-
ous place, I expect, but worth a visit if only to drink their
beer.*

*Of course, heaven is a long shot after what I've done in
my life, and the worst deed of all is what might occur after
my death. My clever, wicked plan may destroy thousands—
no, tens of thousands—of innocent people. It only needs the
right spark to set a fire that will rage across India. And for
what purpose but to replace the rule of one empire with that
of another? I wish to God that I could undo what I have
done, but that would be impossible even if I were not en-
tombed in this cell. I can only pray that my damned scheme
never reaches fruition.*

*Aye, I deserve to burn in hell. At least I'll probably see
more of my old friends there than I would in heaven.*

Laura frowned at her transcription. There it was again,
that reference to a fire that might destroy India. She really
must speak to Ian and see if Pyotr had ever mentioned his
"clever, wicked scheme." It was hard to imagine what he
might have done that could cause the kind of disaster he
referred to. She suspected that he exaggerated the importance of his work.

With a sigh, she flexed her fingers to ease a cramp. The
more of her uncle's journal she read, the more she regretted
not having known the old reprobate better. Would he have
discussed the nature of paradise with her if they had met
again when she was grown, or would he have kept such
irreverent speculation to himself? Now she would never
know. Just as she was unlikely ever to know what his
"clever, wicked scheme" was.

She and Ian had decided to stay over the day after the ball

in order to recover from the occasion, and to take care of remaining business. After breakfast—when Ian had not only eaten a sizable meal but asked for seconds—the two of them had gone separate ways. Laura had paid farewell calls on the most senior wives, including Blanche Baskin, who teased her about midnight swims with her handsome husband. Then she returned to the bungalow, packed her belongings, and was free for the rest of the day. She was glad to have the time for her uncle's journal.

3rd May. Ian still hasn't been returned to the Well. If they made the same offer to him as to me, did he take it? I don't know, can't even guess, though we have come to know each other so well. He may have done as I once would have, thinking himself obliged to take any chance that might lead to freedom. But he's a stubborn lad, and may instead have told the tempters to do something rude and anatomically impossible. So he may be free, or he may, God forbid, have been executed. I pray that it is the former, and that he will find his way home.

5th May. Selfish of me, but I miss Ian's company terribly. The cold seems colder, the darkness blacker, the loneliness well-nigh unbearable. I try to sleep as much as possible.

6th May. Ian is back, raving and horribly beaten. They lowered him down like a slab of meat. There's a viciousness to the injuries that turns even a stomach as hardened as mine. If he survives he may be blind, and there might be other permanent damage. I have done what I can to help, but it is so pathetically little that I weep from frustration. I am an old man with little time left—why could they not have wreaked their havoc on me?

Pen clamped between bloodless fingers, Laura stared sightlessly into space, the anguish of the Black Well more real than the brilliant Indian sun. So this was when Ian had lost his eye, and probably suffered the injury that had changed his life.

Afraid of what she might see but unable to stop herself, she looked at the next brief entry.

20th May. Ian has survived the crisis, at least physically, but barely speaks and will say nothing about what they did

*to him, or why. Damned fool Englishman must have defied
them and is paying the price for it.*

I now fear more for his spirit than I did for his body.

Hands shaking, Laura closed the Bible. It would be a pity
to blur her uncle's words with her tears.

Chapter 16

❦ ❦ ❦

IT HAD BEEN sheer chance that Ian had found Georgina visiting at her parents' home the day he first returned to Cambay. He had never been to the bungalow that Georgina and her husband occupied, but David had given him instructions, along with a curious glance, and the place proved easy to find.

Within two minutes of giving his name to the Indian butler, Ian was summoned to the greenery-filled veranda on the side of the house. Georgina had been pinching dead blossoms from a hanging geranium plant, but as Ian entered she turned to face him, her face pale. She wore a pink morning gown and was very lovely, but there was a brittle vulnerability about her that Ian had never seen during their courtship.

Not bothering with greetings, Georgina said stiffly, "What brings you here today, Lord Falkirk?"

"I wanted to talk to you before I left." Ian regarded Georgina searchingly. He remembered very clearly the laughter and passionate kisses they had shared, yet now he felt no real kinship with her. Had their relationship been so entirely based on physical attraction that without desire there was nothing left? With Laura, he had felt emotional closeness almost from the beginning, even though there was no physical desire.

Georgina's memories must have been more disquieting, for she colored under his gaze, picked up a pair of gardening shears, and began to clip some trailing vines with unnecessary violence. "I met Lady Falkirk last night. She was very gracious."

"Yes, she is." Even if she had pushed him into the lake after her encounter with Georgina, Ian added silently. Deciding to go directly to the purpose of his visit, he said, "I owe you an apology for how I behaved when I returned from Bokhara."

She lowered the shears and looked at him, her face stark. "They said you were dead, Ian. How could I know otherwise?"

"You couldn't," he said gently. "Even then I knew that, but I was so devastated at finding you married that I couldn't be reasonable. It wasn't until I calmed down that I saw that the false report of my death must have been the working of a benevolent fate, because it ended our engagement."

She looked down at her hands, turning the shears over and over. In a small voice, she said, "Are you saying that you never cared for me and are glad that we didn't marry?"

Wanting to free her from the past and spare her pride without encouraging futile regrets, he said carefully, "What was between us was very real, Georgy. If I hadn't foolishly volunteered to go to Bokhara, we would have married and dealt very well together. When I was in prison I thought of you constantly—you stood for everything that made life worth living. But the man who left, whom you promised to marry, is not the same as the one who returned. Now we are almost strangers to each other, and as I am now, I would not make you a decent husband. You deserve better than that."

Uncertainly she studied his face. "How have you changed, Ian? You don't seem so very different."

He hesitated, unsure how to convey what he had never defined even to himself. "In prison I looked into the abyss and that changed the way I see life," he said finally. "I don't know if that's good or bad, but it's a profound, very real difference."

Her brows knit in puzzlement. "What do you mean by the abyss?"

"It's what's left when everything you value has been stripped away." He gave a thin, humorless smile. "The experience was . . . educational, but I think that whatever knowledge I gained came at too high a price."

Georgina frowned, and he saw that she didn't really understand. He hoped she never did. Instead, she asked, "Your wife—has she also looked into the abyss?"

"Yes, she has," Ian said, a little surprised at his own certainty, but not doubting the truth of his words. "Laura and I fit each other as you and I no longer would, but as you and Gerry can. He is the best of men—be happy with him.''

It was absolution, and tears formed in Georgina's eyes as she understood. "Thank you, Ian,'' she said quietly. "I hope you and Laura also find happiness. Or if that's not possible after what happened, at least contentment.''

One last thing needed to be done. Ian pulled the diamond ring from his pocket and held it out to Georgina. "I bought this for you and no one else. I can understand that you don't want to wear it, but perhaps you can keep it for your oldest daughter. Tell her it was from someone who . . . admired you very much.''

"I'll do that.'' As she accepted the ring, she gave him the bright smile that had helped sustain him through so many dark months. He felt a surge of affection, different from how he had once felt about her, but equally real. Taking her hand, he kissed her fingertips lightly. "Good-bye, Georgy. Please give my very best wishes to Gerry.''

Then he turned and left. As he vanished through the door, Georgina sank into a wide cushioned chair and curled up like a child. It had been difficult to see Ian again, but now that the interview was over, she felt a profound sense of relief. Ian was right. He had changed and she could feel the differences, though she couldn't define them. Very likely he was also right when he said that they would no longer suit. Not that she didn't still feel some pangs. It was no accident that she had originally chosen Ian over Gerry; Ian was special and a small part of her heart would always regret what might have been. But now Gerry was her husband; bonds had been forged between them by daily living as well as in the privacy of their bed. They had both rejoiced at the knowledge that she carried their child.

Nonetheless, their marriage had been severely strained by Ian's return. She had felt guilty, almost sinful, for having accepted Gerry so soon after the reported death of her first fiancé. Ian had honored her by asking her to be his wife, and she felt as if she had betrayed his trust. She suspected that Gerry's feelings were similar, though she wasn't sure, since the subject was one they hadn't been able to discuss. Perhaps part of his unhappiness was because he feared that he was losing her to Ian for the second time, emotionally if not literally.

She was still on the veranda when her husband returned for lunch and sought her out, with the expression of longing and wariness that had characterized him for weeks. He stopped in the door when he saw her. "Is something wrong, Georgy?" he said uneasily. "You've been crying."

She rubbed her eyes with the back of one wrist. "Ian Cameron was here."

"Damnation," Gerry swore, his face darkening. "What did he say this time? I won't allow him to keep upsetting you."

Georgina shook her head, then rose and went to link her arms around her husband's neck. "He didn't upset me," she whispered. "He came to give me permission to be happy with the man I love."

At first Gerry didn't understand, but when Georgina's lips met his, everything suddenly became clear. He crushed his wife to him and the barrier of guilt and doubt that had risen between them shattered like the walls of Jericho.

A good imagination was in many ways a blessing, but it made reading Pyotr's journal a wrenching experience. His sparse words conjured up the Black Well more effectively than more lurid descriptions would have. And empathy was equally a curse in this case, where the two men who suffered were both so close to her.

Deciding she'd had enough for one day, Laura thumbed idly through the Bible, counting the number of entries left and reading an occasional phrase of the text, the Russian words echoing in her mind with a resonance rooted in the stones of the St. Petersburg cathedral where her family had worshipped.

She was almost ready to set the volume aside when her own name unexpectedly leaped out at her from the last page of the book. Pyotr's regular entries had ended about two-thirds of the way through the Bible, but the blank page at the end of the volume contained a letter written directly to Laura. It was dated early in August, the month Pyotr had been executed.

The hair on the back of Laura's neck prickled as she read it through, stumbling over the translation, for Pyotr's cramped handwriting had deteriorated badly. Once she had the words straight in her head, she wrote them down in English so that she could show the letter to Ian.

2nd August. Ah, Larissa Alexandrovna, my little Lara, last of the Kushutkins and the Karelians, is there any chance that this volume will ever find its way to your hands? I fear not, yet it is not quite impossible. I heard of an Englishman who left a prison journal not unlike mine. Twenty years after his death, it miraculously arrived in England at the home of his sister.

So there is a chance you will someday read my musings, particularly if Ian survives, for I have charged him to try to see that you get this. Perhaps you two might meet some day, in India or England. I like that thought, for you, my only niece, are the closest thing to a daughter I have ever known, and Ian, my friend and brother, is the closest to a son that I will ever have. I think that you would like each other.

But I must not waste this blank paper and my failing strength on maunderings. If this journal reaches you and the journey is safe and possible, I want you to go to Dharjistan, in northwest India. I became friends with the maharajah, Rajiv Singh, as much as an ordinary man can be friends with a prince. I met him while visiting India. Before I returned to Central Asia on this journey that has cost me my life, I left a casket of personal effects, mostly papers, with him. That casket is my bequest to you. If you identify yourself as my only surviving kin, Rajiv Singh will give it to you. Not only is he an honest man, but there is nothing in it to tempt a prince to theft.

Examine the casket and its contents carefully, and I think you will find the results worth the journey.

God bless and keep you, child. Remember that you are Russian, but use your pride as a source of love, not hatred.

Business done, Ian was cantering back to David's bungalow when a shout stopped him. "Major Cameron Sahib!"

He reined in his horse and turned. "Zafir?" he said incredulously as he recognized the turbaned man who galloped toward him with the recklessness of a frontier tribesman.

As the newcomer pulled his horse up with a wild flourish, Ian laughed aloud. "You old Pathan bandit. I had not thought to see your face again. I asked for you in the regiment and was told you'd gone on leave and wouldn't be back for two months."

Zafir grinned, a flash of strong white teeth against dark

skin and black beard. "Such was my intention, Cameron Sahib, but I heard that you had returned so I turned my horse south again. I wished to see if you had indeed survived or were just a *jinn* come to see if your troops were living up to your standards."

Rather belatedly, Zafir gave a respectful salaam. Ian responded by taking the other man's hand and shaking it heartily. Zafir had been his orderly for several years before the trip to Bokhara, and Ian had regretted that the two men would not be able to see each other. "I'm no longer an officer so you needn't worry about my standards. But I fear this must be a short visit, for tomorrow I leave for Bombay, there to sail for home."

"I shall accompany you," Zafir announced without an instant's hesitation. "I have a wish to see Bombay." He smiled slyly. "They say the women there are very fine."

A little taken aback, Ian said, "Do you truly wish to spend your leave in such a way?"

Zafir had the surprising gray eyes sometimes found among his people, and now a distinct twinkle showed in the smoky depths. "It is as good a way to spend a leave as any other. If you have hired another servant, discharge him. I will do the job better."

Ian laughed again. False modesty had never been Zafir's strong suit. "I have no servant but I have taken a wife."

The Pathan's shaggy black brows rose. "Then truly you need a servant. A man should not waste his time on mundane matters when he has a new woman."

Ian debated for a moment. There had been a pleasing intimacy in traveling alone with Laura, but the journey to Bombay was long. It would be convenient to have a servant, especially one so capable. As he came to a decision, Ian recognized that his need for solitude was diminishing, for, quite simply, he also liked the idea of traveling with a man whose company he enjoyed as much as Zafir's. "If you're willing to make the journey, I'd be delighted to have you."

The men spent several minutes more catching up on news, and a time was set for Zafir to join them the next morning. Then, whistling softly, Ian rode the rest of the way home, eager to see Laura and tell her of his day. Eagerness was as new as laughter.

A pleasant breeze was blowing, and he found Laura taking advantage of it by sitting on the veranda. He went up

the steps two at a time, then gathered her into his arms for
a hug. She was a delightful armful, soft and faintly scented
with jasmine. After the ball last night, he'd slept the whole
night through with her in his arms. It was the best rest he'd
ever had.

Though Laura seemed abstracted, she smiled up at him.
"You're in tearing high spirits. You've had a successful
day?"

"I made the arrangements for Leela and her son." Ian
perched on the veranda railing, one leg swinging. "And you
were right that I should talk to Georgina. Not only does she
feel better now, but I do as well."

"Really?" Laura cocked her head. "Why is that?"

He toyed with his topi as he thought about it. "I think it
was another step in putting the past behind me. Accepting
what I have rather than being angry about what I haven't.
A simple concept, but as you once said, it's the sort of thing
that one must put into practice over and over again." He
gave her a rueful smile. "Sorry I've been such a slow
learner."

Laura didn't answer, just nodded, her topaz eyes glowing
with warm approval. She was the most restful woman, except when she was furious. He liked her that way, too. "The
last news of the day is an unexpected bonus—we've acquired a servant for the last leg of our journey," he said.
"My Pathan orderly, Zafir, came back from leave to see if
I really was alive. Since I am, he has decided to accompany
us to Bombay. I was glad to see him, and he'll do an excellent job."

She bit her lower lip. "There's something we must discuss. I was translating more of Uncle Pyotr's journal and I
found this at the end of the Bible. It's a sort of letter to
me." She handed him the English transcription she had
made.

As soon as he hit the word "Dharjistan," a vision of fire
flared through his mind. "Bloody hell," he swore, closing
his eye against a wave of disorientation.

He felt Laura's hand on his arm. "Is something wrong,
Ian?"

Her touch steadied him. "I'm not quite sure," he said
slowly, opening his eye and seeing her concerned face.
"When I read 'Dharjistan,' I saw fire."

"What was burning?"

He took a deep breath and thought about the image, which was much clearer than the vague flashes that had haunted him since Bokhara. "This will sound strange, but what I see is like a map of India, only more real. Flames shoot up in the northwest, then sweep across the whole country, destroying everything in their path."

"A fire across India?" she said, startled. "Several times in his journal, Pyotr used that phrase." She flipped through the journal, then read aloud what her uncle had written.

"So that's why I've had nightmares of fire for months!" Ian rubbed his temple. "It's beginning to come back to me. I was out of my head with fever when Pyotr was taken to be executed. He tried to tell me something, but because I was delirious, the only thing that stuck in my mind was the fact that he was going to his death. Now I can hear him saying, 'a fire across India' as clearly as if he were standing here on the veranda." Ian spent several minutes searching his memory, then shook his head in frustration. "He said more, but damned if I can remember what."

"From the way you reacted, he must have mentioned Dharjistan as well," Laura said thoughtfully.

Ian sighed. "Very likely, but I have no idea what he said."

"Now that you've started remembering, perhaps the rest will come back," she said encouragingly. "Can you tell me something about Dharjistan? I know nothing about the place."

"I've traveled through several times because it lies across the main route to Afghanistan. Dharjistan has great strategic importance for that reason." He paused to marshal the important facts. "As you know, it's a princely state with its own native ruler rather than being under British administration. The maharajah, Rajiv Singh, has always been a solid supporter of the Sirkar."

"What kind of man is he?"

"As Indian rulers go, he's considered very humane," Ian said cynically. "That means he'll have a man's nose or ears cut off where another ruler would order execution. Still, that's progressive by local standards. Now that Ranjit Singh has died in the Punjab, Rajiv Singh is the most influential prince in northern India. He's a Rajput, which is a warrior caste known for honor and fighting ability. His wife, Kamala, is said to be the most beautiful woman in India."

Laura thought about that. "Do they have anything to do with a fire across India?"

"I have no idea." Ian glanced at the paper in his hand. "But I do wonder how a Russian agent came to be such good friends with Rajiv Singh."

"Why shouldn't they be friends?" she asked with a touch of defensiveness. "Uncle Pyotr was a charming, cultivated man."

"So he was," Ian agreed, "but if Pyotr Andreyovich was in India, it was in hopes of causing trouble for the Sirkar. He probably spent his time in Dharjistan trying to subvert the maharajah. Rajiv Singh has always seemed to recognize that it's in his own best interests to get along with the British, but perhaps he is less loyal than thought." Ian's brows drew together as he reread the end of the letter. "Or perhaps someone wants to overthrow Rajiv Singh. Most Indian courts are rife with intrigue, and Pyotr may have secretly aided a potential usurper. If an anti-British ruler came to the Dharjistani throne, he could cause real trouble for the Sirkar."

"Why would Pyotr involve himself in the politics of an Indian state?"

"His ultimate goal would be to help Russia get a foothold in India," Ian said grimly. "Russia has always resented the British presence here. Several times they've unsuccessfully sent expeditions in the hopes of pushing us out. That's why Central Asia is so important. If the terrain weren't so appalling, there would be Russian troops sitting at the other end of the Khyber Pass, waiting for a chance to march through."

She looked uncomfortable with the thought. "You really think my uncle could have been involved in something like that?"

Knowing that Laura had never really made the connection between the uncle she loved and the work that he had done, Ian said, "Furthering Russian interests was his job, and he was very good at it. I was a soldier first and a rather poor diplomat second, but your uncle was a true political agent, dedicated to doing whatever was necessary to achieve his country's aims."

"At the end, he obviously regretted what he had done." Laura frowned, then said with determined optimism, "Still, it's been over three years since he was in India, so surely his scheme must have come to nothing.''

"Probably," he agreed. "If I thought there was a chance that Dharjistan was about to go up in flames, I wouldn't take you there, bequest or no bequest.''

"You won't mind going, Ian?" she asked. "It will delay our return to Scotland.''

"Between Pyotr's legacy and his dark hints of past plots, it would be impossible not to go." He glanced back at the translated journal and skimmed the last several entries, chuckling when he read Pyotr's speculation about the nature of heaven. Then he came to the description of his own beating, and his face stiffened. Thank God that when he was raving he had said nothing about the interval when he was out of the Well. The events of those four days were something he had no desire to have known, especially not to Laura. He would rather that she maintained the few illusions she might still have about him.

He looked up to see Laura regarding him with disconcerting intensity. Not wanting her to ask any questions about the beating or the missing days, he handed back the journal. "How do you feel about the covert conflict between Russia and Britain? Since you've spent so much of your life in England, I tend to think of your loyalties as entirely English, but perhaps that's an unwarranted assumption.''

"I don't want to see my native and adopted countries come to blows," she said tartly. "If I have a loyalty, it's to peace.''

Ian got to his feet. "I think I'll get the cook to find some food to keep me until dinner. Do you want anything?''

"Does this mean you're beginning to enjoy eating again?" Laura said, her full lips curving into a smile.

"I do believe I am," Ian said reflectively. "Just remember that if I end up weighing twenty stone, you're to blame.''

She laughed and Ian laughed with her. As he went into the bungalow he realized that he was now enjoying food, sleep, laughter, and the companionship of a delightful woman. It was far more than he had thought possible a few short weeks earlier.

Most important of all, he had learned not to dwell on what was forever out of his reach.

Chapter 17

❦ ❦ ❦

As THE ROAD crested the high hill, Ian pointed out a straggling collection of houses on the floor of the valley. "That should be Hirsar, the village where the dak bungalow is."

"I hope so," Laura said. "I'm ready to call it a day."

Ian gave her a quick glance. "Have I been pushing the pace too hard? You've seemed to have no trouble keeping up."

"The pace is perfect," she assured him. "Faster would be too fast, and slower would be tedious."

He chuckled. "When you said you were an agreeable woman, you were telling the truth. Don't make it too easy for me to be unreasonable." He took off his topi and looked into the cloudless sky. "Today the season has changed from the hot weather to the cool. Can you feel the difference in the air?"

She gave the sky an inquiring glance, but it didn't speak to her as it had to Ian. "It has been pleasant today, but does that mean that the heat has broken for the year?"

He nodded. "About my fifth or sixth year in India I learned to sense the difference. One day in October, it's as if a lever is thrown. The change occurs almost in the blink of an eye."

"I hope you're right—it will make the rest of our traveling much nicer." Laura looked across the countryside with renewed interest. "The months between October and March are so lovely that it's almost enough to make one forget the hot weather."

"I always felt that way during the cool season," Ian agreed wryly, "but changed my mind as soon as the hot weather came back. Once a northerner, always a northerner."

Laura agreed; though she had learned to tolerate murderous heat, she still disliked it intensely. "Will you miss India?"

"Some," he said slowly. "There's something about this country that calls to anyone with a drop of Celtic blood. Maybe that's why there are so many Scots and Irishmen here. I'll certainly miss the sense of magic one sometimes finds, though I can do without the disease, filth, and poverty. Still, if travel between Europe and India improves so that the trip is quicker, I wouldn't mind returning for a visit. Would you like that?"

"Yes." She grinned. "It isn't just Celtic blood that responds—the Slav in me feels the same way that you do. I'd like to visit again, as long as it's during the cool season."

They continued into the valley in friendly silence, Zafir ambling some distance behind and leading the pack horse. Laura had wondered if having the Pathan along meant that the men would be constantly talking of things and people she knew nothing about, but that wasn't the case. The easy familiarity between Ian and Zafir didn't seem to require much speech.

She had never known any Pathans since they lived in the mountains of the northwest, far from Baipur, but Zafir's affable directness was very likable. Though Laura's behavior might be brazen and bizarre by Pathan standards, as Ian's woman she received the same courtesy and loyalty that Zafir gave to Ian. And the Pathan was wonderfully efficient, which was useful in this sparsely settled country where they often had to camp out.

Half an hour more of riding brought them into the little village. They were met by a welcoming committee consisting of most of the village's inhabitants. A villager must have seen them coming and informed the headman of their approach.

An elderly man of great dignity emerged from the center of the waiting group and greeted them. "Namaste, sahib. You will be spending the night at the dak?"

Agreeing that they would, Ian dismounted, introduced himself, and began exchanging courtesies. Eventually the headman said, "Forgive this impertinence, Cameron Sahib, but the nobility of your bearing suggests that you are an officer in the army."

"Your honor is perceptive," Ian said politely. "Though I'm in the army no longer, I was for many years."

The headman nodded with satisfaction. "A dispute has arisen which should best be resolved quickly. Will you judge it?"

Surprised, Ian said, "But I am not trained in the law. Wouldn't a judge of your own district be a better choice?"

"It will be long before one visits again, and it would be a great burden for everyone to journey to the court," the headman explained. "As an officer of the Sirkar, sahib, we know you will be just. If you are willing to act, the case could be heard right now. All parties involved are here in the village."

"Very well. If everyone concerned agrees to accept my judgment, I will hear the case." Turning to Laura, Ian said in English, "This will probably take at least a couple of hours. I assume that you prefer to go to the dak and relax?"

"Yes, great wise one," she said demurely. "So convenient in this case to be a mere woman." Laura remounted and she and Zafir continued to the dak, which was a small one with no resident servants. While Zafir went off to buy food, Laura decided to go for a walk to loosen muscles tightened by a day of riding.

She felt at peace with the world as she strolled along the road away from the village. She and Ian had been on very easy terms since leaving Cambay, and mutual laughter was commonplace. Though Ian still withdrew into himself for long spells, she no longer sensed that his remote manner concealed desperation.

The only difficulty was her increasing physical attraction to her husband. She had become accustomed to the slow burn of longing that occurred whenever Ian touched her—and as his state of mind improved, he was becoming steadily more affectionate. Sometimes at night she woke up feeling restive and too warm, her body intertwined with her husband's solid sleeping form.

The discomfort wasn't anything she couldn't tolerate—compared to the Indian hot season, it was a minor inconvenience—but she sometimes wondered what would happen if her longing continued to strengthen. Would she grow hotter and hotter until one day she incinerated, leaving only a small char of ash?

Smiling a little at her exaggeration, she rounded a bend

in the road and saw a sadhu sitting cross-legged with half a dozen villagers around him. Sadhus were holy men who had renounced all material possessions and traveled the land with only a few rags and a begging bowl to sustain them. This one appeared to be a Bengali from eastern India. Like most of his fellows, he was half-naked and sported a wild beard and a mane of grizzled hair.

Laura was about a hundred yards away and hadn't been noticed, so she decided to withdraw rather than intrude. But before she could, a woman carrying a baby flushed with fever stepped forward and laid the limp child on the ground in front of the sadhu. Laura frowned, for the infant appeared critically ill.

The holy man laid one hand on the infant's head and the other on its tiny chest, then closed his own eyes. Though he said nothing, the air around him seemed to shiver with unseen forces. As Laura watched, utterly engrossed, the child's unhealthily high color began to recede and it began moving its small hands and feet restlessly. After about five minutes, it gave a healthy wail of infant indignation. Weeping with gratitude, the mother dropped to her knees and thanked the sadhu profusely, then lifted the child in her arms again.

A little shaken, Laura reminded herself that children's fevers could break very quickly. Miracles might take place in other times and places, but they didn't occur in front of one's very own eyes, even in India.

Once more she was on the verge of retreat when the sadhu raised his head and looked straight at her. "Eh, Larissa Alexandrovna," he said in fluent English with only a slight singsong accent. "You don't believe the evidence of your own eyes?"

Laura's jaw dropped. The English was surprising enough, but there was no possible way that the sadhu could know her Russian name. On the other hand, he had just spoken it. Weakly she said, "I don't know what to believe."

He beckoned for her to come closer. She did, though part of her wanted to run away and pretend that this impossible, unsettling incident had never happened. The villagers drew back as she approached. Uncertain what to say, she pressed her hands together and bowed her head over them. "Namaste, holy one. You speak English very well."

"I worked for the Sirkar as a clerk in Calcutta for many

years. Then, with my children settled and my wife dead, it became time for me to turn to higher thimgs.'' The holy man's black eyes were piercing, seeming to look into her very soul, but Laura felt no sense of menace.

"How did you know my name?"

"Knowledge is all around us." He made a deprecatory gesture. "Learning your name was a mere parlor trick. Such things are useful to get the attention of the unenlightened."

"Why would you want to get my attention?" she asked. "I'm just a foreign woman, and most assuredly unenlightened."

He smiled. "True, but you have an open mind and a caring heart. The proof of it is that you have not already flounced off in anger because of my nigger impertinence."

Laura winced, sure that the sadhu had heard the ugly phrase from a British mouth. "I was raised to respect all spiritual beliefs, even when I do not understand them."

He nodded. "Aye, your father of the heart was a fine man. Would that all British in India had his understanding." He smiled again, ironic amusement in his dark eyes. "I wish to offer you a bit of unsolicited advice. Seekers such as I should not do such things, but I, alas, am still far too human. I shall not free myself from the wheel in this lifetime."

More and more intrigued, she said, "What is your advice?"

"There is darkness in front of you. When it seems invincible, you can find light by accepting a truth demonstrated by the gods of India." Anticipating protest, he raised a hand. "It will not interfere with your Christian faith. You need only be open to views different from those you were raised with."

Laura thought about his words, then shook her head. "I'm afraid that I don't understand."

"You will in time, Larissa Alexandrovna." Then, audience over, the sadhu turned back to the villagers.

"Thank you, Father," she said softly, as she would have to a priest of the Orthodox Church. Though she didn't understand his methods or message, his spiritual quality was evident. She dug into her purse and left a generous donation in the begging bowl.

Then Laura walked slowly to the dak bungalow. Yes, there

was magic in India, and a rather alarming commodity it
was.

Ian's impromptu stint as a judge took nearer three hours
than two and he was tired and hungry when he finally
made his way to the dak. As he entered, Laura walked
into his arms, freshly bathed, sweetly scented, and wearing a loose white gown. He gathered her close, luxuriating
in her soft, womanly feel.

"Was the case a complicated one?" she asked.

After nuzzling her silky hair, Ian said, "Not really.
Most disputes involve women, property, or land, and this
was no exception. There wasn't even much disagreement
about the facts."

Laura smiled. "Was most of the village sitting and watching the trial as if it were a stage show?"

"Exactly, and offering comments as well. It was probably
the most exciting thing to happen in Hirsar in months." Ian
linked his arm around Laura's waist and drew her down on
the shabby wicker sofa. "A man called Manoj claimed that
his wife Rithu had been abducted by a fellow called Kasturi.
Kasturi denied that there was an abduction and insisted that
Rithu was living with him of her own free will. Rithu agreed
and flatly refused to consider returning to Manoj, then listed
her reasons why not in embarrassing detail."

Laura chuckled. "Women must be independent in these
parts."

"Rithu certainly is," Ian said, amusement in his voice.
"Manoj was resigned to losing her, but since she had cost
him seventy-five rupees, he demanded that amount in compensation."

"That's a lot of money to a villager."

"She was a very handsome wench," Ian explained. "I
agreed that compensation was in order and there followed
much dickering over price. Everyone in the audience had an
opinion. Even though she must have known it was a nego-
tiating position, Rithu herself was quite insulted when Kasturi said she was worth only twenty-five rupees since she
was no longer new. Finally I decided that fifty rupees was
a fair price and ordered Kasturi to pay that. He didn't have
that much money, but friends contributed the rest and Manoj received his compensation.

"All well and good—until a haggard woman stood up and

asked what would become of her, Kasturi's wife? With tears running down her face, she explained that she was ill and without relatives in the village. Now that her husband had taken a younger wife, was she to be put out to starve and die?''

Laura frowned. ''The judge's task became more difficult.''

''Actually, the situation solved itself in the most unexpected way.'' Ian ran his hand down Laura's arm, momentarily distracted by the feel of firm, smooth flesh beneath the light fabric. ''No one had mentioned that Kasturi had a wife already, and I was wondering what the devil to do when Rithu went up to the older woman and hugged her, saying that they would be as sisters. Rithu will care for Tetri and share Kasturi's gifts equally. But the strangest twist was still to come. Manoj stood and said that since Kasturi now had two women to care for, he would return the fifty rupees, for Kasturi would need the money.''

A catch in her voice, Laura said, ''What can one say about such generosity?''

''As a judge, I gave my heartiest approval. As a man, I decided that there is hope for the human race.'' Ian got to his feet. ''I'll wash up now. I assume that once again dinner will be an aged and leathery fowl rendered palatable by long stewing in a curried sauce?''

Smiling, she also rose. ''Yes. I'll be joining you, since I decided I'd rather eat with you than alone. Later I'll tell you about the sadhu I met.''

''A paragon among women,'' he murmured. Without thinking he ran an appreciative hand over Laura's round backside. His wife gave him a surprised glance when he touched her, but didn't protest. She really had the most delectable curves imaginable.

Whistling softly, he went off to the spartan washroom. The world was a fine place.

He began to rouse from sleep when Leela turned in his arms, her hand moving drowsily down his torso. He responded to her touch instantly, for it had been too long since they were together. But he took his time, knowing that traveling the road was as important as reaching the destination. Tenderly he ran his hand through her flowing black hair and inhaled the scent of jasmine. Leela was still half asleep, her

*bare knee tucked between his legs, her warm breath caress-
ing his shoulder. The night air was heavy with sensual
promise. As desire grew, he kissed her temple and moved
his hand to her breast.*

The breast beneath his hand was not that of petite Leela
but the lusher curve of a larger woman.

The realization jarred Ian into wakefulness with a shock
like ice water. There was an instant of violent disorientation
when he thought that he was in prison, dreaming of happier
times. But the hair that tickled his face was real, and when
he saw that it was lustrous bronze rather than shining black,
reality snapped into focus. He was in a village called Hirsar, and the woman in his arms was his wife, not his former
mistress.

Yet wakefulness included a stunning shock: his sexual
arousal was genuine. The blood burned in his veins in a
way he had almost forgotten, and had thought he would
never know again. Incredulous, he slid a hand down his
body and confirmed that he was not still dreaming. His
erection was real; he was a whole man again.

His first reaction was transcendant joy. Looking back, he
realized that there had been subtle signs of improvement for
some time. He had always enjoyed Laura's closeness, but
what had at first been simple physical pleasure had gradually developed sexual overtones. In fact, the spice of desire
was brightening the whole world. Today's evaluation of Rithu, the runaway wife, had included a distinct element of
masculine admiration.

Ian's first impulse was to bend over and kiss Laura with
deep, sexual possessiveness. He wanted to share his joy
with the woman who had had so much to do with his recovery, and express his gratitude with all the skill and passion
at his command. His head was inclining to her when he
stopped as abruptly as if he had run into a brick wall.

Laura had married him precisely because he was incapable of physical intimacy. Time and again she had repeated
that the situation was exactly what she wanted, and she
would never have accepted him under any other conditions.
The restored potency that was a source of exulation for him
would mean fear and repugnance for her. A deep shudder
passed through him. His whole body throbbed with desire,

all of it focused on the lovely, warm woman by his side—but to act on that desire would betray his wife and destroy what few shreds of honor remained to him.

Had passion always been so insistent, so irrational, so dangerously hard to control? Knowing that he must get away from Laura before he did something unforgivable, he rolled away and slid from the cot. The plank floor rough beneath his feet, he stumbled to the window, then stared into the night. Wearily he rubbed at his aching temples, his brief exhilaration turning bitter as bile when he tried to assess the implications of what had happened. On some deep, half-unconscious level, he had vaguely thought of his impotence as both punishment and symbol for the appalling cowardice he had shown in Bokhara. He had even grimly accepted that there was a certain fitness to the idea.

Now it appeared that his punishment was going to be far subtler and crueler. Laura had given her warmth and acceptance unstintingly when he had needed it. She trusted him, or she would not have become as relaxed with him as she was now.

He turned and bleakly regarded his wife. To betray the covenant they had made would be despicable, yet there was no way in heaven or hell that he could spend the rest of his life sharing a bed with her chastely. If he tried, sooner or later—and, depressingly, he knew that it would be sooner—passion would overcome honor and shatter the foundations of the marriage they had made.

For a moment he considered the possibility of seeking physical release elsewhere, then dismissed it. Such a solution might be less immoral than violating his wife's trust, but his Calvinist conscience rebelled at the thought of lying with another woman, and not only because he would be futilely pretending that the woman was Laura.

Nonconsummation was grounds for annulment, and perhaps ending the marriage would be the wisest course. But an annulment would be as much a betrayal of their agreement as physical intimacy. He had pledged to support and cherish his wife, and doing so was a pleasure as well as a duty.

Laura lay curled on her side, one hand tucked under her husband's pillow. In the dim lamplight, she was all soft curves and mysterious shadows. His heart twisted as he studied her. He could never let her go, even if annulment was legally possible.

Silently he crossed the room and stood over her, thinking how lovely she was. While sharing a bed had given him a general idea of what lay beneath her modest white gown, he would much prefer to slide the garment off and see for himself. Then he would press his lips . . .

When he realized that his hand was reaching out to her, he spun away from the bed before he lost what sense he had left. After a spell of restless pacing, he concluded that his best hope was that, in time, he could help Laura overcome her aversion to the idea of marital relations. Though she might fear sex, she was not a cold woman; already she was far more at ease with him that she had been at first. In time, she might be willing to allow intimacy, if only for the hope of children. If that happened, he was confident that she would find lovemaking rewarding for its own sake. Perhaps a little gentle caressing when appropriate might interest her in further explorations.

With grim humor, he realized that he was contemplating the seduction of his own wife. And that was something he dared not attempt, because once he began, he might not be able to stop. For the time being, he must keep his distance from Laura, for coercing her either physically or emotionally would be despicable. Though he wanted her desperately, mere submission would not be enough. She must give herself freely.

His gaze was irresistibly drawn back to his wife's peaceful face. He felt closer to her than he ever had to anyone, except perhaps his sister and Pyotr Andreyovich, in different ways. Yet he could not tell Laura of his miraculous recovery, because doing so would damage their developing relationship. She would become wary of him. And justly so.

He couldn't possibly share a bed with her any longer. He would have to concoct some plausible reason for sleeping separately.

The prospect did not enthrall him.

Wearily he perched on the windowsill and looked out into the softly rustling trees. How many other dark nights of the soul had he endured since returning to India? It seemed like dozens. The Black Well had been appalling, but there had been a certain bleak simplicity to life there. Now he must deal with the dreadful irony of the fact that he was finally capable of making love to his wife, but honor prevented him as thoroughly as disability had earlier.

Among all of his uncertainties, one thing was absolutely clear. He must find a solution to his dilemma within the bounds of the marriage they had made between themselves.

Chapter 18

❦ ❦ ❦

RUEFULLY LAURA DECIDED that it had been bad luck to congratulate herself on how well things were going, for the very morning that they left Hirsar, Ian had withdrawn into another dark silence. Though polite, he spoke scarcely a word all day to either of his companions. Laura regretted his remoteness, but philosophically accepted that life consisted of downs as well as ups. Soon his mood would lighten again.

Philosophy vanished that night when Ian's state of mind turned out to have deplorable repercussions. They had been invited to stay in the home of a prosperous landowner and the room assigned to Laura and Ian was the most comfortable they had seen since leaving Cambay. She changed into her nightgown and slid under the covers, feeling an unseemly amount of eagerness as she waited for Ian. She loved the quiet intimacy of the night. To sleep with another person required trust, and the hours they spent in each other's arms were weaving a bond between them.

But instead of joining her, Ian said, "I've been having trouble sleeping again, Laura. I'll make up a bed on the floor." He took a pillow and blanket and arranged them a few feet from the bed, then lay down.

"I'll be with you in a minute." Laura sat up and pushed the covers away. The prospect of lying on the floor was no hardship, for other nights she'd rested very well on the cold earth. What mattered was having her husband next to her.

Ian looked up, and something taut and unreadable flickered in his eye before his face shuttered. "You stay where it's comfortable. I think I'll sleep better alone," he said expressionlessly. "Good night." Then he wrapped himself in the blanket and rolled on his side so that he faced away from her.

At first she just stared at his uncommunicative back, feeling a ridiculous desire to whimper. Maybe *he* would sleep better alone, but she certainly wouldn't.

Quietly she lay back on the bed, telling herself that she mustn't take Ian's defection personally. He had improved so much in the last few weeks that it was easy to forget that it hadn't been that long since he had been enduring unimaginable horrors. The road to full recovery was bound to be a lengthy one.

In fact, when she thought about it, sleeping alone was more sensible than bumping elbows, and other things, in a crowded bed. Laura was a sound sleeper, but Ian wasn't. He probably found it disruptive to have her wrapped around him all night.

It was all perfectly logical. That being the case, why did she feel so much like hurling her pillow across the room?

The old merchant Mohan was dying. As the end drew near, his ailing body was taken outside so that his spirit could wing freely away to heavenly spheres when the time came. He was a wealthy man and his household was large, so as morning dawned, many women were keening their grief at his approaching death.

Yet the woman who had most reason to mourn was silent, for fear was greater than grief. Meera was Mohan's second wife, an expensive indulgence that the merchant had acquired to amuse his later years. She was of mixed caste and would never have been acceptable as Mohan's first wife, but she was beautiful, which was all that was required of a concubine. For three years she had been a pampered bride. Now, at the tender age of seventeen, she must pay a dreadful price for the benefits she had received.

Mohan gave a last, rattling sigh and then breathed no more. The chorus of female voices rose to a chilling, ear-shattering crescendo that announced the death of the master of the house. Meera began to weep for the loss of Mohan and his kindness, but even more she wept for herself, for within a few hours it was likely that she, too, would be dead.

Though the odds were against her, Meera had been a stubborn child, the despair of her mother, and she fought for her life against those who wanted her to die. No sooner had the death wail subsided than Pushpa, wife of Mohan's eldest son, said with false solicitude, "Come, Meera, you must prepare for *suttee*."

Voice wavering but determined, Meera replied, "I will not go to the pyre with my husband."

There was a horrified intake of breath from those close enough to hear. Pushpa said sharply, "You must! Your death will bring honor to the family. Your sacrifice will spare Mohan from any burdens on his soul."

"My husband was a good man and his soul does not need my sacrifice," Meera said rebelliously. "At this very moment, I'm sure he is in heaven with Ruppa, the mother of his sons."

Voice hardening, Pushpa said, "Do you wish to spend the rest of your life living behind a curtain with a shaved head and eating only a handful of rice a day?"

"Yes," Meera cried, "for at least I will still be living!"

Voices muttered disapproval. Someone said that she valued life too much, while Pushpa's husband, Dhamo, growled that he'd not support a useless woman for the rest of her life. "A husband is as a god to his wife," the Brahmin priest said persuasively. "It is right that you join your soul to Mohan's so that the two of you can spend eons together in your own paradise."

Stubbornly Meera said, "A widow must become suttee voluntarily, or it means nothing. I do not consent, nor would Mohan have expected me to." Her words were defiant, but as she looked at the angry eyes that surrounded her, she feared that her strength would not be enough to preserve her life.

Throughout the day, the men made preparations for the cremation ceremony while the women of the household did everything they could to coerce Meera into consenting to become suttee. To Meera they seemed like crows, anxious to feast on her corpse. Yet in spite of her exhaustion, she steadfastly refused to give in until midafternoon, when finally she faltered.

In a voice like poisoned honey, Pushpa said, "As Mohan's wife you have been treated like a high-caste woman, but if you refuse your sacred duty you will become an object of loathing. The very pariahs will avoid your shadow. You will choose such vile disgrace merely for the sake of a few miserable years of existence, when to become suttee will guarantee you bliss?''

Meera knew that the bleak prospect described by her stepdaughter-in-law was horribly likely. Dizzy with exhaustion and confusion, she raised a hand to her head, trying to clear the cobwebs that clouded her thinking. ''Perhaps,'' she said hoarsely, ''perhaps I should . . .'' Then she thought of the flames. Terror gripped her, but it was already too late. Her gesture and stumbling words had been taken as the consent needed.

It was now the obligation of all good Hindus to ensure that she died at her husband's side.

Eyes covetous, Pushpa brought Meera's jewel box and set it down by the new widow. ''Tell us how you want to bequeath your jewelry. I shall see that your will is done.''

Meera lifted her numb gaze to her stepson's wife and saw that Pushpa was already wearing a pair of Meera's best earrings. A spark of angry defiance broke through Meera's resignation. She opened the box and began to remove the glittering contents. ''I shall wear it all to the pyre.''

A horrified murmur rose from the surrounding women. ''But you can't!'' one exclaimed while another mourned, ''Such a waste.''

Meera looked around and saw no sympathetic faces. ''None of you were my friend in life.'' She clipped an exquisite *meenakari* necklace around her throat, then slid on heavy silver cuff bracelets. As she reached for a lotus blossom chain, she said flatly, ''If you want my gold and silver, you can dig through my charred bones for the melted fragments.''

Fury rippled through the room. Pushpa raised a hand as if tempted to rip the valuables away, but Meera snapped, ''Touch anything I wear and I'll curse you with my dying breath.'' No one else dared dispute her decision.

Passive as a doll, Meera allowed herself to be dressed in her best scarlet silk sari, the one she had been married in. All too soon, it was time to join the procession to the riverbank where the burning would take place. As she left her home forever, Meera dipped her hand in red paint and left a print on the lintel beside the faded marks of other hands. Dully she wondered if those long-forgotten women had become suttee willingly, or whether, like her, they had been forced.

As the sun dropped toward the horizon, Meera walked in the middle of the procession, surrounded so that she would be unable to flee if she chose to disgrace herself and the family. She would have run away if there had been any hope of escape, but there was no such hope. With her own eyes she had once seen a woman try to escape the pyre, only to be shoved back into the flames by her own son. No, there was no escape, and Meera was resigned to the fact that she must die. Who was she, a mere mixed-caste female, to rail against the unfairness of fate?

The pyre was made of stacked sandalwood that had been packed with oily, ghee-soaked cotton. It would burn quickly, though not fast enough to kill Meera without agony. Numbly she endured the ceremonies, knowing that she should be praying or even desperately savoring these last moments of life. But all she could think of was the fire. If a man's wife must die at his side, why did it have to be so painfully?

Then Dhamo was roughly pushing at her. Remembering that she must circle the pyre three times, Meera dutifully performed her part, though her feet dragged. The moment came for her to ascend the ladder to the top of the pyre. When she faltered, a hard hand shoved her upward. Curiously, Mohan's flower-decked corpse seemed welcoming as none of his family had. Perhaps it was right that she send her soul to join his.

Trembling so hard that her jewelry jangled discordantly, Meera lay back on the piled wood and waited bleakly for the fire.

Laura would be glad to reach Manpur, the capital of Dharjistan, because traveling with a mute man was getting a little tedious. More than tedious; for the last several days, she'd had the uneasy feeling that something was wrong. Ian's gaze was brooding, almost angry, and he avoided even the most casual contact. Yet his courtesy was unflagging, and there was a kind of tenderness in his behavior, as if he were subtly apologizing for his difficult mood.

Since it was getting late, Laura brought her horse alongside Ian's. "Will we stay in another dak bungalow tonight?"

He shook his head. "No, we're almost out of British-controlled territory—there will be no more daks. Unless some dignitary in that town ahead insists that his life will be blighted if we don't honor him with our company, we'll camp out."

Chanting sounded in the distance. Ian listened a moment. "A funeral. Judging by the amount of noise the mourners are making, it's for an important man. There's a river to the right—they must be carrying the body to a burning *ghat* there."

Laura murmured, "Rest in peace."

While she wondered how to prolong this conversation, which was the longest that they'd had in days, Ian said, "Speaking of pyres, did you know that Pyotr Andreyovich burned Moscow down?"

"What?" Laura said incredulously.

"It's true. I'm sure you know the story of how Moscow was evacuated before Napoleon and his troops could occupy it?"

"Of course. Every Russian schoolchild knows that the residents and the army withdrew ahead of Bonaparte. On the very night the French occupied the city, a great fire struck. But I never heard that it had been set deliberately."

"I suspect that the governor of Moscow wasn't anxious to admit that he ordered the destruction of the greatest city in Russia," Ian said dryly. "Pyotr was one of a handful of young officers who hid and waited for the French to arrive. He said the deserted city was eerie, like a haunted dream. That night, after the French had taken possession, he and the others who had stayed set Moscow ablaze, running through the streets with torches. Since most of the buildings were wooden, virtually the whole city burned, except for the Kremlin."

"I had no idea," Laura said softly. "It must have been harrowing to be the instrument of destroying Moscow."

"Pyotr said that seeing the city go up in flames was like watching the funeral pyre of a nation. Yet afterward, Mother Russia arose from the ashes like a phoenix." Ian's glance was respectful. "You come of fierce people, Larishka. By having the courage to destroy everything that might aid the enemy, Russia brought down the greatest conqueror Europe had ever known. Britain was instrumental in administering the coup de grâce to Napoleon, but it was the Russian campaign and the Russian winter that really broke him."

"I'm a little envious that you knew Uncle Pyotr so much better than I," she said wistfully.

"Prison is a wonderful place to learn to know another person in depth," Ian said, voice dry again. "Amazing how much detail one can recall when there is nothing else to do."

He withdrew again, but the conversation had lifted Laura's mood. Yes, there would be better days ahead—and better nights.

After Meera took her place, Dhamo thrust his torch into the stacked wood. A wisp of smoke trickled lazily upward. Then the cotton ignited with a crackle of sparks and a surge of vicious heat. Her stepson began to circle the pyre, stabbing the torch in repeatedly. Clouds of smoke billowed into the air, incongruously scented with the spicy tang of burning sandalwood.

Meera's resignation lasted until the first yellow flame shot upward, fed by the oil-soaked cotton. The hem of her sari flared and pain blazed along her lower leg, shattering her numbness. She screamed and hurled herself frantically away from the flames. Unable to wait passively for an agonizing death, she scrambled down from the pyre, even though she expected that remorseless hands would seize her and hurl her back into the inferno.

But the billowing smoke provided unexpected cover. When her feet hit the ground, instinctively she darted toward the thinnest section of the surrounding crowd. As she blundered through the clouds of heavy, eye-stinging smoke, she crashed into a man who muttered a curse. A woman hissed at Meera for her rudeness, and a hand clutched at her wrist, but she broke away.

Miracle of miracles, she managed to get through the ring of watchers before anyone realized who she was. As she bolted into a grove of trees, furious shouts began rising behind her. The sound grew until it was like the howling of jackals. Meera threw one quick glance back and saw that the men were overcoming their incredulity and starting to follow. But she had played with her brothers as a girl and could run with unfeminine speed. Soon it would be dark. If she could hide until then, she might win free.

Even if she became a beggar and starved, it would be a better end than what she was fleeing. Driven by fear and desperate hope, she lifted the hem of her charred sari and raced away from the burning ghat.

* * *

Laura glanced toward the river, where a plume of smoke marked the site where the funeral they had heard earlier must be reaching its culmination. She heard shouting but thought nothing of it until Ian suddenly reined in his horse and threw up a warning hand. "Do you hear that?" he said sharply. "Something's wrong."

Laura also stopped. Zafir, who had been a little behind, moved briskly forward to join the others so that the party was in a compact group. As the shouting rapidly drew nearer, someone exploded from the bushes about fifty feet ahead. Laura had only time to register that it was a running woman in a red sari before half a dozen howling men appeared close behind her.

As the fugitive stumbled into the road, she raised her head and saw Ian. Hatless and a dozen feet ahead of Laura and Zafir, he was easily identifiable as a European. Instantly the woman veered toward him, "Please, sahib!" she cried frantically. "Do not let them burn me!"

As more people poured into the road, Ian spurred his horse forward past the woman. When he was between her and her pursuers, he shouted, "What's going on here?"

Laura caught her breath, startled and a little unnerved by her husband's transformation from casual traveler to soldier. With his height and air of command, he effortlessly dominated his surroundings. The men in the crowd skidded to a confused stop in the middle of the road.

Ian was not the only one to change, for as Zafir eased his rifle from its holster, the Pathan's usual laughing expression vanished, leaving the fierce gaze of a mountain warrior. Deciding that she should contribute something, Laura pulled her own rifle from its holster and laid it across her lap, trying to look dangerous. Though she didn't cock the hammer, her regular target practice had improved her skill to the point where she might actually be of use if worse came to worst.

Having regained his composure, the man who had been leading the pursuers said belligerently, "Continue on your way, Englishman. This is no concern of yours."

Ian looked over his shoulder at the fugitive, who stood between Laura and Zafir. "Why were they chasing you?"

The length of sari that was usually draped over a woman's head had fallen away, showing that the fugitive was very

young, hardly more than a girl. Voice shaking, she said,
"My husband's family is forcing me to become suttee
against my will, sahib."

Turning to the group, Ian said harshly, "Is that true?"

The leader spat. "Meera, the sacrilegious slut, consented
to suttee, then changed her mind. She has disgraced herself
and the family by her cowardly flight. Only by returning to
the pyre will honor be redeemed."

"Please, sahib, do not let them take me," Meera begged.
"If you protect me, I will be your willing slave."

As the front edge of the crowd began inching forward,
Ian set his horse into motion. It began prancing back and
forth across the road with short, mincing steps, a masterly
display of horsemanship that created an effective equine barrier between the girl and her pursuers. "You are breaking
the law," he said, his harsh voice carrying to everyone present. "The Sirkar forbade suttee a dozen years ago."

A Brahmin priest worked his way to the front of the group.
"Suttee is our ancient custom, Englishman," he said furiously. "Neither you nor your filthy Sirkar have the right to
forbid it."

"And it is ancient English custom to hang men who burn
women," Ian said with menacing cordiality. "By all means
let us act according to our national customs."

"You are no longer in British India, Englishman," the
leader snarled. "This is Rajputana—the Sirkar has no authority here. The woman consented to become suttee, and
now she must burn. If you don't give her back to us, we
will take her."

A voice from the back of the group shouted, "And if you
don't hand her over now, that isn't all we'll take, Englishman!"

Laura sucked her breath in, chilled. A potent combination of religious fervor and hatred of the British was rapidly
turning the crowd into a vicious, unpredictable mob. She
swallowed hard, determined not to give in to her fear. Softly
she said, "Zafir, take the girl up with you. We may need
to run for it."

Zafir lowered his rifle and snapped his fingers to get
Meera's attention. When she turned, he extended one hand.
The sight of his fiercely bearded visage made her hesitate
until he smiled. "Come, little dove. You are safe now."

Reassured, the girl grasped the Pathan's hand and he

swung her up behind him. With a metallic clatter of jeweled chains, she settled sideways and wrapped shaking arms around his waist.

Laura had been watching Meera, but she snapped her attention back to the crowd when someone roared, "English swine!"

The first shout triggered a roar of similar epithets. As fury rent the dusky sky, Laura saw a man at the right of the crowd scoop a jagged chunk of sandstone from the ground and wind up to throw at Ian. Terrified, because the attacker was on his blind side, she shouted, "Ian, look out—to your right!"

Ian spun and saw the missile launched at him. Cobra-swift, he whipped his revolver from the holster and fired without seeming to aim. The sandstone shattered and fragments showered on the crowd, provoking howls of dismay. He shifted his aim and shot again. The second bullet struck between the feet of the leader and sent up a whirlwind of dust and gravel. The man blanched and jumped backward, belligerence vanished.

As the crack of the reports echoed across the plain, Ian raised one hand and ripped off his eyepatch, exposing the blind eye. "If you do not value your lives, at least have a care for your souls." Slowly he scanned the group, glowering at each man in turn. When he was done, he continued in a voice that cut like a lash, "Anyone who tries to injure the widow Meera shall have an eternity of time in which to regret it."

A pall of horror settled over the group, and everyone gaped at Ian as if he were the devil incarnate. The silence was so profound that the jingling of a bridle rang like a church bell. At first Laura didn't understand. Then she remembered what Ian had told her soon after they met. To the superstitious, a blind eye was an evil eye, with the power to inflict curses. Already men at the back of the crowd were fading away, faces ashen.

Ian said quietly in English, "Time for us to be on our way. Laura, circle around the crowd to the left."

She nodded and set her horse to scrambling up the sloping embankment. Zafir, Meera, and the packhorse followed. Ian came last, holding his revolver ready as they rode around the group, then returned to the road a safe distance ahead.

When they were in the clear, Ian ordered, "We'll put a few more miles behind us before we camp for the night."

They set the horses into a fast canter. Zafir led the way, the Indian girl clinging like a limpet. Ian moved forward until he was riding even with Laura. "How are your nerves holding up?"

Laura was not surprised to see that he had already managed to replace his eyepatch and looked as calm as if he were riding across an English meadow. "Reaction has set in and I feel ready to fall to pieces, but basically I'm fine," she said in a voice that was less steady than she would have liked. "Do you think they'll try to follow?"

"Most unlikely. I've always suspected that much of the reason for suttee is to get rid of inconvenient women," he said cynically. "Now that the family has gotten rid of this one, there is no real reason to hunt her down, especially if they believe that they'll incur a curse in the process."

"That was very cleverly done," she said admiringly. "But weren't you at least a little anxious?"

He shrugged. "None of them had guns, so there was no danger."

They had had rocks and had been willing to use them, but Laura didn't bother to point that out. Obviously quelling a near-riot was all in a day's work for her husband. Lightly she said, "I was surprised that you didn't correct that fellow when he called you an Englishman."

Ian grinned. "Even a pigheaded Scot knows that sometimes one must avoid being distracted by side issues."

His auburn hair shone like dark fire in the setting sun, and altogether he was irresistibly attractive. If they had been standing rather than riding, Laura knew that she would walk up and kiss him whether he was willing or not.

Needing to change the direction of her thoughts, she said, "I'm ready to concede that you had a point about learning to be a decent shot."

"Of course I was right," he said, voice bland but expression mischievous. "Does this mean I can now expect perfect wifely obedience in all things?"

"No," she said cheerfully. "But I will work harder on my marksmanship."

His laughter was almost as good as a kiss. Almost.

Chapter 19

❁ ❁ ❁

AFTER THEIR ENCOUNTER with the mob, they followed the road to the northwest, not stopping until well after sunset. As Laura slid stiffly from her saddle, she noted that Ian had chosen a campsite that was protected on three sides.

Zafir helped the Indian girl from his mount, then set about collecting fuel and building a fire. With Ian tending the horses, Laura could deal with the young widow in relative privacy. After introducing herself and the men, Laura said, "Do you have any burns or other injuries, Meera?"

The girl examined the scorched silk of her sari, then said in an admirably even voice, "My leg is a little blistered, memsahib, but nothing more."

Laura went to her medical kit for a jar of salve. "This will help ease the pain." After handing over the salve, she began unpacking the food and utensils needed for dinner. "Though it's against the custom of your people to eat with those of other faiths, you are welcome to share what we have."

Meera raised her small chin. "Now I am out-caste, memsahib. I will eat whatever you grant me and be grateful for it."

When Laura set the griddle over the fire to heat for baking bread, Meera said, "Let me do that, memsahib. I told your husband I would be his slave, so it is right that I serve you."

Laura sat back on her heels and said doubtfully, "You should be resting after such a ghastly experience."

The girl gave a wry smile. "I am no frail lotus blossom, memsahib. Though my husband was wealthy and of high caste, my own birth was lower. I know how to cook and clean as well as any woman." As proof, she knelt and began mixing water with flour to make bread, her jewelry swaying incongruously in the firelight when she began expertly kneading the dough.

"It's good of you to help," Laura said, "but you won't want to be a servant forever. Can you return to your own family?"

Meera shook her head. "No. My eldest brother would be willing to accept me, I think, but Mohan's sons might make trouble for him if he did." She looked earnestly at Laura. "An English lady should not travel without a maid, memsahib. Allow me to serve you—I swear I will work very hard."

Laura bit her lip as she considered what to do with this resourceful young woman. "My husband and I will not be in India much longer. After a short visit to Dharjistan, we will go to Bombay. If you wish, you can work for me until we leave. With a reference, it won't be hard for you to find another position." She shook her head as she studied the slim, expensively dressed young woman. "But it will be a great comedown for you."

"Compared to death, memsahib," Meera observed, "being a lady's maid is not so bad."

Laura couldn't argue with that.

With Meera baking chapatis on the griddle and Laura cooking the pot of pilaf, dinner was ready by the time the men had finished their chores. After the meal, Laura persuaded the girl to tell them about her background, and how she had managed to escape from the pyre. When the young widow was finished, Laura added, "Meera will serve as my maid until we reach Bombay. Then she'll seek another position there."

Ian nodded approval. "Tomorrow we'll be passing through a town where we can pick up clothing and a pony for her to ride."

Meera ducked her head. In a choked voice, she said, "You are as generous as you are brave, sahib."

Ian looked mildly embarrassed. "I could hardly stand by and watch them drag you off to be burned alive."

Laura knew he was speaking the simple truth; she could not imagine Ian allowing such a crime to proceed. It must be tiring to always feel responsible for everyone. Laura herself had been another of his projects; perhaps he was wearying of the project and that was why he was pulling away.

As Ian banked the fire, he said, "Zafir, tomorrow evening we'll be near the compound of your Uncle Habibur. Do you think he'll be willing to put us up for the night?''

Zafir grinned. ''If you come so close without visiting and Habibur finds out, he will swear a blood feud against you.''

''It will be good to see the old reprobate again.'' Ian gave a reminiscent smile. ''When I visited on the way to Bokhara, it took me two days to recover from his hospitality.''

''Think of how much more exhausting it is to be his nephew,'' Zafir said with deep feeling.

As the men drifted into a discussion of the colorful Habibur, Meera shyly approached Laura. ''Memsahib, there is nothing that a humble creature such as I can do for your husband, so I must express my thanks to you.'' Deftly she removed from her neck a long chain made of filigreed gold wire in abstract floral patterns. ''Please take this as a mark of my gratitude.''

Laura's eyes widened as the beautifully wrought necklace shimmered in the firelight. ''This is too valuable, Meera. You must keep your jewelry for your future. You will need it for a dowry should you decide to marry again.''

''I have enough other jewelry to ensure my future.'' Meera's youthful face became sardonic. ''I do not know if I will ever take another husband, memsahib, but if I do, it will be a man of a lower caste that does not require suttee.'' She laid the glittering, sinuous chain in Laura's hand. ''As for the value of this—my life is worth a great deal, too.''

Seeing that it was a question of honor, Laura said gravely, ''Thank you. I shall cherish this necklace always.''

Pleased, Meera went to make up a bed on the far side of the fire while Laura did the same on her side. Ian's manner had been so relaxed that she hoped he might lay his blankets within touching distance of her. To her disappointment, he said, ''Though I doubt it's necessary, I think we should post a guard tonight. Zafir, I'll take the first watch.''

Exasperated, Laura burrowed into her blankets. The damned man had eluded her again. Just wait until they were sailing back to England, she said to herself, half joking and half serious. Even the best stateroom didn't have enough space for him to maintain much distance. Then he'd be at her mercy.

But until then, the nights would be long and lonesome.

* * *

As Ian expected, his watch was quiet, undisturbed by anything but the sounds of nocturnal wildlife and the ache of his own frustration. Time and again his gaze went to Laura's shadowed form. Each time it took a major act of will to prevent himself from crossing the campsite and taking her in his arms. His motive was not only passion, compelling though that was. He was equally hungry for the easy, affectionate companionship that had grown between them.

His body, which lacked subtlety, simply translated all the nuances of physical and emotional longing into rampaging lust.

After they escaped from the mob, he had wanted to sweep Laura from her horse and cradle her until she no longer felt ready to "fall to pieces," as she put it. Unfortunately, soothing her nerves would have the opposite effect on his. As he had recognized in Hirsar, he couldn't trust himself where she was concerned, and the situation was getting worse, not better.

It was easy to understand why men had been riveted by her at the ball in Cambay, for her unconscious sensuality was enough to drive men mad. Certainly Ian was becoming a little madder each day. If Laura were even a little flirtatious, she would be drawing men from five hundred miles around. He supposed he should be grateful that she was unaware of the effect she had; if she did, she would be even more dangerous than she was now.

Needing a distraction, he began to clean his revolver. He would never be able to endure the present situation for the six months it would take to return to Scotland. That meant he must try to renegotiate his marriage contract before then. But when? After a moment's thought, he decided on Bombay. The city was civilized and had a large British population, so Laura wouldn't be isolated as she was now. She could decide whether she was willing to have a true marriage based on how she felt, not because she thought she had no choice.

Again he studied Laura, who was a pleasantly curving mound in the firelight. Yes, Bombay would do very well—though perhaps it was more accurate to say that restraining himself until then might be possible. Scotland was out of the question. As he reassembled his revolver, he began mentally calculating how many weeks before they arrived in Bombay.

He refused to think about what the devil he would do if Laura was unwilling to change the terms of their marriage.

Meera curled up in her borrowed blankets, unable to believe her luck. She had been right to feel that it was not her karma to die so young. Perhaps that belief was why she had struggled so hard against death. The English sahib (Scottishness was a subtlety that Meera was never to grasp), had been splendid in his wrath when he drove back the mob that wanted to burn her, and the memsahib was a kind woman who would make a good mistress. Though the great bearded Pathan had alarmed her at first, his touch had been gentle. She had felt safe when he carried her away.

She had known more kindness today than in all her years in her husband's house, save for the affection of Mohan himself. It was strange, she thought drowsily. The night before she had been a respectable wife with a rich, though dying, husband. Now she was a serving maid with only the possessions she carried on her body. Yet she was happier and more hopeful than she had ever been in her life. She fell asleep on that thought.

Meera awoke to fire and sparks flaring up into the night. Terrified, she shot bolt upright and looked around wildly until she saw that the sparks were only the result of Zafir replenishing the campfire.

The Pathan's head turned when she moved. Softly, so he wouldn't waken the sleeping sahib and memsahib on the other side of the fire, he said, "The fire frightens you, little dove?"

She unclenched her fists. "I . . . I shall soon become accustomed again. I must, for one cannot live without fire." Then, curiously, she asked, "Why do you call me little dove?"

He smiled, his teeth white against his dark beard. "You are small and graceful like a dove, and you flew like one. But perhaps I should call you little falcon, for it took courage to escape the pyre. Never have I heard of a widow who did that."

Like most Pathans, Zafir was taller and more fair-skinned than the people of the plains, with aquiline features that made him look fierce even when he smiled. Meera was glad he had been on her side. "I wasn't brave," she said honestly, "I was terrified."

"Of course. You are only a woman," he said graciously. "But your fear became a source of strength rather than weakness. Go to sleep, little dove. None shall harm you now."

Before taking his advice, Meera said cautiously, "Does Falkirk Sahib really have the evil eye?"

"No." Zafir chuckled. "He doesn't need it. He has no fear, and he rides and shoots as well as a Pathan."

Daring to tease a little, she said, "I thought no one could match a Pathan warrior."

"The best of the British are very nearly our equals. That is why I am willing to serve the Sirkar. That, and because there is much to learn from them." With an abrupt change of subject, he asked, "Was your husband good to you?"

"Oh, yes. He gave me many jewels and treated me kindly. He said I was clever, so he had me taught Persian so I could read the great tales and poems to him," she said with pride.

"A woman of accomplishments," Zafir observed. "A great pity to waste such skills on a pyre."

"My feeling exactly," she said tartly.

The Pathan chuckled. Then he gestured toward the sky. "Look, little dove. A demon dies."

Meera looked up in time to see the flash of a shooting star. "A demon?"

"My people say that a shooting star shows that an angel has vanquished a demon in the endless struggle between good and evil," Zafir explained. "Perhaps that one marked your escape from evil today, for surely an angel aided you."

She cocked her head curiously. "I knew that Pathans were warriors, but not that they were poets."

"The two go together, for war is the greatest of poetry." His voice softened. "Sleep, little dove, and do not dream of fire."

Meera settled back in her blanket with a contented sigh. Tomorrow she would perform a devotion for Ganesha, to thank the blessed god for having interceded on her behalf.

The last thing she thought of before falling asleep again was the way the Pathan's gray eyes caught the firelight.

The household of Habibur the Pathan reminded Laura of nothing so much as a carnival. The enormous mud-brick compound consisted of rooms built around a central court-yard, and was home to several generations of related families. Laura didn't even try to puzzle out the interconnections of the residents. She couldn't speak to all of the women, for many spoke only Pashto, the Pathan language. But they were a friendly lot, and welcomed Laura and Meera into their midst. Laura's fair hair was a particular source of fascination. It was patted and stroked so often that within fifteen minutes all of the pins had fallen out and it was about her shoulders.

Laura didn't mind their curiosity. After several days of Ian's remoteness, it was pleasant to be among people who were enthusiastic. Nonetheless, the need for a familiar face kept her and Meera together at first. The young Hindu widow was now wearing a simple cotton sari; with her jewelry concealed, she looked the part of a humble servant. At first she was even shyer than Laura, but there were several other Hindu women present, and soon Meera was talking easily with them.

The whole inside of the compound, which included trees, a well, poultry, and three bullocks, was a purdah area where women could go unveiled because the only males allowed in were relatives. Outside the ten-foot high walls females were required to wear totally enveloping robes that made them look like swaddled ninepins, but at home they delighted in bright colors.

Though Ian was an honored guest, even he was not allowed in the compound. Instead, the men sat outside under the trees, smoking, talking, and feasting on roast goat. Inside the compound, the women enjoyed their own festivities.

Since Ian wasn't going to share Laura's bed even if they were together, she had no objection to spending the night in purdah. It was a surprise when Darra, Habibur's wife, gestured for her to follow, saying in broken Urdu, "Men sleep now. You go to husband in guest room."

As they went across the wide courtyard, Laura felt a spatter of unseasonable rain, which explained why the men's outside gathering was breaking up early. Just past the clay-built bread oven, Darra stopped in front of a wooden door that showed a crack of light at the bottom. "Husband." She gave Laura a broad, suggestive smile and patted her arm. "Fine tall ferengi," she added, using the general term for a European.

Laura made a deep curtsy to her hostess, then entered the

guest room. The windowless chamber contained no furniture except a table with a flickering oil lamp and two of the web-strung beds called *charpoys*. Ian sat on the edge of one of the beds, wearing the loose sashed robe he slept in. When Laura entered the room, he glanced up from the map he was studying and gave her a brief smile. "What was purdah like?"

"Jollier than I expected." Laura's gaze was caught by the curling hair visible at the V-shaped opening of Ian's robe. It was an effort to wrench her eyes away. As she walked over to her baggage, she heard the sound of a bar being laid across the door on the courtyard side. Glancing back, she said with surprise, "Are they locking us in for the night?"

"Only in one direction. There are two doors and the other leads outside, so we could leave that way if we wanted." Ian gestured at the opposite wall, where the second door was almost hidden in shadow. "Visitors enter directly from the tamarind grove so that they needn't cross the purdah area."

Laura gazed at the locked door to the courtyard. "Pathans really take this separation business seriously, don't they?"

"They do indeed," Ian said. "A woman who accidentally allows an unrelated man to see her unveiled face will probably be killed by her husband because of her 'infidelity.' After he has dispatched the offending man, of course. Though Habibur welcomed me like the prodigal son, if I sullied the honor of any woman of the house, he would shoot me himself."

Laura winced. "That's as bad as suttee. Here I was thinking that the Pathan system was reasonable by comparison."

"It is in many ways, but honor is everything to them." He smiled without humor. "The British aren't much different."

"Why is Habibur living here, so far from his tribal lands?"

"Traditionally Pathans live by extorting money from travelers in return for safe passage through the mountains. Habibur, however, has a more commercial turn of mind," Ian explained. "He started a horse fair in the nearest town. Now it's a major livestock trading center for northern India. After he became successful, he moved his whole household down here. Some non-Pathans have been added, but everything is still run pretty much along tribal lines.''

Ian glanced back at the map and Laura took the opportunity to study his face, thinking that this was the first time they had been alone in days. In spite of the subtle strain visible in his expression, he looked very well, all lean, pantherish muscle. He would never be fat, but he had put on enough weight so that he no longer seemed too thin. Her gaze drifted to a charpoy. It was wide enough for two people if they didn't mind being close, which she certainly wouldn't.

Before her brief hope had a chance to take root, Ian said, ''Do you have a preference for one of the beds?''

''Either will do.'' She suppressed her sigh. ''How much longer until we reach Manpur?''

''Barring the unforeseen, we'll be there in three days.'' He folded the map and returned it to his baggage, then straightened and surveyed the guest room without enthusiasm. ''I'm half-tempted to sleep outside even if it is wet.''

Even a philosophical disposition has its limits, and Laura couldn't keep hurt from her voice when she said, ''Is it that unpleasant to be around me?''

Ian swung around and he took a step toward her before halting. ''That isn't what I meant, Laura,'' he said tightly. ''In Bokhara I developed a deep antipathy to windowless rooms. Even with a lamp lit, I feel as if the walls are closing in on me.''

Chastened, Laura bit her lip. ''I see that I jumped to the wrong conclusion. But you've been so . . . so remote lately.''

''I'm sorry,'' he said uncomfortably. ''That's me being difficult, not a reflection on you.''

The atmosphere between them was charged with unsaid words, and Laura knew that changing the subject would be the wise thing to do. Instead, Larissa Alexandrovna reared her imperious head and persuaded Laura to do what she had been longing to do for days. She walked up to Ian, stood on tiptoe, slid one hand around his neck so he couldn't escape, and kissed him.

She intended to make it a brief goodnight kiss that would also wordlessly express how much she missed being with him, but as soon as their lips touched, intensity flared. Ian's arms encircled her and he drew her close, his mouth hard against hers. She sighed with pleasure and melted against him. And fatigue and loneliness evaporated like mist in the morning.

Chapter 20

❦ ❦ ❦

FOR A MOMENT, Ian's logic and control went out the door, propelled by a virgin's kiss. Laura was so warm, so soft, so willing. . . . But she was also an innocent who didn't understand the reaction she was provoking—a trusting young woman whose actions were based on the belief that he was incapable of doing what she feared.

Ian broke the kiss but couldn't bear to release her quite yet. He stroked her back with one hand and rested his cheek against her temple. When he could trust his voice, he said, "Too much traveling is a strain on the disposition. I know that sometimes I'm like a bear with a sore paw, but don't ever think it's your fault. I hope you can be tolerant of my shortcomings. I don't want you to regret having married me."

She chuckled a little, as he had hoped she would. "I don't regret it, though I won't be sorry when your paw heals. I won't be sorry to reach Bombay, either. Once we're on a ship, I won't have to unpack again for weeks."

He gave a wry laugh and released her. "I'll be glad to reach Bombay, too." There, God willing, he would be able to persuade her of the advantages of a real marriage. But in the meantime, he must—*must*—keep his distance.

He realized that this was the first time they had stayed in a place where Laura had no privacy to undress and don her nightgown. Knowing that doing the gentlemanly thing was also the best way to maintain his sanity, he said, "If you're ready to change and go to bed, I'll move this table and lamp to the corner so the light will disturb you less during the night."

Keeping the table level so the lamp wouldn't tip, he lifted it over his bed and placed it by the wall. Then he knelt by his baggage and began unpacking his soap and razor for use in the morning. Behind him, Laura took advantage of his turned back to remove her riding clothes.

Though Ian's hands were busy with shaving equipment, his imagination was running rampant about what his wife looked like without her layers of cotton and leather. Nonetheless, it was pure accident that when he lifted his shaving mirror to set it on the table, the mirror caught a reflection of Laura removing her divided riding skirt. With a wiggle she pushed it over her hips, then stepped out, neatly folded the garment, and laid it on top of her saddlebags.

Ian froze, eyes riveted on the mirror in his hand as she unbuttoned her white linen shirt. Luckily Laura was standing with her back to him so she didn't notice that he had been transformed into a statue. Though it was perfectly legal to watch his wife undress, he felt absurdly guilty. Not, however, guilty enough to stop.

He had wondered what she wore under her unorthodox riding costume. It proved to be a pair of lightweight, knee-length drawers and a sleeveless chemise that came to the top of her hips. Both garments were trimmed with dainty white embroidery. Before removing them, she bent over and rolled off her stockings, revealing her shapely ankles and calves. She was moving with brisk efficiency, and he had to suppress an outrageous urge to tell her to slow down so he would have more time to savor the sight of her graceful, scantily clad figure.

His mouth dried as she lithely swept the chemise up over her head, revealing creamy skin and the long, lovely arc of her spine. For an instant he caught a glimpse of a round breast as she folded the chemise, then laid it on her other garments. His fingers clenched the mirror so hard that the edges scored ridges on his fingers.

Finally she untied the ribbon that secured her drawers and slipped them off, revealing the beautiful curves of her hips. Round, womanly hips, perfectly designed by nature to incite male desire. Ian felt himself hardening and knew that he would pay for this with a night's torment. Yet even so, he could not make himself set the mirror on the table, or even move his hand a fraction to tilt the glass to a different, safer angle.

When she stepped to one side to pick up her nightgown, he tracked her with the mirror, shifting it to keep her in his sight until she dropped the gown over her head. For a moment he stayed absolutely still, fighting the impulse to cross the room and remove the damned gown. The impulse vanished when Laura finished fastening the small buttons that closed the garment, then turned back to the center of the room. Hastily he set the mirror on the table, then bent over and blindly searched for his comb.

Innocent of the fact that Ian had been watching her as if she were the holy grail, Laura sat down on her charpoy and began brushing out her tawny hair. As she untangled a knot, she said, "Can Zafir be trusted around Meera?"

His thoughts entirely elsewhere, Ian said unintelligently, "What do you mean?"

"Meera's a widow and not of his race and religion," Laura said patiently. "Under the circumstances, he might consider her fair game for seduction. I've noticed how he looks at her. It isn't hard to tell what's on his mind."

Ian had to smile. "Male minds are often easy to read when there's an attractive female in the vicinity. I gather that you're appointing yourself Meera's chaperone?"

"I'm less interested in morality than in the fact that she is very vulnerable now," Laura said tartly. "Meera has been separated from the only life she's ever known, and she faces an uncertain future. Though she's bearing up remarkably well, the last thing she needs is to have a man take advantage of her loneliness and confusion."

Ian sobered. "As I did with you after your father's death?"

Laura raised her head and regarded him with cool cat eyes. "The circumstances are nothing alike." Resuming her brushing, she said, "No doubt Zafir's honor is impeccable where his own womenfolk are concerned, but Meera is a different matter. I don't want to see her hurt again. In particular, a pregnancy would make her life much more difficult."

Ian gave serious thought to her concern. "I really can't predict what Zafir might do. You're right that in Pathan terms Meera is fair game, but I've never known Zafir to be callous or cruel to a woman." An alarming thought occurred to him. "I sincerely hope that you're not going to ask me to talk to him about reining in his manly lusts."

She smiled a little. "I can see where that wouldn't be appropriate, but I might have a word with Meera. Fortunately, the opportunities for seduction are limited the way we've been traveling.''

''Very true.'' Ian did his best to keep regret from his voice.

Laura gave him a slanting glance, then slid under her quilt. ''Good night.''

More slowly, Ian did the same. He had been wise to avoid being alone with Laura over the past week. A mere half hour in her company was almost enough to convince him that this was the perfect time to try to woo her into his bed. But that was desire speaking, not logic; his mind still said that it was too soon. When the time came to try to change her mind, he wanted to do it with champagne and roses in Bombay, not on a narrow cot in a mud-brick cubicle.

It wasn't easy to relax when his delicious wife was just a few feet away. If he had any sense at all, he would go outside and sleep in the tamarind grove in spite of the rain. Sense, however, was something he conspicuously lacked at the moment.

After the intoxication of Ian's embrace, Laura had not thought she would fall asleep, for her whole body pulsed with the longing to be closer to him. She wanted so much to sleep in his arms that she seriously considered joining him in his charpoy, but caution prevailed. Somehow she didn't think he would welcome an invasion of his bed as much as he had welcomed her kiss. Having him kick her out, even politely, would be unbearable.

But after a long day's travel, sleep would not be denied. Soon she drifted off, though her dreams were not peaceful ones. In her imagination she and Ian continued to kiss, and her clothing mysteriously dissolved under his caressing hands. Together, still kissing, they fell gracefully to the bed, like drifting leaves. His robe had also magically evaporated and his warm, hard flesh was pressed against her. Something was going to happen, was happening, only she didn't quite understand what. . . .

A shattering crash jolted Laura into wakefulness. The air was close and pitch black, and for a moment she had no idea where she was. Memory returned when she heard Ian mutter a string of muffled oaths. Hearing a note in his voice that frightened her, she scrambled out of bed and crossed the narrow space that separated them. ''Ian, what's wrong?''

Misjudging the distance in the darkness, she stumbled against his charpoy and half-fell onto it. As she sprawled across Ian, his arms came around her, hard. His body was rigid with tension, and she felt the pounding of his heart against her breasts. Laura shifted to a more comfortable position so that they lay face to face on their sides. After pulling the quilt up, she put her arms around him, holding him so that this breath warmed her throat and shoulder. "What's wrong?" she asked again.

"Nothing really. It's just . . . just the damned, suffocating darkness," he said in a frayed voice. "Sorry I disturbed you. That crash was the lamp breaking. I forgot to check the wick before going to bed, and it burned out. I woke up when the light went out. Then I knocked the lamp to the floor while trying to find the matches on the table. Stupid clumsiness on my part."

For someone who hated the dark, this windowless room must be a nightmare, for it was black and close as a cavern. With the night sky covered with rain clouds, there were not even cracks of dim light around the doors. "Easy to make a mistake in such darkness," she murmured. "Is there another lamp in the room?"

"There's one in my baggage. In a minute I'll get up and look for it." He made a palpable effort to regain control of himself. "It's ridiculous—in my head I know I have nothing to fear from what is only a lightless bedchamber, but my insides are churning like a desert sandstorm."

"Yet the storm has not overpowered your reason."

"Not quite." His embrace eased and he ran his hand down her back, as if reassuring himself of her presence. "It helps having you here. It helps a great deal."

"I'm glad." Hoping that talking might relieve his distress, she asked, "Was the Black Well entirely without light? I've wondered how Uncle Pyotr could see to write in his journal."

"The Well was a pit twenty feet deep, with no windows and a hatch over the top," Ian explained. "For the first year or so, the hatch was an iron grid that let in a little daylight from the room above, which had a small window. It wasn't much, but eyes become incredibly sensitive to any light that's available. It was enough for Pyotr Andreyovich to read and write in his Bible. Even more important, it kept us in harmony with the natural cycle of day and night."

He was still trembling, but less so than he had been at first. "You said that for the first year there was a grid," Laura said. "Did something happen later?"

"Not long after Pyotr's execution the hatch was changed to a solid slab of wood. After that, the only light I ever saw was when food was lowered down."

"I can't imagine what it is like to live in constant darkness," she said softly. "Tell me about it."

He gave a bitter laugh. "Why would you possibly want to know a thing like that?"

She brushed a light kiss on his cheek. "To understand you better, *doushenka*. To know why your paw is sore."

"You're a glutton for punishment, Larishka," he said wearily. "If you really want to know, living in endless night is a special kind of hell that completely severs all connection with reality. Without light, there is nothing."

"Like Genesis, where it says 'The earth was without form and void, and darkness was upon the face of the deep'?"

"Something like that. I now understand why God decided to create a world to fill all that empty space," Ian said with a shadow of humor. After a long pause, he went on, "Time was distorted until it vanished. It was impossible to know whether minutes, hours, or days had passed. The result was a form of madness, a disintegration of mind and spirit that words can't describe. Even filth, cold, and hunger hardly seemed to exist."

Again there was a long pause before he said painfully, "Sometimes I fell apart and cried for hours."

Laura knew intuitively that he could never have admitted such a thing in the light, but the darkness created a profound heart-to-heart intimacy that made his bleak honesty possible. "If Pyotr had still been with you," she asked, "would it have been easier to maintain your emotional balance?"

"Yes, I would have managed much better. God knows I was already in poor shape when Pyotr died. With him gone, the combination of isolation and darkness wreaked havoc. Later I was surprised to learn that I'd been alone only about six months. It seemed like much longer—years."

"Given the condition you were in, how did you endure an exhausting escape across the desert that would have been difficult for a man in perfect health?"

"I had no choice," he said simply. "It was a matter of

pull myself together or die. Worse, weakness would have endangered my companions by holding them back. As it was, Ross had to tie me to a horse for the first stretch. But the longer I was free, the stronger I became. At least, physically. Unfortunately, the mental damage is harder to repair. At times like this, it seems impossible.''

''Surely your strength and honesty and courage are more than just an illusion.''

''Those things *are* an illusion,'' Ian said harshly. ''I feel as if I'm hollow—an actor playing at being what others expect me to be. Pretending to be brave, pretending to be strong.''

His words were so at odds with how Laura saw him that at first she didn't know how to respond. At length she said hesitantly, ''I'm only a feeble female, so perhaps I can't understand, but what is the difference between *acting* as if one has courage and really having it? You seemed brave enough yesterday when you were facing that mob.''

''That sort of thing is easy. Real bravery is mastering the darkness within one's own soul.'' He gave a shuddering sigh. ''And that I cannot do.''

His stark words were wrenched from some bleak, solitary depth far beyond Laura's understanding. Sadly she accepted that she would never truly understand what Ian had endured. But she could reassure him that he was not alone now—that he need never be alone again as long as she lived. She turned her head and touched her lips to his.

He caught his breath and his body went taut. Then his hand slid around her, coming to rest, warm and wide, on the small of her back. As he pulled her pliant body against himself, her mouth opened under the pressure of his, and he teased her lips apart with his tongue. The resulting kiss was beyond anything Laura had imagined—sweet ravishment and wildfire, both end and beginning—and she welcomed it with surprised wonder.

As she responded, he made a rough sound deep in his throat and rolled her onto her back, surrounding her with his strength. Yielding utterly, she accepted all that he gave, then returned the gift to the best of her ability. Though dimly she recognized that such behavior might not be wise, she didn't care. Here in the intimacy of absolute darkness was freedom and safety. She could pretend that this madness was not quite real—that this was a moment out of time where they could do things that would be unthinkable in the light.

And darkness had an unexpected benefit, for all her senses were sharper. She was acutely aware of the rough sounds of his breathing, the faint brushing contacts of flesh and fabric as his warm hand caressed her arm. His scent was a dusky masculine essence uniquely his, laced with accents of night rain and wood smoke. It intoxicated her. And his taste, ah, his taste, sensual beyond belief. Darkness enhanced the kiss with dimensions she would never forget.

Best of all, without the distractions of sight, touch expanded into a mesmerizing universe of sensation. Body heat was tangible, a physical guide to location and closeness. As his lips moved to the sensitive flesh beneath her ear, she raised one hand and buried her fingers in the crisp waves of his hair. Did auburn feel different from blond or brown? She didn't know, did not ever want to touch another man's hair to find out. Her fingertips glided over his jaw and corded throat, the prickle of whiskers provocative, silently etching the difference between male and female.

His linen robe had a nubby grain. Sliding her hands beneath the fabric, she skimmed across the width of his formidable shoulders, feeling the contoured hollows and the straight, strong length of his collarbones with the heels of her hands.

Enchanted, she drew her open hands down the broad expanse of his chest. Springy hair, the flex of hard muscles beneath taut skin, all a thousand times more vivid to her palms and fingertips than they would have been to her eyes. She discovered a thin ridged scar, and traced it along his ribs toward his left hip, pushing his robe back so that she could follow the arc until it ended in a hard knot.

As she brought her hand back, she touched the small tight nub of his nipple, then rolled it experimentally between her fingertips. He shuddered, then exhaled, his breath shaking. "I'm sorry," he said hoarsely. "We—I shouldn't be doing this." The charpoy rocked as he pulled away, and the thick quilt fell back. "I'll look for the other lamp."

The air was as richly opaque as black velvet. Moving heat and the compression of air signaled the passage of his arm as he lifted it over her torso. Once he left the charpoy he wouldn't return and she couldn't bear the thought. She shifted with involuntary protest, accidentally bringing her breast into the path of his hand.

When his fingers grazed the swelling curve, he paused, arrested, unable to continue his retreat, his hand rigid except for a faint tremor. Before he could bring himself to withdraw, she caught his hand and pressed his palm against her breast. Warmth burned through the thin fabric of her nightgown.

He groaned, "Laura . . ." as his fingers tightened.

"Don't," she whispered, knowing that words would shatter the spell. "Don't talk. And don't stop."

And before logic or doubt could intervene, she closed his mouth with a kiss.

Chapter 21

❦ ❦ ❦

A BATTLE BETWEEN passion and restraint had been raging inside Ian, but Laura's command ended the conflict. With joy and humility, he realized that his perceptive bride must have deduced that he was now whole. Now she was willing—more than willing, eager—for them to become truly man and wife.

He was free to fully savor every wondrous aspect of Laura's sweet body and spirit. Even as a hot-blooded youth astonished by his first experience of passion, he had never been so completely bewitched. Her supple softness, her instant responses, her quick wondering breaths, were all miracles, for he had never expected to know them again. And like anything that one has thought lost forever, he valued passion all the more for having regained it.

But tonight was not only for his pleasure; he must also give his wife her first, vital lesson in the art of making love. Because his hunger was great, this first union would not be a prolonged one. And so he must take special care to help Laura discover her own capacity for passion.

With leisurely skill he trailed kisses across her flawless cheek from her lips to the tender hollow beneath her jaw. Her braid was coming undone, so he completed the process and loosened her hair into a spun-silk cloud. Then he buried his face in the gossamer strands, finding a faint, sweet floral fragrance.

With his tongue, he toyed with her ear, and was rewarded with a startled exhalation of breath that tickled him with warmth. His hand still rested on her breast, so he gently squeezed it while he nibbled his way down the vibrant arc of her throat. The tightening of her nipple against his palm proved so erotic that he replaced his hand with his mouth and teased the delicious hardness with his tongue.

She pulsated against him, her hands restlessly kneading his shoulders. Her gown was so sheer that he could feel the pebbly texture of her areola through the muslin, but that was not good enough. Remembering that the garment was secured by small buttons, he located the first and began unfastening, slipping the smooth spheres from their loops one by one.

After struggling with far too many buttons, he spread open the panels of her gown, releasing a luscious essence of sultry female and slumberous warmth. A man could drown in such delight, and go to his maker with a smile on his face. Perhaps later he would, but now he must do homage to her breasts, which fitted his palms as lushly as he had imagined they would. He cupped both and molded them together, kissing the scented cleft he created.

Even though he was experiencing her in a multitude of ways, he longed to see as well as touch the woman who had miraculously become his wife. But seeing must wait for another time. Though he chafed at the darkness, now it was his ally, allowing her to respond with a lack of inhibition that she would not otherwise have known.

As he suckled her breasts, she made a choked sound and her nails dug into his back. Suddenly feverish, he slid his hand downward from her waist, following the rounded contours of stomach and hips to the firm mound between her thighs. She gasped and rubbed against his palm. Impatient with the nightgown, he caught a handful of fabric and raised the skirt, baring her lower body to the cool night air. Then he untied the sash of his own robe and tugged the garment off.

He licked the warm ivory curve of her belly. It was firm and gently yielding under his tongue, subtly different from the blossom texture of her cheek, the taut smoothness of her throat, or the voluptuous depth of her lips. Slipping his hand between her knees, he began massaging the fragile skin of her inner thighs. Her legs opened as naturally as the petals of a flower greeting the sun, and urgent tremors pulsed through her as he caressed higher and higher.

After tracing the supple junction between abdomen and thigh, he trailed his fingertips through tangled downy hair until he could touch her intimately. She stiffened for a moment and made a raw, startled noise. But as he delicately probed into the warm, moist secret folds, her body eased again.

Ah, God, he had forgotten what joy there was in pleasuring a woman. Or perhaps he had not dared remember. With smoldering hunger, he bent forward to capture her mouth again. In the dark, he found first her cheekbone, then her welcoming lips. His fingers continued their ardent explorations, learning exactly what pressure and rhythm pleased her best, what hastened her breathing and the frantic cadence of her blood.

His deft touch was both wondrous and frightening, for it was dissolving Laura's sense of herself. She would whirl away, lost forever, if Ian were not anchoring her to the present with his taste, his strength, the pressure of his hard chest against her breasts. Her body began throbbing. She didn't understand what was happening to her, and was more than a little afraid, but she would not have stopped even if she could.

When the startling, urgent release swept through her, she twisted her mouth away from his, tasting the saltiness of his shoulder as she shuddered against his hand. In the aftermath she was so weak that she could do no more than press an exhausted kiss against his collarbone.

There was a long, still pause, and vaguely she registered the fact that he was as tense as she was limp. In one quick movement he raised himself and moved between her legs, his hand still on her, stroking, separating, triggering new shocks of sensation. His fingers glided through heated moistness until they penetrated a place for which she had no name.

She did not know, she truly did not understand, even when his searching fingers were replaced by a hotter, harder pressure. At first she thought only that he was caressing her in a different way. Then her mind snapped into wakefulness, stunned and disbelieving. No, it wasn't possible. He couldn't . . .

But he could, and he did. The slow, inexorable pressure abruptly ended in a quick rip of pain, and suddenly he was inside her. They were joined as intimately as the figures in the cave temple, and for a shocked instant she went rigid. Then he kissed her again, his open mouth familiar and silently soothing. Slowly she relaxed, first accepting the invasion, then finding surprising pleasure when he began to move deeper.

Curious, she raised her hips against him, intrigued by the way her slick heated flesh adjusted around his. He sucked his breath in and went still as a statue, so she pressed again, harder. He gasped, his control disintegrating, and his weight came down on her as his hips began moving convulsively, thrusting over and over in a rough, compelling tempo. His breathing lost all semblance of rhythm, and after a handful of moments she felt a potent throbbing deep inside her. At the point of deepest penetration all motion stopped. He groaned, a visceral, drawn-out sound that filled her with profound satisfaction.

His crushing weight lifted as he sagged to his side on the thin mattress. Then he pulled her close, kissed her on the forehead and cradled her against him, murmuring her name worshipfully, his palm cradling the nape of her neck.

At first, Laura lay content and almost mindless as his heartbeat slowed from tumult to normal, and then to the relaxed rhythm of sleep. They had consummated their marriage and were truly wed in the eyes of God and man. But how? She would swear that Ian had spoken the truth when he said he was incapable of marital relations. Certainly during the first weeks of their marriage there had been no sign that he had lied. Perhaps the lifting of his melancholy had restored him.

As she considered his situation, she felt rueful sympathy. Having married her on the premise that their marriage would be nonsexual, recovery must have put Ian in the devil of a quandry. In fact, that must be why he had stopped sharing her bed.

In the past Laura had always been able to sense desire from other men, so why had she completely missed the changes in Ian? She must have been blinded by her belief that he was incapable of intercourse. Looking back, she realized that she *had* felt differences in him, but had interpreted his feelings as anger or distress. Strangely, though other men's yearning had always made her uncomfortable, Ian's desire had not bothered her at all. Was that because she did not fear him? Yes, and also because she wanted him, as she had never allowed herself to want any other man.

The thought gave her a sudden chill as she abruptly realized the implications of the night's events. She, who had forsworn passion, had broken her vow. Dear God, the fact that she had completely forgotten what was at stake was conclusive proof of her weakness. What had seemed like wonder and discovery was in fact the prelude to disaster.

In spite of the warmth of Ian's embrace, she began shivering. Tonight she had succumbed to her own worst nature, and in doing so had opened Pandora's box. Her mind flooded with nightmare images, but this time she was wide awake, unprotected by the blurred unreality of dreaming. Her parents clawing at each other, passion making them savage as animals. The vicious threats, screamed in furious Russian. *"If you do, I'll kill you, or I'll kill myself."* Her own hysterical, dangerous reaction to the betrayal of the young man she had loved and trusted.

Though Laura tried to deny it, she was much—too much—like her parents. In Cambay she had felt the first ugly stirrings of jealousy, and she knew she was capable of much worse.

And Ian. At first she had thought him like Kenneth, always calm and rational. But with a deep stab of fear, she admitted that there was also much of her first father in Ian—the passion, the intensity, the lethal capacity for violence. Like Laura, Ian had also succumbed to jealousy at the ball, and his irrational anger had been even worse than hers. If they were lovers, how long would it be until they consumed each other?

How long would it be before she drove Ian to his death?

Desperately she fought to prevent madness from overwhelming her. Yet though she told herself that the future needn't be the same as the past, her frantic mind was no longer capable of logic. Reason was drowned by the tortured voices of her memory, a frenzied chorus that promised catastrophe.

As panic disintegrated her control, she slipped from his arms and stood, the rough planks cold beneath her bare feet. She had doomed herself; infinitely worse, she had also doomed Ian. What should she do? *Dear God, what could she do?*

Frantic for air, she fumbled her way to the outside wall, stubbing her toes on a saddlebag, then scraping her fingers over the coarse plaster until she found the door. Her shaking hands could barely work the latch, but finally she managed it. Outside, rain drummed steadily from the lightless heavens.

Yet the air was fresh and pure after the dark, suffocating room where she had betrayed her hard-won wisdom. She turned her face upward, and cool raindrops mingled with her hot tears. Would rain wash away her fatal weakness? Would fire purify her flaws?

"Die, damn you, die!" Harsh, uncontrollable sobs began racking her body. In her mind's eye, she saw the hideous brilliance of blood on the walls, but this time it wasn't her father's, it was Ian's. And it was her fault. May God have mercy on her soul, it was her fault.

Blindly, tears streaming down her face, she tugged the door shut behind her and fled into the sheltering night.

Ian had drifted into sleep in a state of awed happiness, sure that everything was miraculously working out in spite of his failures. But joy lasted for only a handful of sleeping moments. He awoke abruptly with a gut-wrenching sense of foreboding. The obvious cause was the outside door, which had swung open with a bang and was now admitting a blast of wet, frigid air. He was also alone in bed, but neither of those facts was the source of his anxiety.

Propelled by the instinct that had saved his life many times over, he swung from the bed. "Laura?"

There was no answer.

Aided by the dim light that came through the open door, he fumbled on the floor until he located the matches he had dropped earlier. He struck one and the flare of light confirmed what he already knew: Laura was nowhere in the small room.

Swearing under his breath, he found the spare lamp in his luggage and lit it. Alarmingly, Laura's clothing was still folded on top of her luggage. The only garment that seemed to be missing was the nightgown she had worn to bed. Even her boots were neatly set against the wall.

He pulled on trousers, shirt, and boots with violent haste and plunged into the stormy night while he was still tugging on his coat. Rivulets of water streamed across the muddy soil and the biting cold was a sharp reminder that winter was closing in.

Except for his last months in prison, Ian had always had a reliable mental clock. Now it told him that not much time had passed since he had fallen asleep. Laura couldn't have gone far. Ferociously clamping down on his fear, he quartered the tamarind grove as fast as he dared, thinking that if she wasn't there, he would make his way to the stables.

He found her at the far end of the grove, her white nightgown so soaked and muddy that she was almost invisible among the shadows. It was her faint, despairing whimper that first drew his attention. He found her huddled against a tree trunk, one bare, vulnerable foot protruding from below her sodden hem.

He stopped stock-still when he saw her, a wrenching pain constricting his heart. This was far worse than anything he had imagined. Merciful heaven, what had he done?

The answer was simple: he had broken his word. And, in the mindless urgency of passion, it appeared that he had also broken his marriage and his wife.

There was no time to think of that. He dropped to his knees beside his wife and said softly, "Laura—Laura, can you hear me?"

When she didn't respond, he brushed the heavy, soaked hair from her throat and searched for a pulse. For a moment he couldn't find it, and his heart spasmed with fear. Then he found the thready beat. Grimly he slipped his arms under his wife. As he straightened and lifted her from the ground, she came alive and began thrashing feebly. "Don't touch me," she gasped. *"Don't touch me!"*

"I must, unless you can walk, and it doesn't look like you can," he said, trying to sound calm. "I certainly can't leave you out here."

She quieted, but as he carried her across the soggy ground, silent sobs shook her slender frame. After entering the guest room, he kicked the door shut behind him and laid her on top of her charpoy. Then he searched her baggage until he found a dry shift. She cringed away when he stripped off her saturated, blood-marked nightgown, but didn't struggle against him.

Ian vigorously rubbed her with a coarse towel, his guilt burning through him like poisoned fire. When she was dry, he pulled the dry shift over her head, added a pair of his own woolen socks to warm her feet, and wrapped her in his own robe.

After tucking her under her quilt, he went to his baggage and retrieved the small flask of brandy that he carried. Laura pulled away again when he sat on the edge of the charpoy. His mouth tightened to a thin, hard line. He yearned to hold her, to shelter her from all harm with his own body, but it must have been his unruly body that had brought her to such dire straits.

He lifted her with an arm behind her back, then held the flask to her lips. "Drink some," he commanded. "Slowly."

She did, choking a little at first, but it helped revive her. When she had had enough and waved the flask away, he took a deep swig himself. As the brandy scorched its way down his throat, he numbly realized that, like Laura, he was cold to the bone, and the soul. He permitted himself another mouthful of spirits before asking quietly, "Can you tell me what's wrong?"

She lifted her head and gave him one quick, haunted glance from her slanted eyes. Then she dropped her gaze to her clenched hands and shook her head.

"If you can't say it, I suppose that I must," he said in a voice harsh with self-loathing. "I broke my word to you. In my selfish lust, I misunderstood what you meant and raped you. Violation both moral and physical."

Very gently he lowered her back against the stacked pillows. Then he turned, made a fist, and slammed his left hand into the wall as hard as he could. The brittle plaster crushed under his knuckles and pain exploded through his hand, yet, surprisingly, no bones broke. For a moment of mad lucidity he studied the blood that flowed across his hand.

He was drawing his fist back to smash it into the wall again when Laura cried, "Stop it, Ian!"

Earlier tonight it had been "Don't stop," and her words still rang in his mind. He halted, his breathing ragged, caught between past joy and present anguish.

He heard Laura scramble from the bed, then she caught his arm and turned him toward her. She looked like a lost child in the voluminous folds of his robe, but she faced him with determination. "What happened wasn't your fault, Ian, it was mine," she said intensely. "It's true that I didn't realize that you had recovered, so I didn't quite understand what was going to happen. But you did nothing that I didn't want you to do."

He stared down at her, trying to read the distraught amber

depths of her eyes. In a voice that wasn't quite a question, he said, "You did seem to enjoy what we were doing."

"I did, even though I knew it was a mistake." She closed her eyes, her face tight with misery. "In the darkness it was easy to pretend that I was dreaming—that I was safe because what we were doing wasn't real."

"But it was real," he said bleakly, "and it can't be undone." Then, because he had to know, he asked, "Was making love as hateful as you thought it would be?"

She shuddered, then said haltingly, "That wasn't the problem. You guessed that I feared the physical side of marriage, and I didn't say otherwise." She gave a bitter laugh. "What I really feared was not that I would hate it—but that I would like it too much."

He shook his head helplessly. "I don't understand."

She tried to speak again but failed. He drew her into his arms and folded her close against his chest. This time she didn't pull away. Her head fell wearily against his shoulder, damp wavy locks of hair spilling to his waist. She smelled of jasmine and pain.

"For me, passion brings madness," she said in the voice of a desolate child. "If I succumb, I risk bringing disaster on both of us."

He still didn't understand. "You really think that the joy of sexual fulfillment would cause worse problems than we have already?"

She began sobbing again. Every word sounding as if it were wrenched from the depths of her soul, she whispered, "Forgive me, Ian, but I dare not allow this to happen again."

Outside the rain continued to fall, splashing against the flat roof and wooden doors. The low bawl of a bullock sounded from the courtyard. How could the world sound so normal when Ian's life had shattered again? Aching with regret, he held his wife close, fearing that he would never be able to do so again. Even now, in the midst of emotional chaos, desire hovered in the shadows. Under less drastic circumstances, he would not be able to trust himself to touch her.

In spite of Laura's generous attempt to absolve him, guilt settled into a lethal, indissoluble lump in his midriff. She might not have understood what she was doing, but he had. Yet, caught in the iron grip of passion, he had made no attempt to talk to her, to be sure that she understood, even though he had known that she feared physical intimacy. In his male arrogance, he had believed that his irresistible charm had magically eliminated her deep-seated fears. Now he must live with the consequences of his mistake. His mouth twisted bitterly. Though he might deserve what he was getting, why did his punishment have to be at Laura's expense?

The basic facts could not be denied. Quite simply, he had broken his word and betrayed the woman he had pledged to protect. And what he had thought was a new beginning was in truth the end, for where in the name of heaven could they go from here?

Chapter 22

❦ ❦ ❦

LADY FALKIRK ACCEPTED her topi from Meera, then gazed at it blankly, as if unable to remember what to do with it. Then she donned the hat, gave her maid a vague, gentle smile, and crossed to her horse, where Zafir was waiting to help her mount. Meera frowned as she watched her mistress, then clucked her tongue and went to her own placid pony.

Zafir came to help her also, but instead of linking his hands together to make a step, as he had done with Lady Falkirk, he grasped Meera's waist and lifted her directly to the broad back of the pony. His gray eyes danced when Meera gave him a quelling look, but she smiled when he turned away to his own horse. Though he was an arrogant Pathan who was all too aware of his own handsomeness, she had to admit that she rather enjoyed his playful attentions. Not that she would ever ruin herself with such a man, but his teasing was pleasant after the unremitting hostility of Mohan's sons.

Meera's amusement faded as they began the day's journey. Lord Falkirk was riding beside his wife, but they didn't speak. They didn't even look at each other, yet emotions pulsed between them with such strength as to be almost visible. It was as if the lord and his lady were holding a gigantic, fragile glass ball between them, and both were terrified because the least slip would shatter it.

The sahib and memsahib had been like this for a day and a half, ever since the party had left Habibur's compound. Each was achingly polite and they watched each other with haunted eyes when it could be done discreetly. Meera sighed and shook her head in disapproval. It was not at all like the anger or sulking that would have resulted from a normal argument between spouses.

After they made camp that evening, she voiced her disquiet to Zafir. It was still light and the memsahib had decided to walk to the top of a nearby hill to investigate the ruins of an old fortress. Saying that it was not safe for her to go alone in this wild country, her husband had accompanied her since Zafir was not available as escort.

A few minutes after they disappeared from sight, the Pathan returned from watering the horses. Chores finished, he sat by the fire and lounged back against his saddle so he could watch Meera prepare the evening meal. Meera picked up an onion and began chopping it for the goat stew. With a gesture in the direction their employers had gone, she said, "Things are not going well with those two."

"Aye," Zafir agreed. "Women always bring a man trouble."

After dumping a handful of chopped onions into the stewpot, Meera scowled at her companion. "If women are such trouble, why do men always pursue them?"

He grinned. "A real man likes trouble, and a woman is the next best thing to a good battle."

She snorted to hide her smile. "Then may the gods preserve women from men. Certainly the memsahib should have kept away from Falkirk Sahib. Yesterday when she was brushing her hair I heard her say to herself that she should never have married."

For a moment the Pathan's usual cheerful manner slipped, revealing concern, but he quickly masked an emotion that could be considered weak. "Don't forget that the man you are insulting saved your valueless hide, woman."

"So he did." She began slicing a carrot. "I'm not denying that the sahib is brave, but he's making the memsahib miserable."

"She is equally making him miserable. I served Cameron Sahib for years, in battle and out, and never saw him eviltempered until he met his cat-eyed lady," Zafir commented. "Mind you, as a man I can see why he thinks her worth the trouble, but the English make things difficult for themselves. The women have too much freedom."

"Women need more freedom, not less," Meera retorted as she scooped up the sliced carrots and dropped them in the stew. "I suppose you think we should all be penned up like goats in a cage, the way Pathan women are."

"Our women have freedom and influence within the home, where it matters," Zafir said reasonably. "And outside, the veil protects them from the advances of strangers."

Meera knew that what she was doing was hazardous, like teasing a tiger, but she couldn't resist saying, "Women wouldn't need protection if men weren't such beasts."

"So we are," Zafir agreed. With one swift motion he sat up, caught Meera's left wrist, and pulled her across his lap.

She gasped as he kissed her. He was very strong, but it wasn't just his strength that kept her draped across him like a shawl. Though he was a barbarian, he knew a great deal about kissing. He was also in the full flower of manhood, not in the sunset of his years like Mohan had been.

Meera was unable to prevent herself from responding, but when he released her, for pride's sake she skittered out of his reach. "Fool!" She adjusted her disordered scarf over her head. "I should have put my chopping knife through you."

"But you didn't, little dove." He gave her a lazy smile. "And you wouldn't."

"Try that again and I'll add a few pieces of Pathan to the stew," Meera retorted. When a gleam showed in Zafir's eyes, as if he were considering testing her threat, she hastily retreated to the other side of the fire and dug into a pouch for seasonings. As she began grinding spices together, she vowed that the next time Zafir tried to kiss her, she would show him that she was not a weak slut who would roll onto her back for any arrogant rooster who showed interest in her.

Rather to her disappointment, he didn't try again.

They were about five miles from Manpur when a troop of cavalry came galloping down the road toward them, scattering pedestrians and bullock carts. Seeing Ian frown, Laura asked, "Is this trouble?"

"Shouldn't be," he said slowly. "I've never heard of Rajiv Singh bothering Europeans traveling through his state."

Nonetheless, Laura noticed that her husband had come sharply alert, ready for anything that might come. She herself was glad of a distraction, for the three days since they had left Habibur's compound had been sheer torture. Daytime was difficult, for her awareness of Ian was a constant ache, but night was worse now that experience had transformed her vague longings into painful desire. She remembered every kiss and caress Ian had given her, and she wanted more.

Which was precisely why she must keep her distance. The fierceness of her yearning confirmed her resolution that they must stay apart, for it was frighteningly clear how quickly passion could get out of hand. A single night had filled her with dangerous, unstable emotions and desires, and more such nights would make her even more dangerous. Only God knew where that would end.

Much as physical separation hurt Laura, she suspected that it hurt Ian even more. It was hard to be sure. He was better at concealing his emotions than she was, and he had retreated behind an impenetrable wall of detachment. Still, he couldn't hide the force of his desire, which emanated from him with the intensity of a bonfire. That was bad enough, but she had an unhappy suspicion that frustration was not his only problem. In spite of Laura's attempt to explain that the fault was hers, she guessed that Ian blamed himself alone for what had happened. It was bitterly unfair that he was tied to a woman incapable of being a wife to him. In the darkest hours of the night, when her guilt was as sharp a pain as her desire, she considered telling her husband that he should seek physical satisfaction elsewhere.

Yet the mere thought of Ian with another woman was enough to send Laura half out of her mind with jealousy. If Ian had even once turned his desire toward Meera, Laura would have become a hissing virago. Fortunately he did not. It was his wife he watched; again and again during the day she felt the pressure of his hooded gaze. Probably, she thought with depression, he was wondering what the devil he had done to merit the misfortune of marrying a crazy Russian.

No one had ever told Laura that marriage was like two people sharing a narrow single bed—one made of nettles. They couldn't spend the rest of their lives at such a pitch of tension. One way or another the situation must change, but she had no idea how. For her to leave Ian was unthinkable; the possibility that he might leave her was even worse.

Before her thoughts could go any further in such a profitless direction, the contingent of Dharjistani horsemen arrived, reining in their mounts with a flourish. The officer called out, "Do I have the honor of addressing Lord Falkirk?"

"You do, sir," Ian replied, showing no surprise at the question. News traveled quickly in this part of the world, and Ian's distinctive appearance made him easy to identify.

The officer salaamed gracefully. "I am Ahmed of the royal guard. Maharajah Rajiv Singh has heard of your coming and invites you to stay at his palace. You are going to Lahore?"

"No, our destination is Manpur," Ian said. "My wife has a small matter of business that pertains to the maharajah, if His Royal Highness will condescend to receive us."

The officer's surprised glance went briefly to Laura. "Rajiv Singh will surely rejoice at the opportunity to receive you both. Permit us to escort you the rest of the way."

The horsemen divided, half staying in front and the other falling in behind Zafir and Meera. As milling hooves raised a cloud of dust, Ian muttered something under his breath. Only Laura was close enough to hear, and she said quietly, "What was that?"

"Nothing," he replied. "Just an old eastern proverb. 'Beware of the man who has no ax to grind.' "

"What's that supposed to mean?"

He shrugged. "Nothing much. Just that it's a bit surprising that a maharajah would go to so much effort to welcome unknown private travelers of no particular importance."

"You're a lord. Perhaps he thinks you have influence with the Sirkar. Or maybe he's just bored and wants company."

Ian gave her a sardonic glance but didn't answer. They rode the last few miles in silence.

Laura's eyes widened when they passed through the massive gates into the palace of Rajiv Singh. Outside, the land was flat and dusty, but within the high walls was a lush green pleasure garden that stretched as far as she could see. Gaudily colored birds sang in the trees and a cluster of tiny, elegant deer drifted by less than fifty yards away.

The palace itself, when they finally reached it, was even more impressive. Laura had been in the homes of wealthy natives, but this was luxury on a scale she had never imagined. Like most grand Indian architecture, the building was in the Islamic style that was a legacy of the Mughal rulers

and was a symphony of white walls, slim towers, and graceful arches.

They were ceremoniously passed to a household official
who bid them to follow him. The walk was a lengthy one
that took them through a maze of courtyards, lofty chambers, and passages. The palace bustled with servants and
courtiers, none of whom showed more than mild curiosity
about the visitors.

As they walked, Laura wondered if once again she and
Ian would be forced to share close quarters, as at Habibur's.
She needn't have worried. They were given a whole suite
of rooms on the second floor. Because the apartment was
in a corner of the building, an abundance of windows gave
it an airy, spacious feel.

The official bowed himself out of the reception chamber,
which was the equivalent of an English drawing room. He
took Zafir and Meera with him so they could be shown to
their own quarters before returning to help their employers
unpack.

As Laura took off her topi, she surveyed the embroidered
hangings, cushioned couches, and exquisite Persian murals.
"Queen Victoria wouldn't feel slighted at laying her royal
head here."

"This is far more impressive than the royal palace at Ken-
sington." Ian indicated a Moorish arch. "Shall we explore?"

Laura walked past him and found herself on a balcony
that overlooked a quiet courtyard with a fountain in the middle and cooing doves in a tree. The scene was so charming
that she impulsively leaned over the railing and cooed back.
As soon as she heard herself, she stopped, embarrassed at
her silliness.

"Were you cooing in Urdu?" Ian said with interest.

"In Russian," she said, blushing. "I always liked talking
to the doves in the park when I was a child." At least her
husband's expression was amused rather than contemptuous. It was the most relaxed he had appeared in days.

Looking as dignified as possible for a woman who had
been caught talking to a dove, she left the balcony and went
to the first of the two arches in the end of the reception
room. She found an opulent bedroom, with a silk-covered
bed large enough for four people. Laura hastily averted her
eyes from the bed and went to the next arch, where she was

grateful to find an identical bedroom. Though the two chambers connected through a doorway, at least she and Ian could sleep separately.

As she tossed her topi on the bed in the second room, Ian called, "I've found something I think you'll like."

Laura went to investigate and sighed rapturously at the sight of the incredible bath chamber. A tub that was easily six feet square was sunken into a floor of glazed ogee tiles, and stacks of thick towels and vials of perfumed oils sat ready for use. "Oh, my," she said reverently as she looked up at the ceiling, where a translucent dome admitted gentle aqueous light. "Like a Turkish bagnio. This is positively sinful."

"Spoken like a good Scottish Presbyterian," Ian said. "Does that mean you won't bathe here for fear of imperiling your immortal soul?"

Laura grinned. "Not on your life. I'll meditate on my sins of sloth and gluttony while I'm immersed in steaming water."

As she glanced back at the tub, a little maid entered from a service door hidden behind a screen in the corner. The girl bowed. "Would the memsahib like to bathe?"

"Yes, please." Laura turned to leave so the maid could arrange the bath. She almost collided with Ian, who was closer than she had realized. He sucked in his breath and stepped back into the drawing room, his face rigid. He hadn't touched her in any way for three days, and now she knew why: proximity triggered a flash of sizzling heat between them.

She drifted back toward the balcony, not looking at Ian. To obliterate that moment of painful awareness, she asked, "What happens now that we're here?"

"We wait to be summoned by the maharajah. The chamberlain will pass on our request to see him." Ian surveyed their sumptuous surroundings without enthusiasm. "I hope Rajiv Singh will receive us before too many days have passed."

Though he didn't say so, Laura knew that he was thinking how stressful it would be for them to be together with nothing to occupy their time. As she went into her bedroom to prepare for her bath, she silently echoed Ian's hope that the maharajah would not delay long in summoning them.

* * *

Their hopes were fulfilled with startling speed. Laura had barely completed her bath when a chamberlain entered and announced that His Gracious Majesty Rajiv Singh, son of heaven and ruler of earth, was ready to receive his guests. There followed a frantic ten minutes while Meera helped Laura dress.

In honor of the occasion, Laura donned a conventional day dress, complete with corset. She hoped Rajiv Singh appreciated her efforts on his behalf. Then Meera hastily coiled Laura's hair into a tawny knot at the back of her head. A picture of respectable British womanhood, Laura joined her husband in the drawing room, where he was patiently giving the chamberlain his full name, titles, and honors, for use in announcing him to the maharajah. He had also changed his clothing and looked as distinguished as a man with a rakish eyepatch could.

As they left the apartment, Ian seemed his usual imperturbable self, but as Laura looked at him from the corner of her eye, she thought his expression was too controlled. Speaking under her breath in English, she said, ''Aren't you glad that we'll be getting this over so quickly? You look dubious.''

''I just have an overly suspicious mind,'' he murmured. ''Amir Nasrullah of Bokhara was very affable when I first called on him. In fact, his hospitality was splendid right up to the moment he had me tossed into the Black Well.''

Her brows knit in concern. As they went down the stairs, she said, ''Is your intuition saying that something is wrong, or is this just natural caution?''

''The latter,'' he said without hesitation. ''The situations are entirely different. Nasrullah was known to be mad and he hated all Europeans. In contrast, Rajiv Singh is one of the cleverest, sanest princes in India.''

They spoke no more until they reached the vast chamber where the maharajah held audience. Called a *durbar* room, it glittered with crystal, gilding, and shining marble. Dozens of chattering, lavishly dressed courtiers lounged around the edges. Laura had the dizzy impression that there were more jewels present in this one room than could be found in all of England.

Amidst so much dazzle, she almost missed seeing a raised step ahead of them, for the diffuse light in the durbar room cast few shadows. Immediately she realized that if it was hard for her to see, it was probably impossible for Ian. She took a firm hold of his arm, as if she were nervous and wanted his support. Ignoring the fact that he stiffened when she touched him, she said under her breath, ''A step upward, about two strides ahead.''

With her warning, he was able to avoid stumbling. ''Thanks,'' he murmured after they had both negotiated the step successfully.

Though there were no more steps, she kept hold of his arm until they reached the Persian carpet in front of the dais that held the throne. The chamberlain announced, ''Ian Cameron, Lord Falkirk of Falkirk, fourteenth Baron Falkirk and seventh Baron Montieth, late of the 46th Native Infantry, and Lady Falkirk.''

Ian bowed and Laura curtsied. Then she raised her head and looked at the maharajah. From across the room he had been just another glittering figure, but now her eyes widened. Though she had heard of Rajiv Singh's power and intelligence, no one had mentioned that he was handsome enough to earn any woman's admiration. Tall and fit, he was probably in his late thirties. Under a scarlet, bejeweled turban he had humorous dark eyes that studied his visitors with shrewd interest.

The maharajah said in flawless English, ''Welcome to Dharjistan, Lord and Lady Falkirk. I understand that you wish to speak with me?''

He was of the warrior caste of Rajputs and had the natural authority of a born leader of men. He also had the directness of a military man, and Ian responded with equal directness. ''Yes, Your Highness. My wife is the niece of Colonel Pyotr Andreyovich Kushutkin, who claimed acquaintance with you.''

The Rajput's face lit up as he transferred his gaze to Laura. ''Ah, you must be the one he called 'his little Lara'?''

''Yes, Your Highness, though I use the name Laura now.''

''How is my old friend Pyotr Andreyovich?''

''I regret to say that he is dead.''

Rajiv Singh sighed. ''A great pity, but not a surprise. It was a dangerous trade your uncle plied.'' He regarded her with interest. ''Pyotr Andreyovich said his young niece played chess very well. Are you as good as he was, Lady Falkirk?''

''Uncle Pyotr taught me,'' she said demurely.

A gleam showed in the maharajah's eyes. "That's a strong recommendation." His expression became thoughtful. "I had half forgotten, but your uncle left a small casket of personal effects here. Is that why you have come?"

"Yes, Your Highness," Laura replied. "Before his death, he wrote me a letter wherein he mentioned the casket, saying that he had left it with you."

"It will be delivered to your chambers as soon as it can be located." Rajiv Singh gave an engaging grin. "It's somewhere in the treasure room. Quite safe, but the place is cluttered, so some searching will be required."

His gaze returned to Ian. "You're a soldier, Lord Falkirk?"

"I resigned my commission when I inherited the title," Ian explained, "but before that I was in the army."

"Very good. You should be interested in a troop review that I will be holding in a few days." The Rajput smiled. "I'm rather proud of my army. I hired the best officers in Europe to train it, and I've provided the finest weapons. With the Punjab in turmoil and the frontier tribes always a threat, I must be prepared. If you have suggestions for improvements in drill or equipment, I shall be glad to entertain them."

"Your Highness is most gracious," Ian said. "Though I have no special expertise beyond that of other officers, I would be honored to watch the troop review."

His face as eager as a boy's, the maharajah leaned forward in his massive gilded throne. "Have you experience with artillery?" When Ian nodded, Rajiv Singh said, "I have been told that Russian cannon can fire twelve times a minute, but I have trouble believing that. Is such a rate possible?"

"Whoever said that exaggerated," Ian replied. "The best crews I've seen can only do about seven rounds a minute and for accuracy, four rounds a minute is better. Why waste one's fire?"

"Certainly the number of hits is more important than sheer speed," the Rajput said thoughtfully. "Do you think . . . ?"

Laura's attention wandered as the conversation became technical. Then a richly dressed lady-in-waiting came forward and beckoned her to come up on the side of the dais. "Please to come, Lady Falkirk," she said haltingly.

It seemed rather bold to move so close to the maharajah, so Laura glanced at Ian. He had seen the interchange and nodded that it was all right, so Laura followed the lady-in-waiting up the steps and across the level surface of the dais, less than a dozen feet from the throne. Absorbed in his conversation with Ian, Rajiv Singh ignored her, and none of the heavily armed guards paid any attention at all.

It appeared that her guide intended to walk straight into the wall. Then Laura realized that what she had thought was a mural was actually an embroidered fabric panel that covered an opening about six feet wide. It was a purdah curtain, designed to protect a highborn Hindu lady from the stares of the vulgar. The material was so sheer that light and dark could be distinguished on the other side.

Without hesitation, the lady-in-waiting parted the curtain and walked through, then turned and again gestured for Laura to follow. Alive with curiosity, Laura stepped through the curtains, and found herself in another world.

Chapter 23

❦ ❦ ❦

THE SMALL ROOM behind the purdah curtain was decorated with a richness that would have made Aladdin's cave seem plain, and the air was redolent of a complex, haunting perfume that implied both innocence and age-old wisdom. Yet it was the woman sitting calmly on the cushioned divan who made Laura catch her breath in wonder. She must be the maharani, and she was the quintessence of eastern loveliness, with dusky skin and huge, dark almond eyes that seemed to see and understand everything. The tiny, starlike gems that spangled her white silk bodice and sari made her look like an Oriental version of the queen of fairyland.

Laura dropped into her deepest curtsy. As she straightened, she searched her mind desperately for the correct etiquette for dealing with royalty. If she made a mistake, would she and Ian be tossed into the nearest dungeon and forgotten? Asiatic rulers could be an arbitrary lot. Deciding that basic courtesy was a good start, she joined her hands and bowed her head. "Namaste."

With a delighted smile, the woman in white returned the greeting, then said in painstaking English, "I am Maharani Kamala. I am wanting to welcome you to Manpur, Lady Falkirk."

"Thank you, Your Highness." Laura wondered if she should say more; it was royalty's right to lead the conversation.

Kamala tilted her head to one side, her torrent of ebony hair shimmering beneath her transparent veil. "You are most lovely, Lady Falkirk, but not in the usual way of Britishers. More, more . . ." With a twinkling of gold bangle bracelets, she waved her hand as she searched for a word.

Switching to Persian, Laura said, "In fact I am not British but of Russian blood, Your Highness, with some Tartar ancestry."

The maharani's face brightened. "Ah, you speak my language beautifully, Lady Falkirk," she said in Persian. "My husband wishes me to learn English and I have been studying it for some time, but I have much to learn." Gracefully she indicated a cushioned footstool. "Pray take a seat. Another day we might converse in English so that I can practice, but now it is a pleasure to speak freely. Though I have longed to make the acquaintance of a lady of your nation, few of your countrywomen come to Dharjistan, and I've never met one who spoke Persian well."

"It will be my pleasure to answer your questions, Your Highness." Laura soundlessly crossed the thick carpet, then seated herself. "But pray forgive me if I make an error in court etiquette, for I am unfamiliar with the ways of royalty."

The maharani gave a delightful laugh. "I shall take that into account, but you need not worry—I am not easily offended." She was even lovelier close up, with delicate features like a Michelangelo Madonna. "What brings you to Dharjistan?"

Remembering that the exchange in the durbar room had been in English, Laura said, "My uncle, a Russian colonel called Pyotr Andreyovich Kushutkin, left his personal effects in the keeping of your husband. Since he is dead, I am here in his place."

The maharani's expressive face clouded. "What a pity. The colonel was a delightful man. I enjoyed his visit enormously."

"You met him face to face?" Laura asked, surprised.

"Though I maintain purdah for public occasions, I usually go unveiled around the palace and in front of friends, as now." Kamala grinned with a mischievousness that made her look very young. "Of all the castes of India, we Rajputs are the most independent. Some say brazen. Did you know that Rajput princesses often choose their own husbands?"

"No, I didn't," Laura said, intrigued. "Did you choose Rajiv Singh?"

Kamala gave a reminiscent chuckle. "There was no real choice. My father, the Rajah of Stanpore, invited a dozen princes of suitable rank, but Rajiv Singh surpassed the others like the sun surpasses the stars. Perhaps you know that 'singh' means lion. Usually it is no more than a name, and a common one at that. But as soon as I saw my Rajiv, I knew he was a lion in truth, and that we were destined to be together.''

The expression of shining love on the other woman's face gave Laura a sharp, unworthy pang of envy, but she said only, "How old were you then, Your Highness?"

"Fifteen. Rather a great age to become a bride, but my father was reluctant to let me go." The maharani tilted her head again. "It shall become very tedious if you are always calling me 'Your Highness.' In private, you must call me Kamala."

"I am honored. In return, please call me Laura."

Sadness showed in the maharani's dark eyes. "I have not been blessed with children. Do you have any, Laura?"

Laura found herself blushing. "My husband and I have been married only a few weeks, Kamala. Even among my people, I was not a very young bride."

Making a quick recovery, Kamala said reassuringly, "It was worth waiting for your husband. A pity about his eye, but still a very striking man. Such an air about him! Like a soaring falcon, a prince of the air. Have you had your horoscopes cast?"

When Laura admitted that they hadn't, the maharani said, "If you give me the place and time of birth for you and your husband, I'll have a priest calculate your horoscopes—the karmic bonds, areas of compatibility, the areas of discord." She laughed again. "By this time you have doubtless discovered those yourself! Still, it is interesting to hear what horoscopes say." With a quick change of direction, she asked, "You must live in India to speak Persian so well. Where is your home?"

Since even such simple questions required complicated answers, there was no danger that the two women would run out of conversation. Kamala was a stimulating companion, and by the time she dismissed her visitor, they were well on their way to being friends. Yet as Laura was escorted through the palace labyrinth, the thought that occupied her mind most was a curiosity about horoscopes, and whether they could really tell her something useful about her marriage. She rather hoped so.

* * *

After being dismissed by the maharajah, Ian returned to the apartment and went onto the balcony for some fresh air. The sun was setting, and he found it relaxing to watch the shifting shadows in the courtyard while he pondered the day's events.

It was almost dark when Laura returned. Seeing Ian on the balcony, she came out and joined him, leaning crossed arms on the railing a careful distance away. "Did you and Rajiv Singh come to any conclusions about artillery?"

"Apart from the fact that it's better to hit your target than just make noise, not really," Ian replied. "But his knowledge of the subject is substantial. I'm looking forward to seeing the military review next week."

"The maharajah is an impressive man," she said. "Forceful and magnetic. One can see why he's such an effective ruler."

"I agree." Though the courtyard was deserted, Ian automatically dropped his voice. "Let's hope that he's as solid a supporter of the British as is generally supposed."

Voice equally low, Laura said, "Do you think he might be plotting against the Sirkar?"

"I hope not—as an opponent, he would be formidable." Ian frowned as he thought. "We both need to listen carefully to the people around us. I think I'll also ask Zafir to strike up the acquaintance of some Dharjistani soldiers. They might provide useful information—I never cease to be amazed at how much common soldiers know about what is going on among their superiors."

Laura nodded, then turned and leaned against the railing, her face sober. As she moved, the rippling folds of her gown released a faint, rich perfume that reminded Ian of marzipan and lilacs. It wasn't surprising that he often thought of his wife in edible images, since she was the most appetizing female he'd ever known. He glanced at her delicate profile and found himself wondering how many pins secured that great coil of tawny hair, and how it would look cascading around her. Realizing that his body was tightening, he deliberately returned his gaze to the fountain below. He was making admirable progress in self-control; he hadn't even come close to pouncing on her.

Though Laura seemed to have forgiven him for what had happened at Habibur's, Ian could not forgive himself. He had known it would take time to overcome her fear of physical intimacy, yet he had rashly allowed passion to cloud his judgment and had hurt her deeply.

Nonetheless, he found it impossible to believe that the damage could not be undone, for no woman who responded to lovemaking with such sweet ardor would want to forswear it forever. Though Laura's despair and confusion later that night had vividly demonstrated how deeply rooted her problem was, he was sure that time, patience, and understanding would overcome her terror. The key to a happy future was patience on his part.

He sighed. What a pity that patience had never been his strong point. "What is the maharani like? I assume that it was she who summoned you behind the purdah curtain."

"Kamala really is the most beautiful woman in India, and quite possibly the most charming. Though she must be about my age, she reminds me of my mother." Laura considered. "It must be her quality of wise, womanly warmth. My mother had that."

Ian turned and leaned against the railing. "Kamala and Rajiv Singh are one of the great Indian love stories. Among the common people, it's said that they're the reincarnations of Shah Jahan and Mumtaz Mahal." When Laura looked blank, he explained, "Shah Jahan was the ruler who built the Taj Mahal as a memorial to his beloved wife, Mumtaz Mahal."

Laura smiled. "And Kamala and her husband are their reincarnations? That's a romantic thought. Perhaps this time around they'll be luckier and have more years together."

Ian heard wistfulness in her voice. He understood, for he felt the same way. Being part of a legendary romance must be a good deal more enjoyable than inhabiting a marriage that was cursed by too much desire and too many intractable problems.

He heard the soft sound of footsteps in the reception room and looked indoors to see two servants entering with trays of food. Since high-caste Hindus wouldn't share a table with those not of their own rank, Ian and Laura would probably be eating all of their meals in their rooms.

After washing their hands, they took seats by the low, round table. As a servant placed a dish of curried lamb on the table, Laura said, "I'm surprised that meat is being served. I thought all upper-caste Hindus were vegetarian."

"Many are, but some, like the Rajputs, are meat-eaters.

Also, this is a vast and complex household, with people of many religions and ranks, and they must all be fed.'' Ian nodded toward the servant. ''This chap is a Muslim, so he won't be defiled by contact with our food unless pork were to be served, which I'm sure it won't be, any more than beef would be on the menu since it would offend all good Hindus. It's part of Rajiv Singh's skill that he can effectively lead men of all different backgrounds. His army has regiments of Hindus, Muslims, even Sikhs. They share quarters only with their own kind, yet all will fight and die for the maharajah.''

Laura swallowed a bite of rice pilaf. ''Isn't that what the British Indian Army does?''

''Exactly, which is one reason it's the most powerful army India has ever seen.'' Ian used a piece of nan bread to mop up his lamb sauce. ''As you know, the vast majority of the Company's soldiers are natives. What makes them superior to the armies of most Indian rulers is training, weapons, and leadership. Rajiv Singh is clever enough to take the best of modern European military theory and blend it with native warrior traditions.''

They had just finished eating when a royal chamberlain entered with two palace guards. The chamberlain set down the box he carried and bowed to Laura. ''With the compliments of Rajiv Singh, here is the property of your uncle, which is now yours.'' Then he and the guards withdrew.

Delighted, Laura examined Pyotr's legacy. The humpbacked, leather-bound chest was European, about two feet long and roughly eighteen inches deep and high. In spite of its battered appearance, the lock was still sound. She frowned as she examined it. ''Ian, do you have a key that might work on this? I'd rather not break the lock if possible.''

He set the chest on a table and studied the lock, then went to his room and located a piece of stiff wire in his collection of useful oddments. After a few minutes of carefully probing inside the keyhole, the lock sprang open.

''You have some interesting talents,'' Laura said, impressed.

''An officer and a gentleman should be prepared for anything,'' Ian said blandly.

Her brows arched. ''Surely you didn't learn how to do that as a cadet at Addiscombe.''

He grinned. "One boring winter on the frontier, when there was nothing better to do, a sergeant with a colorful past taught me how to pick locks. It was mostly a way to pass the time, but occasionally the knowledge has been useful."

Smiling appreciatively, Laura lifted the casket's lid. The box was full to the brim with papers and journals. "Uncle Pyotr did say that there was nothing here to tempt a prince," she said with a trace of disappointment. "But I guess I was hoping for something a bit more exotic than journals."

"Why not take the papers out?" Ian suggested. "There might be more interesting items farther down."

Laura began removing the papers and piling them on the table, careful to keep them in order. As she neared the bottom, she said, "You were right—here are several intriguing objects wrapped in cotton."

She removed the padding from the first item, revealing a fine gold pocketwatch. "I remember this!" she said with delight. She wound the stem, then opened the case. Several notes chimed a musical phrase. "The watch originally belonged to my grandfather Kushutkin. Family tradition said that it was made by a man who was watchmaker to the kings of France."

"Pyotr must have left it here so it wouldn't identify him as a European when he went to Central Asia."

Laura studied the inside of the case, where an inscription was carved in Cyrillic characters. "I remember my uncle dangling this in front of me, swinging it back and forth to catch the light while the notes played. I was very small and was probably being perfectly dreadful, and he thought this would distract me." She closed the case and weighed it in her hand, her expression nostalgic. Then she handed the watch to Ian. "Here—I think he would have liked for you to have it."

Startled, Ian said, "You're giving it to me?"

"In his prison journal, Uncle Pyotr once said that you were like the son he had never had, so the watch should be yours." She smiled mischievously. "And giving it to my husband means I can see it whenever I like."

"Thank you." Ian stroked the burnished gold. "I don't think I have to tell you what this means to me."

"No, you don't." Laura gave him a sweet, satisfied smile. It was one of the moments of perfect understanding that made Ian hunger for a physical closeness that was equally strong.

Sensing his yearning, she dropped her gaze and began unwrapping the other objects in the chest. There was an antique enameled snuffbox, probably of French origin; a Chinese jade carving of a graceful female figure; a flat silver case that still held several small, desiccated cigars; a pen-knife whose handle was inlaid with gold wire patterns. Perhaps oddest of all, there was a deformed lead rifle ball.

Laura looked down at the collection wistfully. "I don't recognize any of these things. I suppose I'll never know just where they came from, or what they meant to Uncle Pyotr."

Ian fingered the rifle ball. "There's a good chance that this was dug out of Pyotr Andreyovich at some point in his career. Men tend to have oddly sentimental feelings about the bullets that don't quite kill them. I have a couple like these in the trunks that are being shipped from Cambay to Scotland."

She made a face. "So this is one of those famous bullets that had a man's name on it?"

"The bullets I worried about were the ones that said 'to whom it may concern,' " Ian said dryly. "There are a lot more of them, and they'll kill you just as dead."

As Pyotr had said, there was nothing especially valuable in the assortment; at most, the market value would be a few hundred pounds. The colonel's papers, however, might be very interesting indeed. Ian eyed the stacks. "I wish I read Russian. Any information about Pyotr's 'fire across India,' is probably somewhere in there. How long do you think it will take you to skim through the lot?"

"I'm afraid it will take quite a while." Laura lifted a journal from the top of a pile and looked inside. "At least he had all the paper, ink, and light he needed so that the text is easier to read than his prison journal." Closing the volume, she said, "It has just occurred to me that he must have been in India at the same time I was, but he didn't come to see me."

"It's a long way from Dharjistan to Baipur," Ian said. "Even if he had the time, visiting you might have endangered him."

"I have trouble remembering that he was England's enemy even though he was my uncle. Papa and I would both have loved seeing him." She sighed. "Ah, well, no point in brooding about it."

As she moved a tilting stack of papers, the top section slid to one side, revealing a packet of letters tied with a faded ribbon. "Love letters do you think?" She picked the packet up, then said with surprise, "Good heavens, these are letters I wrote to him. To think that Uncle Pyotr kept them all these years." She thumbed through the stack. "Some are from my mother, too. Lord, reading these will turn me into a watering pot."

Remembering that Pyotr had emphasized that Laura should study his legacy carefully, Ian said, "There's a couple of inches of disparity between the inside and the outside of the casket, so there could be secret papers concealed beneath a false bottom. Mind if I investigate?"

Without looking up, Laura said absently, "Be my guest."

The interior had been rather clumsily lined with a patterned Indian fabric that was much newer than the chest itself. Ian opened the penknife and carefully cut around the inside bottom, then tried to loosen the base. After several minutes of cautious prying, the bottom panel suddenly popped up, revealing a cavity packed with raw cotton wool.

Ian felt a twinge of disappointment. Still, though there were no secret plans, other things might be hidden here. He probed the fluffy white material with his fingertips and immediately located two small objects swathed in blue silk. He opened the first one, then gave a stunned whistle.

In the center of his palm lay a ruby as large as a walnut and as crimson as heart's blood. Impatiently he unwrapped the second object. This time he found a diamond as large as the ruby, with icy brilliance coruscating in its depths. "Laura, my dear," he said when he had caught his breath, "Pyotr did include something more exotic than papers."

She glanced up, her mind still in the letters, then gave a startled gasp. "Merciful heaven, are these what I think?"

"If you're thinking gemstones, the answer is yes," Ian replied. "Shall we see what else is tucked in here?"

After ten minutes of scrabbling through the cotton wool, an emperor's ransom in jewels lay glittering on the table. All of the stones were large and unmounted, and at least to Ian's untrained eye, they looked flawless. "How do you suppose Pyotr got these?" Laura asked in a hushed voice.

"In the course of his duties in Central Asia, he would

have found occasional opportunities to make money," Ian said. "Once in Afghanistan I traded a pistol in return for a sizable ruby. The Afghan and I were both pleased with the bargain. I sold the stone and invested the proceeds, and over the years it's become a tidy little nest egg. Multiply that a few dozen times, and it's plausible that Pyotr could have built a sizable fortune, then converted it into jewels as the most portable form of wealth. Since India is the world's great treasure house of gems, he could buy them here for half what they'd sell for in Europe."

"I like that explanation," Laura decided. "Much nicer than thinking that my uncle robbed a temple."

Ian smiled a little and touched a huge sapphire with his forefinger. "He did say that if you came to Dharjistan, you'd find it worth the trouble."

Laura scooped a handful of jewels into her palm, watching the way the lamplight lit them into a gaudy rainbow of colors. "It's certainly an unexpected dowry."

"Instead of a dowry, it would also have made you a woman of independent means rather than a governess." Ian felt a deep pang when he looked at the jewels. He had been able to comfort himself with the thought that marriage had improved Laura's financial situation even though it had caused her distress in other ways. But now his support was a benefit she no longer needed; in fact, her fortune must be greater than his.

Laura glanced up at him, the depths of her Oriental eyes shimmering with sherry-colored light. "If it hadn't been for you, *doushenka,* I would never have known of this. The casket would have stayed in Rajiv Singh's treasure room indefinitely, and perhaps someday been discarded, jewels and all. Worse than that, with Pyotr's watch inside."

Her perception was so uncanny that he had a brief desire to duck for cover; one of these days, she might see all the way through to his greatest shame. Instead, he gave her a wry smile. "How do you manage to read my mind so well, Larishka?"

"It's a Russian talent," she said loftily. "Designed to strike terror into the hearts of more rational beings."

"Certainly you strike terror into my heart," he said, only half teasing. He picked up the largest topaz in the collection, an enormous square-cut gem that sparkled amber and gold, and held it below her throat. "Whatever you decide to do with the rest of the stones, this one must be made into a pendant for you. I'll pay for the setting and have earrings made to match.''

''I'd like that,'' Laura murmured, her gaze holding his. Eyes of gold and amber and sherry, deep enough to mesmerize a man. Lips full and soft and kissable—and wanting to be kissed.

Ian stared down at Laura, unable to look away. It had been premature to congratulate himself on his control. His wife was capable of riveting the attention of men from across a crowded room; this close, her intense sensuality was devastating.

Though her mind might think no, her body was shouting a resounding *yes*. If he kissed her, at first she would quiver, caught between yearning and dismay, but she would not withdraw. Instead her arms would creep slowly around his neck. Then passion would crackle out of control, hot, quick, and fierce as detonated gunpowder.

Simple and satisfying, right up to the point when lust was satisfied. Then she would despise both him and herself.

It would be simpler for Ian. He would despise only himself.

Why did doing the right think have to be so agonizingly difficult? It took all his discipline to step away and say evenly, ''Putting the jewels back where they came from is probably safest for now.'' Wrenching his gaze from his wife, he began burying the bright gems in cotton. A pity that passion could not be as easily obliterated.

Chapter 24

❦ ❦ ❦

THE VAST PLAIN outside Manpur churned with dust from the feet and hooves of the Dharjistani army, but those who watched the review from elephant back were above the worst of it. Ian's view of the exercises could not have been improved, since he shared the *howdah* of the Maharajah of Dharjistan.

Since arriving in Manpur, Ian had spent much of his time with Rajiv Singh, discussing every aspect of military science. In the process a genuine, if slightly wary, friendship had grown between the two men. Mutual respect and liking were tempered by a tacit acknowledgment that their values and loyalties might not always be the same. As a result, their conversations were laced with verbal fencing that was half humorous and half serious.

Out on the plain, the last of the infantry regiments finished their maneuvers and marched away, to be succeeded by a battalion of lancers. Riding at full gallop, the lancers wheeled to their right, their lines dressed in perfect order, a huge cloud of dust rising behind them. The Royal British Household Cavalry could not have done better. Ian said, "Magnificently trained, Your Highness."

"I thought you would be impressed." The maharajah glanced at him thoughtfully. "Do you think them the equal of your British native lancer companies?"

"They may well be," Ian replied. "Though I trust that question will never be put to the test."

"As I do," the maharajah said blandly. Nodding toward the plain, where camels were hauling light artillery pieces into position, he continued, "Drill is vital, for without discipline an army is just a rabble, easily broken by troops who can keep better order, who can stand fast without breaking under the worst assault. Your British Army has proved that again and again. Yet even so, the true test of a warrior is still courage, not drill.''

"Perhaps, yet courage is not a simple thing that one either has or doesn't have,'' Ian said. ''In my experience, I have found that a soldier will almost always prove equal to what is asked of him when he is well trained, well commanded, and surrounded by comrades whom he doesn't want to fail.''

"I have also found that.'' Rajiv Singh frowned. ''My army does not lack courage, training, or weapons, but it will be severely tested if my neighbors decide to march on Dharjistan. The Punjabi army is equally well trained and well armed. It is also, regrettably, much larger than my army, and spoiling for a fight.''

The light artillery discharged into the empty plain, sixty cannon blasting so closely together that the effect was of one monstrous, deafening explosion. Four salvos were fired in a minute, and the last was only slightly more ragged than the first. The gunners had also learned their lessons well.

The cannon blasts temporarily numbed all listening ears, and Ian waited before replying to Rajiv Singh's last comment. ''The treaty you signed with Britain assures that aid will be sent if Dharjistan is attacked.''

"With so many British troops tied up in Afghanistan, your army is stretched very thin. Do you think there would be enough left to help me stop the Punjabis?''

"Yes,'' Ian said without hesitation. ''Even if regiments have to be pulled from as far as Calcutta and Madras, Britain will honor its commitment to Dharjistan.''

"Doubtless you are right.'' The Rajput's expression was sardonic. ''But even if you are, I have a certain lack of enthusiasm for having British troops enter Dharjistan. It is all very fine when the tiger comes to defend you, but it could be difficult to persuade the tiger to leave later.''

"I wish I could say that your fears are groundless, but you and I know better than that,'' Ian said ruefully. ''There are certainly men in the Sirkar who would welcome an opportunity to annex Dharjistan. However, there are more who believe that a strong, independent state under your rule is British India's best defense against Afghanistan.''

The maharajah raised his brows. ''That's a remarkably frank admission for a Britisher. Don't you feel compelled to defend your government?''

"The English government has done many things that can't be defended," Ian said tersely. "My own people, the Scots, have suffered greatly at English hands."

"You sound like a man with a grievance that is more personal than political," Rajiv Singh said, eyes bright with interest. "Was your inheritance the only reason you left the army?"

Like Laura, the maharajah could be uncomfortably acute. "No, it wasn't," Ian said with some reluctance. "I was imprisoned while on an official mission to Bokhara, and held captive for a year and a half. The amir said he would release me if he received a letter from the British queen verifying my status."

Immediately guessing what was coming, the Rajput said, "And from pride or indifference, your government did nothing."

"Nothing at all," Ian said, not quite able to suppress his bitterness. "It was easier to think me dead and turn to more pressing matters. I would have died in Central Asia if it were not for the efforts of my family. Even before I learned of the inheritance, I had decided to resign my commission."

"So your government failed you," Rajiv Singh said pensively. Then his gaze sharpened. "No wonder you no longer wish to serve it. Would you be willing to serve me, Falkirk?"

"Sir?" Ian said, startled into military terseness.

"As you said, soldiers need to be well led. Would you like to command my army? You have a fine grasp of strategy and tactics and the ability to lead men." The maharajah gave a charming smile. "It seems a pity to waste such gifts on being a farmer back in your own country."

It was a breathtaking offer. Ian doubted that it was made as casually as it appeared. No wonder Rajiv Singh had spent so much time talking to Ian over the last days; it had been an undeclared job interview. Ian considered the possibility. He would have wealth, power, and the chance to use his hard-won military skills fully.

But for what purpose? In peacetime, a soldier's challenge was to maintain razor-edge readiness in the face of endless, boring drill. In war, his task was to deal the maximum in death and destruction. Neither of those things were what Ian wanted for his future.

Having seen the abyss, what he most wanted was a loving marriage and the chance to sink roots in the land of his ancestors. And if life became too peaceful, he could use his seat in the House of Lords to chastise the British government when it became too overbearing. Commanding an army wasn't on his list. "It's a great honor you are offering, Your Highness," he said formally. "But I must decline."

"The offer remains open, Falkirk," the maharajah said, unperturbed. "Either way, I would like you to accompany me on a short tour of my frontier fortresses. The journey will give you time to consider the advantages of becoming my commander."

"I'll be happy to come with you, but don't expect me to change my mind."

The Rajput fixed Ian with a dark, hypnotic gaze. "You would have power, Falkirk—the ability to mold and lead men, to make your mark on history. Can you honestly say that the prospect is entirely unappealing?"

Ian smiled. "The real power is yours—I would be but a servant. My estate in Scotland is tiny compared to Dharjistan, but it is *my* kingdom, and there I will be the ruler."

Rajiv Singh laughed. "That is hard to argue with. Yet there is also much to be said for taking my salt and serving me. Unlike the Sirkar, I have never betrayed a man who served me well." He gestured at the nearest elephant, whose howdah was screened with a curtain to protect Kamala and Laura from the eyes of the world. "Talk it over with your wife. She seems happy here, and the maharani loves her. If you become commander of the army, Lady Falkirk will also benefit by your position. All women like jewels—you can deck her in diamonds if you like."

"I'll discuss the matter with her," Ian promised, "but she is not a woman who can be persuaded by diamonds."

On the plain, the light camel-guns had been replaced by heavy cannon drawn by elephants. When they had been lined up, they fired one after another at one-second intervals. Ian automatically began counting and came up with a hundred shots—enough artillery to blast a major city to dust in a day.

When his hearing had recovered, he repeated what he had said to Laura several days earlier. "Your army seems to incorporate European science with the best of the Rajput warrior tradition, Your Highness. The results are formidable.''

''That is perceptive of you, Falkirk.'' Rajiv Singh's expression became reflective. ''India is the great mother. Her strength is her ability to accept all that comes, and to make it part of herself. Every invader, every religion that has ever reached this land still remains, absorbed by Mother India.''

Ian nodded. ''The result is probably the most complex society in the world.''

''What makes it possible is the caste system, which so many of the English sneer at. Here there is a place for everyone, even those who are not Hindus, like the Parsis and the Muslims.'' The maharajah gave Ian a challenging glance. ''Though the English rule, there are too few of you to have much effect on a land so large and dynamic as this one. You will have your brief day of power and then be gone, leaving little mark of your passing.''

''But we will leave some traces.'' Ian indicated the army in front of them. ''Discipline, justice.''

The maharajah snorted. ''Discipline has its uses, but your British justice is a narrow, small-minded concept, best suited to tillers of the soil.''

''Which is as it should be,'' Ian said tartly, ''for they need it most. Your country has never been kind to the weak. They are preyed on by landlords, bandits, priests, and princes. In British India, life is far less hazardous, taxes are more fair, and every peasant can have his day in court and receive justice.''

Rajiv Singh's eyes narrowed. ''I won't deny that such things have value, or that most of your administrators are men of integrity. But taxes, thieves, litigation about whose bullock has eaten whose garden—those are trivial issues. What matters is the richness of Indian culture, the diversity of her society. No matter how hard the Sirkar tries, it can never eliminate that.''

Ian had never seen the Rajput so intense. Wanting to ease the situation, he said, ''Nor do we wish to. Like the Romans, we rule without trying to change people's ways.'' He thought of suttee and child sacrifice and amended, ''At least, not usually.''

Rajiv Singh snorted. ''You are tolerant, Falkirk. Because of men like you, the English yoke weighed lightly for many years. But more and more of your countrymen seek to 'improve' us, to change our heathen ways. They despise the gods and customs that make us what we are. The more such Britishers there are, the more Mother India will chafe at the harness."

"I agree," Ian said. "The best of my countrymen know that our time here is limited. I hope that when the time comes for the British to leave, we will do it in peace, not anger. India and England have learned much from each other. It would be a great pity if that legacy were to be marred by violence."

On the plain, two battalions of cavalry were making a spectacular charge through each other's ranks, but the maharajah kept his penetrating gaze on Ian. "You are among the best of your race, Falkirk. That is why I want you by my side." Then he returned his attention to the spectacle in front of him.

Ian did the same, but his mind was not on the quality of the Dharjistani troops, nor Rajiv Singh's blandishments. It was becoming increasingly clear that the maharajah was not a man who was overly fond of the Sirkar.

The day of the military review was a holiday for many of the palace servants, and the atmosphere was festive. Meera had found the review a grand and thrilling sight. Afterward she was still excited, not ready to return to the women's quarters, so her expression brightened when she saw Zafir approaching through the chattering crowd. Meera hadn't seen him since they arrived in Manpur, and she rather missed scolding him.

The tall Pathan looked as always: arrogant, bold, and barbaric. He was also, when he smiled, quite sinfully handsome. "Greetings, little dove. Since we are both at liberty, would you care to walk with me in the park?"

She debated a moment. But she and Zafir were both members of Falkirk Sahib's household, which was rather like being family. Besides, she wanted to go. In a tone of carefully cultivated indifference, she said, "Very well, I've nothing better to do just now, but I must be back by the time darkness falls."

The palace grounds were enormous, with seven formal gardens representing the different sectors of paradise, as well as kitchen gardens and a more casually landscaped park. While the formal gardens were reserved for the use of the royal family and their court, servants were free to enjoy the park. Many were doing just that; however, the farther they strolled from the palace, the fewer people they saw.

Meera suspected that her companion had explored the area earlier to find a place of relative privacy. Still, though the Pathan might hope to seduce her, she was sure that in his company she would be as safe as she wanted to be.

As the two wound their way through lush flowering shrubs, they exchanged news of what they had done since arriving in Manpur. Meera found that she had a gift for verbal caricature that kept her companion laughing. He seemed to enjoy her tart tongue, which was a pleasure after the restraint of her years in Mohan's household. Her husband had preferred her demure.

When the sun began dipping to the horizon, Meera said regretfully, "It will be dark soon, so it is time to turn back. Has Falkirk Sahib told you when we will leave Manpur?"

"Tomorrow he goes on a tour with the maharajah and I go with him," Zafir said. "The major said we would be absent for five or six days. We leave for Bombay a few days after that."

"So tomorrow you are off again," she said, unable to conceal a note of disappointment.

He grinned. "Have you missed me, little dove?"

"Miss such a great, rude lout? Of course not," she scoffed.

Meera should have known the dangers of teasing the Pathan, for he immediately swept her up in his arms. As she squealed, he deposited her on the branch of a tree that stretched parallel to the ground at a height that put her face level with his. She grabbed the limb for balance, which left her with no hands free to fend off Zafir. He leaned forward to kiss her, murmuring, "I shall remind you what you have been missing."

By the time he had finished reminding her, she had lost all desire to push him away. As she relaxed, he moved forward against the branch so that her knees were straddling him. Meera found the position wickedly exciting in spite of all the clothing that separated them. She let out a long sigh of pleasure when he caressed her breast, but when his exploring hand moved below her waist, she jerked her head back and inhaled sharply. "Stop, you mustn't do that."

His hand paused but did not withdraw. She said,

"Please,," a little desperately, for she knew her will was weak.

To her relief he eased back, though he kept his hands on her waist. "I was hoping you were a lusty widow who cared nothing for conventions," he said sadly. "Instead, you have a boring determination to preserve your virtue."

"I most certainly do!" she sputtered indignantly. "Why should I ruin myself with a ruffian of a hill bandit?"

He chuckled. "Then I have no choice. I must marry you."

Meera was so startled that she would have fallen off the branch if Zafir hadn't steadied her. "Are you serious?"

"Yes, little dove, I am." He kissed her lightly. "For one of the few times in my life, I am. Will you be my wife and bear me strong warrior sons who will laugh in the face of fire?"

Her immediate reaction was to say a resounding, "Yes!" But common sense prevailed. "Which interests you more," she said warily, "me or my jewels?"

"I'm glad you're not penniless, but I come of a good family and have done well as a soldier of the Sirkar. My wife will never be reduced to selling her jewelry to survive." His expression became tender. "But if I didn't love you, all the jewels in India would not persuade me to make you my wife."

When he looked at her like that, she would agree to anything. She inhaled shakily and reminded herself of one of the major obstacles to marriage. "Would I have to become a Muslim?"

"Yes," he admitted. "Myself, I would not mind if you kept to your own ways, but my children must be raised as believers. I will not try to persuade you that Islam is better than your own beliefs, but remember—Muslims do not burn widows."

"But Muslims do take more than one wife." Meera's eyes narrowed at the thought. "Do you have other wives?"

"Ah, my little dove is jealous!" he said with delight. "No, sweet one, I have no other wives. Though the Koran allows four, it is not Pathan custom to have more than one, except sometimes if the man is rich, and his first wife has borne him no sons."

That reminded Meera of another potential problem. "I

might be barren—I was married for three years without conceiving.''

"Mohan was an old man,'' Zafir said simply. "I am not.''

She had to smile at his sublime confidence. "I do not think I am barren. But if I am wrong, will you put me aside?''

"No, you would still be my chief wife, the head of my household,'' he assured her. "If I die, you will always have a home and position with my family.''

"Won't they resent me as a foreigner?''

"Not since I have chosen you. In particular, my mother will be glad that I am finally taking a wife.'' His gray eyes gleamed wickedly. "If you are concerned that you are barren, I can help you find out.'' Once again hands began gliding over her hips.

Meera swatted at him. "Behave yourself, barbarian. The only way I will lie with you is if we marry.''

"I'm willing.'' His expression sobered. "Marrying me will mean giving up the life you know, and you will lose some liberties that a Hindu woman has. But you will gain other liberties, along with security and protection. Though Pathan women must be veiled when they venture into the outside world, within the compound they have influence and respect. If you accept me, I will do my best to make it easy for you to become one of us.'' He raised her hand and kissed her fingers. "And I do love you, little dove, not just because you are beautiful, but because you have the heart of a lioness.''

Meera thought of Habibur's household. Their ways had been different from what she was used to, but she had seen nothing that repulsed her. And there had been much that she liked.

As she hesitated, Zafir grinned, his teasing self again. "You'd best accept me. How many other men would be willing to marry a woman with a tongue like a viper?''

"You'd be surprised,'' she said loftily.

His hands clamped on her wrists. "Are you being courted by another man? Shall I have to abduct you?''

She was not at all displeased by his show of possessiveness, but knew better than to tease him about this. If she did, she might find herself slung over the back of his horse, being carried to the Khyber Pass like a sack of grain. "There have been several men who have shown interest, but I paid no attention to them. None could compare to you.'' When Zafir began to smile, she said, ''I am inclined to accept your proposal, but as you said, marrying you will mean many changes. I must think more before I give an answer.''

His eyes gleamed and he gathered her into his arms. ''Let me give you something else to think about.''

And so he did.

Chapter 25

❦ ❦ ❦

KAMALA HAD EVENTUALLY tired of the lengthy military review, so she ordered their *mahout* to take them away before the end. Laura didn't mind, for the cannonade had given her a headache.

When Laura reached the apartment, she took a long bath. She never tired of the luxury and still hadn't sampled all of the perfumed oils available. Afterward she brushed her hair and put on a loose robe. She was looking forward to spending the evening quietly with Ian. They had both been kept so busy by Rajiv Singh and Kamala that they had hardly seen each other in days.

This late in the year night came early, and it was already dark when Ian returned. Laura glanced up from the journal she was skimming. "You're even dustier than I was."

"After the main review, we switched to horseback and rode among the Dharjistani regiments," Ian explained. "I'll tell you about it later." While he bathed, Laura ordered dinner.

As they sat down to eat, he had the alertness that she recognized as a sign that something was in the wind, but he spoke little until they had finished. As Laura poured tea, he said, "Rajiv Singh offered me a position."

"What kind?" Teacup in hand, she curled up on the divan.

Ian lounged back on a sofa. One booted ankle rested on the opposite knee, but as Laura studied him, she saw that he was much less relaxed than his posture implied. "He wants me to become commander-in-chief of his army."

"Good heavens! That's quite an offer." Her brows drew together as she considered the implications. "Have you given him an answer yet?"

"I said I'd had enough of soldiering, but Rajiv Singh isn't giving up. He pointed out how much you're enjoying your visit, so I said I'd discuss the subject with you." Ian took a deep swallow of tea. "Would you like to stay in Dharjistan as one of the most important ladies in the land?"

Laura hesitated, wondering if Ian wanted to accept the position. She didn't doubt that he'd be a superior general if he chose to be. Had he initially turned the offer down because he thought she would object? After several fruitless moments of trying to decipher his expression, she mentally shrugged and decided that she was wasting her time; the only feelings she could be sure of were her own.

"Kamala is wonderful and our visit has been like an Arabian Nights fantasy, but I wouldn't like living in a royal court," she said. "I can feel how much the other women resent the fact that I'm in the maharani's favor. It's not so bad now, for I'm just a visitor, but if we were to stay, it would become much worse. I'd be isolated except for Kamala." Her voice dropped to a whisper. "And what about the possibility that Rajiv Singh might be plotting treachery against the Sirkar?"

He started to answer. Then his gaze swung around the room, as if searching for listening ears. "It's been a long day. Let's go to bed."

When she shot him a startled glance, he gave his head a small shake to indicate that his words were not to be taken at face value. She swallowed the last of her tea and left the cup on the table, then rose and led the way to her bedroom.

When they were both inside, he made a thorough check of the room before coming to Laura. She stood by the interior wall that separated her bedroom from Ian's, the spot in the apartment where a conversation would be hardest to overhear.

Ian stopped only an arm's length away so they could speak in undertones. After weeks of keeping a careful distance from each other, she found his nearness distracting. He was too close. Too attractive. Exasperated by the low tenor of her mind, she asked quietly, "Now that you know Rajiv Singh, do you have an idea where his loyalties might lie?"

Ian frowned. "At the review he said some things that I found rather disturbing. I suspect that if the odds were favorable, he might turn that excellent army of his on the

British. But there's no real evid nce that he has ever planned to take arms against the Sirkar ''

"Today, during the review, Kamala casually mentioned something that might have be :n Pyotr's scheme," Laura said. "About two years ago, a general who was a cousin of Rajiv Singh's made an attempt to take over the throne. The plot was caught almost before it started, and the conspirators were executed. The general, Janak, was known to be anti-British."

Immediately catching the implication, Ian said, "So perhaps your uncle was trying to help this Janak to the throne. If so, his scheme was foiled by the maharajah."

Laura's brows drew together. "Another piece of evidence that suggests that Rajiv Singh is on the side of the British is the fact that he wants to put you in charge of his army. Surely he would never expect you to fight your own people."

"He might." Ian summarized his earlier conversation with the maharajah. "I didn't mean to mislead him, but he attached too much importance to my anger toward the government, and to my comment on how England has oppressed Scotland. He might have thought I'd be happy to oppose the English."

Laura smiled a little. "I'm sure there are members of Her Majesty's government whom you'd like to send to a Central Asian prison for a year or so, but I can't imagine you bearing arms against your former comrades."

"Out of the question," he agreed. "Though Rajiv Singh is perceptive, he misjudged me on this and showed more of his true feelings about the Sirkar than he would have otherwise."

She sighed. "So we're back where we started. Maybe he's anti-British and was hatching plots with Pyotr. And maybe not."

"That's about it." Ian's mouth quirked ruefully. "I like Rajiv Singh. I don't want him to be an enemy, and that may be clouding my judgment." He stopped speaking, his expression distant.

She waited patiently for him to continue. She was perfectly content to study the dark chestnut strands that curled temptingly into view at the open throat of his shirt. Another of those fascinating differences between men and women. She remembered the textured feel of his chest hair against her palms, and the recollection created small spirals of warmth deep inside her. Needing distraction, she asked, "If Rajiv Singh *is* plotting against the British, what might he do?"

As Ian considered her question, he absently braced one arm against the wall above Laura's shoulder. He was so close that she could feel the warmth radiating from his solid frame. Instead of war, her thoughts moved irresistibly to love. She knew that she should move away from him, but could not bring herself to do so. Her hands curled into fists, for it took all her willpower just to prevent herself from touching him.

"As things stand now, I don't think there's much likelihood of Rajiv Singh attacking British India," Ian said slowly. "He's too intelligent to send his troops into battle without a decent chance of winning. But that could change if fighting breaks out elsewhere. For example, if Afghanistan rises against the British garrisons, Rajiv Singh might take advantage of our weakness and try to overrun northern India. If he could persuade the Punjabis to join him, together they could do considerable damage."

Reminding herself that serious issues were at stake, Laura wrenched her eyes away from her husband's tanned skin. "Do you think any of that might happen?"

"It's not likely." Ian shrugged. "I'm worrying too much. The attempt to overthrow Rajiv Singh must have been what your uncle tried to bring about. If successful, it could have caused considerable trouble, but it failed." After more thought, he added, "Still, I'll talk to the authorities in Bombay so they can keep an eye on this area. And keep looking through Pyotr's papers. I wouldn't mind more information on what he was up to."

"Very well. I'll do that." No longer able to restrain herself, Laura raised her hand to the bare, tantalizing skin of Ian's throat. His heart accelerated under her fingertips.

He caught her gaze with his and they stared at each other, mesmerized. Politics vanished in the face of older, more primal, needs. Moving as if in a trance, he put his hands on her shoulders and drew her close, then bent and touched his lips to hers. The desire that had been smoldering between them for days ignited like tinder.

He was unable to disguise his hunger, and she responded in kind, wanting to absorb him into herself. When his arms

came around her waist, she shivered and pressed herself
into him, her softer body compressing against hard muscle
and bone.

With a groan, he lifted her from her feet and carried her
to the nearby bed, then laid her across the mattress. Coming
down beside her, he resumed the kiss, his tongue thrusting
deep with a rhythm that she now recognized as the promise
of another, more profound, possession.

As his hands moved unerringly to the most sensitive,
yearning parts of her body, she yielded eagerly to the sensations that surged through her. She wanted to be swept
away, to drown the warning voice at the back of her
mind. . . .

More of his weight came onto her, crushing her into the
mattress. She ground her pelvis into his, feeling the hot,
hard bulge of him between her legs. Sensing how she burned
in secret places, he shifted to one side and raised her gown,
the fabric skimming teasingly up the length of her bare legs.
Then he slipped his hand between her thighs.

When he touched her moist, heated flesh, she gasped and
stiffened, shaken by her shatteringly intense response. It
would take very little for her to reach that frightening crescendo of need that she had experienced once before, and
which she now craved with heedless urgency.

It was that very urgency that jolted her back to awareness.
Dear God, she was once again on the verge of succumbing
to madness. With sick certainty, she knew that every time
she surrendered, the madness would grow stronger, until
she would be incapable of mastering it. Already she was
near that point.

Passion. Blood. Disaster. The terrified child inside her
thrashed out, futilely trying to twist out from under him as
she cried in a suffocated voice, ''No! This is wrong. I
mustn't!''

Ian went rigid, his mouth still on hers, his fingers inside
her. In a wanton, greedy corner of her soul, Laura prayed
that he would ignore her protest and finish what they had
begun. Later, after their mutual hunger was sated, would be
soon enough to agonize about consequences.

But he was too strong for her. Groaning, ''Bloody, bloody
hell,'' he rolled away and stumbled to his feet. Then he
leaned against the wall, burying his face against his up-
raised arm. He was shaking, but as Laura watched, his con-

trol clamped down. Inch by inch, the long line of his body became still and taut as marble. Without lifting his head, he said with lethal restraint, "You had really better explain what your problem is, Laura, because I can't bear much more of this."

She curled around herself, face flushed and breathing ragged as she tried to calm her outraged body. "I don't think I can explain," she whispered.

He dropped his arm and pivoted toward her furiously. "You had bloody well better try! If this happens again, I'll end up either forcing you, or leaving you." His eye narrowed. "Or is being forced what you want? If so, you'll have to find another man to give you what you want, because it's not a game I'm willing to play. I have enough shame in my life already."

His anger was like a splash of ice water. Fighting the irrational, childish panic that had overwhelmed her, she pushed her trembling body to a sitting position and tugged her gown over her bare legs. In spite of her choking fear, somehow she must find the strength to tell him everything.

She wiped her eyes with the back of her hand, then haltingly began in the most obvious place. "At Habibur's, I told you that it wasn't that I feared passion, but that I feared I would like it too much. That's the truth, Ian. For most people, I think desire is only part of life, sometimes welcome, sometimes a nuisance, but basically manageable. For my parents, though, passion was madness." She drew in a shaky breath. "It destroyed them, and I'm sure that if I allow it into my life, it will eventually destroy both of us, too. That's why a passionless marriage was the only kind that I dared attempt."

She didn't mention that that was exactly why she had agreed to marry Ian. She didn't need to. Ian's anger faded and he became very still, with a cool, hard clarity like black glass. "Ideas like that don't come from nowhere. Why do you believe that passion is so dangerous?"

Going back to her earliest nightmare, she said, "It began when I was four or five years old. My parents had gone to a ball. It was very late when they returned, but I woke up when the door opened. I got out of bed and went into the hall and peered through the balusters, thinking that if they were in a good mood, not fighting, I'd go down and see them."

She swallowed hard. "As the door closed behind them, my father said something I couldn't hear. My mother hit him. They began fighting like animals, tearing at each other with teeth and nails, making horrible, inhuman sounds. I was terrified." Her mouth twisted. "Now, of course, I realize what they were doing. They were probably having a wonderful time, even though it looked as if they were murdering each other. But as a child, I didn't realize."

"You certainly should understand now," Ian said dryly. "A few minutes ago, we were behaving exactly the same way."

She flushed and dropped her gaze. "I know. That's why I became so frightened." She took a deep, steadying breath. "That night, I crouched on my knees and watched in horror, my hands locked around the balusters, convinced that the two people I loved most were going to kill each other right in front of me. When he dragged her to the floor and they began . . . began coupling, I got up and ran back to my room and hid under the blankets and cried. The next morning, I couldn't believe that everything was normal. My mother wore a high-necked gown and a satisfied expression, my father was in one of his most exuberant moods."

"It's not surprising that you were frightened and confused," Ian said soberly. "But surely that one incident was not enough to make you believe what you do."

Her hands knotted into fists and dug into the mattress at her sides. "There were other incidents. The worst was several years later, when . . . when my father died." Her throat closed, and she couldn't continue.

When the silence grew too long, Ian said, "You told me that your father committed suicide. Wasn't that what happened?"

"What I told you was the truth, but not the whole truth." For a moment she hid her face in her hands as she searched for the strength to reveal what she had never before spoken of. Raising her head, she said, "The day that he died, they had a ghastly row. They were in the drawing room, and I was reading in the library that opened off of it. The door was open so I could hear every word, but they didn't know I was there."

"You seem to have been unlucky in your eavesdropping."

Laura grimaced. "It was more that my parents were profligate with their emotions. Growing up in that house, it was impossible not to know how matters stood between them. If I'd been upstairs in my room, I'd probably still have heard every word of what they said—none of the servants were home that afternoon, so they saw no reason to be moderate.

"The fight was about the fact that my mother had just learned that Papa had been unfaithful to her. Not a real affair, just a quick tumble with a married woman in their circle. I think the woman must have wanted to make trouble, because she immediately came to my mother and tearfully confessed her sin.

"My mother became insanely jealous and confronted my father when she found out. She threatened to carve him up with a knife so he could never betray her again. Instead of denying her accusation or admitting it and asking her forgiveness, he stupidly tried to brazen it out, saying that the act had been meaningless and Tatyana was a fool to carry on so. After all, it was she whom he loved, so she should stop acting like a shrew.

"I couldn't see what was happening, but judging by the sounds, she threw the poker at him," Laura continued. "Then she said that if sex was so meaningless, she'd go and spread her legs for Count Vyotov, who'd been trying to seduce her for years. My father exploded, shouting that a man had the right to bed other women, but no decent woman could do the same. My mother laughed and said why should she be decent when her husband wasn't?"

Laura's voice cracked as the scene replayed in her mind, as vivid as the day it happened. "Papa called her a whore and hit her—I heard her scream and crash into a piece of furniture, then fall to the floor. Her voice dropped into a hiss, the most terrifying sound I've ever heard. She said she was going to leave the house that minute and go straight to Count Vyotov. Papa threatened to kill her if she tried to leave. She told him he'd better get a gun, because nothing but death would stop her."

Once again Laura choked to a halt. His voice deep with compassion, Ian said, "Did they get into a struggle where she accidentally shot him, and you've been concealing the truth all these years?"

"No, that would have been horrible but would have made a certain ghastly kind of sense," Laura whispered. "Instead, Papa said that he couldn't kill the woman he loved, but he would kill himself if she betrayed him. Cold as ice, my mother said it was a pity that he had valued love so little, for his infidelity had destroyed her love and he had no one to blame but himself. Then she stormed out of the house.

"I thought of going to my father, but he was in such a rage that I didn't dare. Instead, I slipped out the other door of the library and hid in my room, trembling." Forcing herself to continue, she said, "The rest is as I told you. I had almost convinced myself that this was only another fight, like all the others, and that the next day everything would be fine again. Then . . . then I heard the shot and went downstairs to the library. When I found my father's body, my first thought was that if I had gone to him, he would not have done such a thing."

"You mustn't think that!" Ian said sharply. "No child has that kind of responsibility for a parent."

"How could I not think it?" she cried in anguish. Wrapping her arms around the pain in her midriff, she tried to speak evenly. "But I didn't waste time on guilt then. When Papa fell across the desk, he had knocked his suicide note on the floor. It was in front of me when I walked in. I picked the note up and read it, and it was almost the worst part of all. He said that he couldn't bear Tatyana's unfaithfulness, and that he had killed himself to prove how much he loved her." Laura's voice took on the brittle edge of hysteria. "Can you believe that is what he said? He destroyed all of our lives and said it was for *love*!"

"Your father was suffering from a spell of madness," Ian said, his calm voice pitched to bring her back to earth. "He was a melancholic, prone to despondency, and what happened that day pushed him over the edge into suicidal despair."

"Oh, I don't doubt that he was mad that day," Laura said bitterly. "On the other hand, my mother was sane, except when she was in the grip of passion. Then she became as wildly unbalanced as my father. Though she didn't shoot him, it wouldn't have surprised me if she had. She was capable of it."

"But she didn't, and you are more like her than like him."

Ignoring his interjection, Laura said, "When I saw the note, I knew instinctively that it mustn't become public, so I hid it in my room. The official verdict was that my father had accidentally shot himself while cleaning his pistol, so that he could be buried in holy ground.

"Several days after the funeral, I gave my mother the note. It seemed that she should know—certainly the knowledge was more than I could bear alone. I think she had guessed why my father killed himself, but when she saw the proof, complete with dried bloodstains, she broke down, crying that it was all her fault. She hadn't gone to Count Vyotov that day, but to the house of a female friend. After she had calmed down, she came home prepared to forgive my father if he was suitably chastened. Instead, he was dead. She told me that passion was the culprit, that it was a viper that destroyed all that was good and true. That she would never let herself be ruled by passion again, because it was a form of madness."

"You are not your parents," Ian said firmly. "Your mother married again, but there was no disaster the second time around."

"Tatyana had learned from what had happened. Also, my stepfather was too steady—too sane—to allow another tragedy. But that doesn't mean that I am a safe person." Laura shivered. "The blood of both parents runs in my veins, and I carry the seeds of violence in me."

"That would be a heavy burden to bear, if true." He shook his head. "Why are you so sure that passion will turn you into a madwoman? You have a temper, but I've seen nothing that suggests that you could be a danger to yourself or others. Pushing me off a dock was hardly a homicidal act."

She gave a twisted smile. "The proof is in the last of my nightmares. I've never told anyone this, but when I was sixteen, I became infatuated with a student at Haileybury College. Edward said that because my stepfather was one of his teachers, we must keep our feelings secret until he finished the course. I was stupid enough to think the situation was wonderfully romantic. Edward was the younger son of a viscount. Later I learned that his family had sent him to Haileybury in the hopes that India would cure his wildness. Or if not that, at least he wouldn't be causing scandals in England."

"He tried to seduce you?" Ian said, his face like granite.

"Yes, and very nearly succeeded." She stopped, hot color flooding her face as she remembered what easy prey she

had been for a handsome face and sweet, lying words. She
had melted like wax at his touch, bewitched by her discovery of desire.

In a torrent of words, she continued, "I fancied myself
in love with him, and with the arrogance of a sixteen-year-
old, I was sure that I knew exactly what I was doing. I was
different from my parents—wiser, my love more true." She
shuddered. "Even though I knew it was wrong, I finally
agreed to meet Edward in the woods one afternoon, because
I trusted him. That was when I discovered how powerful,
how dangerous desire can be. All my judgment, all of my
knowledge of right and wrong, dissolved when he kissed
me. I very nearly . . . let him have his way with me.

"Fortunately, before it was too late, I made some idiotic
remark about how we really should wait until we were married. He was so startled that he blurted out that foreign-
born dollymops like me were for play, not marriage."

Her voice failed again as the humiliation of that moment
came back to her. "I realized immediately what a fool I had
been. I don't know what he saw in my face, but he drew
away as if I'd turned into a cobra. Then he stood and ran
off. I never saw him again. I found out several days later
that he had dropped out of Hailleybury. Not long after, I
heard that he was killed in a brawl in London."

"Which the swine obviously deserved," Ian said grimly.
"It was a horrible thing to happen to a young girl who gave
her trust and her love. But the fact that you made a youthful
misjudgment doesn't mean that passion will doom you."

"No. It was my response that did that." Her hands
clenched, the nails biting into her palms. "At first I was
numb. My main desire was to conceal what had happened
from my parents, because I was afraid of what they might
do. I had a horrible vision of my stepfather challenging Edward to a duel. Or, more likely, the possibility that they
might insist that he marry me.

"The next day, I was doing some embroidery in my room,
pretending everything was normal. But I couldn't help
thinking about what he had done to me—and how much I
had *enjoyed* it . . . ! A kind of madness came over me, like
a furious scarlet fog. The next thing I knew, I was kneeling
on the floor with my sewing scissors in my hand. In my
rage, I had slashed the upholstery of a wing chair into ribbons."

She closed her eyes for a bitter moment. "I wanted to kill Edward. If he had been there, I would have. That's when I realized that I was truly my parents' child. I swore then never to allow myself to get into such a situation again. Then I met you, and it seemed like it might be possible to have a marriage that would be safe." Raising her gaze to her husband, she said, "But it hasn't worked out that way. Once, briefly, I considered telling you that you should seek physical satisfaction elsewhere. The very thought of it made me murderous. I'm dangerous enough now. If I surrendered to the wild, Russian side of my nature, God only knows what I would be capable of."

Ian leaned against the wall, looking as drained as she felt. Choosing his words carefully, he said, "Everyone has the capacity to be violent in the right—or wrong—circumstances. That doesn't mean you're incapable of a normal married life. Though you are your parents' child, you are also yourself. At sixteen, passion burns like wildfire in almost everyone—it's part of being young. I did things at that age that I'd rather not think about, and would certainly never do again. You can't predict the rest of your life based on how you behaved then."

"Perhaps, with another man for whom I had milder feelings, it would be possible," she said bleakly. "But not with you, Ian, for I care too much. And you aren't an entirely safe person, either. Remember how furious you were when you thought I was too flirtatious at the ball? The night ended in farce, but it could as easily have been tragedy."

"I'll admit that the thought of wringing your neck has crossed my mind more than once. A woman like you could unbalance a stone saint," he said with a trace of acid humor. "But that's exasperation, which is a long way from real violence. Though I acted like an idiot in Cambay, I didn't hurt you. I don't think I could, no matter what you did."

"Perhaps you couldn't. Unfortunately, I'm not at all sure that I would never hurt you, or myself. I fear that the two of us together would create a folie à deux, a mutual madness that would destroy us both, as happened to my parents." Her voice broke. "I can't allow that. I *can't*."

He rubbed his temple, his face gray. "Never having seen my father's brains sprayed across the wall, I'm not in a position to refute that. Very well, so be it. At least now I understand your reasons."

"I'm sorry, Ian," she said wretchedly. "You don't deserve to suffer because of my weaknesses."

"We are what we are, Laura. Don't apologize. I was the one who changed the rules of our marriage by recovering." He smiled humorlessly. "It's ironic. I was overjoyed when I realized I wasn't permanently incapacitated. I thought that any other differences could be solved and that very soon we would have a real marriage. But obviously I was wrong. It would have been far better if I had remained as I was. As for whether or not I deserve to suffer . . ." His expression closed. "If my stern Calvinist ancestors are right, this is a just punishment for my sins. To have remained a eunuch would have been too easy."

Laura bit her lip. "Perhaps, when I have had time to become more accustomed to the idea, I will be able to accept your having a mistress." The mere thought caused stabs of pain and fury, but she continued doggedly, "Other women learn to live with such arrangements, so I should be able to also. Particularly if I don't know the details."

"Somehow I don't see adultery as the answer. There are worse things than celibacy, Larishka. Falkirk is a spacious place and we should be able to rub along tolerably well. But you'll have to do your part. I can, barely, manage to control my own appetites, but it's too damned much to expect me to control yours as well. While I acquit you of deliberate teasing, your vacillation is making it very difficult for me." His face became harsh. "Not difficult—impossible."

"I think that part of me did want to be overpowered so that I wouldn't be responsible for what happened. Now that I've faced that, I'll do better in the future." She hesitated, then said painfully, "I love you, Ian. That makes it hard to be moderate."

She hoped that he would be gratified by her declaration, perhaps even say that he loved her. Instead his face became even more remote. "If you love me, you will learn to control yourself. Otherwise we will be unable to live together." He pushed himself away from the wall. "Rajiv Singh has asked me to go with him tomorrow on a tour of his defenses.

By the time I return, we should both have cooled to a manageable level."

As Laura studied her husband, she saw that there was a new kind of blackness in him—not the hopelessness that she had felt when they first met, but a grim determination that separated them as effectively as a granite wall. If this was what was necessary for them to survive together, the solution might be as painful as the problem. She drew a shaky breath; she could only hope that in time they would recapture the relaxed friendship that had grown between them. "I'll work on my discipline while you're gone."

"Excellent idea." He turned to go into his own bedroom, then paused on the threshold of the connecting door. "I know the possibility is remote, but is there any chance that you might have conceived that night at Habibur's?"

With all her heart, she wished she could say yes, but she couldn't. "No," she said sadly. "I didn't."

"A pity. A child would have . . . made up for a great deal. Good night." He stepped into his own room and the curtain fell in place behind him.

Shaking with tension, Laura dowsed the lamp and crawled under her blankets. She knew that it was good that the situation between them had been clarified. But she felt empty and miserable, and her body pulsed an angry beat of frustration from their uncompleted lovemaking.

She must learn to live with that, for Ian was right; they couldn't survive unless the lines of separation were clearly drawn. She must learn to control desire for her husband.

Impossible, yet she must do it. Either that, or she must accomplish the even more impossible task of freeing herself from the prison of her fears.

Chapter 26

❦   ❦   ❦

LAURA ENTERED THE maharani's private reception room and curtsied. "Good day, Kamala," she said as she rose. "Your message said you have a surprise for me?"

The maharani smiled mischievously. "Indeed I do, Laura. The priest has completed the horoscopes for you and your husband." She gestured to a small, wizened Brahmin, who wore plain white robes and a face of imperturbable calm. As he bowed, she added, "Now Srinivasa will interpret them for you."

Laura had almost forgotten that she had given Kamala the birth data needed for the horoscopes, but she felt a spark of interest at the prospect. Heaven knew that she needed guidance.

After performing the introductions, Kamala said, "Would you prefer for me to withdraw so you can hear Srinivasa in private?"

"Please stay," Laura said as she sat on a cushion on the opposite side of a low ebony table from the Brahmin. "I don't even know the right questions to ask."

He indicated two sheets of paper in front of him, each showing a square diagram marked with unintelligible symbols. "A horoscope is a map of the sky at the time and place you were born, Lady Falkirk," he explained. "Each moment in time is unique. A person born in it is imprinted by the special quality of that moment, at least for the length of the current life."

Laura was a little bemused by such matter-of-factness about reincarnation, but nodded obediently. "You can really tell about a person's life from reading that chart?"

"Oh, yes, and not merely about the life." He looked up

at her, his dark eyes mildly inquiring. "Shall I tell you the
day and hour of your death?"

She thought the Brahmin must be joking. When she realized that he was serious, she exclaimed, "Good heavens,
no! I wouldn't want to know." She thought of her stepfather, who had been told of his own impending death. If he
had not believed in it, might he have fought harder against
the disease that killed him? She repressed a shudder; these
were matters too deep to contemplate now, or perhaps ever.
"For a European, such knowledge would be unbearable."

He nodded understandingly. "It must be difficult to believe that one has only a single chance to learn all the lessons of existence. Still, while Christians do not believe in
reincarnation, all men are subject to the same universal
laws."

"Srinivasa," Kamala said warningly from the nearby sofa
where she reclined.

The Brahmin inclined his head. "My apologies, Lady
Falkirk. The maharani said I must not speak of spiritual
beliefs, but I forgot. For me, mind, body, and spirit are so
intertwined that it is difficult to think of them separately."
He flicked a finger toward one of the charts. "I assume that
you will not be sorry to know that you will have many
happy, prosperous years before you leave this body behind."

"That's good to hear," Laura agreed, "but what do the
horoscopes say about my marriage?"

"The aspects between you and your husband are very
powerful," he replied. "You were born to be together,
memsahib."

She thought back to the circumstances of her first meeting
with Ian. "I have trouble believing that. It was the merest
accident that our paths crossed."

"There are no accidents," the priest said firmly. "From
the moment of your births, you were both caught in a river
of events that would bring your paths together, even though
you were born in different lands." He looked back at the
chart. "The most important link was an older man whose
death drew you together—a man whom you both loved. You
met your husband soon after you experienced a great loss."

Laura's eyes widened. "You can tell that from a horoscope?"

"That and much more," he replied. "This is not the first

lifetime you have shared with your husband, nor will it be the last. Though the rewards will be great, there is much difficult karma that must first be overcome. You are each other's debtors from the past, and you each have power to hurt or heal the other. It will not be easy to separate those two things.''

After thought, she said apologetically, "I'm sorry, I find your explanation rather abstract. Can you be more specific?''

"I shall try.'' Srinivasa studied the diagrams pensively. "Mars and Saturn, courage and duty, are very strong in your husband. He is a warrior, with a warrior's strength, and a warrior's weakness, which is the inability to accept that his strength has limits. He torments himself because of his own perceived failings, not seeing them as necessary steps on the path. Jupiter, planet of faith and joy and growth, is also inherently strong, but it has been heavily afflicted for the last two years or so. An imprisonment of body, and now of spirit.''

The chart had given the priest an understanding of Ian that was in some ways better than Laura's. A little afraid of what she might learn about herself, she said, "What are my strengths and weaknesses, Srinivasa?''

He smiled. "The feminine strength of Venus and the moon, of warmth and instinct and acceptance. You also have the strength of Mars and Saturn to command, but there is an imbalance of the masculine and feminine energies and a fear of your own power. A fear of all passion.'' He tapped the chart with his nail. "Events are now forcing you to confront the imbalance. Very soon you will begin to master the energies, though you will not be fully in balance until the birth of your son.''

Laura caught her breath in disbelief. "Ian and I will have a son?''

"Yes, and . . .'' His words were cut off when Kamala gave a warning cough. Regretfully the priest said, "Again I forgot that you do not want to know the future in too great detail. But you will not be surprised to hear that soon you will travel across the sea to a home that is very old, but new to you.''

Laura nodded, a little dazed. Before today, she had vaguely assumed that astrology was a superstition that had died out in Europe and good riddance, but the Brahmin's skill was rapidly making a believer of her. He was saying things that no stranger could know, things she had not hinted at even to Kamala.

Srinivasa looked back at the diagrams and his brows drew together. "There is an ill-omened fixed star that I do not fully understand," he murmured, stroking his chin. "The planet of war will soon afflict critical points in the charts of you and your husband." Frowning, he glanced at Kamala for a moment. Then slowly, as if he was thinking out loud, he continued, "Great danger is imminent, but you will survive unscathed. "Your husband . . ." He pursed his lips. "Very soon your husband will be beneath the earth."

It took a moment to absorb the meaning of the statement. Then Laura realized that he had just predicted that Ian would soon die. As terror swept through her, she exclaimed, "No!"

When Srinivasa glanced up, mild surprise on his face, Laura sprang to her feet, her knee hitting the low table and jarring it so that the horoscope papers rustled across the ebony surface. "This is superstition and I won't listen to any more," she said with horror. "It can't be true and I won't believe it!"

Then she turned blindly and rushed through the arches that led into the courtyard. Ian beneath the earth, dead and cold, his strength and laughter stilled forever. No, she would not believe it, for belief was unbearable.

Yet she could not dismiss the prediction no matter how much she wanted to, for the priest had been right about so many other things. *Very soon your husband will be beneath the earth.* How soon was very soon? If the Brahmin spoke truly, there was enough time left for her to conceive a child. But how could that happen? She wasn't pregnant yet, and she and Ian were physically more estranged now than they had ever been.

She stopped under the mulberry tree that provided shade for the courtyard and pressed a hand over the tight pain in her chest, too confused and unhappy to know what to think. The Brahmin had referred to Ian's death as calmly as he had mentioned the voyage over the sea, but then, the priest seemed to view death as not much more significant than changing one's clothing. Perhaps in a spiritual sense he was right, but Laura wasn't detached enough to take the broad view. She wanted Ian alive and happy, preferably with her, but if not, at least somewhere on God's green earth, breathing the same air that she breathed. He deserved some happiness, after all he had endured.

Kamala's soft voice sounded behind her. "Laura, are you all right? I thought you would find the horoscopes amusing and perhaps enlightening. I'm sorry you were upset."

Laura closed her eyes and made an effort to regain her composure before turning to her friend. "I'm sorry, Kamala. I hope Srinivasa doesn't feel insulted," she said in a voice that was almost even. "Perhaps he should do horoscopes only for Indians. As a European, I'm uncomfortable with the idea that the future is fixed and immutable."

Undeceived, Kamala studied her face. "Walk with me, Laura. You are troubled, and not only because of what the priest said."

Laura accepted the suggestion gratefully, and the women made their way through the palace and into the grounds. The park seemed to stretch forever, and it was a realm of peace and ever-changing beauty. Elegant pavilions were hidden amidst lush greenery, little brooks made music of falling water, and the brilliance of the flowers was rivaled by the bright birds that flashed through the trees and sang to the sky.

Walking helped Laura regain her equanimity. As they crossed a bridge that arched over a small waterfall, she said, "I'm sorry to have reacted so foolishly to what Srinivasa said. His comments about our characters and problems were very interesting, but I can't believe that future events can be predicted."

"It's true that East and West view the world differently, so horoscopes might not have the same meaning for Europeans," the maharani said reflectively. "Perhaps what would be fixed for an Indian is only a possibility for you." She glanced at Laura, her almond eyes teasing. "I think you should accept the predictions of a son and a long, happy life and dismiss the rest."

"I don't know about the long life, but I don't believe that we'll ever have a child," Laura said bleakly. "There are . . . problems in our marriage that make it unlikely. And it's all my fault."

"Do you want to tell me about it?" Kamala said in her gentle voice. "As a confidence from one woman to another?"

Laura hesitated, wondering if discussing their marriage with an outsider would be an unpardonable violation of Ian's privacy. But she desperately needed to unburden herself to someone wiser in matters of both the heart and the body. "If you have the patience, I would love to hear what you think. If ever a woman has been completely at ease with herself and her femaleness, it's you." Laura tried to smile. "But I warn you, you'll think I'm very foolish."

"Nothing that happens between friends is foolish," the maharani said serenely. "Come, one of my favorite spots is ahead. No one will disturb us there."

Another minute of walking brought them to a small clearing where pollen danced in the sun and the scent of flowers hung heavy in the air. Laura's gaze immediately went to the two swings that hung side by side from the branch of a massive tree. Thick ropes of twisted silk and seats cushioned to protect royal derrieres from discomfort showed that they were not playthings for children, but amusements fit for a princess.

Kamala perched on the right-hand swing, her small, sandal-clad feet skimming the velvety grass. "Now tell me why you think you're foolish."

Laura perched on the other swing and pushed her feet against the ground to set herself into motion. "One thing Srinivasa said that was certainly true is that I fear passion." As she swung back and forth, she repeated what she had already revealed to Ian. This time, the words came a little more easily.

After revealing her background, she described the curious matching of needs that had led her and Ian to marry. Kamala gave a startled glance at the mention of Ian's impotence—since it was no longer true, Laura felt that her original promise of silence was no longer in force—but made no comment beyond an occasional sympathetic sound. She simply listened, face gravely attentive, her silk sari fluttering gently as she swung back and forth.

When she finished her story, Laura asked, "What do you think, Kamala—is the situation hopeless?"

"Nothing is hopeless, Laura, and certainly not your marriage." The maharani tilted her head as she considered. "I think that in your mind, you have confused two different fears—not surprising given the example set by your parents. The lesser, normal fear is of your own longings. All innocents are a little afraid of passion—not only women, but men, too. It's frightening to know that one's will and judgment can be swept away by the embrace of the beloved, and that is doubly true for someone of strong emotions, like you. Yet I think that if you had had different parents, your fears would have been no more than those of any young woman.''

Laura sighed. She had hoped that Kamala would have some magical answer, but apparently that wasn't to be. "But I did have passionate, destructive parents. I share their blood, their flaws, and their doom—the inability to control passion. The proof is in the way I behaved about Edward.''

The maharani wrinkled her nose. "I think you attach too much weight to that experience. You were an innocent then. Never again will you be so vulnerable, or so angry. The problem was not passion, but betrayal.'' She smiled a little. "Remember, you didn't actually hurt him, only the chair.''

"I'd like to believe that I would never behave so wildly again, but the example of my parents terrifies me.''

"The problem in their case was not passion itself, but rather jealousy and immaturity, which are not at all the same thing,'' Kamala said calmly. "Your father behaved like a child, your mother responded in kind, and like children they destroyed the object of their conflict—in this case, their marriage.''

"Is it possible to have passion without jealousy?'' Laura asked with honest bewilderment.

"But of course. This is exactly where your confusion lies. If your parents had loved and trusted each other enough, there would have been no problem.'' Kamala thought for a moment. "They must have enjoyed the childish games and fights, and it is true that such things can sometimes be amusing. But when real trouble arrived, they didn't know how to act wisely. Your father, with his melancholia, was incapable of balancing passion, and your mother allowed herself to be caught up in the same destructive dance. But your mother's second marriage was happy, was it not?''

"Yes, but I've always thought that was because it was less passionate.''

"Perhaps, perhaps not, though my guess is that there was more there than you realized.'' Elbows around the ropes, the maharani let her swing drift to a stop. "Tatyana had become wiser. Also, her second husband must not have found jealousy amusing. He sounds like a man who knew how to use passion wisely rather than lashing it about like a child. Hence, they were able to love each other without destruction.''

"It took a catastrophe for my mother to learn her lesson. Do you think I can do better than that?'' Laura said wistfully.

"The key, as I said, is trust.'' Kamala raised her feet and leaned back against the ropes so that the swing moved in longer arcs. "Did you know that Rajiv Singh has several concubines?''

Shocked, Laura said, "I had no idea. How can he, when the two of you love each other so much?''

"It is expected of a man in his position,'' the maharani replied. "As is just, he spends one night a month with each. The other nights he sends for me. I could allow myself to be jealous, but what purpose would that serve? I am the love of his heart, his body, and his soul. That is what truly matters.''

It took some time for Laura to absorb that. "That is a very mature attitude,'' she said at last. "I'm not sure I'm capable of that much maturity.''

"You don't have to be—your husband is not an Indian prince,'' Kamala said, a gleam of humor in her dark eyes. "Is Falkirk Sahib a dishonorable man who will betray your trust, or a deceitful man who will break his marriage vows?''

Without a moment's hesitation, Laura said, "Never.''

"Then where is the cause of jealousy?''

Laura frowned, her hands knotting around the silk ropes. "You make it sound so simple.''

"Perhaps,'' the maharani said shrewdly, "you have been making it too complicated.''

Laura felt the shock of recognition that occurs when an idea strikes instantly to the heart of an issue. "You said that I was confusing two different things,'' she said hesitantly. "Does the complication come in because my normal fears have become entangled with the disaster that my parents brought on themselves?''

"Exactly,'' the maharani said with satisfaction. "In this area, the West has less wisdom than the East. You look on male and female as being opposite, and think passion is a separate thing, like a wild beast that must be caged. But all opposites are part of each other, and passion is part of man's—and woman's—nature. Have you noticed how Hindu deities are always couples, one male, one female? To worship the god, one also worships the goddess. Vishnu and Lakshmi. Siva and Parvati. Krishna and Radha. Wholeness lies in balancing both. This is why images of men and women coupling, becoming one, are sacred.''

''Srinivasa said that my feminine and masculine energies were out of balance,'' Laura said, trying to fit the pieces together into a coherent whole.

''With parents who were so intemperate, of course it's difficult for you to achieve your own balance. Whenever passion appears, you become once again a terrified child.'' Kamala glanced across the space that separated them, her expression earnest. ''You try so hard to control yourself that the result is exactly the opposite of what you want. By attempting to suppress passion, you increase its power and make it dangerously unstable. I think that if you accept desire openly, soon it will find its natural place in your life.''

Allowing the swing to slow, Laura asked, ''What is a natural level for passion?''

Kamala grinned. ''Ask any couple that has been wed for a long time if desire is as compelling at ten years as it was at six months. In many ways mature, married intimacy is better—deeper and richer—than youthful ardor, but it has become a normal part of life and is no longer madness. The madness only returns under certain conditions, such as separation. When Rajiv Singh and I are parted, we come together again with the same craving we had when newly wed. But most of the time, desire is simply one part of life.'' After a moment, she added, ''Mind you, it's always a particularly nice part.''

Laura smiled acknowledgment, but her mind was on the ideas Kamala was giving her. ''So passion that has no outlet is the most compelling. In other words, by holding myself apart from my husband, I am making the situation worse for both of us?''

''Very likely,'' the maharani said. ''While your intentions have been honorable, even noble, if you continue on your present course you are more likely to precipitate disaster than if you do what your heart and body hunger for.'' She made a rueful face. ''It may be a mistake to give advice, for I am an outsider who has known you only a little while, and your husband I scarcely know at all. But I think it probable that if you can overcome your fears and become a real wife, very soon passion will cease to frighten you. Karma already binds you and your beloved together, so you might as well have the pleasures as well as the pain of that connection."

For Laura, Kamala's insights were like sunlight chasing the shadows from a room that had been closed for too long. It was all too true that whenever Laura thought of passion she became a terrified, irrational child. The time had come to use what wisdom she had acquired in her twenty-four years. She must try to understand herself as well as she understood others.

For the first time, she looked at her parents and was able to separate their passion from their tragedy. The two things had been irrevocably intertwined ever since she had witnessed their violent sexual union when she was an impressionable child. Yet as Kamala had pointed out, it was not passion as such that had caused her father's death, but infidelity, jealousy, and despair. And it was not sensual yearning that had caused Laura's rage at Edward, but his despicable behavior.

Once she had established that, she reexamined the jealousy she and Ian had both felt in Cambay. His had been rooted in his impotence, Laura's in the fact that she was neither his lover nor his beloved. Their fight would never have happened if they had been truly man and wife, and had been sure of each other.

To love Ian freely, without fear—could the solution really be that simple? Laura thought of the holy man in Hirsar, who had spoken to her after healing the child. He had said that when darkness seemed invincible, she would find light by accepting a truth demonstrated by the gods of India. Such truth was exactly what the maharani had given her.

With hope, rising, she said, "You may be right, Kamala. Lord knows that what I'm doing now isn't working. Worse, it's making Ian and me both miserable. It's time to take a chance."

"Good." Smiling wickedly, the maharani dismounted from the swing in one fluid motion. "You have said that matters are strained between you and Falkirk now, for he is an honorable man and strives to do the honorable thing. But

I'm sure that you are woman enough to find a proper balance in your marriage.''

The idea of becoming a real wife was terrifying. Yet it also felt powerfully right, in a way that Laura's desperate confusion never had.

Her resolve was briefly shaken when she remembered Srinivasa's reference to Ian's imminent death. She felt another shiver of the childish terror that had ruled her life. Grimly she decided that she must suppress all memory of what the priest had said. Otherwise, she would go mad.

Enough had been said about her problems, but Laura thought that it was a good time to ask about something else that had been on her mind. As they strolled through the woods in the direction of the palace, she said, "I never know what to make of the Hindu religion, Kamala. It contains much beauty and wisdom, but also things that I can only see as barbaric.''

"That's because Hinduism is not a religion in the western sense, but a way of life,'' the maharani replied. "There is not a single belief that a person must hold to be a Hindu—the only way to be Hindu is to be born one. You could not become one of us even if you sat at the feet of a guru for the rest of your life. Unlike Muslims and Christians, we do not try to convert others to our beliefs, for there is salvation in all true belief.''

She picked a golden flower and inhaled the scent. "Yet our way of life has room for everyone. For the simple people, there are primitive rituals, for the sophisticated there are noble concepts of great subtlety.'' She chuckled. "Me, my beliefs are somewhere in the middle. Not too high, not too low. I will not be freed of the wheel of rebirth in this lifetime, but then, I don't want to be. I would be happy to have a thousand more lifetimes like this, with Rajiv Singh.''

"Aren't you disturbed by things like suttee?'' Laura asked, thinking of Meera. "Many women are burned against their will.''

"That is wrong, of course,'' Kamala said firmly. "Anyone who forces a woman against her will is a murderer who will pay for it in the next life. But for a woman who chooses it, suttee is a rite of great holiness. If Rajiv Singh dies before me, I will certainly accompany him to the pyre.''

"You, Kamala?'' Laura was so surprised that she stopped

walking. It seemed impossible to reconcile such a terrible death with the serene, beautiful woman beside her.

The maharani smiled gently, as if talking to a child. "When Rajiv dies, my spirit will die with him. What is the point of preserving my body when we can be together in death and also in our next lives? When the time comes, I will go without doubts."

"I hope it doesn't come anytime soon," Laura said fervently.

"Srinivasa says we have many years still." After a few more steps, she added, "There is an old tale of a Rajput princess whose husband was called to battle on their wedding day. He was killed, and the next day she went to the pyre with him, virgin, bride, and widow, her nuptial flowers fresh on her breast."

Laura shivered a little. "That is a story of great power, but I am too much of the West to truly appreciate it. I would rather live for my husband, or even die to preserve his life, than follow him into death."

"Then live fully and without fear, Laura," the maharani said gently. "For him, and for yourself."

They emerged from the woods onto the wide green lawn that surrounded a small open pavilion. Laura was admiring the structure when she saw a flicker of movement from the corner of her eye. She turned her head, expecting to see a deer or monkey, then inhaled in horror. Somehow a black panther had gotten into the park. Swift as dark lightning, it bounded across the green turf toward the two women, its lithe muscles fluid with power. Struggling to keep panic from her voice, she gasped, "Kamala, we're in danger."

Laura looked around, wondering if there was help in sight, or if there would be time to reach the pavilion, but it was too far. Besides, if they turned their backs to run, the panther could bring them down as easily as lambs.

"Do not fear, Laura," the maharani said quickly. At the same moment, the panther swerved around Laura, then gathered its feet together and leaped straight at the maharani.

Before Laura could scream for help, she saw that the panther was not biting, but butting. It drove its round head into Kamala's ribs so hard that she was almost knocked from her feet. Smiling, she reached down with both hands and began roughly scratching behind the sleek ebony ears.

Incredulously Laura said, "It's a pet?"

"I'm sorry you were frightened, Laura," Kamala said contritely. "I forgot that you had never met Tika. Black panthers are very rare, and another rajah gave her to me when she was a kitten. I kept Tika in the palace when she was small. Now that she's full-grown, she has very fine quarters in the park. Still, whenever she scents me, she leaps the fence and comes immediately. Come, rub her chin. She is very fond of that."

Her heart still pounding with her reaction, Laura obeyed and was rewarded with a very loud, very unnerving, rumble of pleasure. Not a true purr, she decided, perhaps panthers weren't equipped for that. More of a focused growl, a sound that would have terrified anyone hearing it outdoors at night.

Laura had heard that black panthers were a variation of the regular leopard, and now she saw that the leopard pattern did indeed show up as blacker spots on the glossy fur. It was all most interesting. As Laura scratched the panther's chin, it closed its eyes in ecstasy and leaned into her hand so hard that she had to brace herself. It was much like a tabby cat, only larger. Much, much larger.

Kamala glanced up from her pet. "Passion is very like this," she said seriously. "Treat it as a wild beast and it has the power to destroy you. But make it your friend and it becomes a source of great pleasure."

Laura looked down at the panther and smiled. "Perhaps Srinivasa was correct in saying that there are no accidents. Certainly Tika came at a perfect time to illustrate your advice."

The panther was more than an illustration; it was an omen. As the two women resumed their walk to the palace, the panther twining between them, Laura realized, with a heady mixture of fear, determination, and hope, that she was going to follow Kamala's advice and try to make passion her friend. Then, God willing, she and Ian would find peace together.

Chapter 27

❦ ❦ ❦

THE MAHARANI WAS making perfume. Her labors filled her private sitting room with a dizzying blend of aromas—flowers and spice, sandalwood and herbs. Not quite satisfied, Kamala blended a single drop of oil into her latest mixture, sniffed the result, then sighed rapturously. "Finally." Holding the ceramic bowl to Laura, she said, "What do you think?"

After inhaling, Laura said, "Mmm, what a wonderful fragrance! Delicate, yet sensual."

Kamala nodded with satisfaction. "A truly fine perfume must express the wearer, and this one is perfect for you. It evokes innocent dawn and sultry night, ravishing a man's senses with both lust and tenderness."

"I hope so," Laura said. "It's wonderful of you to make such an effort on my behalf."

"I enjoy making perfume. I've often thought that if I had not been born a Rajput princess, I would have done well in a caste of perfumers." Kamala summoned a servant from the far end of the room and gave orders for the scent to be bottled. "I'll write down the recipe so that you can make it in England. A woman should have a special scent for her person and garments. It will haunt her husband even when she is not there."

"I'll think of you and Dharjistan whenever I wear it." Then, for the fourth or fifth time that day, Laura said, "Do you think the men will be back today?"

"I hope so, but it might not be until tomorrow." The maharani sighed. "I understand your impatience. I shall be very glad to see my husband, too. Even five days of separation are too many, but I do enjoy the reunions. Oh, before

I forget, take a look at this book. I think you'll find it intriguing.''

As the other woman began writing down the ingredients for the perfume, Laura opened the text, but at first she made no attempt to read the Persian script. Three long days had passed since her discussion with Kamala. In some ways, it would have been easier if Laura had been able to act immediately on her resolve to have a real marriage, for the waiting was difficult.

Kamala, bless her, had decided to distract her guest by demonstrating aspects of the education of a Hindu lady. East and West agreed that a gently born female should be able to sing, sew, dance, and play a musical instrument. Laura was adequately skilled in those areas; however, her knowledge of magic, sorcery, and cockfighting was sadly deficient, her ideas of how to adorn the female form were very austere by Indian standards, and she had never in her life made a couch of flowers.

The sessions were interesting and sometimes hilarious. Laura had enjoyed learning how to mix perfume and make sherbet, and being massaged with scented oil had been delightful. That was one skill she would be glad to demonstrate on Ian, for it would be a perfect excuse to run her hands over every inch of his lean, muscular body. She thought that he would like it, too.

The trick would be getting to that state of happy intimacy from the strained situation they were in now. Laura had not yet decided the best way to go about seducing her husband when she had just persuaded him that they must stay apart. It was one thing for her to be willing to lie with him, quite another to make the first move. But she was the one who had turned her marriage into such a muddle, and it was up to her to sort it out.

She hoped that Ian would be back that night, because the delay was making her a nervous wreck.

Telling herself to stop brooding, she looked at the manual the maharani had given her. Within a minute, her eyes shot open. People actually wrote such things down? ''Kamala, does this say what I think, or am I no longer understanding Persian?''

The maharani looked up with a smile. ''I thought you would find the *Kama Sutra* interesting. The pursuit of pleasure, *kama*, is one of the Four Aims of life, so the sage

Vatsyayana wrote a treatise on the subject. Since sex is one of the great pleasures, a good part of the book is devoted to it.''

"The sage seems to have a passion for counting and classifying," Laura said weakly.

"It is rather tedious to read about the eight kinds of love bite and the eight stages of oral intercourse," Kamala agreed. "And he cheats by counting mating after the fashion of deer, asses, and horses as different positions for intercourse. To me, those positions all seem much the same."

"I haven't gotten that far yet. But tell me, is this even possible?" Too embarrassed to read the passage aloud, Laura showed the page to her friend.

"Ah, very difficult. Really only suitable for a trained acrobat," the maharani observed with a twinkle. "If you wish to try it, the sage Suvarnanabha recommends practicing in a hot bath, so that neither of you hurt yourselves."

Laura gasped. "Is that why Indian bathtubs are so large?"

Kamala laughed. "One of the reasons." Her expression sobered. "Don't take everything the *Kama Sutra* says seriously, Laura, but I thought that reading it would expand your horizons. Though the book is interesting and covers many topics other than sexual congress, it's not half so romantic as a verse of fine love poetry. Still, it's useful to know some of the techniques."

"Oh, indeed," Laura agreed, still a little dazed. "I had no idea there were so many possibilities."

"If you were Indian, your education would have started much earlier. In the temple, young girls see and handle *lingams,* stone phalluses, so that they become accustomed to the idea." The maharani chuckled. "Though your education began late, I think Falkirk Sahib will be pleased with what you have learned."

Laura hoped so, too. As she returned to the book, she remembered his Indian mistress, Leela. He must know all about these interesting and athletic maneuvers. She stopped and reread one passage. As Kamala had said, there was nothing romantic about the blunt description, but the thought of doing it with Ian made Laura tingle in spite of her embarrassment.

The maharani rose to her feet. "I must hold audience now, but first I will give you something to aid your endeavors.''

"You've given me so much already," Laura protested.

Kamala's elegant brows arched. "It is easy for me to give, and I take great pleasure in it. Will you deny me that pleasure?"

Laura laughed. "Put that way, I don't suppose I can."

The maharani signaled to the servant. Knowing what was expected, the girl came forward and presented Laura with a folded length of exquisite, lavender-colored silk.

"It's a sari," Kamala explained. "The fabric is so fine that it can be drawn through a ring." She removed one of her gold rings and demonstrated, pulling the whole length of gauzy fabric through the circle. It came out none the worse for wear.

"Thank you, Kamala. It's exquisite." Laura stroked the gossamer silk. "This color is perfect for me."

"I know," the maharani said. "The sari is a very graceful garment, and one as fine as this will drive a man to madness." Her dark eyes sparkled. "I speak as one who knows."

Laura laughed, though she would wait before wearing the sari for Ian. It was too blatant for her at the moment, since she was still the next thing to a virgin. But she was willing to change that.

By midevening, Laura had given up hope that Ian would return when he unexpectedly walked into the apartment. Even dust-covered and fatigued, he looked good enough to eat. The thought brought the *Kama Sutra* to mind, so she said hastily, "You're home! I'd decided you wouldn't be back until tomorrow."

"Rajiv Singh was anxious to return tonight, so we rode through rather than stopping."

Laura considered giving him a welcoming kiss, but decided against it. Though her husband seemed pleased to see her, there was a wariness in his expression that did not encourage her to come closer. She would wait until later, when he was more relaxed. "Shall I order a bath for you?"

"Splendid idea. And some food as well." He ran a tired hand through his auburn hair. "I might as well take advantage of the fact that we're staying in a palace. After a few nights of camping, I'll look back on this luxury with longing."

"Did the maharajah persuade you to take over his army?"

"He tried, but finally accepted defeat." Ian smiled. "We played chess several evenings. I managed to beat him about half the time, which apparently doesn't happen often. It made him even more regretful that I was unwilling to enter his service, but he's been a gentleman about it." He glanced at the journal Laura had been reading. "Have you found anything interesting?"

Grateful that she had been studying Pyotr's papers rather than the *Kama Sutra,* Laura said, "There are lots of interesting things. In fact, I may try to publish Pyotr's memoirs in London—he's very witty and he led an incredible life. But so far, there's nothing like what we're looking for."

"Maybe there's nothing to find," Ian said. "But I like the idea of publishing some of his work. *Memoirs of a Russian Secret Agent* has a ring to it. My brother-in-law Ross is a writer—perhaps his publisher would be interested."

Laura nodded absently, then made the connection. "Good heavens, is the Ross who is your brother-in-law the travel writer, Lord Ross Carlisle?"

"Yes, though he's become the Marquess of Kilburn since his last book was published."

"His work is excellent," Laura said, more awed by the writing than the lordly title. "I've read all his books. It's not just what he says, but how he says it."

Ian grinned, more relaxed than when he first returned. "Tell Ross that and you'll make a friend for life."

Laura made a face. "I don't know. He now sounds as intimidating as the alarming Juliet."

Ian smiled, then went into his bedroom. Laura summoned a servant and ordered a bath and food. While her husband cleaned up, she changed into her prettiest nightgown and robe and brushed her hair out. She wanted to look desirable, in an unobvious way. Apparently she was successful, for when Ian came into the drawing room, his expression shuttered after a single glance. As he ate supper, he avoided looking at her and hardly spoke except for a few terse comments about his trip.

While glad that he wasn't indifferent to her appearance, Laura was also frustrated, for she had no idea what to do next. She couldn't quite bring herself to say, "By the way, Ian, I've changed my mind about lying with you. Shall we adjourn to the bedroom?" A pity that the *Kama Sutra*'s varied advice didn't cover this particular situation.

As soon as he finished eating, Ian got to his feet. "If you'll excuse me, I'm going to bed. We were up riding before dawn to get back to Manpur today."

Part of Laura advised waiting until tomorrow, when Ian was rested, but she couldn't bear another day of delay. Maybe the best approach was to hope that proximity would do the work, as it had in the past. If Ian was too tired, the moment could pass without embarrassment for either of them.

Rising to her feet, she moved around the table until she was standing beside him. Tentatively she laid one hand on his wrist as she looked up into his face. "I've missed you." With relief, she felt his desire kindle, sparking between them like heat lightning. This wouldn't be hard after all.

She opened her mouth to explain her new understanding, but Ian gave her no chance to speak. Face thunderous, he twisted away as if scalded. "You'll have to do better than this," he said grimly. "Remember what I said—I can't control both of us."

Then he pivoted on his heel and vanished into his bedroom. Before Laura could think of what to say, it was too late. She was left standing alone with a sick feeling in the pit of her stomach. She should have known that the line that had been so firmly drawn between them could not be easily crossed. Once more she had misjudged Ian's willpower, and her failure would make it harder to try again. But try again she would; she had no choice.

After taking a long, slow breath, she retreated to her own room. She might be a fool and she had certainly been hopelessly confused about passion, but she had at least one quality on her side: Russian stubbornness. Since subtlety hadn't worked, next time she would try head-on assault.

The next morning, Ian left their suite before Laura was even out of bed. No doubt he was going to find something to keep him busy and out of her dangerous clutches all day. Ah, well, that gave her time to plan the next stage in her campaign. A few minutes later, Meera arrived with a cup of tea, a proper English custom performed by an exotically lovely eastern nymph. After taking a sip, Laura said, "Meera, my husband came home very late last night, so tonight, I'd like to give him a proper welcome—something he'll never forget. Do you have any suggestions? If something exotic is required, the maharani will help.''

With a knowing smile, the young widow offered several ideas that were so imaginative that Laura began laughing. ''There is much to be said for the education of an Indian lady. I wonder if the staid English school I attended would be willing to add courses on 'How to please your husband.' ''

''It would be a very good thing,'' Meera said seriously. ''A wife who can satisfy her man in bed will have a happier life.''

''And so will her husband, I'm sure.'' Thinking of the erotic sculptures in the cave temple, Laura shook her head. ''If my headmistress, Miss Givens, tried to give her young ladies such practical lessons in England, she'd be in jail the next day.'' Laura finished her tea, then swung her feet from the bed. ''I think I'll wear the blue muslin dress.''

''Very good, memsahib.'' But instead of going for the garment, Meera said shyly, ''Zafir has asked me to marry him.''

''He has?'' Laura said, surprised. ''I knew that he admired you, but I hadn't realized that it was marriage he had in mind. Are you going to accept?''

''I think so,'' Meera said with a mixture of pride and doubt. ''Unless you know any reason I should not.''

Hearing a faint question in the girl's voice, Laura said reassuringly, ''My husband has never had anything but praise for Zafir. He is, I believe, a man of courage and honor. Also good-natured, which is a valuable trait in a husband.''

''Don't forget handsome,'' Meera added impishly. ''Or hadn't you noticed?''

Laura chuckled. ''I've noticed. He could turn any woman's head.'' More seriously, she said, ''The only question I have is about the differences in your backgrounds. Do you think that will be a problem?''

''That is also the only question I have. There will be difficulties,'' Meera admitted. ''Yet I no longer have a place among my own people. Zafir wants me and I want him. Do you think that is enough?''

Laura smiled ruefully. ''I'm no expert, Meera—quite the contrary. But wanting each other is a good beginning.''

* * *

Ian stayed out all day, sending a message to Laura tha
he wouldn't be back for dinner and she shouldn't wait up
for him. During his time away, he thought that he had become resigned to the situation, for there was a certain bleak
justice in it. Then he returned, and it had taken almost nothing to trigger his desire again—just a single touch. It was
very hard to deal with Laura's casual warmth when they
were alone together. Her affectionate nature would be wonderful if they had a normal marriage. Under present circumstances, it was harrowing.

It was late when he finally returned to the apartment. As
he stepped in the door, a tidal wave of rose scent engulfed
him. The drawing room smelled as if someone had dropped
a crate of expensive perfume. A good thing he liked attar
of roses.

Laura was already in her bedroom, though a line of lamplight
at the door showed that she was still awake. He went silently
into his room, hoping to get to bed unnoticed. As he was removing his eyepatch, his wife called out, "Ian, is that you?"

Caught. "Yes. Sorry to disturb you."

With an odd note in her voice, she said, "You're not
disturbing me. Could you come in here? I've found something that I think you'll find interesting."

Assuming that Laura's search through her uncle's papers
had finally paid off, Ian went through the curtained doorway
that connected their rooms. "What is it?"

He would have said more, but the sight that met his gaze
rendered him speechless. His wife was not poring over a
yellowed volume but standing in the middle of the room, her
splendid figure swathed in an almost transparent sari, and
her tawny hair cascading luxuriantly over her shoulders. She
was as provocative as a Hindu goddess come to life, or the
ancient Siren whose song bewitched men to their deaths.

And everywhere there were rose petals. No, not everywhere, the bed was clear. But a richly scented carpet of
pink petals covered the floor inches deep, mounding into
drifts and tumbling over Laura's elegant bare toes. The fragrance and color struck him with the impact of a physical
blow, disordering his senses and blurring the line between
reality and fantasy.

Ian knew that he must get out before it was too late, but
already he was too paralyzed to move. Didn't she have any
idea of the effect she was having on him? Yes, dammit, she

dust. "Bloody hell, Laura," he swore. "Are you deliberately trying to drive me crazy?"

"No!" Her slanted amber eyes were wide and anxious. "What I'm trying to do—what I found—is a new understanding."

Slowly she walked toward him, the voluptuous scent of roses spiraling up at every step as petals crushed beneath her bare feet. He couldn't take his gaze off the subtle sway of her breasts, which were clearly visible beneath the translucent silk of her sari. It was obvious that the only thing beneath the garment was enticing woman.

Stopping an arm's length away, she said, "While you were gone, I had a long discussion with Kamala about the nature of passion. It made me realize that I had everything backward—that trying to suppress desire was actually making it more dangerous." She swallowed, the graceful line of her throat taut. "The time has come for me to stop trying to hide from passion and accept that it is an essential part of my nature."

Wondering if his wits were being addled by roses, he said, "You'd better spell out what you mean. When I've tried to interpret your wishes in the past, the results have been wretched."

Color rose in her cheeks. "I know that my vacillation and confusion have been hard on you," she faltered. "You've been amazingly understanding. But now I'm through with vacillating. I hope you're still willing to . . . to make this a real marriage."

Willing? If she wanted him to cut his heart out, he'd ask her for a knife. But this was too sudden. Though he could see in her face that something fundamental had changed, he had learned the hard way that what appeared to be good fortune was probably not. His restored potency had proved to be a bitter blessing, and now his instincts shouted that Laura's change of mind might have equally unpredictable and painful repercussions.

He knew that he should retreat and take the time to think, to examine the black corner of his spirit that was warning him that nothing good could come of this. He didn't deserve unmitigated happiness, and any joy he found with his wife would have to be paid for by a piece of his soul.

But he couldn't draw back, not even to save his life, and that was brutal proof of his weakness. "Ah, God, Laura, you must know that I can't resist you," he said, aching.

"That's what I was hoping," she said with a smile a
tremulous as dawn.

As always, he was fascinated by her combination of fai
coloring and slanted Oriental eyes, as unique and unpre
dictable as the woman herself. He caught a handful of he
shining hair, the color of polished oak, the texture of moon
beams, and brushed it against his cheek, half expecting he
to vanish because this whole magical scene was just a fan
tasy. But she didn't. Instead, she turned her head and kisse
his fingers where they twined through her hair.

Fierce animal passion surged through him. He wanted t
drag her down among the rose petals and mate with mind
less abandon. But that would be too quickly done, and h
dared not waste this priceless opportunity. His mind wa
momentarily too clouded by lust to have room for self
reproach, but once desire had been slaked, bleakness woul
take root, tainting future intimacy. He must make the mos
of tonight. In the future he would never be able to enjoy hi
wife's wondrous sweetness with as much freedom as now
when her darkness was receding and his darkness had no
yet invaded the same space.

He tilted her head up for a kiss. Her arms came aroun
his neck, her breasts crushing against him, and he taste
the hunger in her. He deliberately muted his response, set
ting a pace that would allow them time to savor what ha
passed too quickly the first time they had made love.

He lifted his head and studied her face. In the depths c
her eyes was joy, tempered by lingering anxiety. It couldn
be easy for her to put aside the fears that had ruled her fo
so long. Softly he said, "You are so lovely, Larishka. Be
witching enough to drive a man mad. I don't think I'll b
able to bear it if you change your mind again."

"That won't happen," she said, her eyes wide and ear
nest. "Not this time. Not ever again."

The only jewelry she wore was the necklace that Meer
had given her. The delicate gold chain drew attention to he
flawless skin, which was as finely textured as the petals tha
surrounded them. Delicious. Irresistible. He pressed his lip
to the hollow below her ear, then trailed his tongue alon
her throat until he reached the cool gold links of the chain

Laura exhaled with a breathy sound and her head fell back
her pliant body arching over his supportive arm. She was s

trusting that tenderness immobilized him and became anguish. How could she trust him when he was so undeserving?

Before the thought could take hold and poison his pleasure in the moment, he said, "This time I'm going to see all of you."

The sari was draped in an improvised style, without a blouse, so that one shoulder was bare, the other covered, rather like a Roman toga. The silk was so sheer that the darker circles that tipped her full breasts and the small shadow of her navel were visible even through half a dozen layers of fabric.

He untucked the sari where it was folded across her breasts, then lifted it away from her, unwinding the fabric like thread from a spool. Laura made a dance of it, turning slowly, a seductive smile on her face, her gaze catching his each time she came around. The luscious curves of her body became more visible as every rotation removed another veil of silk.

The last length of fabric slithered away in a rush, landing on the floor as a hazy splash across the pink petals, leaving Laura fully revealed. Mouth dry, he said, "You are even more beautiful than I dreamed. A fantasy come to life."

"My figure used to embarrass me," she said, a little shy at her nakedness. "Too much of everything to be ladylike."

He laughed. "Everything is exactly right. Not a straight line anywhere."

He had wanted to look, but now he had to touch. Placing his hands on her shoulders, he caressed the hollows above her collarbones with his thumbs. "Skin like the very finest polished wood, smooth and alive." He splayed his fingers outward, then skimmed his hands down her sides, trying to memorize all the complex contours. "A waist so slim that I can circle it with my hands." He demonstrated, loving the way her torso tapered down, then flared into ripe, inviting hips. "Gorgeous shapely legs."

Smiling with pleasure, she reached for his shirt. "Now it's my turn to see you." As she undid his buttons, her fingertips grazed his chest, sending hot jolts of sensation crackling through him. He caught his breath, knowing how hard it would be to make love properly when his minx of a wife could dissolve his will with a touch.

She peeled off his coat, then tugged his shirttails loose and pulled the shirt over his head. When his torso was bare, she gave a low sigh of satisfaction and leaned forward to nuzzle her face against his shoulder, her lips soft against his skin, her silky sweep of hair gliding over his chest and ribs. "You're rather gorgeous yourself." She began nipping at him with light, teasing bites that splintered what was left of his control.

With sudden furious impatience, he bent over and dragged his boots off. He was about to remove the rest of his clothing when Laura, laughing, caught his hand and pulled him down to the floor. He went willingly, catching her in his arms and rolling her over for a kiss. The scent of a thousand roses exploded around them, the petals a cushion as soft as crushed silk.

Cutting through the sweet, clear fragrance of roses was the heady aroma of Laura's perfume, an alluring feminine scent that somehow intensified her Lauraness. He molded her magnificent breasts with his hands, then buried his face between them, rubbing back and forth, entranced by the creamy smoothness. A faint rasping sound reminded him that he hadn't shaved since that morning, and when he raised his head he saw that his whiskers had left faint red marks. "Sorry," he said huskily, using his mouth and tongue to solace any soreness.

He couldn't seem to get enough of the sight and feel of her breasts. And the taste, ah, yes, the taste. His lips closed over one dusky nipple. Laura shuddered, her hips rocking against him. As he moved to the other nipple, her nails bit into his back, then slid under his waistband to dig into his buttocks.

Swearing mentally for not having taken the time to get fully undressed, he rolled onto one hip and unbuttoned himself, a process that was complicated by Laura's unskilled but eager fingers. When she slipped her hand into his trousers and touched his hardened flesh, he gasped and his vision darkened. Nothing in his past had prepared him for this degree of desire, for never had he known a woman like this one.

With one swift movement, he yanked off his close-fitting trousers, stirring up a floral flurry in the process. Then, as petals fluttered in all directions, he pressed Laura onto her back and caught both of her hands in one of his, pinning her wrists to the floor above her head so that her breasts lifted. Her golden eyes were feral, and she squirmed against him in wordless demand. "Slow down, lassie," he murmured.

Restlessly she drew up one leg. He leaned over and kissed the fragile skin on the inside of her thigh. She moaned, and the sound vibrated through him like temple bells. He spread his hand over her belly and kneaded the gentle curve, then drew the heel down over soft, curling tan hair. She made a dark, wild noise deep in her throat and began grinding her pelvis into his palm, her desire the sharpest aphrodisiac he had ever known. Another scent joined the enticing potpourri that surrounded them, this one the sweet saltiness of female arousal.

He slid his fingers through the dainty curls and began to caress her intimately. The moist, petal-like mysteries of her body were lovelier than the blossoms around them. She made a choking sound when he began stroking the bud that was the most sensitive spot of all. "Please, now," she panted. "Please."

Knowing that she was as ready, as desperate, as he, he released her wrists and rolled onto his knees, then braced himself above her. Her arms came around his ribs and she opened easily to his penetration, sheathing him with a clasp like hot, liquid velvet. He entered her slowly, but with smooth, inexorable power. At the point of deepest invasion he held still for a moment, his sexual balance as precarious as a tightrope walker.

She gave a low moan of distress as he withdrew, then cried out when he thrust again. Convulsions rippled through her, and she tightened around him in hard, rapid spasms that swept away his balance. He surged into her again and again, until he reached the taut point where madness splintered into peace.

Throbbing and light-headed, he subsided onto her, wondering if he would ever move again. "I'm very, very glad that you didn't change your mind this time," he whispered.

"So am I, *doushenka.*"

With tension released, the only sound was that of their breathing as it gradually returned to normal rhythms. Ian was thinking that he had better move before he crushed Laura when she slid her fingers into his hair and murmured, "I love you, Ian. Thank God you came into my life."

Her words ripped through his surface contentment, baring the darkness below. He would never have answered as he did if he hadn't been physically and emotionally drained. But all of his barriers were down and before he could stop himself, he said, "I wish to God that you wouldn't say that."

Chapter 28

❦ ❦ ❦

UNABLE TO BELIEVE that she'd heard correctly, Laura turned her head and stared at her husband, whose face was only inches away. There was a bleakness in his expression that hurt her heart. Uncertainly she said, "Ian?"

In an instant he masked his emotions so smoothly that it was as if the darkness had never been there. "Just muttering to myself, Larishka." He smiled and kissed her, his expressions so tender that she almost believed that she'd misunderstood. Almost.

Lightly he said, "It's too cool to spend the night on the floor, even with a blanket of rose petals." He raised his head and looked measuringly at the bed. "I wonder if I have enough strength left to get us that far."

Laura could have managed to move, though she was disinclined to try, but no effort was required of her. Ian got to his knees, then scooped her in his arms, stood, and carried her to the bed. His prison gauntness had been replaced by hard, sculpted muscles. Trying to forget her husband's disquieting remark, Laura touched a ragged scar on his bicep. "Did one of your souvenir bullets cause this?"

"Yes. That happened when I was a newly fledged subaltern without the sense to know when to duck." He laid her on the bed, then began brushing petals from her with tantalizing care. "I recall reading that Cleopatra once welcomed Mark Antony in a room knee-deep in rose petals, but the book didn't mention whether they also ended up with petals in such interesting places."

With a soft sigh of pleasure, Laura said, "Having you remove them is part of the fun." She proceeded to brush him off wherever she could reach without having to move from her supine position. "Because you were on top, you don't seem to have acquired as many petals as I did, but your knees are pink."

"A small price to pay." He pulled back the covers and tucked her under, then lay down himself. "I'm almost afraid to ask, but exactly what changed your mind about physical intimacy?"

The rose scent was less obvious now that Laura had become accustomed to it, but it still stirred her nostrils with delicate sweetness. She felt as if they were drifting on a magical sea of blossoms. Turning so that her head was on his shoulder and her arm across his waist, she described her discussion with Kamala.

When she was finished, Ian said pensively, "The maharani was right—passion denied can become so overpowering that nothing else matters. I should have realized that myself, but I was too close to be objective. We owe Kamala a considerable debt. Life will be easier for both of us now, as well as far more pleasurable." His arms still around her, he drifted off, his breathing becoming slow and regular.

But for Laura, sleep wouldn't come in spite of her languid satisfaction. Their physical union had been deeply rewarding and promised to get even better in the future. Her fears of being swept away to madness were largely gone, so remote that it was hard to remember how vivid they had been only a few days before. And though she knew her capacity for possessiveness was great, she didn't believe that Ian would give her cause for jealousy. Not for him the casual sex in which her father had so thoughtlessly, and disastrously, indulged.

She would have been blissfully happy, if it hadn't been for Ian's chilling rejection of her declaration of love. Though he had expertly tried to cover that brief, devastating remark, she knew in her bones that it had been profoundly significant.

For a moment, as his words echoed in her mind, she hovered on the verge of tears. Then her face hardened. She must not surrender to the pain of his rejection. This was simply one more problem, one more veil of the past, that must be removed before they could be fully happy. Clearly there was still darkness inside him. It was not the despair he had been suffering from when they first met, nor was it anger. This was more like the stark withdrawal of the week before, when she had revealed the reasons for her fear of passion.

She found it ironic that her fear was gone, but not his bleakness. It was as if he had conjured up a demon to help him and could not now send it away. The thought produced an immediate twinge of guilt, but after examination, Laura dismissed it. Though her actions had certainly contributed to the problem, the roots lay deeper, in Ian himself.

Thinking back, she remembered his occasional oblique references to shame and unworthiness. Perhaps he had always felt that way about himself, but she doubted it. From the way people who had known Ian before his imprisonment spoke of him, he had once had confidence in abundance. What had Srinivasa said about him? That he had a warrior's weakness, which was the inability to accept that his strength had limits. That he tormented himself because of his own perceived failings.

Yes, that fit. It must have been prison that had changed him. She wondered if there had been one specific incident, or whether the cause was simply the cumulative effects of months of degradation, abuse, and helplessness. For someone like Ian, being helpless must be the cruelest torture of all.

But even if her analysis was true, she had no idea what she could do about it. He had walled part of himself off from her, and she guessed that as long as that wall was in place, he would be unable to love her as she loved him.

The thought filled her with aching grief. She loved him with every part of her being, and she wanted, most desperately, for him to love her the same way. Yet what right had she to complain? In his proposal, he had offered friendship and support. She had those things, and now physical delight as well. To demand love was far beyond the limits of their bargain.

For one brief, raging instant, Laura experienced the passion that destroyed her parents' marriage. She wanted to possess her husband's heart as well as his body, and her failure filled her with the same kind of fury that Tatyana had shown when she discovered her husband's betrayal.

The surge of anger left Laura shaken by the power of her own emotions. It was a sharp reminder that her past fears had not been wholly unfounded, for she was indeed her parents' child. Thank heaven she had avoided the worst of their folly. No, thank her stepfather and Ian and Kamala, who had helped her steer through the stony rapids where she might have come to grief.

But still, her surmise that Ian couldn't love her was acutely painful. She had read books where proud ladies renounced the men they loved because the love was not returned. Though Laura had never understood that in the past, now she did in an utterly visceral way. There was anguish in knowing that she and Ian might never be as close as she wanted. She wondered if the imbalance in loving would prove unendurable, if someday frustration would drive her to leave Ian rather than stay and yearn for what she would never have.

As soon as the thought surfaced, she almost laughed aloud at the absurdity. Perhaps a proud English beauty would refuse to stay where she was unloved, but Laura was Russian, with all the stubbornness of her race. The endless sky and harsh climate had tempered her ancestors, giving them vast patience, tenacity, and a refusal to surrender what was theirs.

That fierce determination had been in Pyotr, who had burned Moscow to keep it from enemy hands. It had been in Tatyana, who survived emotional devastation to build a new life for herself and her daughter in a distant land. It had even, in a tragic form, been in her father, who had taken his own life in a savage testimonial to the strength of his love and his regret.

Determination was in Laura's very marrow. Ian was her husband—*hers*—and she would never leave him. To hell with pride. Rather than walk away, she would spend the rest of her life trying to win the depth of love she craved. Perhaps she would fail, but if so, by God, she would fail like a Russian—without surrender.

The next morning, Laura woke when Ian shifted his arm from under her head. She opened her eyes to find him regarding her gravely. She thought she glimpsed darkness there as well, but he veiled it instantly. "Sorry to have woken you," he said, "but my shoulder is numb."

She began massaging the afflicted area, enjoying the feel of his hard muscles. "You do make a lovely pillow, though."

"You're good at that." He smiled lazily. "In fact, you're getting all of my blood stirring."

His expression made it clear what he meant, and for a moment Laura was willing to begin her next lesson in the pursuit of kama. But her reflections of the previous night were still vivid and before she had time to evaluate the wisdom of her question, she asked, "What happened to you in Bokhara that haunts you so, Ian?"

His eye color shifted from its usual warm blue-gray to a cool, steely shade like winter water. Impassively he said, "Between what I've said and Pyotr's journal, you should have a general idea of what the Black Well was like."

"Yes, but the details elude me." Remembering what Srinivasa had said, she continued, "I keep thinking that something happened that you can't forgive yourself for—something that made you feel like such a failure that it's like a river of ice in your soul." Remembering the part of her uncle's journal that had raised the most questions, she said hesitantly, "Perhaps it was during that time when you were taken from the Well for days and beaten so badly?"

Her words struck home, triggering a reaction that he couldn't conceal, though he tried. For a moment Laura thought that he was going get up and walk out. Then his expression solidified into a mask of ironic detachment. "Whatever happened to that demure, well-behaved young female whom I proposed to, whose greatest goal was to be a ladylike nonentity?"

"She married a man who encouraged her to give her Russian nature free rein," Laura said, unrepentant.

"You took my advice with a vengeance," he said dryly.

"So I did, and I find that I'm much better at being emotional than I ever was at being stoic." She propped the pillows behind her and sat up against them. "I'm not asking from idle curiosity, *doushenka*. One by one, I've admitted my dark secrets, and the results have been all to the good. But though I know you far better than I did, I feel as if I am still missing some vital key to what made you what you are. If you can bear to talk about it, perhaps some of the darkness might dissipate."

He pushed up the pillows as she had and leaned against them. Then he lifted his eyepatch from where he had dropped it on the bedside table the night before. Laura suspected it was no accident that he was putting the eyepatch on again; it was like watching a knight don armor.

"What happened was in some ways so trivial that it hardly seems worth mentioning," he said slowly. "And speaking of it isn't likely to help. Some things can't be mended after they're broken, Larishka."

"Perhaps, but how can you be sure if this is one of them?"

He folded his hands behind his head and stared at the opposite wall. Laura began to think that she shouldn't have raised the subject, at least not when they had just reached a new level of understanding.

She had given up expecting an answer when he said, "Bokhara is considered a holy city, and there's a strong vein of religious fanaticism there. Several times I was told that if I would turn Muslim, I would be released and given a position in the amir's army." Ian's sardonic gaze went to Laura. "The offer usually included a plump, rosy wife or two. Don't know how I managed to resist. Pure Scots bloody-mindedness, I suppose.

"The first few times, the subject was dropped after I declined, but on this particular occasion, they decided not to take no for an answer. When I again refused to convert, three guards began beating me under the direction of one of the Bokharan ministers, a weasly little fellow called Rahmin who was the amir's chief hatchet man. I kept saying no, and they kept beating."

He pulled his hands from behind his head and laid them on the counterpane, his fingers moving restlessly. "I was rather flattered that they thought three guards were needed—with my hands tied behind my back I really wasn't much of a challenge. My right eye was destroyed, my left damaged to the point that I could barely see at all, some ribs were cracked. They took special pleasure in kicking me in the genitals. That's why it was easy to believe later that the damage was permanent."

Ian's flat delivery was harrowing. Laura felt tears stinging her eyes, but when he glanced over and said, "Do you really want to hear more?" she nodded for him to proceed.

"I knew that I was going to die. Not thought, *knew*. The pain was so great that mostly I hoped that they would hurry up and finish the job. I knew that the end was near when they dragged me outside—I couldn't walk—to a patch of land be-

tween the royal palace and the city jail. Rahmin gave me a
shovel and told me to dig my own grave. The sadistic little
bastard was having a wonderful time. The guards had to do
the digging since by then I wasn't good for much. When there
was a decent-sized hole, they asked me once more if I would
reconsider and join the brotherhood of the faithful.''

Ian still spoke in a voice of unnatural calm, but his nails
were digging into the counterpane. "As you can imagine,
my enthusiasm for becoming a Bokharan was low at this
point, so I said no, adding a couple of juvenile insults in-
volving the probability that their mothers had mated with
wild hogs. Rahmin shoved me into the grave and I thought,
'Finally it's over. I haven't disgraced myself, and soon I'll
know whose ideas about heaven and hell are the most accurate.' I was ready to die. Damned eager, in fact.''

He stopped speaking, his chest rising and falling rapidly.
Laura bit her lip so hard that the metallic taste of blood was
in her mouth. Then she laid her hand over his. He caught it,
squeezing her fingers so tightly that they hurt, though he
seemed unaware of the gesture. "One of the guards had a
jezzail, one of those long-barreled Asiatic rifles. He raised it,
held it about six inches from my head, and cocked the hammer. I was glad—it would be quicker and a little neater than
being hacked up by swords, which I assumed was the alter-
native.

"But Rahmin had a better idea. He told the guard not to
shoot. Instead, at his order . . .'' Ian stopped again, the
pulse in his throat beating like a triphammer. "The guard
used the jezzail to club me into the hole. Then they . . .
they began to bury me alive. The soil was loose and sandy,
easy to shove in. That's when I broke.''

He swallowed convulsively. "I've been afraid many times,
but this was beyond fear—it was panic so profound that it
squeezed out everything else. There was no room for pain
or pride or anger—only terror. Not because I was going to
die, but because of how it would happen. The thought of
being buried alive—of suffocating under the earth, of feeling
the weight and the blackness crushing down, but still being
alive. . . . ''

He stopped speaking for a long time, and when he resumed, his voice was once more utterly flat. "I was completely shattered. Ian Cameron died in that moment. The
pity of it is that his body wasn't killed at the same time.''

Chilled by his inhuman detachment, Laura said softly, "But you didn't die."

"No, I didn't," he agreed. "Which is how I learned that some prices are too high. I screamed, I wept, I begged, I groveled. I said that I'd do anything they wanted. If they had brought out Pyotr and told me to shoot him, I would have. Instead, they simply repeated the request that I convert. And this time I agreed. It's very easy. All one has to do is say the *Kulna,* the Muslim profession of faith: 'There is no God but God, and Mohammed is His Prophet.' So I did."

His grip on Laura's hand was so tight that her fingers were numb, but she didn't pull away. "If you converted, how did you end up back in the Well so soon?"

He shrugged. "I didn't even have the courage of my cowardice. As soon as I said the Kulna, I was taken into the palace and a doctor was sent for. I was cleaned up, fed, and treated better than I had been in a year, though I was in so much pain that I hardly noticed even when they circumcised me. I spent three days wallowing in self-loathing that was as bad as the fear of being buried alive—so bad that I knew that only death could wipe out my failure.

"Then Rahmin called and said that the amir was looking forward to putting me in charge of his artillery. I knew I could never do that, so I said that it would be a cold day in hell before I would work for the amir—that I recanted my conversion and they would have to finish killing me. Rahmin was so furious that I thought he would order me to be cut down on the spot, for Muslims hate a heretic or lapsed convert far more than they do infidels. But he managed to control himself. I assumed that he would revert to his original plan and have me buried alive, since he'd seen how I reacted to the prospect of that.

"It was a surprise when they dumped me back in the Black Well. Probably the amir needed time to decide the most effective way of finishing me off. Ultimately they decided on a public execution." There was a long lapse before Ian added the final, anguished sentence. "Which is how a couple of months later Pyotr Andreyovich had the privilege of dying for my sins."

Though she doubted that any words of hers would reduce his guilt for that death, Laura said, "Pyotr was already dying, and the chance that you would be spared gave his death meaning."

"Perhaps, but his courage doesn't diminish my cowardice, or my culpability," Ian said, his voice dead. "Though I had never been a very deep thinker, I did believe that when the time came I would be able to die like a man. Not necessarily unafraid, but at least with honor. But I couldn't do it. The one, rather simple thing that I had to do in order to be the man I thought I was—and I couldn't do it."

On one level Laura could almost understand, but at the same time, the way he was torturing himself made her want to shake him. "So now you can't forgive yourself because pain and horror briefly overcame you—even though within a few days, you were willing to face the same death that had terrified you before? I have trouble believing that God will blame you for such a lapse."

He let go of her hand and rolled from the bed, then walked across the room. In the early morning sun, the wilted rose petals were turning brown around the edges.

He halted by the window, rubbing his temple as he stared out blindly. "I told you it sounded trivial. Admittedly it's hard to imagine that a God powerful enough to create the universe is very interested in my lapses—He's probably too busy keeping track of all the sparrows that fall. But while it might not matter to God, it matters to me."

He drummed his fingers on the windowsill. "I never paid much attention to religion—it was simply there, a duty to be performed when necessary and avoided when possible. But I denied the faith of my fathers as well as betraying myself, and by doing so, I destroyed a vital part of my spirit. Now the broken pieces won't go back together." His voice cracked, and he drew a long, shuddering breath. "Pyotr died in my place. My sister and her husband risked their lives to save mine. So much effort on behalf of a man who should have died. Who did die, but didn't get the details quite right."

What had Srinivasa said? *He torments himself because of his own perceived failings, not seeing them as necessary steps on the path.* Unable to bear Ian's grief, Laura slipped from the bed and went over to join him by the window. "It's true that after all you've endured, you can't go back to being the man you were, but you have the capacity to be better and stronger."

"Have you ever seen a piece of pottery that was better after it broke?" He scooped up a handful of rose petals, then let them trickle through his fingers and drift crookedly to the floor. "Doesn't matter how good a job of patching you do, it will never be the same again."

"A man is not a piece of crockery," she said sharply.

"No," he agreed, not looking at her. "A broken plate is fortunate enough to be thrown out. A broken man is supposed to go on living."

With sudden, searing fear, Laura said, "You will, won't you? Keep on living?"

He turned to face her, his face stark. "Don't worry, Larishka. Since I haven't done myself in by now, I won't in the future. I promised that to David, and I'll extend that promise to you. Duty has kept me alive—duty to those who risked their lives for mine, duty to my family, which has suffered enough on my behalf. And remember, you wanted to hear all this. I'm not complaining, for I'm a lucky man. I have much more now than seemed possible two months ago."

He took her hand and lifted it to his lips, then clasped it to his chest, above his heart. With self-mocking humor, he said, "Since getting out of prison, my life has been one obsession after another. The first was to get back to India, to Georgina, so that everything would be all right. That didn't work, so I latched on to the idea of Falkirk. I was needed there, and it would give me a chance to expiate my sins. And then I met you." His clasp tightened. "The last and best obsession. You're not only a reason to go on living, Laura. You've made it possible to enjoy the process more than I dreamed possible."

Laura had wanted to know what haunted him, yet now that she knew, she had no idea what to say. Or no, perhaps she did. Softly she said, "I don't care if you think you're broken and badly mended. I love you as you are, far better than I could have loved you as you were."

He drew her into his arms then, resting his cheek against her temple. "In Cambay, I told Georgina that she and I would no longer suit because I had looked into the abyss and it had changed me," he said quietly. "She asked if you had also looked into the abyss. I said yes. I was right, wasn't I?"

She nodded, her face pressed against his shoulder.

He stroked her hair with gentle fingers. "I, too, am glad that our lives have come together. I'm sorry, Laura, that I can't give you all that you want from me."

At that, the tears that had been hovering began to flow.

Fiercely she repeated, "I love you as you are, Ian." Then she raised her face and kissed him, hard.

Their bare bodies were pressed so closely that she could feel the first stirrings of response. His hands slipped down to cradle her buttocks and he pulled her against him. Desire went from a spark to a bonfire in moments.

The night before, Laura had deliberately set out to create the most romantic scene she could, using flowers and scent and seductive clothing. This morning there were none of the trappings of romance, and none were needed. They made love in the light, with only themselves and their desire.

Ian swept her to the bed and proved that he already knew the techniques of sensuality. Using hands and breath and tongue, he demonstrated all of his knowledge of what pleased her, and then went beyond. When he kissed her intimately, she froze at first. The *Kama Sutra* had described this in cool, bland words that did nothing to convey the stunning sensations. When she was incoherent with desire, he entered her. Her sense of completion was magnified now that she better understood what a miracle it was that he was whole, and that he was hers.

She crushed his moisture-filmed body to hers, and very soon she reached the level of shattering exaltation that she was coming to recognize. The climax started where they joined, then spread through her in scorching waves, filling her belly and breasts and limbs. His culmination echoed hers, passion resonating back and forth between them so that she could scarcely tell her body from his as he spent himself inside her.

When it was done, they lay limp and quiescent in each other's arms. This time Ian didn't withdraw when Laura said that she loved him.

Perhaps he would never be fully at peace with himself again, though she was unwilling to accept that as the final truth. But now that the two of them knew everything worth knowing about each other, the result was a new level of intimacy.

If it wasn't love, it was the next best thing.

Chapter 29

❦ ❦ ❦

THEY ATE BREAKFAST late that morning. Ian enjoyed watching Laura; she had the contented expression of a purring cat. He envied her ability to put the past behind her. Having decided to accept physical passion into her life, she now seemed entirely comfortable with her decision. Not that he was complaining, since he was the prime beneficiary of her change of mind. With her tawny hair loose over her shoulders and her natural sensuality no longer suppressed, she was a sight to gladden any man's heart. Among other things.

He was content merely to look, for their early morning discussion and lovemaking had left him mentally and physically drained. Describing his unforgivable cowardice had been even harder than revealing his impotence.

Still, though his opinion of his behavior had not miraculously improved, he did feel unexpected relief at having told his wife the worst. Subconsciously he had expected a stronger reaction from her: disgust or shock, or perhaps anger that her uncle had died in such an unworthy cause. But once again, she didn't look back. Pyotr was dead and would have died anyhow, and Laura clearly wasn't going to tie herself into knots worrying about what-might-have-beens.

Pity would not have surprised him, though he would have hated it, but he was glad that her response had been empathy. Pity was offered by those who were above the fray, and perhaps just a little contemptuous of the sufferer's weakness. Empathy was for equals who had both looked into the abyss and survived.

Yes, he was a fortunate man. His bitter regret over his self-betrayal had not vanished, but he had lived with it so far, and he would continue to live with it. In the meantime,

devoting himself to making Laura happy was an endeavor
that was almost as rewarding for him as it was for her.

Since neither of them had any special plans for the day,
Ian was about to suggest that they ride into the city of Manpur. Before he could, a messenger from the maharajah entered with an urgent summons for Falkirk Sahib. Ian
frowned. "I wonder if something has happened." He got
to his feet. "Well, only one way to find out."

He gave Laura a quick kiss, then followed the messenger
outside and into an unfamiliar section of the gardens. The
barking of hyenas showed that the royal menagerie was
ahead.

Confident and regal, Rajiv Singh stood on a low bluff
overlooking a rhinoceros wallow, a marshy area adjacent to
a stream. Happily ensconced in the wallow were two of the
single-horned Indian rhinos. As Ian approached, the maharajah turned. Without preamble, he said, "I just received
a dispatch which will interest you, though it's not news
you'll welcome. It will be simplest if you read it yourself."

The information in the lengthy dispatch was staggering.
Ian read it once, then again, his blood congealing. Without
any real hope, he said, "Is your source reliable? It's hard
to believe that the whole British Army in Afghanistan
—almost five thousand trained soldiers—has been destroyed
except for one single man."

"My informant is very reliable." A hint of contempt entered Rajiv Singh's voice. "The details speak for themselves. Your British commander, General Elphinstone, was
utterly incompetent and made mistakes that would shame a
schoolboy. Once your forces left Kabul to retreat to Jalal-
abad, their fate was sealed. You know what that countryside
is like."

Ian stared blindly at the dispatch and tried to control his
expression. Though the message was couched in flat, un-
emotional language, his mind supplied vivid details of the
carnage that had taken place. The withdrawing troops, some
British, more of them native, would have been accompanied
by thousands of camp followers. Many were women and
children, and the column would have moved with hideous
slowness. It was full winter on the high plateau of Afghanistan, and bitter winds and snow would have lashed at the
struggling multitude.

The Afghans were some of the finest riders and marksmen in the world. They would have harried the column every step of the way, darting in to slash and kill, then racing away before the British troops could retaliate. Ian had traveled through those mountains and knew exactly how treacherous they were. Once the demoralized column reached the mountain passes, they were doomed. The Afghans would have held the heights, and the soldiers and camp followers below would have been easy prey.

According to the dispatch, a single officer, a surgeon called Brydon, had reached the British fort at Jallalabad to tell of the massacre. Ian glanced at the date and saw that the sole survivor had stumbled into sanctuary only two days before. The maharajah's source was excellent; Ian probably had the dubious privilege of being the first Briton in India to hear the news.

"I'm sorry, Falkirk," Rajiv Singh said. "Did you have friends among the Kabul garrison?" Though the sympathy was real, the maharajah had an air of suppressed excitement about him.

Tersely, trying to keep the pain from his voice, Ian said, "Yes, I had friends there. I wish to God that one of them had had the sense to shoot Elphinstone. This never should have happened. Never!"

"Though only one man reached Jallalabad, it's likely that other survivors will eventually turn up," the Rajput said. "Some of the Indian soldiers will have gone to ground among the hill people, and the Afghans might have taken prisoners."

"I hope so. But a few more survivors won't alter the fact that this is one of the greatest disasters ever to befall a British army, and it's one that shouldn't have happened." Ian's lips twisted bitterly. "Perhaps this is a judgment on my countrymen for their arrogance. It was the height of stupidity to remove a capable ruler like Dost Mohammad from the throne simply because he had received Russians at his court. I see that it was his son Akbar who led the forces that drove the British out. There's justice in that."

"You're admirably objective about your nation's failings." The Rajput looked down at the rhinos. One heaved itself from the wallow, then began scratching against a tree trunk with a force that made the tree quiver. "The British went into Afghanistan like that rhino, heavy and stupid. They were able to shake the country briefly, but they forgot that even a rhinoceros can be brought down by an angry tiger.''

Ian handed the dispatch back to the other man. ''You don't regret this, do you?''

''It's a pity when brave men die because of inept leadership, but apart from that, I'm not sorry.'' The Rajput began walking along the path with a gesture for Ian to accompany him. ''I have been an ally to the British because it is good policy, and there are individuals such as yourself and your lovely wife whom I like and respect. But I do not love the conquerors of my country, nor do I weep when they reap the rewards of their arrogance.''

Obviously the time had come for honesty. They walked in silence for several minutes. Abruptly the maharajah said, ''There is talk that in the future, the Sirkar will annex any independent state whose ruler dies without leaving an heir of his body.'' Rajiv Singh gave his companion a fierce glance. ''I have no such heir. If I adopt one, according to the custom of my people, will the Sirkar take Dharjistan from him when I die? And if that happens, is that your British justice?''

Ian was rocked by the other man's intensity. ''I didn't know that such a policy is being considered.'' He grimaced. ''But if it is enacted, I would not call that justice.''

''Nor would I.''

They rounded a bend and came upon a huge enclosure containing several white tigers. The area included trees, grass, and a waterhole. A ditch surrounded it, with a high, pointed fence on the outside edge to keep the beasts from escaping. Ian had heard of white tigers, but never seen any. They were magnificent and a little unreal, like powerful ghosts of their golden cousins. Wanting to ease the tension, he remarked, ''Splendid creatures. They appear comfortable with their lot in life.''

''But they would rather be free,'' Rajiv Singh retorted. ''Just as India would. Someday India *will* be free, not held in thrall by European invaders with superior guns.''

''Undoubtedly that will happen, but not in our lifetimes.''

''Don't be too sure of that, Falkirk. Who would have thought the British could be pushed out of Afghanistan as they have been?''

Warning signals went off in Ian's brain. The maharajah

was not talking in the abstract, but like a man with something very specific in mind. "The situations are very different," Ian said in a deliberately neutral tone. "To most Indians, one set of foreign rulers is much like another. The British are no more alien than the Mughals were when they came. Men serve the Sirkar with pride. The Company army has more volunteers than it can accept. But in Afghanistan, the British presence was resented right from the start. It's not surprising that they rebelled."

Rajiv Singh's head swung around and he said in a low, dangerous voice, "If the Sirkar isn't gone from India in my lifetime, Falkirk, I will come back again and again until it is. I swear that I shall be one of the men who helps put an end to it." His tone lightened. "That's how reincarnation works, you know. We must keep trying until we get it right."

"I hope Hindu beliefs are correct," Ian said with wry humor. "There are a number of things I don't think I'm going to get right in this lifetime."

The atmosphere eased, and when one of the tigers stood up they both turned to look at it. The beast stretched its powerful body and yawned, showing an enormous mouth with amazingly long teeth. Then it strolled lazily across the grass to the water hole and went for a swim, as peaceful as a house cat.

"That particular tiger killed at least thirteen villagers before it was captured and brought here," the Rajput said thoughtfully. "Given how the situation has changed, no doubt it is fortunate that you refused my offer and are leaving India. Like that tiger, you might prove more dangerous than you look."

The implications of that were distinctly unsettling. Ian wished he knew what the maharajah had in mind; certainly it was nothing that would benefit the Sirkar. Wanting to keep the conversation light, Ian said, "Like the tiger, I would rather lie in the sun with my mate than fight."

Perhaps thinking that he had said enough about political matters, Rajiv Singh began walking again. "The next enclosure contains some very rare Chinese bears called pandas, which will eat nothing but bamboo shoots. I had hoped they would breed, but they seem reluctant."

Ian made a humorous comment and they continued on. But as they did, his thoughts returned again and again to the question of what was on the maharajah's clever, Sirkar-hating mind.

After Ian left to see Rajiv Singh, Laura wrote a note to Kamala to say that the effort to achieve a more intimate relationship with her husband had been smashingly success-ful. Then, after a longing glance at her copy of the *Kama Sutra,* which the maharani had said she could keep, Laura returned to her uncle's papers. Surveying the material had been fascinating and she looked forward to the time when she could translate it in detail. However, she had found nothing relating to the work he had done in India. As Ian had said, perhaps there was nothing to be found. Neverthe-less, Laura dutifully kept looking.

It was almost an accident that she found the paper at all. Pyotr's Indian journal had been the first item she had skimmed, but it contained only innocent travelogue, with no information about his secret work. Hoping that she would find something she had missed before, she decided to go through it more carefully.

A quarter of the way through she came to a dog-eared paper that had been folded and used as a bookmark. She was setting it aside when she noticed faint traces of ink that showed through from writing on the inside. More from a desire for thoroughness than hope of finding anything, she opened it.

Eureka. If she hadn't had the experience of reading Pyotr's cramped, abbreviated prison account, she might not have been able to decipher the cryptic notes which he had prob-ably scrawled to himself when he was working out his ideas. Perhaps he had intended to destroy the paper, then had ab-sentmindedly tucked it into his travel journal. Whatever the reason, as she read, her lips tightened. In her hands she held the outline of her uncle's plan to drive the British from India.

After they finished viewing the royal menagerie, Rajiv Singh said, "I will not have time to see you again before you leave, Falkirk, so I will say good-bye now. I hope you and your lady have a safe journey home." As a mark of favor, he offered his hand, as a European would.

Ian shook it firmly, then returned the Hindu "Namaste,"

which meant farewell as well as greeting. "I'm sure we will. Many thanks for your hospitality."

Then the two men separated, the maharajah to his audience chamber and Ian to his rooms. To the end, there had been that intriguing mixture of affinity and challenge that made them not quite friends, though not yet enemies.

As he made his way through the labyrinthine palace, Ian's thoughts obsessively returned to the massacre in Afghanistan. He could not stop himself from trying to total up the number of men he knew who must have died during the retreat. At one point, the road from Kabul to Jallalabad led through a gorge that was less than twenty feet wide. With snipers above, it would have become a slaughterhouse. How many had died? How many women and children had been taken into slavery? His stomach knotted with misery and irrational guilt that he had been safe and comfortable while friends were dying only a few hundred miles away.

Ian wanted nothing more than to get back to Laura and her warm understanding. Yet as soon as he stepped into their drawing room and she looked up, he knew something had happened.

"I found it, Ian," she said in a hushed voice, speaking in English. "And it's worse—much worse—than we suspected."

He caught his breath. "Have you written out a translation?"

She shook her head. "I thought it better not to write it in a language that someone here might understand."

"Good thinking." Raising his voice, he said, "Shall we adjourn to the bedroom? After two hours away, I find that I'm missing you fearfully."

She smiled, but her eyes were still grave. They went into her bedroom, which maids had cleaned that morning. There was not a single rose petal left, though the scent lingered wistfully.

Ian sat on the sofa and pulled his wife down beside him. "Incidentally, I really have missed you." He kissed her, and duty was almost forgotten. She was so warm, so soft, so giving. He pulled away with great reluctance. Keeping one arm around her shoulders, he said, "What have you found?"

She opened a paper covered with chaotic Russian scribbles. "Essentially Pyotr was organizing a coalition of forces that would attack the Sirkar when conditions were ripe, which he defined as a combination of two things. First, it would have to be after Ranjit Singh died, because he held the Punjab together and was our best ally in the north. Second, the Sirkar would have to be weakened by something such as fighting in eastern or southern India, or a European war that would require troops to be withdrawn from India.''

Ian sucked his breath in. "The first condition was met when Ranjit Singh died two years ago, and the second happened two days ago.'' When Laura glanced at him inquiringly, he said, "I'll explain when you've finished. Continue.''

"Pyotr spent months talking to chieftains in the Punjab and Afghanistan,'' she said. "He found many who would be happy to join in a *jihad,* a holy war, to push the British out. He also talked to princes in some of the central Indian states who would rise if there were a chance that the Sirkar could be overthrown.''

Ian frowned. "If all those groups would fight together, they would be a formidable force.''

"Exactly what Pyotr thought,'' she agreed. "And the key to the plan is Rajiv Singh—a natural leader, an experienced general who has expanded his own domains considerably, and a prince who resents British rule. He is the one man who might be able to hold the rebel forces together.''

"And in doing so, he would light a fire that would burn across India.'' Ian gazed sightlessly at the wall as the pieces fell into place. "This is what Pyotr tried to explain before he was executed. His plan was to create a situation where the right spark would set off a whole series of disturbances. The Sirkar could handle one or two, but not outbreaks on all sides.''

"It gets worse,'' Laura said tersely. "He had some diabolical ideas for arousing people against the British, including ways to persuade our native troops to mutiny.''

Shocked, Ian said, "How the devil could that be done?''

"Rumor warfare, I suppose you'd call it.'' Laura consulted the list. "I don't quite understand this, but he said there was talk that a new rifle would soon be issued to the army. It would use a paper cartridge that contains both powder and a ball?''

"The cartridge is bitten to release the powder,'' Ian explained. "Then the powder is poured into the barrel and the ball rammed in on top of it."

Her eyes widened. "Now I understand. Pyotr said that the cartridge is covered with grease. His idea was to spread a rumor that the coating contained both beef and pig fat."

"Damnation!" More quietly, Ian said, "So when a soldier bit the cartridge, he would be defiled—by the beef fat if he was Hindu, the pig fat if he was Muslim."

"Exactly." She scowled. "And he planted the idea with both Hindu and Muslim holy men that if such a gun was issued, it would be a deliberate attempt by the British to break caste so that soldiers could then be converted to Christianity."

Ian frowned. "Twenty years ago a rumor like that wouldn't have done much damage, but the number of missionaries and zealous Christian administrators is increasing all the time. Many of them would like to abandon the policy of religious tolerance and try to turn this into a Christian nation."

"That will never happen," Laura said flatly. "Hinduism is too much a part of the fabric of Indian life and culture."

"You and I know that, as does any European in India who pays attention to the society around him, but there are enough zealots to make Pyotr's rumors devastating. Is there anything else?"

She looked at the notes again. "Apparently Pyotr heard that British officials are considering a law that a princely state could not pass to an adopted son, only an heir of the body. If there isn't one, the Sirkar will annex the state. Pyotr mentioned the possibility to every native prince he met."

"So that's where Rajiv Singh got the idea. Just today he told me that such a policy is in the wind. Fear that Dharjistan will be annexed increases his resentment of the Sirkar. Pyotr did his work well." Ian shook his head ruefully. "I wish your uncle hadn't been so damned clever. Is there anything else?"

"I'm afraid so," Laura said. "In Afghanistan, he learned of a minor pass through the mountains near the Khyber Pass. It's very narrow, scarcely more than a goat track, so it's used only by local Pathan tribesmen. However, because the pass is so little known, it's not guarded like the Khyber. Pyotr speculated that when the time came, the Afghans could invade through that pass and be in India before the British knew they were coming.''

"Bloody, bloody hell," Ian swore. "New rifles and cartridges haven't been issued, but the other conditions have been met. If Rajiv Singh wants to strike at the Sirkar, now is the perfect time.'' Briefly he outlined the news from Afghanistan that he had learned that morning. "And there was something about his mood this morning that makes me think he is ready to move.''

Laura's face paled when she heard the news. "So you think the Afghans might follow up their victory by coming down onto the plains and joining Pyotr's jihad?''

"I think it's very likely—they'll never have a better chance.'' Ian analyzed the plan, looking for the weak link that might head off the enterprise before it could begin. "Is there any hint of where that mysterious pass might be?''

"There's a rough set of directions that could probably be followed by someone actually in the mountains. And a name—Shpola. Does that mean anything to you?''

"There's a village by that name between the Khyber Pass and Jallalabad, so one end of Pyotr's pass is probably near there," he said slowly. "I'll ask Zafir if he's heard of it.''

She shivered. "And the time is ripe. The Afghans victorious and angry. Turbulence in the Punjab, so the leaders there might be happy to turn the attention of the army outward.''

"And Rajiv Singh ready, willing, and able to serve as the spearhead,'' Ian finished. "The slaughter of a British army has proved that the Sirkar isn't impregnable, and that becomes another important factor. In the East, there's a belief in *iqbal*. If that belief falters, the jackals will close in.''

"What exactly is iqbal?''

"Preordained good fortune. One's luck, one's fate,'' he explained. "If it looks like the British star is faltering, everyone who has ever had a grievance—every landlord who was ever stopped from squeezing murderous rents, every prince who has ever lost power, every man who has ever suffered from the Sirkar's greed, or felt that his religion was being threatened—they'll join together in a hunting pack that could slaughter every European in India.''

Laura's face went white. "You think it could come to that?''

"I'm afraid so. There are only a few thousand Europeans

compared to tens of millions of Indians. We survive here only because our rule is acceptable to most of the people we govern. But that could change, especially if someone as clever as Rajiv Singh acts on the plan that Pyotr developed.'' Thinking hard, Ian ran his hand through his hair. ''Was your uncle only interested in getting rid of the British? I would have thought that his ultimate goal would be Russian domination.''

''I'm sure it was,'' she answered. ''There's a hint that he had a double game in mind—persuade Rajiv Singh to lead a rebellion and hope that the coalition fell apart after victory. Then the Russians could move in.''

''That could easily happen, given the tension that exists among Hindus, Muslims, and Sikhs,'' Ian said. ''Without a common enemy to fight, the leaders could end up at each other's throats after destroying the Sirkar. I think your uncle underestimated Rajiv Singh's ability to hold the different groups together, but I would rather not find out for sure.''

Laura refolded her uncle's notes and smoothed the creases with her thumbnail. ''I see why Pyotr wrote in his prison journal that he had come to regret his cleverness at devising this scheme. Tens of thousands of people will die if the Afghans invade and the other states rise up to join them. How could a kindly man like my uncle think this up in the first place?''

''The simple answer is that it was his job to protect and extend Russian influence.'' Ian sighed. ''But the true reason is that it's dangerously easy for a man to get caught up in the excitement of the work. As you know, the British call this secret warfare the Great Game. Pyotr said the Russian term is 'the tournament of shadows.' In both cases, the metaphor is sport. Be the quickest, the cleverest, the most dangerous, and win the game.''

''And God only knows how many innocent people might die as a result,'' she said bitterly, thinking of all of the Indian villagers she had known who wanted only to be left in peace to live their lives. ''What do we do now, Ian?''

''That's simple,'' he said. ''We obey Pyotr's last wish, and make sure that this is one fire that is never kindled.''

Chapter 30

❦ ❦ ❦

WHEN MEERA WENT to her mistress that morning, there had been no need to ask if the attempt to establish a more intimate relationship with her husband had been successful; one look at the memsahib's glowing face gave her the answer. After arranging for the rose petals to be removed and delivering a note from the memsahib to the maharani, Meera was at liberty, so she decided to walk a bit. It was pure coincidence that she chose to do so near the section of the palace where male servants were quartered.

She was a little piqued that Zafir, the great scoundrel, had not yet sought her out after returning to Manpur. Considering how much thought she had put into the question of whether or not to accept his proposal, it was disagreeable to think that the Pathan might not be terribly interested in her answer.

She had prepared a number of sharp comments for use in the event that she happened to see him. Yet when their paths did cross, the dazzling smile he gave her drove all criticism from her mind. "Little dove, you are a sight for weary eyes."

Rallying, she retorted, "Your eyes don't look weary. You look like a bright-eyed fox that is eyeing a fowl for dinner."

"Exactly! The fowl in this case being a dove." He looked hopeful. "Shall I have you for dinner?"

Heat rose in Meera's face. She had certainly opened herself up for that. "I shall be nobody's dinner. I was going for a walk since the memsahib will not need me for several hours."

"Then I shall accompany you and guard against foxes."

Which of course was exactly what Meera had hoped for. It wasn't until they were well away from the palace that

Zafir said, "Have you considered what I asked you, Meera?"

She glanced up, surprised. "I think that is the first time you have ever used my name."

"Rather than Meera or even little dove," he said gravely, "I would prefer to call you wife."

Mesmerized by the intensity of feeling that she saw in his clear gray eyes, Meera said, "Then I shall call you husband."

Zafir whooped. Catching her around the waist, he lifted her into the air and swung her around three times. By the time a laughing Meera was returned to the ground, she was convinced that her answer did matter to him.

"A pity I don't have my rifle," he said regretfully. "A proper Pathan celebrates by shooting into the air, but I shall do the happy fire another time. Perhaps when we are wed."

Trying without success to look severe, she straightened the scarf that covered her hair. "Speaking of wedding, I think we should wait until Falkirk Sahib and my lady reach Bombay."

He pulled her close and kissed her. "Must we wait so long?"

"Yes," she said rather breathlessly after surfacing from his kiss. "The sahib and memsahib have done much for me. To leave her now would be ungrateful."

He kissed her again and this time his hand covered her breast. "We can wait for the wedding, but do we have to *wait?*"

Catching his meaning, she cuffed his wandering hand. "Yes, we do, you wicked creature. Not until we're married."

Undisturbed by her refusal, he laughed and picked a crimson flower from a bed by the path. "A prudent woman—exactly what a man wants in his wife." He tucked the blossom over her ear.

"You are always so good-natured," she said curiously. "Isn't there anything I could say or do that would give you offense?"

He grinned. "I would have been offended if you had refused me. Come, let us walk in the royal section of the gardens."

Meera had not been paying attention to where they were walking, but now she saw how close they were to the restricted area. "This is only for the royal family and their chief courtiers. Won't we get in trouble if we're found here?"

"We are visitors in Dharjistan and could plead ignorance. At most, we would be scolded and told to leave the garden," the Pathan said carelessly. "The maharajah would not have the servants of his guests executed for such a trivial reason."

Though Meera was not entirely comforted by this speech, she couldn't resist the idea of seeing the private gardens. She glanced around uneasily as they walked, but they saw no one else. Soon they were deep in the royal preserve.

"Ah, that must be the famous banyan tree," Zafir said, gesturing ahead.

Banyan were the most distinctive trees in India, for the aerial roots that dropped from the branches turned into additional trunks where they touched the soil. Those in turn shot off more branches and aerial roots. The result was as complicated as a wooden spider's web, with trunks and roots going in all directions. The area under a banyan was often used as an open bazaar, and a large one could shelter hundreds of people.

"What's famous about this one?" Meera asked after careful study. "It looks like any other banyan to me."

"They say the maharajah had a throne built into the tree, and that he sometimes receives visitors here," the Pathan explained. He began circling around the massive perimeter of the banyan, Meera following nervously.

On the far side they found the throne, which had been carved from a root, then decorated into a seat fit for a king. Zafir promptly sat on it. "Not bad," he said. "Come, give me a kiss so we can tell our grandchildren that you were fancied by the man who sat on the throne of Dharjistan."

Part amused, more horrified, Meera hissed, "Idiot! If anyone finds us here, the maharajah might decide to slit your nose or remove your ears."

Grinning, the Pathan pulled her onto his lap. Even as her body melted in response to his embrace, Meera thought with exasperation that men were excited by the most alarming things.

He whispered in her ear, "Better yet, shall we see if we can conceive our first child on a throne?"

"No, you barbarian," she exclaimed, scrambling off his lap. "I want to leave right now!"

With a chuckle, he got to his feet. Then his amusement abruptly evaporated. He cocked his head, listening. "Too late," he said softly. "Someone's coming."

As Meera listened, she also heard the voices of approaching men. Zafir grabbed her around the waist and boosted her into the branches over their heads. A moment later he swung up beside her, then guided her higher yet to a place where the interwoven branches formed a crude platform. As birds squawked angrily at the humans who had invaded the tree, he settled down with his back against a trunk and drew her into his arms.

The branches and dark green leaves would prevent anyone below from seeing them, but as Meera lay still as a mouse in the arms of her beloved, she plotted hideous punishments on him for getting them into this. For one of the men below was the maharajah himself. She recognized Rajiv Singh's voice speaking in the formal Persian used by the court. It was the same language that Mohan had had Meera learn so she could read to him.

Unsubdued, Zafir tugged Meera's scarf off and began nibbling her ear. She caught her breath to prevent herself from gasping out loud. As desire curled through her, she decided that she would definitely murder him some day. But not just yet.

Greatly daring, she slipped a hand through the folds of his clothing and stroked his bare chest, which she had been longing to do. The taut muscles rippled under her touch. Wondering how he would react to being sensually tortured under such conditions, her hand began to move lower.

Suddenly she stopped, shocked by what the men below her were saying. Zafir, who didn't understand court Persian, wanted to continue their game, so his hand moved toward her breast. She grabbed it and shook her head, her face deadly serious, when he looked at her questioningly.

Dislodged by the vehemence of her head shake, the red flower behind her ear tumbled loose with mocking slowness. Zafir made a lightning grab that just missed. The blossom dropped between two branches and continued falling, its progress marked by faint, almost inaudible rustling sounds. Though Meera prayed that the flower would be caught in the tree, it made its way all the way to the ground.

The men below stopped speaking for a moment. Then the maharajah barked a sharp question.

For a heartstopping instant there was silence. Meera was so frightened that she stopped breathing. Though trespassing in the gardens might be a minor crime, eavesdropping on a prince could be lethal. Then a monkey shrieked directly over their heads. It was answered by another. A furious squabble broke out, which sent twigs and leaves tumbling to the ground. Since a monkey might have brought the flower into the banyan, the men, reassured that they were private, resumed their discussion.

Meera listened hard as the maharajah summarized his earlier instructions so there would be no mistake. "Remember to tell the Afghan chiefs that they *must* invade at once, for the Punjabi generals won't move without Afghan support and I haven't enough men to take on the British alone," he said, his voice taut. "I've sent another messenger to Nabil Khan and Tejut Singh in the Punjab to tell them to be ready to move as soon as the Afghans reach the plains. We must act together, or not at all, and we must do it quickly, before British reinforcements arrive from the east. We shall never have such an opportunity again."

"I shall emphasize that they must come at once, Excellency," the other man repeated, "and by the Shpola Pass."

The messenger took his leave and departed with a faint crunching of gravel. Several minutes passed. Then the maharajah said in a low, icy voice, "The ferengis shall not take my Dharjistan into their greedy hands. *They shall not.*"

There was a long silence before Rajiv Singh's receding steps could be heard. Meera and Zafir waited patiently, all playfulness extinguished. Finally the Pathan descended the tree, checking carefully every step of the way. Then he reached up and helped Meera to the ground. "What were they saying, little dove?"

Words tumbling like a torrent, she repeated the conversation as exactly as she could. Zafir's face darkened as he listened. When she was done, he said sharply, "Come, we must tell Falkirk Sahib about this immediately."

His words filled Meera with relief. Falkirk Sahib would know what to do. He had saved her; surely he could save India.

* * *

"How does one go about preventing a war?" Laura asked, her fingers drumming nervously on her knee.

Ian took her hand, his calm flowing into her. "The best way would be to bring a large force of British troops to the frontier so that the rebel forces can't get together. Their weakness is that initially they will be uncoordinated and under a number of different chiefs. Given time, I think Rajiv Singh could overcome that and get the combined armies to unite under his leadership, so we must move quickly. If he wins a victory or two here in the north, uprisings will be triggered all over India."

She shivered. "If that happens, it will be hard to stop."

"Which is why our best hope is to prevent the rebellion from starting. With a large enough British presence in northern India, there's an excellent chance the disaffected groups will give up the thought of challenging the Sirkar."

"So the key is getting the Sirkar to move swiftly, before the news from Afghanistan becomes widely known."

"Exactly." Ian frowned, thinking. "The nearest large British force is at Cambay. That's fortunate, because it's the one place in India where I have the influence to get a quick response. Even more fortunate, the Cambay commander-in-chief, General Rawdon, is an officer who can be counted on to act on his own, without higher authority, in this sort of emergency. He can also move troops faster than any man I know."

" 'Roaring' Rawdon? Even I've heard of him." Laura gave a sigh of relief. "So all that's necessary is to get to Cambay, tell our story, and let the army do the rest."

"Exactly. We'll leave here tomorrow as planned. Once we're out of sight of Manpur, we ride like hell, and within a week there will be Company regiments on the way to the Khyber Pass. And, of course, that Shpola Pass of Pyotr Andreyovich's." Ian gave her a half smile. "Be grateful that the powers that be still haven't adopted the new rifle that Pyotr was talking about. Sometimes official sluggishness is a real blessing. In this case, it means that the Sirkar won't have to worry about the sepoys rebelling because they think their faith is being compromised. All we have to do is make sure that the Afghans, Punjabis, and Dharjistanis can't come together."

"You make it sound so simple." Laura bit her lip. "Ian, what will happen to Rajiv Singh and Kamala?"

He shook his head, his expression grave. "I'm not sure. If the serpent's fangs can be drawn without bloodshed, Rajiv Singh may well be able to keep his throne, though I'm sure the Sirkar will set sharp limits on the size of his army and will use force to ensure that he doesn't exceed them."

"He's a warrior, a prince of the Rajputs," she said sadly. "Do you think he'll sit tamely by and let his fangs be drawn?"

Ian sighed. "I don't know. I hope so, not only for his sake but for Kamala and Dharjistan."

Laura was about to ask another question when they heard footsteps in the drawing room outside. For a second she tensed, wondering if they had been overheard. Then she heard Zafir call, "Major Sahib, are you here?"

There was a note in his voice that she had not heard before. Ian must have recognized it, because he immediately rose and threw open the bedroom door. "In here. What's wrong?"

Zafir stepped into the room, Meera beside him. "We must speak to you, *huzar*." The fact that the Pathan used "huzar," the formal equivalent of the English word "sir," was uncharacteristic and did not bode well. "On a matter of great significance."

"Then speak freely."

"We . . . happened to be in the royal banyan tree."

Ian's brows went up. "What on earth were you doing there? No, never mind, I can guess. Did you overhear something?"

Zafir nodded. "A conversation between the maharajah and an Afghan. They spoke in Persian, which Meera understands. She says they spoke of an invasion of India."

"Bloody hell!" Ian shared a look with Laura, both of them thinking the same thing: disaster was much closer than they realized. "Meera, tell me exactly what you heard."

Laura listened, her stomach tight. The girl's report brought Pyotr's scribbled notes from the realm of theory down to gritty reality. Within a matter of days, the Afghans would be invading, joining with tens of thousands of well-armed Dharjistani and Punjabi troops into a fire that would sear India. How many Europeans would survive such a holocaust? How many peaceful natives would die once the dogs of war were unleashed?

Unlike Laura, Ian was growing progressively calmer as the situation worsened. She had never seen him look so dangerous. After telling Zafir and Meera what he and Laura had learned, he said, "Do you know where the Shpola Pass is?"

The Pathan shook his head. "I have heard the name, but I don't know exactly where it is, only that it lies somewhere in Afridi territory. That is why I have never been there."

Ian thought for a moment, his brows drawn together. "Very well. Tomorrow, we'll leave Manpur. Once we're away from the city, you and the women will ride south. For the sake of safety and speed, leave Laura and Meera with your Uncle Habibur. When you get to Cambay, find my brother and give him the report I'll write tonight, detailing what we've discovered. I'll go up to the frontier and try to find this Shpola Pass. Then, when troops arrive, I can guide them right to it. A pass that small can be closed by a single company of soldiers."

Zafir said, "Very good, huzar." His frivolity was gone and he had become a cold-eyed, deadly warrior.

Ian continued, "When you leave here, go to the city bazaar and buy tribal clothing for me, the ingredients to make skin stain, native harness for my horse. Go to a number of different shops so no suspicions will be aroused. You know the drill."

Before the Pathan could acknowledge the order, Laura said explosively, "No!"

Both men turned toward her, Zafir startled, Ian, who knew her better, looking distinctly wary.

Ignoring the Pathan, Laura fixed her husband with a steely eye. "If you're going to the frontier, Ian, I'm going with you."

Her words dropped into the room like stones. Voice calm but inexorable, Ian said, "That's out of the question."

She glared at him, equally inexorable, and much less calm. "No, it isn't. You're not going without me."

She was about to say more when Ian snapped, "Enough!"

When his gaze went to the Pathan, Laura realized that to quarrel with Ian in front of a subordinate was bad policy. Since her chance of changing his mind was much better in private, she held her tongue as he said to Zafir, "I'll get money for the bazaar so you can be off."

Laura used the next few moments to marshal her arguments. As soon as Ian said that she was to be sent to safety while he went north alone, she had been struck by violent anxiety. Though she refused to think about Srinivasa's nonsense, her own emotional, irrational nature was shouting that her husband would be safer if she stayed with him.

And maybe camels had wings and could fly like eagles. Insane to think that she could make a difference if the hand of fate was on Ian, and insane to even *think* of accompanying her husband to the frontier. So be it; she might be insane, but she was damned well going with him.

Zafir left and Ian turned to her. Seeing her determination, his face became implacable. "I appreciate your loyalty, Laura, but this sort of mission is no place for a woman."

"How dangerous will it be?"

"Not very," he said. "I used to find straight military duty a little boring, so sometimes I got myself seconded to the political service. I've been over the frontier a number of times, and I can pass as a native reasonably well."

"With your coloring?" she said dubiously.

His mouth quirked. "You'd be surprised how convincing I am with my skin dyed and a turban over my hair. My beard even grows out the same red as the henna dye some Muslims use on their beards. More important, I know the languages and customs. But I'm not going to be in any danger, Laura. This is simply a short reconnaissance to locate the Shpola Pass. Then, when British troops arrive, they'll be able to bottle up the Shpola and the Khyber and send reinforcements to the fort at Jallalabad."

"If it's so safe, why can't I go?"

"You'll slow me down. Also, I'll worry about you, which will diminish my effectiveness," he said, beginning to show impatience. "There's no good reason for you to go, and dozens of good reasons not to. Why the devil are you so determined?"

Laura didn't think he would be impressed if she said she hoped to prevent him from being killed. Ignoring the question of why she wanted to go, she said, "I won't slow you down. I've crossed half of India with you, and I can ride as well as most men. Thanks to your foresight I can also shoot, not brilliantly, but well enough to be of help in a tight spot. I speak Persian and several dialects of Urdu. With skin dye and the right clothes, I should be able to pass for a native at least as well as you—my eyes are brown and Oriental, not Highlander blue."

His gaze went over her. "Even loose native clothing isn't

going to make you look like a boy," he said dryly. "And your eyes aren't brown, they're a highly distinctive amber."

"Then I'll wear a *burqa* like the Pathan women do when they leave the compound," she retorted. "You could disguise a water buffalo under one of those."

He shook his head, unmoved. "No, Laura. This isn't subject to discussion. I'm not taking you to the frontier."

Trying a different tack, she suggested, "Wouldn't it make more sense to send Zafir instead of going yourself? That's Pathan country, so he should be able to locate the pass more easily than you. You're also the best person to explain the danger to the authorities in Cambay. Zafir won't be taken as seriously, even though he's carrying a message from you."

"With David's backing, he'll be believed," Ian said. "And I can't send Zafir to look for the Shpola Pass. It's controlled by the Afridi tribe, which has a blood feud with Zafir's tribe, the Mohmands. Asking Zafir to go in alone would be sending him to his death. Besides, I have a better eye for the tactical possibilities than he does."

Appalled, she said, "But won't it be death for you?"

"No, because I'll go dressed as a Punjabi tribesman. Since the Afridis have no feud with me, I won't be shot on sight."

"Then why can't Zafir go dressed like a Punjabi?"

"He would consider going into Afridi territory disguised as an act of cowardice," Ian explained. "He'd much rather be shot."

Men! They didn't have the sense to cross the street without female help. Curbing her exasperation, she said, "Ian, you know the territory and the tribes, you're the best shot I've ever seen, and it's only a little reconnaissance mission. Surely I'll be as safe with you as I would be going south with Zafir. After all, that road also goes through fairly wild country, and with only one man to protect two women, I'd be better off with you."

Amusement showed on his face. "Flattery won't work, Laura. I could be the best shot in the history of mankind, but that won't save you if we're ambushed by fifty bloody-minded bandits. The answer is still no."

She glared at him, furious but undiscouraged. She was sure in her Slavic bones that going with him would make a crucial difference. Then she realized that the trump card was in her hand. "The directions to the Shpola Pass are written in Russian, and I won't translate them for you." She held up the sheet of notes and tried not to sound smug. "If you want to find it, you'll have to take me along."

Exploding with the forcefulness for which redheads are known, Ian roared, "Then I'll find it without you! Hell and damnation, this isn't a game, you idiot female!"

"You're damned right it isn't," she yelled back, as furious as he. "It's life and death, and I'm going with you!"

As he stepped toward her, Laura wondered if she was about to find out how Tatyana felt when her husband hit her. But Ian was not Laura's father. He put his arms around her, tilted her head back, and kissed her. Her wildfire response made her shockingly aware of how thin the line was between fury and passion.

Laura kissed him back, aching with protective tenderness. She wanted to love him, not fight with him. Then, as his hand moved expertly down her body, she realized what he was doing. With a gasp of outrage, she turned her face away from his. "Do you really think you can seduce me into obedience?" she snapped. "That's a double-edged sword, you pigheaded Scot."

She fumbled with his trousers. He was already partially aroused. As she undid the buttons and slipped her hand inside, he went rock-hard, his whole body stiffening.

He began to laugh. No, Ian was not like her father. "You little witch. I knew you were dangerous, but I hadn't realized quite how much so."

Sobering, he lifted her chin and looked into her eyes. "Laura, why are you so hell-bent on going with me? You're not usually an unreasonable woman."

"I'm worried about letting you out of my sight," she said. "I know I'm being ridiculous, but I feel as if nothing too terrible can happen to you as long as I'm there."

He studied her face. "I know what you mean. Part of me—the stupid part—wants to keep you nearby."

Sensing victory, she said persuasively, "If this trip really isn't that dangerous, where's the harm in my going?"

"Anytime one travels into wild country, there's an element of unpredictability. Ninety-nine chances out of hundred, we'd be able to go up there, locate the Shpola Pass, and come back without a problem." He grimaced. "It's the hundredth chance that bothers me."

"Ninety-nine out of a hundred isn't bad. And the hundredth could happen even if I went with Zafir." She was about to say more, but decided it would be more effective to hold her tongue and let Ian analyze the odds on his own.

Finally he sighed. "Very well. This really shouldn't be dangerous, so you can go if it's that important to you." His face hardened. "But there's one condition. You're going to have to promise to follow orders like a subaltern. If something goes wrong, arguing could cost us our lives. Do I make myself clear?"

"Yes, sir," she said with a surge of relief so strong that it weakened her. "You're the commander of this expedition." For a moment she rested her head on his shoulder. With fear out of the way, other emotions began to manifest. She began stroking him mischievously. "Now that we've settled that, can we finish what we started, only with no hidden motives?"

He laughed again, then took her hand and led her over to the bed. "Since you're going to be doing a lot of riding in the next few weeks . . ."—he lay on his back and drew her down on top of him—"you might as well practice."

What followed proved to be as enjoyable as it was educational. Laura decided that it didn't really matter whether she finished reading the *Kama Sutra* or not. She was learning everything she needed to know from her husband.

Later that afternoon, Laura made a farewell call on Kamala. She was worried that knowledge of Rajiv Singh's plot would make it hard for her to act naturally, but the maharani made the visit easy. After dismissing her women, Kamala pulled Laura down to the cushion beside her. "Even if you hadn't sent a note," she smiled, "I would know that you have found your heart's desire."

Blushing, Laura nodded. "The suggestions you and my servant Meera made were wonderful. In particular, the rose petals were an inspiration."

The maharani waved her hand grandly. "What's a garden for, if not to provide pleasure for one's friends?"

Caught between laughter and tears, Laura said, "I'm going to miss you, Kamala."

"And I you." Shyly the maharani added, "Will you write me?"

"Of course," Laura said warmly. "It will be good for me to practice my Persian. And perhaps someday Ian and I will come back for a visit. Every year, the trip becomes swifter." Then she fell silent. A year from now, it was possible that the British would be gone from India. Or Rajiv Singh and even Kamala might be dead, or exiled. The friendship between two women could become just another victim of the cataclysm that was forming.

Not understanding the reason for her guest's sadness, Kamala said, "I, too, weep in my heart. A queen has many subjects but few friends." She gnawed on her lip, then said in a rush of words, "I shouldn't speak of this until I'm absolutely certain, but I must confide in someone, so I will tell you."

Good Lord, did Kamala know of her husband's plan and want to discuss it? Torn between friendship and patriotism, Laura said uncertainly, "If it's a state secret, I shouldn't know it."

Kamala gave her a luminous smile. "It isn't a state secret, it's my heart's desire." Her voice dropped to a whisper. "Laura, I think I am with child. Srinivasa said sometime back that it might happen, but I have been afraid to hope."

It took a moment for Laura to shift mental gars. Then she gasped, "Oh, Kamala, after so many years? That's wonderful!"

"I daren't speak of it yet to anyone, for it would break Rajiv Singh's heart if I'm wrong. There is a young cousin he has been thinking of adopting as his heir, but he has held off, still hoping." The maharani smiled bashfully. "I am an old woman, but not so old that I cannot still give him a son."

"Old—you?" Laura laughed. "You are the embodiment of womanly beauty. Once you have discovered the knack of childbearing, perhaps you shall have more. Does Srinivasa have anything to say about the possibility?"

Kamala's face became grave. "He said—and this is most unusual—that the issue is clouded and could have more than one outcome. In fact, I also asked him to look again at the charts of you and your husband, since you were so concerned." She caught her visitor's hand. "There is a cloud over all of our futures," she said earnestly. "Be careful, Laura."

"And you also, Kamala," Laura said, her voice choked. She rose and gave the maharani a hug, then a deep "Namaste. I will pray for both of us, my friend."

There were tears in her eyes when she left. She hoped to God that the events that were shaping up would not make it impossible for both of them to have their hearts' desires.

Chapter 31

❦ ❦ ❦

MEERA CLICKED HER tongue disapprovingly. "It isn't proper for a memsahib to dress like an Indian boy."

"Let's hope that no one will suspect that a memsahib would even think of such a thing," Laura responded. Having already donned baggy pants and light boots, she layered two enormous shirts over each other and tied them around her waist with a sash. Even with her breasts flattened by a close-fitting undershirt, she was beginning to appreciate Ian's remark that she didn't have the sort of body that was easily disguised as a boy's. Luckily it was late autumn; by the time she added a couple of loose coats to her costume, she would be thoroughly sexless.

Shivering in the chilly air, Laura put on the last coat. They had left the royal palace before dawn that morning and ridden south toward Bombay. Five miles from the city, they had veered off the main road and ridden into this dense thicket, where she and Ian were to change their identities. Meera had helped her apply stain to every visible bit of skin, then had braided her hair and tucked it around her head in a coronet.

Tying the turban proved tricky; it required a knack that she didn't have. A good thing she also had an all-encompassing burqa to wear when passing through towns. It would be more prudent to wear it all the time, but a burqa was a suffocating garment, with only a small square of mesh to see through, so she intended to avoid it whenever possible.

Laura thrust a scabbarded knife in her sash, then slung her rifle over her shoulder. "How do I look, Meera?"

Meera clicked her tongue again, her head shaking back and forth. Laura thought that meant failure until the girl

said, "I would not know you for a ferengi, memsahib, nor
a woman. Here, look at yourself in the mirror."

Laura caught her breath when she saw her image in the
hand mirror. With her slanting eyes and stained skin,
she looked like a genuine Asiatic. The skin dye even had the
effect of making her eyes look darker, more brown than
amber. From what Mongol ancestor had she inherited her
eyes? Probably a Tartar warrior who had casually raped a
Slavic woman. Europe and Asia met in Russia, and in Laura.
For the next fortnight or so, she must draw on that ancestry
and think like an Asiatic.

"Time to see how the men are doing," Laura said. They
made their way through the bushes to the clearing where the
horses were, Laura trying to walk like a man. In the clearing, Zafir and a *badmash,* the local term for a ruffian, were
in the process of changing the saddles and harness from
European to Indian.

Laura blinked, not believing her eyes. Though she knew
the second man had to be Ian, she wouldn't have recognized
him if she had passed him on the street. He had changed
not only his clothing and skin color, but his whole de-
meanor. He no longer carried himself like an officer; in fact,
he didn't even move like a European, though she couldn't
define the difference. He had also discarded his black eyepatch for a cruder version in tan leather that was almost the
same shade as his skin. Even the color of his other eye
seemed different, less blue, closer to the gray tone sometimes found among fair Asiatics.

Ian turned and examined Laura critically. "Not bad," he
decided, "as long as you don't get too close to anyone. You
look rather like a Gharhwali."

"What are Gharhwalis?"

"A tribe from the foothills near Nepal. They have a fair
amount of Mongol blood, but tend to be a little taller and
lighter in build than Ghurkas." He chuckled. "If anyone
questions your appearance, I'll say that Gharhwalis are also
noted for their pretty girlish faces. No one will be the wiser,
since I doubt many Gharhwalis are seen in these parts."

Laura checked her baggage, hoping she wasn't forgetting
something vital. Though she was used to traveling very
lightly by British standards, now their supplies were pared
to the bone. Most of their possessions were going with Zafir, to be left at Habibur's with Meera, while they carried

only basic provisions and ammunition, with nothing to identify them as Europeans.

Then it was time for the two couples to separate. While the men shook hands and exchanged a few last words, Laura hugged Meera and wished her Godspeed, then swung onto her horse. As they cut through the trees to the road, she felt vulnerable, shorn of her identity. Uncannily reading her mind, Ian said, "It's not too late to change your mind, Larishka. If you're having second thoughts, don't let pride stand in the way."

She gave him her best duplicitious smile. "Wouldn't dream of missing this trip, *doushenka*. After a fortnight or so of sleeping rough in the Himalayas, that drafty castle of yours is going to seem as luxurious as Rajiv Singh's palace."

"More spunk than sense," he said in a resigned tone, but the respect in his glance warmed her. She was intensely glad that she had insisted upon coming on this trip. Whatever happened, at least they would face it together.

As Meera cleaned up after breakfast, she gave her placid pony a glance of distaste. Though she had become accustomed to riding, the pace they had set the last few days had been bruising. In one way, she'd be glad to reach Habibur's. But only in one way.

She glanced over at Zafir, who was loading the pack pony. There was an odd kind of intimacy on this hasty journey, for in many ways they were behaving like husband and wife, each taking care of their share of chores, relying on each other. But that was the only intimacy, for Zafir was withdrawn, not the teasing man she had fallen in love with.

She got to her feet and scanned the ground to make sure that nothing had been forgotten. It was a pleasant little campsite, private and protected in a grove of trees well off the road. It was the last privacy they would have. Walking over to Zafir, she said, "We'll be at Habibur's today?"

He nodded. "We should be there not much after noon."

"Will you stay the night?"

He shook his head. "No, little dove. I'd like to, but I can't afford the time. Matters are grave, and a half day might make a critical difference."

She made a wry face. "I knew the situation must be perilous, for you haven't tried to seduce me once since we left Manpur.''

That caught his attention and his abstracted gaze sharpened. ''It would not be honorable to try when you are under my protection. Besides, you have made it clear that you are waiting for our marriage bed.''

She lifted her head, her face stark. ''Then I was sure we would have a marriage bed. But there is danger now. You are a soldier. You might be killed.''

''It's possible,'' he agreed. ''Danger is my job, little dove. If war comes, I must return to my regiment immediately. But if anything happens to me, you will have a place with my uncle for as long as you wish. Or if you choose to return to your own people, my aunt and uncle will help you.''

''It isn't my own people that I want,'' she said vehemently. ''It's you.''

She moved close and laid a hand on his wrist, soft and graceful. ''Perhaps you cannot spare a half day, but surely you can spare an hour?''

He stared at her, realizing that his lovely little dove had something specific in mind. She made it clear exactly what with her next sentence. ''Give me something to remember, beloved,'' she whispered, raising her arms and sliding them around his neck.

He didn't need a second invitation. All the playfulness and teasing of their relationship fell away, leaving only this, the urgent need of a man and woman to be together. And as he kissed her, he knew that this was the ultimate reason men went to war. Not just for glory, or greed, compelling as those things were, but because of this fierce tenderness, the need to protect his home and woman, with his own life if need be.

As he laid her down in the soft grass, he knew that as urgent as his message was, this was equally urgent. Falkirk Sahib would not begrudge a man an hour with his beloved if it might be the only hour they would ever have.

Laura shifted stiffly in her saddle, thinking ruefully that Ian had spoken the truth when he said she'd be doing a lot of riding. This sort was nowhere near as enjoyable as the gallop they had had their last afternoon in the palace.

Though less than a week had passed, Dharjistan seemed like another world.

Ian had also taken Laura at her word that she could ride as well as any man, and he set a hard pace. They crossed the flat, dusty plains of the Punjab without incident. On the occasions when they went through a sizable town, Laura donned the dark, all-encompassing burqa and attracted no notice at all.

Occasionally Ian struck up conversations with villagers or other travelers, expertly extracting information without seeming unduly inquisitive. Word had spread of the British loss in Afghanistan, and it was a frequent subject of discussion. The Punjab had never been under British rule so the natives did not feel directly affected, but most took a certain malicious satisfaction in the downfall of the ferengis.

They were also very curious about how the Sirkar would respond. Laura, who listened but never spoke, could see for herself how critical the situation was. Weakness on the part of the British now could trigger an avalanche of opposition.

After three days of hard riding, they had entered the stony hills. It was the most desolate country Laura had ever seen, so barren that it was hard to see how anyone could live in it. The mountain peaks were covered with snow and everything else seemed to be jumbled rock, with only the most tenacious plants clinging to a precarious existence. No wonder the Pathans needed banditry to survive; for centuries, their chief source of income had been charging travelers for the right to pass unmolested.

Following the sparse clues in Pyotr's notes, Ian and Laura had swung south from the main route, which ran through the Khyber Pass. Now they had run out of information and were on their own. Though they must be within a dozen miles of the eastern end of the Shpola Pass, it would take months or years for them to find it without help. They must find someone who could guide them to it.

The trick was to find a guide before the location of the pass was revealed by an avalanche of Afghans.

Zafir could hardly believe his eyes when the dusky evening light revealed an encampment of Company cavalry just off the road. He squinted at the banners snapping in the dry Punjabi wind. Allah be praised, it was even a regiment headquartered at Cambay, the 39th Native Lancers. A pity Zafir had no personal friends in the 39th because the regiment had only recently been posted to Cambay. Still, it should be easy to establish his identity, and finding a cavalry regiment already on the march to the northwest meant that several priceless days had been saved.

Zafir turned into the camp. When guards stopped him, he identified himself as a sepoy of the 46th Native Infantry and asked to be taken to the commanding officer of the regiment. The guard in charge sneered, "You think we allow any badmash that wanders in to see the Colonel Sahib? Be off with you."

Zafir hadn't expected this, and for a furious moment he was tempted to raise his rifle and force his way past the guards. But military discipline paid off, and he managed to repress his Pathan instincts. Instead, he snarled, "You misbegotten spawn of a pig and a scorpion, I am the orderly of Major Ian Cameron and I carry the future of India in my hands. Summon an officer!"

The guards conferred and Zafir heard the name "Cameron" mentioned several times. One man left, and the other said, "We'll see if you're telling the truth. Wait right here and keep your hands away from your jezzail."

For ten interminable minutes, Zafir paced restlessly. Then an authoritative voice said, "You have a message from Major Cameron?"

Zafir recognized the voice with a burst of relief. Turning, he saw David Cameron striding toward him.

The captain recognized him at the same moment. "Zafir—it really is you. Has something happened to my brother?"

"He was in good health when we parted, huzar, and if Allah is merciful he continues to be." Zafir extracted the papers from under his shirt. "Here is the major's message. I was to take it first to you, then to General Rawdon."

The captain opened it and skimmed it by the light of the guardpost lamp, his face hardening as he read. When he was done, he said, "Come along, Zafir. We're in luck— General Rawdon is traveling with the 39th."

"Yes, huzar." When they were out of earshot of the guards, Zafir said, "Why are you with the 39th rather than the 46th?"

"Because I've been in Afghanistan and know Pashto. None

of the officers of the 39th have such experience, so I was temporarily seconded to the regiment,'' the captain explained. ''Word of the massacre in Afghanistan reached Cambay several days ago, along with the news that the fort at Jallalabad is besieged. Rather than wait for orders from Bombay, General Rawdon decided to dispatch reinforcements immediately. Several infantry regiments, including the 46th, are also marching this way, but of course they're several days behind.''

''May Allah preserve Rawdon Sahib,'' Zafir said reverently.

''I resented being taken from my own men, but it appears that this will work out for the best.'' The captain looked at the message that he still carried, then shook his head. ''Trust Ian to go off on his honeymoon and find a hornet's nest instead.''

General Rawdon lived up to his reputation for decisiveness by instantly grasping the significance of this new information, then issuing orders to deal with it. First thing in the morning, a detachment of cavalry would leave and ride to the frontier at top speed with instructions to locate and close the Shpola Pass. And at his own request, David Cameron was placed in command.

They rounded a bend in the road and came on another small, straggling Pathan village, no more than half a dozen houses. Laura considered putting on the burqa, then saw that it was too late, for a man had seen them. She slouched in her saddle, trying to look tired and nondescript. It wasn't difficult. For several days they had been looking for a guide to the Shpola Pass, but without success. Though all of the men Ian had questioned had heard of the pass and several had a vague idea of the location, precise information had been lacking, or deliberately withheld.

The Pathan who had spotted them was sitting on the ground, leaning lazily back against a mud wall as he sharpened a wicked-looking knife. When the strangers halted their horses, he got to his feet and ambled into the road, his expression not unfriendly but his long-barreled rifle lying over his arm. Laura would sooner expect to see a Pathan naked than without his jezzail.

Ian nodded politely and gave the Pathan greeting, ''May you never tire.'' His beard grew quickly, and after a week

without shaving, he looked like a genuine hillman, with
only the details of his costume to mark him as a Punjabi
rather than a Pathan. Wanting to appear as a man of peace
rather than one searching for trouble, his own rifle was holstered on his saddle rather than slung over his shoulder.

"May you never see poverty," the villager returned.

Knowing better than to ask immediately for what he
wanted, Ian began a rambling discussion. Fortunately the
Pathan spoke a form of Urdu. Though Ian himself was fluent in Pashto, the Pathan language, whenever possible he
made his inquiries in Urdu so that Laura could understand.
After touching on mankind's favorite topics, politics and
weather, and agreeing that both weren't what they used to
be, Ian said, "Tell me, brother, do you know a small pass
through the mountains near here? I know of it as the Shpola
Pass, though it may have other names."

The Pathan's eyes narrowed. "It's scarcely a pass—more
like a path for marmots, which is why it's almost never
used. If you want to go through the mountains, take the
Khyber. It's not worth risking the Shpola to save a few
coins."

"Only the Shpola will do." Ian touched his eyepatch and
launched into the story he had been using. "A *hakim*, a
doctor, told me that he could make a salve that would restore sight to my eye, but he needed an herb that grows only
in the Shpola Pass. A winter herb, tiny and bitter."

"And you believed him?" The Pathan snorted. "Precious little grows in the Shpola, and I've never heard that it
included magical herbs."

Ian looked shamefaced. "No doubt you're right, but, well,
there's this woman I would wed. She favors me, but for the
eye. Says she'll only marry a man with two good eyes. No
other hakim holds out any hope. The trip has been long and
likely a waste of time—but the lady is very beautiful."

The Pathan gave a coarse guffaw. "If you're mad enough
with love to go up there, I might be able to find the way."

Recognizing his cue, Ian dug a coin from his pocket and
tossed it over. "Allah's blessings on you, brother."

For the first time, the Pathan glanced at Laura. "Good-
looking boy. Where's he from?"

"A Gharhwali, from the eastern hills. Not very bright, but a
good servant. He claims he'll know the herb when he sees it."

Curiosity satisfied, the Pathan said, "Follow me." Turn-

ing, he trotted through the village, then took them up a track
so steep that Laura and Ian had to dismount and lead the
horses. In keeping with his role as master, Ian didn't spare
Laura a glance.

The Pathan moved with amazing speed and stamina. After two hours of following him deeper into the mountains,
Laura was exhausted. The snow-capped peaks were still
sunlit but the lower reaches were in shadow when the Pathan
finally halted at the foot of a narrow track. "Follow this
path around the mountain, and it will take you into the pass.
Once you're there, you can't get lost, for there's no place to
turn. Unless there has been a recent rockslide you'll be able
to get your horses through, but it will be slow going. When
you descend on the other side, you'll be about an hour east
of the village of Shpola."

"I don't intend to go that far. Allah willing, I'll find what
I'm looking for and soon be on my way home." Ian gave
him another coin. "Wish me luck, brother."

"You'll need it." The Pathan gave a crack of laughter.
"If you fail, remember that there are other beautiful women
in the world." He turned and bounded down the mountain
like a goat.

Closing up behind Ian, Laura muttered, "Not very bright,
but a good servant?"

He grinned. "I got that reversed. Should have put it the
other way around."

After a few minutes of riding, they came to a relatively
level and protected patch of ground. Ian pulled in his horse.
"Water, fuel, and forage. We won't find a better place to
camp, so we might as well stop here. It's getting late and
the path is only going to get worse ahead."

Laura dismounted, creaking in every joint, then surveyed
her surroundings. Though it was the best campsite they were
likely to find, it was still incredibly bleak, consisting mostly
of cold, gray, tumbled rock. "This looks like the scraps
God had left after creating the rest of the world."

"It's hard country, which is why it produces hard men."
Ian dismounted and tethered his horse in a spot between
two boulders that offered some protection from the abrasive
wind. "I hope our guide has brought us to the right place.
I have the itchy feeling that we're running out of time."

As she tethered her horse, she said, "Will we go all the
way through the pass?"

"No. The Khyber is something like thirty-three miles long, and I suspect that the Shpola may be longer. Going the whole length and then back would take two or three days if the path is bad, and we can't afford that much time. We'll go into the pass far enough to make sure that it's what we're looking for, and to get an idea what conditions are like." He unlashed his saddlebags and swung them from his horse. "If we're really lucky the pass will be closed by snow, but there's a good chance that the elevation is low enough so that it stays open through all but the worst winter storms. The Khyber is like that."

"Then what?" Laura asked as she unloaded her own horse.

"We head back into the Punjab and hope that soon we'll run into Company troops marching to relieve the fort at Jallalabad." He unhitched his saddle and removed it from the weary horse's back. "I'll identify myself, guide a company or so up here to insure that no Afghans will use this as the royal road to India, then you and I head to Bombay. As I said, a simple, not very dangerous mission. My favorite kind."

Laura shivered and hoped it was from cold, not a premonition that they wouldn't get through this so easily. After settling her horse for the night, she made a fire with the fuel Ian gathered, then prepared a simple supper of tea and chapatis wrapped around fried onions and melted goat cheese. It wasn't half bad, she decided. Nothing like hunger to sharpen the appetite.

Night fell quickly, and so did the temperature. As they split the last of the tea between them, she began shivering in earnest. "After this, Falkirk is going to seem tropical."

"Come over here and I'll warm you up," Ian said.

She looked at him doubtfully. "Now? Here?"

He chuckled. "What a lewd mind you have. I was speaking literally, not euphemistically."

Laura circled the fire to where he was perched on a low rock. When she joined him, he turned her around so that she was sitting on the ground between his legs with her back tucked cosily against him. "Mmm, much more comfortable than the rock I was on." With a sigh of pleasure, she relaxed against his warm body. "You mentioned in Manpur that you had worked as a political officer. Exactly what does that mean?"

He finished his tea and set the tin cup down, then wrapped his arms around her waist. "Political officers work directly with the natives, both for liaison and to gather information on what people are thinking and doing. They're often drawn from the army. The best can pass for natives."

Laura gave a nod of understanding. "So with your Persian childhood and language skills, you were a natural for such work."

"In skills but not temperament," Ian said ruefully. "A lot of the work is essentially spying. Though I was rather good at it, I didn't fancy a life of full-time subterfuge. Whenever the head of the political service asked me to join permanently, I refused. On the other hand, sometimes I found the life of an army officer—a few hours of drill and a lot of hours of sports, hunting, and gossip—a little tedious. That's why so many officers overindulge in drink or drugs. Not good—India tends to kill the overindulgent rather quickly. So, whenever I became too restless, I would volunteer for some political work, which is how I ended up in the Black Well." His voice lightened. "Next time I feel restless, I'll go for a swim."

Intrigued by this new facet of her husband, she said, "I can't decide whether you're a naturally direct man with a devious bent, or a devious man with a streak of compulsive honesty."

He chuckled. "Some of both."

They sat in silence for a while longer, watching the small fire. As it subsided into embers, Laura rested her head back against Ian's shoulder. "This is the warmest I've been all day."

"It will go below freezing tonight," he said. "There's enough fuel to keep a small fire going, but even so, we'd better sleep together for safety's sake."

When she stiffened a little, he said, "Just sleep." He tightened his arms around her but the embrace was protective rather than passionate. "You feel it, too, don't you? That under these conditions, with the threat of war hanging over India like the sword of Damocles, too much joy would be out of place."

"That's it exactly," she said, startled at how well he understood. "If I were personally threatened with death, I'd probably want to make love with you as often as possible in the time remaining. But this is different. With India on the verge of going up in flames around us, private passion seems selfish.''

'' 'To everything, there is a season, and a time to every purpose under heaven,' '' he quoted softly. '' 'A time to kill, and a time to heal.' I forget the exact order, but 'a time to embrace, and a time to refrain from embracing' are on the list.''

Reaching back to her childhood Bible study, Laura went to the last lines of the famous passage. '' 'A time to love, and a time to hate. A time of war, and a time of peace.' '' After a pause, she said, ''The dancing Siva means the same thing, doesn't it? Life's eternal cycle.'' After Ian agreed, she continued, ''I'll be glad when the 'time for peace' returns, not to mention the 'time for embracing,' but I'm rather enjoying this opportunity to see you in action. Not many women have the chance to see their husbands like this.''

''Most women wouldn't want it,'' he said dryly. ''This is quite a honeymoon I've brought you on. Ever since we met, your standard of living has been declining, until now you're living like a hill bandit. Wouldn't you have preferred Paris?''

She laughed. ''Wherever you are is the right place, *doushenka.*''

He rested his chin on the top of her head. ''While I'd prefer knowing that you were safe in Bombay, I must admit that I've rather enjoying this trek, too. I was only about five years old when my sister Juliet taught me never to underestimate the strength and determination of a female, but I'm still impressed by your stamina and good nature. Pyotr Andreyovich would be proud of you.'' He kissed her temple. ''And so am I.''

Laura was sure that his words were making her glow brighter than the fire. Perhaps it was not the time to make love, but that didn't mean there was no love present, for every day she loved Ian more, even if he could not love her back in the same way. Perhaps Srinivasa had been right to say that there was no accidents and that she and Ian had been born to be together. He felt like the other half of her soul, and in a surge of optimism she saw their lives intertwined for decades to come.

The shiver she felt then *must* have been from cold.

Chapter 32

❦ ❦ ❦

THE WARRIOR DIDN'T know how long he had been stumbling through the mountains, for he had been out of his head for much of the time. In some ways delirium was better, for then there was no pain. But now his awareness cleared, and he saw that he had managed to make his way through most of the Shpola Pass. Surely it was the hand of Allah that had kept him on the treacherous track when he could so easily have pitched into the abyss. Would it be blasphemy to hope Allah might also send some food? He couldn't remember the last time he'd eaten, but it had been days. Soon he would not have the strength to continue.

Yet continue he must, for much depended on him. He wavered to a halt and leaned against the cliff face. The pass was a haunted place and the wind wailed eerily, like the voices of doomed men. Not far beyond the eastern end of the pass was his home, where there would be food and warmth and someone to bind his wounds. But the remaining distance might as well have been a thousand leagues, for all the chance he had of crossing it.

Then he heard the chinking sound of hooves echoing through the pass. For a moment panic surged through him, clearing his head. They had caught up with him and there would be too many to fight. But no, the sound came from ahead, not behind. He listened carefully. The stony cliffs distorted sound, making it hard to judge how many horses were coming, but he decided that it was only a single traveler. Allah had not forsaken him, for soon he would have transportation as well as food and water.

It didn't occur to him that the approaching rider might be a friend, not after so many days when every man's hand had been turned against him. He retraced his steps to a spot

where the trail was a little wider and a jagged boulder reared
up to a height above a rider's head. Slowly, pain stabbing
through his shoulder, he crawled onto the boulder and hun-
kered down so that he would be concealed from the rider's
view.

Then he drew his knife and waited.

Ruefully Laura decided that the Pathan guide hadn't been
joking when he called the Shpola a marmot track. The pass
wasn't much more than a steep-sided, winding slash in the
rocky mountains. At best, the track was wide enough for
two men to ride abreast. Usually it was narrower than that.
This section they were currently traversing consisted of a
ledge clinging precariously to a cliffside. Far below tumbled
a narrow river of violent, white water rapids. The way the
wind whistled between the cliffs made her exceedingly
grateful that she wouldn't be here during a storm, for it was
all too easy to imagine being blown into the gorge. She kept
most of her attention fixed on the track directly in front of
her, though her sure-footed horse was doing most of the
hard work.

But it wasn't only the obvious physical dangers that made
the pass disquieting. It seemed a place of ill-omen. Laura
rode with her rifle ready, though she doubted that it would
be of much use against ghosts.

She glanced up for a moment, wanting a sight of Ian. If
her husband was uneasy, it didn't show. He rode about sixty
feet ahead of her, as calm as if he were showing off a new
hack in a London park. She hoped that soon he would have
enough information so that they could turn back; she most
emphatically did not want to spend the night in the pass.

Laura was about to return her gaze to the track when a
dark shape suddenly rose from the top of the boulder that
Ian was passing. With horror, she realized that it was a man
with a lethal blade flashing in his hand—and he was on Ian's
blind side. She screamed, "Ian, above you!"

Two months earlier shouting would have been all she was
capable of, but she was no longer limited by the constraints
of a sheltered young Englishwoman. As the attacker
launched himself at Ian, she whipped up her rifle, cocked
it, and fired.

The attacker shrieked and changed direction in midair,
his knife spinning away into the gorge. Alerted by Laura's

warning, Ian reached for his revolver, but before he could draw, his horse trumpeted with fright and reared onto its hindquarters. For the next minute, he fought a desperate battle to regain control of his mount. Only superb horsemanship kept horse and rider from pitching off the track into the gorge.

Laura's own horse shied when she shot, but mercifully didn't panic. Knowing that she could move faster on foot, she hurtled from her mount and raced down the stony trail. The attack had taken place too quickly for her to feel fear, but she made up for the lack in the moments it took her to reach Ian.

By the time she reached him, he had dismounted and was soothing his nervous horse. The attacker, a Pathan, was lying on his back on the path. A moment before, he had been the embodiment of evil, but now he was only a limp, ragged body. Laura braced herself against the cliff, so shaky she could barely stand now that the emergency was over. "Did . . . did I kill him?"

"Not unless he died from his fall." His horse under control, Ian scanned the narrow pass, his one eye missing nothing. "The fellow appears to have acted alone. If he'd had confederates, they'd be all over us by now."

His words reminded Laura that her rifle was empty, so she reloaded with clumsy fingers. When she was done, Ian put one arm around her shoulders and pulled her against his side. "A superb piece of marksmanship. You shot the knife right out of his hand."

She wiped her perspiring face with the tail of her turban. "Pure accident. I was actually aiming at his body because that was the largest target. My main thought was to make sure the shot was high enough so that I wouldn't hit you by accident."

"You shouldn't have admitted that. I was about to take the credit for being such a great shooting instructor." He chuckled. "I thought I was teaching you to protect your life. Instead, it appears that you saved mine."

His lightness and his touch steadied Laura. As she began to relax, she wondered if this was why she had felt so compelled to accompany Ian. Though it had been more luck than skill on her part, she may indeed have saved her husband from having his throat cut. Thank God for Russian stubbornness.

The moment of tranquility ended when the attacker's eyes opened. Ian immediately released Laura and drew his revolver. But all of the fight had gone out of the Pathan. There were clumsy bandages on his left arm and right calf, and his gaze was hopeless, like that of a man who had bet everything on one last throw of the dice and lost. Nonetheless, Ian kept the gun trained on him. Speaking in Pashto, he said, "Are you alone?"

The man glared but didn't answer.

Ian shifted his aim to the man's abdomen. His tone conversational, he said, "Any idea how long it will take you to die from a bullet through the belly?"

In a raspy but defiant voice, the Pathan said, "Go ahead and shoot, pig. You'll learn nothing from me."

Ian cocked the revolver, wondering whether it would be possible to intimidate the man into talking, or if stronger measures would be required. Then Laura said urgently, "Ian, isn't he wearing the trousers of a Company soldier?"

Ian studied the Pathan and saw that under his ragged brown cloak and blood-stained shirt, he was indeed wearing sepoy trousers. Sharply Ian said, "Do you serve the Sirkar?"

"Aye," the man said sullenly. "A *havildar* and proud of it."

A havildar was the rank equivalent of a sergeant. Beginning to feel excited, Ian said in English, "Laura, get some food and water for this fellow." Switching to the Urdu used in the army, he said, "You were part of the retreat from Kabul?"

For an unguarded moment, the man shuddered. Then he recovered and spat. "You'll get no information from me, you filthy swine," he said again. "Tell your masters that Gulab Khan died as a man—true to his salt."

Ian yanked off his turban so that his auburn hair was visible. "Your masters and mine are the same, Havildar Gulab Khan. I am an officer of the 46th Native Infantry."

Gulab Khan stared at him, his gaze going from Ian's hair to his blue-gray eye and back. Then he wordlessly lifted one trembling hand in a salute.

Laura brought the waterskin and poured a little water into the Pathan's mouth, then gave him two cold chapatis left over from the night before. As the man wolfed them down, she said quietly in English, "Do you think he'd take some brandy? It might help revive him."

Ian looked at the havildar consideringly. Alcohol was forbidden to Muslims and most wouldn't touch it, but there were exceptions. Certainly the man needed something; now that he had found allies, he was on the verge of lapsing into unconsciousness. "It's worth a try. Bring me some."

She poured some brandy into a tin cup. Ian took it and held it before Gulab Khan's eyes. "I need to talk with you about what is happening on the far side of the mountains, Havildar. To ask this of you is a grievous sin, and I shall honor your wishes if you refuse. But for the sake of the Sirkar, will you consider taking spirits this once, in order to restore your strength?"

Gulab Khan hesitated, torn between morality and expedience. To make the decision easier, Ian dipped a finger in the cup, then solemnly flicked a drop of brandy away. "The Prophet said that thou shalt not drink a single drop."

Putting that single drop safely out of bounds was enough to make up the havildar's mind. He drank the brandy in two swallows, and it had a visibly bracing effect on him. "What would you know, huzar?"

"Briefly tell me what happened to the army."

While Laura cleaned and rebound his wounds, Gulab Khan filled out the story that Ian had first read in Rajiv Singh's dispatch. The havildar wasn't sure how long it had been since he was wounded; perhaps ten days. He had managed to keep a small group of his men together during most of the retreat, but a few miles from Jallalabad they had been surrounded and cut down by five times their number of mounted Afghans.

Gulab Khan was wounded, and the body of another man fell across him. The Afghans were so laden by loot that they took only the valuable rifles and didn't bother to search their victims' bodies, so they didn't realize there was a survivor.

Deciding that it was time for a break, the Afghans built a fire next to the sepoy corpses and cooked a meal. As they ate, they had talked cheerfully of their victory and about what would come next. One man was a chieftain, and he told the riders that soon they would go over the Shpola Pass to India. There they would join an army that would sweep the British into the sea as easily as the Afghans had swept them from Kabul.

When he heard that, Gulab Khan realized that he could
not allow himself to die, in spite of his wounds and his
hunger and the fact that he was half frozen from lying in
the snow. When the Afghans left, the havildar got to his feet
and salvaged a shirt and cloak from a dead comrade in order
to cover his distinctive red coat. Then he began limping
onward, determined to tell what he had heard to General
Sale Sahib in Jallalabad.

After the arduous trek to Jallalabad, it had been a crushing blow to get within sight of the fort and discover that he
could not enter. The plains around the fort were alive with
galloping, shooting, shouting Afghans, and trying to make
his way through them would have been suicide.

At that point, Gulab Khan almost gave up. But he was an
Afridi as well as a soldier of the Sirkar, and he would not
lie down and die when he was the bearer of vital news. Sure
that he could not get through the Khyber, he had doggedly
set out for the Shpola Pass, which he knew from his youth.

When he sagged back against the boulder, Ian said quietly, "You have behaved with magnificent courage, Gulab
Khan. The Sirkar is blessed to have such men."

The havildar's eyes flickered open. "The most important
tidings I have saved for last, huzar," he gasped. "The Afghans are less than half a day behind me."

Ian swore. "They have entered the pass?"

"With my own eyes I have seen them," Gulab Khan said.
"When I reached the top of the pass and looked back, I saw
an endless line of warriors, some mounted, some on foot.
And guns, huzar. They are hauling guns."

For a moment, Ian looked at Laura and felt a flash of
disabling fear. He should never have allowed her to come.
The invasion had begun, and the invaders were within a few
miles. He allowed himself only an instant of furious regret
before asking, "Havildar, is there a place in the pass where
one man might hold off an army?"

Gulab Khan thought, then gave a slow, wolfish smile.
"There is, huzar, just a little way ahead."

Ian helped the havildar to his feet, then lifted him onto
his own horse. "Show me."

Ian walked his mount along the path, using one hand to
steady Gulab Khan while Laura followed with her own
horse. Half a mile farther was a spot that might have been
designed with ambush in mind. The track had been rising

for some time, and here it reached its highest elevation before starting to drop again. As the trail fell away, it doubled back around a descending horseshoe bend. The track on the other side was so narrow that literally only one man at a time could come around the bend. A sniper stationed on this side would have a clear shot at anyone coming from the opposite direction. He would also have the advantage of height, and in the mountains, whoever controlled the heights controlled the territory. Not only could Ian hold off an army here, he would have most of the advantages on his side.

"Well done, Havildar. This is perfect."

"No, huzar," the Pathan said. With a wave of his hand, he indicated the mountain above their heads. "*That* is perfect."

Looking up, Ian saw a dark hole that must be the mouth of a small cave. A man stationed there would not only have a clear line of fire at anyone headed east on the track, but he himself would be almost impossible for the enemy to eliminate. Digging a badger out of a hole would be child's play by comparison.

"Excellent, Gulab Khan," Ian said. "With enough food and ammunition, a man in that cave could hold this pass forever."

"So we're going to climb up there and wait for the Afghans?" Laura said as she studied the cave.

"Not 'we.' " Ian braced himself for the argument he knew would come. "I'm going to sit up there with most of the ammunition, and you are going to take the horses and Gulab Khan back through the pass to his village. Then you'll enlist an escort of his grateful kinfolk to take you into the Punjab until you find a British regiment, which you will lead back here."

Her head swung around, and she glared at him with feral golden eyes. "No! I won't leave you here alone."

"You will," he said in a voice that cracked like a whip. "I said you couldn't come unless you were willing to obey me like a subaltern. That time has come, and there will be no arguments. My duty lies here. Yours lies in going for reinforcements."

Smoldering, she said, "So I'm to leave you to face an army?"

"Save your sympathy for the Afghans. Their position is far more dangerous than mine." His voice softened. "Believe me, Larishka, my chances of survival are excellent. That cave is virtually impregnable. It's quite possible that the Afghans will retreat and try to force the Khyber Pass instead. Even at its narrowest, it's hundreds of yards wider than this.''

''What if they decide to fight their way through you?''

''Then I might die here,'' he said coolly. ''But even if I do, I may be able to hold off the Afghans long enough to stop the rebellion from starting. Remember, the Punjabis won't rise unless the Afghans come, and Rajiv Singh won't try anything alone. Isn't that more important than my life? Even, God help me, more important than both our lives?''

Tears stinging her eyes, she stared at him. Never before had she so clearly seen the core of steely strength that had enabled Ian to survive torture, starvation, and endless darkness. In his determination to do whatever was necessary, whatever the price to him personally, she had never loved him more. Throat tight, she said, ''I suppose that is worth more than either of us. Very well, I'll go without any more arguments. But how close do you think British troops might be?''

''If everything went smoothly—if 'Roaring' Rawdon took the bit between his teeth as soon as Zafir and David delivered the news—the advance guard could be here within a few days.''

Laura didn't bother to point out that if things hadn't gone well, it could be weeks until reinforcements were sent to Jallalabad, for Ian knew that as well as she did. She looked up the steep slope to the cave and decided that she could climb it. ''I'll help you carry up supplies.''

''Good. That will speed things up. If you start back soon, you can be out of the pass before darkness falls.''

Laura went to her horse and unpacked the majority of the food and a full waterskin. As she did, Gulab Khan, who had been slumped half-conscious on the back of Ian's horse, revived a little. ''Your servant is talkative, huzar,'' he muttered.

''She's not my servant,'' Ian said dryly. ''She's my wife.''

The Pathan's head came up. ''A woman?'' he said, incredulous.

Ian nodded. ''I rely on you to defend her, Havildar.''

''With my life, huzar,'' Gulab Khan said gravely.

Laura gave both men an exasperated glance. She wasn't

ure if Ian was trying to insure her an extra measure of
protection, or whether he hoped that responsibility would
revive the wounded man, but it seemed obvious that she
was more likely to defend Gulab Khan than vice versa.

Without further words, she slung the sack of supplies over
her back and began climbing. It wasn't quite a cliff and
here were a number of handholds. Even so, she was pant-
ng with exertion when she reached the ledge at the cave
mouth.

Ian was just behind. Swinging up beside her, he set down
his rifle and the heavy saddlebag of ammunition, then looked
along the pass toward Afghanistan. "This is as close to an
invincible position as I've ever seen."

Stepping a safe distance back from the edge, Laura followed his gaze. "If you build a stone barricade with gaps
to shoot through, it will give you some extra protection."

"Good idea. I'll do that while I'm waiting for company."
Ian turned and went back into the cave. His voice sounding
hollow, he said, "This is larger than I expected."

Laura followed. The cave expanded into a chamber high
enough to stand in, then narrowed again and disappeared
back into darkness. Ian indicated a trickle of moisture down
one wall. "Since there's water here, I can hold out indefinitely. The cave might have another entrance as well. Feel
the air moving?"

Laura scarcely heard his words. Her main reason for
climbing to the cave was to give her husband a private farewell, and now her emotions were paralyzed by the knowledge that they were about to part, possibly forever. Voice
choked, she said, "Be careful, *doushenka.*"

He pulled her into his arms and kissed her fiercely. "I
will be. For God's sake, you do the same. Believe me, I
hate the idea of sending you off even more than you hate
the idea of leaving me here."

She clung to him, willing herself to memorize this moment exactly. The feel of his body, the sound of his voice,
the sense of completion she had found only with him—all
were so real that it was impossible to believe that she might
never experience them again. "I love you, Ian," she whispered.

His embrace tightened until her ribs hurt. "I've had a
great deal of good fortune in my life, Larissa Alexandrovna,

but none greater than meeting you.'' His faint accent thickened to a Scottish burr. "God gae with ye, my bonnie lass.''

He gave her one last kiss, aching and sweet. Then they climbed down the cliff to the trail, Ian below so that he could catch her if she slipped. But she didn't slip. She could not afford to falter, for Ian's life might depend on whether she could bring help in time. Though the cave might be almost impregnable, his ammunition was limited, and there was only one of him to an army of Afghans.

Laura mounted and set off, Gulab Khan behind her on Ian's horse. She looked back only once. Ian stood watching her go, as still as the stones surrounding him. He hadn't donned his turban yet, and his hair glowed with dark red fire in the cool winter sun. She wanted to turn and race back to him.

Instead she lifted her hand and blew him a kiss, knowing that she would never forget how he looked at this moment. He smiled, then turned away.

As Laura picked her slow way back through the pass, she was mutely grateful that Gulab Khan knew that she was female. Otherwise he might have sneered at her tears.

Chapter 33

❧　❧　❧

IAN HEARD THE Afghans long before he saw them, for it was impossible for masses of men to move through the mountains soundlessly. At first it was a vague noise, like the buzzing of distant bees. Eventually it resolved into individual components. Voices, including an occasional shouted curse. Footsteps and the clatter of hooves and sometimes the heavy thumps of equipment and supplies. Any soldier would recognize that an army was on the move, though the sounds were curiously thin because they were spread over miles of winding track.

It was midmorning and Ian was waiting patiently. He had made all his preparations the day before. After building a crude defensive wall on the front of his ledge, he had climbed down to the track and piled stones into barricades at several points. The Afghans would have to shift the rocks to pass, and they would have to do it under his rifle. Though such defenses might not be needed, he would rather be overprepared than the opposite.

The night had been quiet. Using dry fuel that wouldn't smoke, he had built a small fire. After cooking all of his flour into chapatis so that he would have a supply of cold food, he leaned against the wall of the cave and watched the fire fall into embers. It was a simple pleasure, the kind that prison had taught him to appreciate.

His mood was a blend of resignation and fatalistic calm. In spite of his reassuring words to Laura, he thought it unlikely that he would escape this engagement with his life. In combat, there were a thousand things that could go wrong. Even if all else went well, eventually he would run out of ammunition.

Yet there was a fitness to dying this way, for sacrifice in

a worthy cause was the only way he might redeem his lost
honor. Not that anyone else would ever know or care how
he had betrayed himself in Bokhara, except Laura, and she
had shown herself to be remarkably tolerant of his weaknesses. But he cared, and his sense of failure had made it
impossible for him to tell his wife how much she meant to
him. Even if he had been poet enough to find adequate
words, he would not have done so. Laura deserved a man
of untarnished courage and integrity, not an all-too-human
failure whose greatest talent was an unheroic knack for survival.

Even though he had hated sending Laura away without
his protection, he was fairly sure that her life was not at
risk. Meeting Gulab Khan had been a stroke of blinding
good fortune. Not only had the havildar supplied vital information, he and his clan were honorbound to protect Laura
because of the assistance she and Ian had rendered. It was
far better to have an Afridi as a friend than an enemy, so
she, at least, would be safe.

The sounds were getting louder. Though it was hard to
judge in the echoing gorge, he guessed that the first Afghan
would come around the bend very soon. He was ready, his
rifle loaded, more cartridges close to hand, a wet rag on
which to rest the barrel of his gun to reduce overheating.
Thank God he had a breechloader, which could be fired
much more quickly than the primitive muzzleloaders carried
by most Afghans.

Though this was not the first time he had fought for survival among desolate mountains, before he had always had
friends by his side. Comraderie was the great compensation
of military life, for facing death together forged a bond like
no other. But this time he would fight, and likely die, alone.

So be it.

The first man rounded the bend. Ian unhurriedly raised his
rifle and squeezed the trigger. The ball sped off, deadly and
true, with a flat report that shattered the air. The Afghan
screamed and staggered sideways until he pitched into the
gorge. As he fell, his voice resonated horribly from the stone
walls until it ended with sickening suddenness.

As Ian swiftly reloaded, another man bounded around the
corner, body crouched and jezzail ready as he scanned the
mountain. Ian fired again. Another shot, another casualty.
This one, luckily, fell on the path rather than off the cliff.

He shot half a dozen men before they stopped coming. Six bullets, six casualties. It was superb marksmanship, but Ian took little pleasure in it. Efficiency in killing his fellow man was grim necessity rather than a source of pride.

There was a long pause. His gaze on the track opposite, Ian sipped some water, for slaughter was dry work. Eventually a voice called out in Pashto, "Who is there? We are not your enemies. If you want tribute for allowing us passage, we will pay it. Then you can join us in our jihad against the British, for we can use a warrior like you."

Ian shouted back, "But we *are* enemies. I serve the Sirkar, and I tell you now, you shall not pass."

Silence. Then, as he expected, a group of them rushed around the corner and scattered, looking for cover from which to return fire. But there was no cover. Methodically he picked them off, one by one. Three managed wild shots before they fell, but they didn't have time to spot his position, and the bullets didn't even come close.

It wasn't war, it was more like the slaughter of tame game birds that English gentlemen called hunting. But it was effective. Very, very effective.

There was another pause. Then a voice shouted, "In the name of Allah, will you allow us to collect our wounded?"

"In His name, I grant you permission," he called back.

The first man came around the curve cautiously, his empty hands in the air. When it became clear that their unseen assailant was honoring the truce, more appeared. Hastily they collected the fallen, then disappeared back around the bend.

A buzz of voices followed. The Afghans were conferring, trying to decide what to do next. Ian felt sorry for the poor bastards. So much courage and fighting skill, yet they were brought to a halt because they could only come at him one at a time. But even though all the advantages were on his side, he didn't hear sounds of retreat.

He settled down to wait for the next assault.

Not surprisingly, Laura was lost. If she weren't so tired and saddle-weary, she might have believed that she was wandering in the landscape of a nightmare, cold and stark and endless. But this was real, as was Gulab Khan, slumped over the pommel of Ian's horse. The night before, when they had made camp, he had had enough strength to dismount

on his own, and he had eaten the humble supper she made
with enthusiasm. But when morning dawned, he was feverish and barely able to get into the saddle again.

Unfortunately, while he could stay on his horse, he was
too delirious to give her directions. She had tried to retrace
their path back to the village of Nushki, where they had
found the guide, but everything looked different when going
in the opposite direction. Now they were well and truly lost.
At the moment, she was following what seemed to be a goat
track, hoping that it might lead to a settlement.

Then, quite abruptly, the situation changed. Three Pathans materialized from behind the rocks and surrounded
her, eyes narrowed and jezzails pointed at her heart. One
of them barked at her in Pashto. Very carefully Laura
stopped her horse and raised her arms, asking, "Do any of
you speak Urdu or Persian?"

No response. As the men drew closer, she tried several
different dialects without striking any chords. But there was
at least one word that they should recognize. She said "*Anglezi.*"

That intrigued them, though they were obviously puzzled
since she didn't look much like an Englishman. Slowly she
raised her hand to her turban, repeating, "Anglezi." Then
she yanked the turban off and her hair spilled over her shoulders.

The Pathans stared. Whatever their feelings about the English, she didn't think they would shoot a woman out of
hand. She pointed at Gulab Khan, who was slouched over
the neck of his horse, oblivious to what was happening.
"Afridi."

One of the men went for a closer look. After looking in
the havildar's face, he exclaimed, "Gulab Khan!"

A babble of comments broke out, and the three Pathans
lowered their jezzails. Thank heaven that Laura and the havildar were close enough to the man's home that he was recognized. Her three captors, or whatever they were, had a
brief discussion, then one said, "Kuram." The others nodded, so the first man went loping off one way while the other
two took the reins of the horses and began leading them
through the hills. Laura was content to let them do as they
wished.

After an hour's travel, they reached a compound that was
much like Habibur's. There were a number of friendly

women who clucked over Laura, touching her hair and petting her. Unfortunately, no one spoke Urdu, and Laura couldn't understand more than a few words of Pashto even though the languages were closely related. It was frustrating, for she felt that comprehension was almost within reach.

Gulab Khan was also clucked over, then whisked away for treatment. Based on the solicitude of the Pathans, if this wasn't his own home, it was surely owned by near relations. She was confident that he would be well cared for.

Though the pampering was pleasant, after Laura had eaten and napped for a couple of hours she began to feel restless. When she tried to convey that she wanted to leave, her hostesses made it clear that leaving was not an option. "Kuram," was repeated over and over again. She hoped that it was the name of an Urdu speaker who had been summoned.

She was almost right. Eventually one of the older women indicated with gestures that Laura was to follow her. They went into the courtyard, then left the compound, the woman covering her face before she stepped outside. "Kuram," she said, gesturing at a tall young Pathan with an intelligent face.

Eagerly Laura said, "Do you speak Urdu?"

He smiled, then said in fluent English, "Yes, but wouldn't you prefer your own language?"

"Thank heaven!" she said fervently. "Are you a soldier of the Sirkar?"

"I once was, until a youthful indiscretion on my part," he said with a trace of wistfulness. "After that, I took salt with a mountain prince and went to England with him. I spent two years there." He gestured to a wooden bench set against the mud-brick wall. "Tell me what an Englishwoman is doing here. You are the amazement of all my kinfolk."

Hoping that Kuram's time in England meant that he had pro-British sympathies, she identified herself. Then she explained the situation, including the fact that she needed to go back through the Punjab to find British troops. At the end, she said, "Will you help me? I'll need an escort and guide."

He considered. "My tribesmen will not be pleased to have British troops cross our lands. Yet even less will they want Afghans to use our territory for an invasion. The Afghans are our cousins, you know, which makes them much easier to hate." He rose from the bench. "I will send word to my kin, suggesting they allow the British safe passage to the Shpola Pass. Most will likely agree that the British are the lesser evil, for they are more likely to leave."

After that, things happened quickly. Within half an hour, Laura and Kuram were riding toward the main Khyber Pass road. Now all she had to do was find an army.

Having found an army, Ian was now wishing that it would go away. The last hours had made him think of a Hindu prayer: *Oh, Lord, from the venom of the cobra, the teeth of the tiger, and the vengeance of the Afghan, deliver us!*

It was easy to see how the Afghans got their reputation. Why didn't these damned fearless idiots concede that they couldn't use the Shpola and leave? But they didn't. They tried rushing out, climbing up, down, and around the opposite cliff and gorge, anything they could think of to get at him.

His opponents had located his aerie. Occasionally one would pop out and take a quick shot, then try to dodge out of sight before he could retaliate. Sometimes they were successful. More often, Ian was. One clever fellow tried a decoy, sticking out a turban wrapped around some other object to draw Ian's fire and waste his ammunition. Ias was fooled once. After that, he waited to see a torso before firing.

Still, no matter how sparing he was of ammunition, by the time dusk fell his supply was beginning to run low. With nightfall, activity on the other side ceased, but there were no sounds of withdrawal. He suspected that they were reluctant to retreat when they had already come most of the way through the Shpola. Turning back now and trying the Khyber would cost them days, and possibly be even more bloody.

He assumed that they would slip out under cover of darkness, with a few of them climbing up to his aerie to put an end to him once and for all. But the night was clear and the moon bright enough to illuminate the track. After he had picked off several men who ventured out, they stopped trying.

The worst time was after moonset, when the pass was lit only by the faint light of the stars. Ian stood on his ledge and listened. It wasn't long until he heard stealthy movements along the opposite track. He waited until they ran into the first of his stone barricades. There was an oath, hastily cut off, followed by the grating noises of rock being shifted.

In prison, his ears and eye had gown uncannily perceptive, and he was able to make a shrewd guess as to which dark shadows were human. He fired, and the sound of a shriek filled the gorge. Reloading by touch, he fired again, then again. He wasn't sure if he made any more hits but his first lucky shot had been enough. The footsteps retreated to safety and he heard a voice cursing him as a demon. But still they didn't withdraw.

Nothing more was tried that night, though he had to stay awake and alert to be sure. By dawn, fatigue was starting to affect him. It was an open question whether his ammuniton or his stamina would give out first.

As he ate cold chapatis and a handful of raisins, he waited and listened. There were still human sounds from the opposite side of the gorge, but no one appeared. They were planning something, he knew it in his bones. The question was, what?

Kuram proved an excellent guide. Laura gave silent thanks. More and more she felt that she and Ian were in divine hands—there had been too much amazing good luck for it to be coincidence. The way they had met; the perfect matching of their needs; Kamala's timely insight that had enabled Laura to free herself of the past. Pyotr's notes; Meera's banyan tree eavesdropping; Gulab Khan; now Kuram. Perhaps it was all what Ian had called iqbal, preordained good fortune. Laura wasn't particular about where help came from, as long as it could stop a war and, she prayed, save her husband's life.

Soon after setting out the next morning, they saw a cloud of dust in the distance. Kuram reined in his horse and peered at the dust, his hand shaded against the eastern sun.

Laura asked, "Is that the road to the Khyber?"

"Not yet." He lowered his hand. "It's a group of Company lancers. Your reinforcements are here, Lady Falkirk."

It was faster than she had dared dream. The troops must already have been on their way north when Zafir met them. Iqbal, indeed. Recklessly she spurred her horse toward the troops, Kuram following behind.

As they galloped up to the approaching lancers, the guide

in the lead whooped and waved his hand. Laura was delighted to see that it was Zafir. But what really convinced her that iqbal was at work was the approaching British captain.

"Laura, thank heaven you're all right," David said when he pulled up beside her. "What about Ian?"

Right in front of the interested eyes of dozens of soldiers, Laura leaned from her horse and hugged her brother-in-law. "He was fine when I last saw him, but we'll need to move quickly to insure that he stays that way."

He hugged her back, though he said, chuckling, "Better behave, or I'll never live this down. Must uphold the dignity of the Sirkar, you know."

"I've given up on being an English lady, but I'll try to control myself for your sake," She gave him an unsteady smile. "Merciful heaven, I'm glad to see you!"

She introduced Kuram, explaining how much he had helped her. Since Zafir was Mohmand and Kuram an Afridi, at first the Pathans bristled at each other. Laura said. "For the purpose of this engagement, can I offer you both temporary British citizenship so you won't be at each other's throats?"

Both men laughed. "Very well, lady," Kuram said. "As long as this curly-tailed son of an unclean beast knows that he'd better not venture onto Afridi land alone in the future."

Equally good-natured, Zafir said something in Pashto, probably some version of, "Your mother's one, too."

But both Pathans had lived in a wider world beyond their tribal lands, and the hostility seemed more pro forma than real. With a truce declared, Laura filled David and Zafir in on what she and Ian had done.

At the end of her recital, David said, "Well done, Laura. Do you think the Pathans who helped you earlier will let you stay with them again while we go into the pass and retrieve Ian?"

Her eyes narrowed. "I'm going with you."

David studied her face for some time. "Mmm, so you are."

She smiled. "You learn much more quickly than Ian did."

He rolled his eyes. "God help my poor brother." Then he turned and lifted his arm as a signal for his men to move forward. Laura stayed at the head of the troops, riding between David and Zafir while Kuram led the way back to the pass.

In a few hours, just a few more hours, she and Ian would be together again. And never again would she let them be separated, she swore, not even to save the British Empire.

Ian found out the hard way what the Afghans' next stratagem was. After several hours of inactivity, something appeared at the bend. When he saw that it was a piece of light artillery, he swore. Then he raised his rifle and aimed at the gunner.

The cannon fired at the same moment he did. His shot was more accurate, clipping the gunner, but the cannon was enormously louder. It discharged with a deafening boom and a ball crashed into the cliff face fifty feet from Ian, setting off reverberations in the cave around him.

Bloody, bloody hell! As cannon went, it was rather small, probably a nine-pounder. It must had been difficult to get even that up the pass. But the gun was plenty large enough to kill Ian if they targeted the cave mouth accurately. Worst of all, the artillery piece offered some protection to the men firing it, so he wouldn't always be able to take them out.

A grim duel began. The cannon would fire, then was dragged out of sight for reloading. Ian would move forward and wait for a good shot at the gunner until the fuse was ignited. Then he retreated into the cave, simultaneously ramming another cartridge into the breech so that he would be ready for the next round.

After half an hour, his ears were numb, and he was beginning to lose some of his accuracy from sheer fatigue. His rifle barrel was already too hot to touch, and there was a very real possibility that the gun might explode in his face. On top of everything else, the afternoon sun was glaring into his face and his eye was stinging from exhaustion and smoke. But if he stopped firing, the Afghans would pour around the bend. If enough managed to get onto the track, he would be unable to shoot fast enough to turn them all back.

Ka-boom! A cannonball smashed into his crude parapet. He ducked instinctively as rocks flew in all directions and stone chips peppered him. The ball itself didn't enter the cave; it must have bounced down the cliff. Ears ringing, he crawled to the end of the ledge and peered over.

The gorge had filled with acrid, vision-obscuring clouds of smoke, but he saw that this time the gunner was reloading in position so the cannon wouldn't have to be aimed again. A man with a jezzail was providing cover, and he fired as soon as Ian looked down. The ball was so close that Ian heard it whistle. He didn't waste time flinching. Instead he squeezed his trigger and shot the *jezzailchi* in the shoulder. Then he swiftly reloaded and fired again. The gunner ducked but managed to touch off the fuse in the cannon.

The cannonball smashed into the cliff just above Ian's head, causing another rain of debris. Yes, they had definitely found the range. As he automatically reloaded, he thought with detachment that the end was near, for he was close to the limits of his endurance, and he was almost out of ammunition. He raised the rifle and fired, this time hitting the gunner. The man fell back with a cry and was dragged away, along with the cannon. A minute later, the reloaded cannon was shoved out by someone else. Christ, these devils were brave.

Ian fired but wasn't sure if he hit the gunner. He retreated into the cave, sliding another cartridge into his rifle.

Ka-boom! The cannonball didn't strike as closely this time; shifting the gun had wrecked the aiming. Instead of moving forward to shoot again, Ian stayed in the back of the cave. He had only a couple of dozen cartridges left. When those were gone, he'd have only his revolver, which wasn't accurate at any distance. Best to stop returning their fire for a while, perhaps lull them into feeling that they had knocked him out of action.

It was a rule of thumb in these parts to save the last bullet for oneself. Good advice, that; if the Afghans took him alive, they would show no mercy, not after the number of them he'd shot. They were inventive people, and death would be a long, painful time coming. The revolver would be adequate for saving him from that. But first, there would be a battle for the cave. The advantages were still on his side. He should be able to take down a dozen or more of the enemy before the end. More important, he would be delaying the invasion a little longer.

The cannon fired, striking closer. They were getting the range again. Time to move forward and shoot another gunner.

Before he could act on the thought, the world exploded into chaos and blackness.

They heard the sounds of gunfire long before they entered the pass. Laura winced at every shot, even though the barrage meant that Ian was alive and holding his own. Because of the difficulty of riding so many horses along a narrow, hazardous track, David had ordered the lancers to dismount and proceed on foot. Most were now snaking their way though the Shpola Pass.

Though pain stabbed her lungs and she was near exhaustion, she refused to give up her position near the head of the line of soldiers. She would have dropped out if she were slowing the advance, but on this rough track dexterity was as important as strength, and she was surefooted. David and Zafir led, Kuram and Laura right behind. She guessed that the Afridi had come along because he couldn't resist a good fight.

Finally they reached the point where she could see the cliff where Ian was making his stand. The edge of his cave was visible, barely, though from this position his opponents were out of sight around the bend. Her heart leaped when she saw a curl of smoke and heard the report of his rifle. He was still alive.

David turned to her. "Stay here while we advance, Laura. They've got at least one piece of artillery up there, and I don't want you within range."

As the cannon blasted, Laura nodded, knowing that the time had come for her to be sensible. Besides, she wasn't interested in fighting Afghans; her sole ambition was to get Ian safely away. She devoutly hoped that he wouldn't feel it was his duty to stay with his brother's troopers.

The cannon boomed again, followed by an indescribable roar, a rumble so deep that it was more a vibration of the earth than real sound. Instinctively Laura looked up at Ian's aerie.

Right in front of her eyes, in agonizing slow motion, the whole face of the cliff collapsed, and Ian's cave with it.

Chapter 34

❦   ❦   ❦

LAURA DIDN'T KNOW she was screaming until David grabbed her and pulled her against him, pressing her face into his shoulder so that she couldn't see the catastrophe. Dust and thunder filled the air, and the earth shook beneath their feet.

Gradually the din subsided to the rattle of occasional tumbling stones and gravel. Laura clung to David, her mind refusing to accept that Ian was dead. Yet no one could have survived what she had just witnessed. The artillery fire must have acted on a fault in the rock until the mountain sheered away. If Ian hadn't been killed outright, he had fallen into the gorge far below and been crushed by boulders. *Ian was dead.*

Her vision faded and she was tempted to sink into darkness. But the pain would still be there when she regained consciousness and a fainting female would be a nuisance. When she was sure her knees would support her, she pushed herself away from David. His face showed the same anguish that must be on hers.

But he was a soldier and would neither scream nor faint, even though he had seen his brother killed in front of his eyes. "Will you be all right here for a few minutes?" he said tightly. "I'm going forward to see what's happened to the Afghans."

When she nodded, he said to Kuram, "Stay with her." Then he led Zafir and his own men ahead while Laura and the Afridi pressed into the cliff face so the soldiers could file past.

Laura wasn't sure how long it was until David returned, for time had no meaning. Nothing did. Quietly her brother-in-law said, "The rockslide has destroyed a huge section of the track and the gorge below is impassable. No one will be traveling through here anytime soon, and maybe never again.''

Shuddering, she pressed her face into her hands. So Ian had succeeded; he had quenched the fire that Pyotr Andreyovich had set, and then lived to regret. There would be no Afghan invasion through the Shpola Pass. The Punjabis could stick to the business of killing each other rather than invading India. Rajiv Singh would have to learn to live with his resentment of the Sirkar, for in the future he would be so closely watched that he would not have the opportunity to get into mischief.

Yes, Ian had succeeded, at the cost of his own life. No doubt he would think that a fair price for stopping a war.

Laura wasn't so sure.

He was being buried alive. Sandy soil filled his mouth, weighing down his body, crushing his lungs until there was nothing in his mind but panic. Ian tried to scream his submission, to say that he would do anything they wanted, anything at all, if only they would give him an easier death.

But his executioners said nothing; there would be no reprieve. Hopelessly he flailed at the dirt, not because he thought it would make a difference, but because it was physically impossible to lie quiet while they filled his grave.

Abruptly one arm broke through into the air, then the other. He thrashed out and a moment later his face was clear. After coughing the dirt from his throat, he was able to breathe, though the air was thick and dusty. But it was dark, so dark, the heavy, suffocating blackness of a tomb.

At first he thought they had finished the job of blinding him. Yet when he touched his face, he felt only a few days' worth of bristles, not the long beard he had grown in prison.

Like a kaleidoscope, the pieces of his life fell into a coherent pattern, and he remembered that he was no longer in Bokhara. Juliet and Ross, then his own return to India. Laura. Marriage, Dharjistan, a plot to bring down the Sirkar, the Shpola Pass, his attempt to hold back an invasion. Had there been an explosion? No, artillery fire. Then what?

He pushed himself upright and cleared away the dirt and gravel that pinned his lower body. Then he stood and explored his surroundings. After a few minutes he identified a squarish knob of rock as one that had been in the back of

the cave. That's right; he had retreated for protection from
the cannonballs. The artillery fire must have caused the front
part of the cave to collapse, so his withdrawal had saved
him from being crushed.

But to what purpose? Dear God, to what purpose? Heart
hammering, he investigated the debris that had fallen, and
found that the tunnel was sealed by boulders too massive to
shift. He was trapped and would die alone in the dark. How
many days would it take for starvation or thirst to kill him?
How many hours and minutes without light?

The panic that had receded a little surged back. For his
sins he must now endure all of his deepest, most shameful
fears. Fear of darkness, of being trapped, of being alone.
Anguish knotted his belly, then rose, expanding until it
wrenched from his throat in a wordless howl.

The sound clamored from the walls, then died away, absorbed by the tons of stone and soil around him. He fell to
his knees, unable to breathe. The weight of the mountain
was pressing down on him, crushing his life inch by hideous
inch.

Another scream ripped from his throat. He jammed his
wrist in his mouth, muffling his terror against his filthy
sleeve.

Escape was as close as the sash at his waist. Beyond
thought, he reached under his loose coat and grasped the
cool steel of his revolver. No one would ever know that he
had taken the coward's way out.

He cocked the hammer, then raised the barrel to his temple and squeezed the trigger.

David's softly insistent voice said, "Laura, can you walk?
We need to get out of the pass."

She still leaned against the cliff face, so she straightened
up. "I can walk," she said dully.

The sun was winter bright. It was a lovely, if chilly day,
but as she started stumbling along the rough track, all she
could think of was Ian, lying still and cold beneath the earth.
Your husband will be beneath the earth.

Shocked, Laura came to such an abrupt halt that David,
who was behind, bumped into her. She didn't notice. *Srinivasa had never said that Ian would die.* Hindus burned
their dead; for a Brahmin priest, the image of being under
the earth would not have the implication of being dead and

buried that it had for a Christian or Muslim. Why hadn't she thought of that before?

Furiously she realized that it was because she had refused to think about it at all. Instead, she had reacted with the same childish terror that had ruled her whenever she thought of passion and her parents' tragedy. Like an ostrich, she had tried to hide from what she could not endure.

"Laura, are you all right?" David asked sharply.

She spun around and stared at the mountain where she had too quickly assumed Ian had died. The time for childish terror was over. If Ian was to have a chance, she must fight for him with English logic and Russian tenacity.

Her brother-in-law took a firm grip on her arm. "We'll rig a litter for you."

She pulled her arm away. "David, he isn't necessarily dead," she said, voice shaking. "The cave he was in was deep. He could have retreated into it, beyond the point of collapse."

"I hope to God he didn't," David said, his own pain showing. "We couldn't possibly get him out in time to save his life, even if we knew where on that damned cliff to dig."

In the throbbing silence, she knew that his thoughts were the same as hers: to die trapped under the earth was too much like Ian's cruel imprisonment in Bokhara. And while David didn't know that Ian had almost been buried alive, Laura did.

She swallowed hard, refusing to think that her husband might already be dead. Far better to remember that Srinivasa had said she would have a long and happy life, which wouldn't be the case unless Ian was alive. He must be—she would not believe he was dead until all hope was gone. "There was air flowing through the cave—Ian mentioned it. Doesn't that mean there's another entrance?"

"There could be," David admitted. "But it might only be a narrow crack that wouldn't help Ian even if he did manage to survive the rockslide."

She frowned, thinking hard. "We must look for the other entrance so we can go in after him."

He shook his head. "Laura, you don't understand what's involved. Cave systems can be enormously complex and run on many levels. Even if we found another cave in the same area, there's no guarantee that it would connect with the one Ian was in.''

Her eyes narrowed with calculation. "You sound knowledgeable.''

"Ian and I explored caves in the Midlands a couple of times during school holidays,'' he said. "That's why I know the difficulties involved.''

"Your experience will be useful—at least, it will be if you're willing to help.'' Her mouth tightened. "And if you aren't, I'll find another entrance and go in alone.''

"It isn't a matter of being willing,'' he said with some exasperation. "I'll do anything I can if there's a possibility that we might find Ian alive. But the chance is remote, and getting more so with every minute. Also, now that the pass is closed, I can't linger here—my men are needed in Jallalabad.''

"Then we'd better get busy, hadn't we?'' she said, icily calm now that she knew what must be done.

David capitulated. "I'll call some of the lancers to help look for caves on that mountain. I'll also go inside with you, if we find one, because I certainly will not allow you to go in alone.'' He fixed her with a steely glance that reminded Laura of Ian at his most determined. "But if and when it becomes clear that further searching is hopeless, I'm going to haul you to safety even if I have to gag you and tie you to your horse.''

She grimaced. "If it's hopeless, you won't have to do that. But as long as there's a chance Ian is alive, I'm staying here.'' Raising her voice, she called, "Kuram?''

The Afridi, who wasn't far ahead, came back at Laura's call. "Kuram, my husband was in a cave that ran deep into the mountain. Do you know if there might be other entrances?''

He frowned. "It's said there are several caves nearby. Perhaps they are really all one. But I know of no one who has gone inside to find out—caves are accursed places.''

So there were other entrances! Beginning to feel hopeful, she said, "Can you help me find another cave that's close enough that it might be part of the same system?''

He shrugged. *"Inshallah.''* God willing.

That was good enough for Laura. She would put her faith in iqbal, for she had nothing to lose and everything to gain.

* * *

Sanity returned in the instant before the revolver fired. Appalled by what he was doing, Ian whipped the barrel away from his head even as his finger completed the reflex action of pulling the trigger. The gunshot was deafening at such close quarters, yet he scarcely noticed the sound or the shower of earth loosed by the vibrations.

Jesus Christ, what had he been thinking of?

He hadn't been thinking—that was the problem. For the second time in his life, he had succumbed to blind, hysterical panic, and his momentary weakness had almost cost him his life.

With trembling hands, he lowered the revolver and thrust it back under his sash. He wasn't dead yet; he wasn't even injured, apart from sundry aches and pains. It was time to confront his fears with the same kind of courage that Laura had shown in conquering hers.

The thought of Laura steadied him. He must do everything he could to survive, not only for his sake, but for hers, for she had lost too much already.

His mind functioning again, he took stock of his situation. The silence was absolute. Either the bombardment had stopped, or the earth was so thick that no sound could enter. The air was moist and faintly fresh, not musty, and there was still a trace of the airflow he had felt before. Though this particular entrance was closed, the cave might have others. He had nothing to lose by trying to find out. The darkness—he wouldn't think about the darkness.

He probed the fallen earth and stones by the cave-in, but found nothing of value. His rifle was lost beyond recall; worse, he couldn't find any food or drink. But water still trickled down the walls, and it quenched his thirst when he licked it.

Time to start moving. The cave was high enough to stand in, so he began walking back into the mountain, slowly moving his arms back and forth in front of his face and testing the ground ahead with his foot before shifting his weight. The cave narrowed rapidly, and he cracked his head when the ceiling lowered unexpectedly on the left. Swearing, he folded over, seeing stars, then told himself with gallows humor that stars were better than the darkness.

He dropped to his hands and knees. The ground became increasingly moist, and soon the opening constricted to a tunnel so small that he would have to crawl on his belly to get through.

He halted, another wave of fear sweeping through him. What if the tunnel ended in a dead end and he became trapped, unable to move forward or back? Reminding himself of the faint movement of air, he gritted his teeth and forced himself forward. Inch by cautious inch, he crawled down the jagged tube of stone.

Follow the air.

Though almost twenty people were combing the mountain for caves, it was the bats that showed the way. David saw several fluttering from the ground and went over to investigate, then summoned the others with a shout.

By the time Laura arrived, David had been far enough inside to know that the cave went some distance into the mountain. Though the entrance was much lower down the slope than Ian's cave, there was a chance the two were connected. She regarded the small dark opening with satisfaction. Iqbal.

A brisk discussion followed. David doubted the wisdom of going into the cave when it was dusk and they had all had a long, tiring day. Fatigue bred accidents. Driven by her sense of urgency, Laura retorted that it hardly mattered whether it was daytime since it would be dark inside either way.

Torn between his better judgment and his concern for his brother, David conceded the point and agreed to start immediately. To Laura's surprise, Zafir said, "I'll go, too."

She was touched that he volunteered, especially since he obviously hated the idea. Caves were a source of superstitious terror, the abode of evil forces. Since the native lancers had never met Ian, she doubted that any of them would have gone in even if ordered.

Kuram was nearby, squatting on his haunches, listening. "Anything a snake of a Mohmand can do, an Afridi can do better," he said after Zafir volunteered. "I will also go."

"You're both sure?" David asked. "This could be dangerous." After they affirmed their willingness, he said, "Very well. Each of us must carry two spare candles as well as one that's lit, matches wrapped in waterproof canvas, food, water, and rope."

Laura gave silent thanks for his experience; she would

not have been as careful. Preparations took only a few minutes since David had already ordered that the necessary supplies be brought from the mouth of the pass, where the
lancers had pitched camp for the night. After putting his
young subaltern in charge of the troops, David crouched
down and entered the small cave mouth, Laura right behind
him.

Inside was a chamber large enough to stand in. As she
raised her candle and studied her surroundings, David said,
"Don't expect a miracle, Laura. The chance that this will
produce results is very remote."

She gave David a crooked smile as she lighted the way
for the two Pathans, who were following. "On the contrary,
I won't settle for anything less."

The tunnel seemed endless. In several locations it was so
tight that Ian could barely squeeze through. As it angled
downward, the moisture was becoming heavier, seeping
from the walls until it formed a noticeable trickle along the
bottom of the tunnel. Eventually the space opened up so
that he could go from wriggling on his belly to crawling on
all fours.

The improved conditions made him less cautious, with
near disastrous results when his right hand came down on
empty space. He pitched forward, and would have gone
headfirst into nothingness if he hadn't caught a crack in the
stone with his left hand. Even so, he teetered for a moment
with his upper body hanging over the edge of the shaft that
had opened up.

After pulling himself back onto solid ground, he
crouched, head on his arms, until the pounding of his heart
slowed. Christ, he hated the dark. But he was no longer
terrified by it.

When he was in command of himself again, he patted
across the tunnel floor with his palms. The opening went
from wall to wall. Finding some loose gravel, he scooped
up a handful and dropped a piece into the hole. Seconds
passed before he heard a tiny, distant rattle. Obviously the
hole was plenty deep enough to kill him.

Could he climb down the side? He felt the face of the
shaft and learned that it was very smooth and offered no
footholds. Climbing down would be impossible, and if it
turned out to be a blind shaft, he would be trapped at the

bottom. Next he tossed a pebble forward. It clattered on
stone opposite him. How far?

For the next several minutes he tossed pebbles with varying degrees of force, trying to roughly map the space ahead
of him. His best guess put the hole at eight or ten feet wide,
and the tunnel seemed to continue on the opposite side,
with the ceiling fairly high. He could jump ten feet, but into
absolute blackness, with no idea what he would be landing
on? Leading an assault against a fortified position would be
easier.

But he didn't have a lot of choices. And if he wanted a
quick death, falling to the bottom of the shaft would provide
it. It was definitely better than being buried alive.

There was just enough space to stand and back up several
steps to build momentum. After drawing several deep
breaths, he wiped his damp palms on his coat. Then he
sprinted forward and hurled himself into the unknown.

Laura's cavern opened with a chamber about the size of
a bedroom, then rapidly narrowed down to a throat hardly
large enough to crawl through. As the four cavers studied
the dark opening, she said, "I'm smallest, so I'll go first."

Though David didn't like the idea, he had too much sense
to dispute her logic. "Very well, but tie a rope around your
waist. If you get into trouble, tug on it or yell and we'll get
you out."

She lay on her stomach and wriggled forward, holding
her candle ahead of her. Shadows flickered wildly along the
walls as the flame wavered. A nuisance, but at least she had
light. What would the cave be like for Ian, who was terrified
by the dark?

She wouldn't think of it.

After several slow minutes of crawling that bruised her
elbows and knees, she emerged into another chamber.
Though she stood cautiously, she bumped her head, which
caused her to drop her candle. It extinguished when it hit
the floor. Blackness. Utter, endless blackness, the only
sound that of dripping water. Was this what the Black Well
had been like? No wonder Ian hated the dark. Grateful that
David had been so adamant about precautions, she drew out
one of her spare candles, then took a match from the wa-
terproofed packet. The match struck easily and she lit her
candle. It was the most beautiful light imaginable.

After retrieving the dropped candle, she examined her surroundings. The chamber was a glittering fairy palace of crystals, columns, and stone icicles. It was also large, perhaps the size of a ballroom but with a much higher ceiling. She went to the mouth of the tunnel and called, "I've found a large chamber, and the tunnel didn't get any smaller along its length. You should be able to get through." Her voice echoed hollowly.

A few minutes later Zafir appeared, followed by Kuram and David. A good thing none of them were fat.

They explored the perimeter of the chamber, and were presented with a quandary when two exit tunnels were found. David said, "Laura and I will take the left, you two men take the right. If the tunnel divides, don't split up again. Choose the most promising direction and use a piece of rock to scratch an arrow on the wall pointing back the way you came. Be careful, and don't let yourself get too tired."

The Pathans nodded and the group split up. As Laura entered the new tunnel, something swooped by her, so close that she shrieked and threw a hand over her face.

"Only a bat," David said reassuringly. "More afraid of you than you are of it."

"I sincerely doubt that," she retorted, her heart thumping.

David chuckled and they continued forward. They made a good team; he gave her the same feeling of safeness that Ian did.

This tunnel was high enough to walk in but narrow, with water trickling along the bottom. It also slanted upward. As they picked their way over jagged stones, Laura's confidence began to fade as she realized just how unlikely an undertaking this was. The cavern system might go on indefinitely and never connect with the cave Ian had been in, even assuming he was alive. No wonder David, with his experience of what lay beneath the earth's surface, had warned her not to expect miracles.

Her mouth hardened. *Remember that you are a Russian. No surrender.*

Ian's leap into the unknown lasted so long that he was sure that he had misjudged and was falling into the shaft. Then he landed hard on a slippery, irregular stone surface.

He lost his balance and went down, sliding on his side across the rock until he slammed into a wall.

Shaken, he did an inventory. Nothing was broken, though he was getting bruises on his bruises. He swayed as he got to his feet and realized that the combined effects of exhaustion, cold, and hunger were starting to seriously affect him. But he daren't stop as long as he was capable of moving forward. If he lay down, he might not get up again.

How long had he been trapped under here? Hours? A day? More? Impossible to tell. As in the Black Well, he was losing all sense of time, though his other senses were acute. He could smell the water and the sterility of the stone, feel the strengthening current of air on his face. He was also getting adept at sensing how near or far away surfaces were. He wasn't sure how he knew; probably the reflections of sound and his own body heat.

He found the next shaft the easy way, by tapping rather than almost falling in. Again he tossed gravel to determine what was ahead, finding that it seemed to be solid rock rather than a continuation of the tunnel. On the plus side, the shaft didn't seem as deep as the first, and the tunnel might continue at the lower level. He debated how to proceed. It wouldn't be easy to go down the shaft, and if he broke a leg he was doomed.

Then he remembered his turban, which was six yards long and made of sturdy cotton. He made a rope by ripping the turban lengthwise into two pieces and tying the ends together. After looping it around a narrow column of stone that rose from the floor, he climbed into the shaft. At the bottom limit of his rope, he lowered himself until he was hanging with his arms straight over his head. At the very limit, his toes touched solid ground, probably the floor of a new tunnel. Releasing one end of the doubled cloth, he pulled the entire length down and wrapped it around his body in case he would need it again.

And so it continued, through large spaces and small, moving through the thick blackness by touch and faint echoes of sound. Once he worked his way down a chimney with his back pressed against one wall and his feet and hands against the other, praying that it wouldn't get too wide for him to support himself. Sometimes he wondered if he was burying himself more deeply, but the air still moved, so there must be an opening somewhere ahead.

The water grew deeper until he was wading through a stream, then a small river. Finally, with a roar, the river plunged into a shaft. Alerted by the intensifying current and the sound of falling water, Ian stopped and made a careful survey. The river, which was now almost hip deep, filled the tunnel. The only way forward would be through the water.

He stood still, water rushing around him, and weighed the odds. If he let the river take him down this subterranean waterfall, he might emerge into a pool in a chamber below. More likely, he would drown or be smashed into the rocks. Not good odds at all, but once again, he didn't see any other choices. There wasn't much point in retracing his steps. He might have passed by dry secondary tunnels, but if he had missed them once, he might miss them again.

Well, he had said that any death would be better than being buried alive, and he was certainly being given a variety of choices. The worst part of going over the waterfall was that his revolver would become saturated so he wouldn't have it in reserve for a final escape; however, since he was probably going to drown, there was no point in worrying about that.

He inhaled deeply several times to absorb every bit of air he could. As he did, he thought of all he would be leaving behind if he didn't survive. Earlier, when panic had driven him to the brink of self-destruction, he had been thinking only of the pain of existence. Yet life had become very rewarding since he met Laura, and dying now would be like leaving a book in the middle of the best part.

Now that existence was stripped down to stark essentials, it was hard to remember why he had been unable to tell Laura that he loved her. It was foolish of him to let his sense of unworthiness silence him, for she deserved to know how much she meant to him. If he survived, he would do better.

During his long journey through the cavern, his irrational fears had ebbed, leaving a curious sense of peace. The darkness was no longer menacing. In fact, it held a warmth that reminded him of the Well when he had shared it with Pyotr Andreyovich. Perhaps the old rascal had come to keep him company. Or perhaps what he felt was that deity whom Pyotr had believed in. Whatever—or Whoever—might be here, Ian no longer felt alone.

The faces of his family passed in front of his mind's eye, beginning and ending with Laura. She was so vivid that it seemed as if he could reach out and touch her. Larissa Alexandrovna, his fierce, loyal, loving Tartar. *Be happy, Larishka, and sometimes remember me.*

Then he lay back and let the current take him into the abyss.

The next chamber was the most beautiful of all, but to Laura's bitter disappointment, it was also the end of the cave. Half the floor of the chamber was taken up by a deep pool with a waterfall plunging into it. She prowled around the perimeter, the stub of her candle so low that it almost singed her fingers, but could find no way out except the one by which they had entered. She felt as if she were trapped inside a Russian cathedral of spires and glittering surfaces.

David was also investigating, scrambling over the uneven floor, but finally the two of them met by the pool. "We'll have to turn back, Laura," he said. "This is the end. Maybe Zafir and Kuram have had better luck. Even if they have, we'd better rest outside before trying another tunnel. We're exhausted, and even willpower has its limits."

She sighed. "I suppose so, though I hate to admit it. I keep feeling that Ian must be here somewhere, if only I knew where to look—if only I tried a little harder."

"No one could try harder than you, Laura—you're the most indomitable female I've ever met." David touched her shoulder. "But now it's time to go back."

She nodded, but when he walked away, she paused for one last look at the waterfall that poured noisily from the wall. No way forward there, for it filled the shaft from which it emerged. She was beginning to turn when she saw an object sweeping down through the veil of water. Something large, a chunk of wood or a drowned animal. It hit with a splash.

Laura stared, sure that she must be hallucinating, seeing Ian in the roiled water because she so much wanted to. Then she began to shout.

Compared to the rest of Ian's subterranean journey, passage through the underground river was almost easy. The water did all the work, sucking him down the stony pipe, the chill numbing his bruises and abraded hands. If only there were air. . . . His lungs began to ache, then burn. He exhaled slowly, using the slight relief to hold back the moment when suffocation would become agony.

Suddenly he slammed into a protruding rock and stuck, trapped by the beating current. Violently he shoved at the stone until he was enough to one side that the water grabbed him again. The river spread out, expanding into a waterfall. His desperate lungs drew in a mixture of air and water that choked more than relieved. Then he plunged into a deep pool. After the waterfall, it was still and calm. And, shockingly, he saw a glimmer of light above.

His first thought, even before the hope that escape was at hand, was that, thank God, he wasn't blind. Weakly he struck out toward the light, kicking upward and wondering if he would last long enough to reach it before he drowned.

When he broke through the surface, the roar of the falls and of blood pounding in his ears eliminated other sounds. It wasn't until a strong arm grabbed him and dragged him through the water that he realized he wasn't alone. He was bumped over the edge of the pool, then landed on a rough stone floor in a chamber feebly illuminated by candlelight.

Reality tilted crazily, for above him he saw Laura's face, which had to be impossible. Nonetheless, he reached up to touch her cheek. The smooth skin was warm beneath his chilled fingers.

She leaned forward and kissed him and his confusion cleared instantly. "Bloody hell," he croaked. "I'm alive?"

"You are indeed."

It was David's voice. Ian shifted his gaze and saw his brother kneeling beside him. After coughing again, he said, "What the devil are you doing here?"

"Trying to find out if I'd inherited Falkirk. I thought for sure I had it this time." David gave a lopsided smile. "You've got more lives than a cat, Ian, but you've really got to stop getting yourself killed. It's too exhausting."

"I couldn't agree more." Shaking his head to clear the water from his ears, Ian pushed himself up. David helped him get to his feet, then enfolded him in a fierce bear hug. Laura was there, too, all three of them wrapped around each other like the aerial roots of a banyan tree.

The combination of physical and emotional warmth restored Ian more than he would have believed possible. It began to sink in that he really was alive, and likely to stay so. With life came curiosity. "Is there a war going on outside?"

"No, you kept the Afghans from getting through. The pass was destroyed when the cliff collapsed," Laura replied. "There's still trouble in Afghanistan, but that's where it will stay."

"So we did it," he said softly. "We put out the fire before it could spread across India."

"Not 'we,' love—you," she said. "You're the one who deduced what the plan was, you're the one who held off an army. Pyotr must be very happy up in that onion-domed heaven of his."

"I'm glad, too." With great reluctance, Ian disentangled himself from his wife and brother. "It's been a hell of a day, and I'm really not in the mood for a war."

While Laura dug into her pack for food and brandy, David wrapped a coarse woolen blanket around Ian's shoulders. "Better use this to keep yourself warm. We still have a fairly lengthy trek out of here."

"The sooner we get out, the better." Ian swallowed a mouthful of brandy, welcoming the burn. As he accepted a rolled chapati from Laura, he added, "If either of you ever hears me express a desire to go into another cave, please hit me on the head with a rock until I change my mind."

Then, with laughter ringing in his ears and Laura's arm around his waist, Ian set off for the land of the living.

When Ian awoke, he ached all over. Nonetheless, he felt wonderful, which undoubtedly had much to do with the fact that a soft, familiar female form was wrapped around him. Opening his eye, he found that they were on a charpoy in a darkened room, with a low-burning oil lamp on a table by the bed.

It was the guest room of a Pathan compound, much like the one at Habibur's. However, this time they were with the Afridis who had taken in Laura and Gulab Khan several days before. Dimly Ian remembered the lengthy, exhausting trip out of the cave. He doubted that he could have made it that far alone.

They had emerged at dawn. Zafir and a helpful Afridi, Kuram, had been outside. They had also reached a point in the cavern where they could go no further. Ian wondered if the waterfall was the only link between the upper and lower caves. He'd been lucky, damned lucky. Or perhaps it wasn't luck; perhaps there was such a thing as iqbal.

Kuram had insisted that they come here, to the home of Gulab Khan's cousin. Ian gathered that he and Laura were entitled to lifetime hospitality because they had helped the havildar through the pass. The fact that Gulab Khan had tried to kill him was tactfully unmentioned; these little mistakes happened.

Once they reached the compound, David had said goodbye, for he must lead his troops to Jallalabad. Zafir, who was still officially on leave, decided to stay with Ian and Laura to escort them back to India. Or at least as far as Habibur's, where Zafir intended to marry Meera as soon as possible.

Ian thought that was a sound plan. He looked down at the bronze hair tumbling over his arm and the curve of Laura's cheek, and thought what an excellent idea marriage was. At least, with a wife like this one. He stroked her hair, scarcely able to believe that they were really together and safe.

Light though his touch was, it woke Laura. Her long lashes fluttered up, showing the amber depths of her amazing eyes. "How are you feeling, *doushenka*?"

"Rather as if I lost a fight with a bull elephant. Apart from that, I feel wonderful. In fact, better than wonderful."

Laura inhaled, her eyes widening. "It's gone—that darkness inside you is gone. What happened to heal it?"

"I should have guessed that you knew it was there." Ian was unsurprised that his wife understood what was going on inside his head better than he did. She was quite right; the vein of sorrow and shame that had run through the depths of his soul was gone. Experimentally he probed around inside his mind. Though he found much that he regretted, there was nothing that he couldn't live with.

"The darkness was fear," he answered, brows knit as he tried to define the mysterious shift that had taken place during his passage through the underworld. "In Bokhara, I was buried alive and died. This time, though I came within a hairsbreadth of destroying myself, I managed to survive all of the things I feared the most, including fear itself. For the first time since I was taken captive in Bokhara, I feel as if I am truly free."

"Even though you're married?"

He laughed. "That's the greatest freedom of all, Larishka, because you've seen me at my worst and are still here.'' He paused to give her a deep, leisurely kiss. "The pieces I thought were broken beyond repair seem to have cobbled themselves together again. Almost as good as new, if you don't mind a plate with lots of seams and scars.''

"That just means you're stronger in the mended places.'' She inhaled with pleasure as he found a particularly tender spot beneath her ear.

"I must be, because before I wasn't strong enough to say how much I love you.'' He opened the front of her gown, exposing her breasts, and kissed one sensitive tip. "And I do love you, Larissa Alexandrovna, my fierce, bewitching, tenacious Russian lady. I can't believe the good luck that brought us together in the face of so many unlikely circumstances.''

She caught her breath as joy spiraled through her. "I love you, too, *doushenka*, my heart and my soul. But I don't think luck had much to do with bringing us together. Kamala's astrologer said there were no accidents. Everything that happened was meant to be.''

"You may be right—the last few months have been too improbable to be the result of blind chance.'' He tugged off his robe and tossed it on the floor. "Now that you and I have peeled away all the layers of each other's secrets and fears so that we are finally down to our bare selves, the only thing left is to be happy. And speaking of bare selves . . .''

As Laura laughed, he deftly pulled her nightgown over her head so that they were flesh to flesh. Voice husky, he whispered, "To everything there is a season . . .'' As he eased into her body, his lips touched hers, warm and infinitely sweet. "And now is the season for love.''

Epilogue

❧ ❧ ❧

Scotland
August 1842

STILL IN HER nightgown, Laura gazed absently out the window of her bedroom and mentally tallied everything that must be done before her visitors arrived in midafternoon. Realistically, she knew that she had done as much as humanly possible to make the old castle comfortable. She was enjoying the task, and the sale of one of Pyotr's gems had provided the funds to do the job right. Nonetheless, she had only been here three months, and much remained to be done.

She hoped that her first house party would go well. Not only would she be meeting Ian's formidable sister for the first time, but another couple was coming. The wife, Lady Sara Connery, was the daughter of a duke, and her husband Mikahl was some sort of Himalayan prince. As she considered the prospect, Laura reflected that she would have been wiser to enter the waters of social life at a less exalted level.

Suddenly her stomach turned disastrously. She barely had time to reach the washbasin before losing the tea, buns, and marmalade which had been served when they were still in bed.

Ian chose this inauspicious moment to return from his dressing room. "What's wrong, Laura?" he said with quick concern.

"I was thinking about our guests," she said feebly.

Ian poured a glass of water and brought it to her, then put an arm around her while she drank. "I knew you were a little nervous," he said, "but not this much. Really, Laura, these are all very nice people. There's no need to tie yourself in knots." He kissed her forehead. "And if any of them have any complaints about your housekeeping, they can damned well leave. Not that they will. You've done wonders.''

Laura smiled, feeling much better, as much because of Ian's embrace as because of his words. ''Thank you for the loyal support. You really are a most agreeable spouse.'' She tilted her head back so she could see his face. ''However, while my hostess nerves are genuine, that isn't the reason I felt ill. You can stop worrying about whether you suffered any permanent damage when you were beaten in Bokhara.''

When Ian stared at her, brows drawn, she elaborated, ''I am just about certain, Lord Falkirk, that you have done your duty to carry on the family name.''

With a whoop, he swept her off her feet. Almost immediately he stopped and set her on the ground. ''Good Lord, you give me wonderful news and I promptly try to make you sick again. How are you feeling?''

''Don't worry, I made a very fast recovery.'' She grinned. ''And what I feel is vastly pleased with myself.''

''You should be.'' He touched her hair as gently as if she were fine porcelain. ''How did you know that I thought that perhaps I had lost the ability to father a child?''

''I am Russki and I know everything worth knowing.'' She put on her best mysterious Oriental expression. ''The priest who did our horoscopes in Manpur promised us a son. He didn't say anything about daughters, but most Hindus consider them not worth mentioning, so we might have one or two of them as well.''

''I'm willing. I hope at least one of them looks exactly like you. And if this is a son,'' he thought a moment, ''shall we call him Kenneth Peter, after your stepfather and uncle?''

''What a wonderful idea.'' Laura set down her glass of water, slid her arms around her husband, and wiggled her hips against him provocatively.

He grinned and lifted her in his arms. ''Just how much better are you feeling?''

''Much, much better,'' she said demurely as he carried her to their massive four-poster bed. ''But I thought you had to go see the bailiff this morning. And you're already dressed.''

''The bailiff can wait, and being dressed can be remedied,'' he said as he laid her on the mattress. Within a minute, it was.

Laura never ceased to be fascinated by the subtle nuances of lovemaking. This morning, as they celebrated the new life they had made, the theme was tenderness. After fulfillment, they lay quietly in each other's arms for a time, stealing the minutes from what would be a full day.

It was a kind of theft Laura enjoyed, for she never ceased to be enchanted by the man she had married. Since the darkness within Ian had healed, his naturally buoyant nature had proved to be a perfect complement to her Russian intensity. She loved his exuberance; at the same time, the fact that he had looked into the abyss gave him remarkable depth and sensitivity.

If the Hindus were right about reincarnation, she must have done something very, very good in her last life to deserve him. She chuckled, drawing a questioning look from her husband. According to Ian, she was still very, very good.

Laura dreamily inserted a carnation into her flower arrangement, thinking that there was nothing like the successful pursuit of kama to dispel a case of nerves. The pursuit had put her behind in her schedule; however, once she finished arranging flowers, she would have just enough time to bathe, change, and turn herself into a model hostess.

She was in a small workroom full of brilliant blooms that the gardener had cut for her. Clipping the stem of a rose, she added it to the vase. She was never able to look at roses without thinking of Kamala and Dharjistan and flurries of petals.

At first she had worried that Ian's actions in preventing a rebellion had ended her friendship with the maharani, but the week before, a letter had arrived from Dharjistan. Kamala had borne a son. Reading between the lines, Laura guessed that finally having an heir had alleviated much of Rajiv Singh's resentment of the Sirkar, for the royal throne of Dharjistan was secure for another generation. She was glad for both of them.

In fact, babies seemed to be the order of the day. A month earlier, a letter from Meera had informed her that Zafir's confidence in his virility had not been misplaced. A little Pathan was expected in the autumn, and Meera had sounded just as pleased as Laura felt.

She was finishing her fourth arrangement when an unexpected occupant of the workroom subverted her efforts. A huge, staggeringly ugly ginger cat leaped on the table and proceeded to knock over all of the vases. "You miserable beast!" she shrieked, her serenity vanishing. "We Russians have ways of dealing with insolent peasants like you."

Unmoved by the threat, the one-eyed tomcat settled in the middle of the table and began washing his face. "You're taking advantage of the fact that I have a weakness for you because of your resemblance to Ian," Laura grumbled as she got down on her knees and began retrieving fallen flowers. "But Ian is much better-looking."

She was crawling under the table to collect the last elusive bloom when the workroom door swung open. Expecting a servant, she looked up, right into the eyes of a very tall, very confident, very red-haired woman.

Hastily repressed mirth in her gray eyes, the new arrival said, "You must be Laura."

As their gazes met, Laura cringed. "And you're Juliet." So much for her intentions of impressing her new relatives with her poise and elegance. Instead she was wearing her oldest gown and crawling around on the floor after having lost a battle with the castle mouser. She gave serious consideration to going back under the table and staying there for the next fortnight.

Her sister-in-law smiled. "Right the first time, though I look so much like Ian that you don't get much credit for guessing." With a graceful flutter of skirts, she knelt so that they were eye to eye. "I'm *so* glad that you aren't the stuffy sort who is always perfect," she said warmly. "When I last saw Ian, he was going to marry a female named Georgina who sounded like the most appalling pattern card of propriety. I knew that she would despise me."

Laura sat back on her heels and began to laugh. "Actually, Georgina isn't a bad sort, though Ian is *much* better off with me. But how could you be intimidated by a mere female? From what Ian has told me about your adventures, it's hard to imagine you concerned about another woman's opinion."

As they both got to their feet, Juliet said dryly, "Only my brothers and my husband have ever appreciated my unusual talents. Most people merely think me hopelessly unladylike."

The comment gave Laura instant insight into her sister-in-law's mind. Yes, they would be friends. "Your brothers and your husband," Laura remarked. "Isn't that enough?"

Juliet smiled fondly. "Yes, it is."

Ruefully Laura examined the wreckage of her flower arrangements. "Ian will be back soon, but now he's off with the bailiff. We thought you wouldn't arrive until after luncheon."

"We rode ahead of the carriage," Juliet explained. "My fault—today I was impatient to see Falkirk and Ian again."

"No such thing, my love," a deep voice said from the doorway. "Today wasn't exceptional—you're *always* impatient."

Laura looked up into the amused face of the handsomest man she had ever seen. Weakly she said, "Lord Kilburn, I presume?"

"Ross to members of the family." He bowed. "Sorry to have disrupted your domestic arrangements. My mother always said that an early guest is among life's worst disasters."

Juliet looked stricken. "I'm sorry, Laura. Having lived at Falkirk as a girl, I think of it as my family home, with no formality required. That's why I decided to go searching for you and Ian rather than waiting." She glanced apologetically at Ross, who smiled at his wife with startling intimacy.

Laura watched in fascination. Did she and Ian gaze at each other like that, as if the two of them were alone in Eden? Very likely. Suppressing a grin, she said, "This is your family home, Juliet, and you must continue to treat it as such."

At that moment, Ian appeared in the doorway, his auburn hair windblown and his tanned face glowing with good health. "I saw the carriage in the distance and hurried back. I should have guessed you'd arrive early, Juliet."

"Ian!" Juliet spun about and launched herself into the arms of her laughing brother. As they hugged, the two Camerons began talking simultaneously, their faces showing identical expressions of vivid happiness.

"They're very alike, aren't they?" Laura said softly. "A remarkable capacity for joy."

Ross nodded, deep satisfaction in his eyes. "After Bokhara I was afraid I'd never see Ian like this again. But now he looks like he's his old self."

She smiled, "No. Better than that."

* * *

One of the modern additions to Falkirk Castle was a patio
in the back, protected from the winds and looking across
the grounds to the sea. As Laura lazed in the sun, she said
to her companions, "When Ian listed his assets and liabil-
ities as a potential husband, he told me all about Falkirk's
inconvenience and draftiness. Yet he never mentioned how
beautiful it is here."

Juliet's brows rose. "Did Ian really propose so cold-
bloodedly? I would have thought he'd have more savoir
faire."

Lady Sara Connery, who was Ross's cousin, smiled. "But
it worked, since Laura thought his pluses outweighed his
minuses."

Eyes twinkling, Laura said, "Actually, a rational analysis
of his proposal told me that I should turn him down."

The other two women turned interested gazes on their
hostess. "But . . . ?" Juliet prompted.

"I threw reason out the window and decided to grab Ian
with both hands," Laura said. "I rather fancied him, you
know."

All three women laughed. As Laura refilled her guests'
teacups, she gave a smile of satisfaction. The house party
was successful beyond her wildest dreams. Not that she
could take much credit. What mattered was the quality of
the guests, who were so full of love and happiness that there
was plenty of both to spare, even for an Oriental-eyed Russian.

Knowing that the others were connected by blood or long
friendship, Laura had assumed that she would feel like
something of an outsider, but that hadn't happened. Though
gentle Lady Sara might be the daughter of a duke, she hadn't
a trace of snobbery in her nature. And her husband Mikahl
was utterly charming, rather in the manner of Kamala's
black panther.

In another one of the coincidences that had persuaded
Laura that there were no accidents, Mikahl turned out to be
the "mountain prince" who had brought the helpful Afridi,
Kuram, to England. Kuram was in the Company army again;
recommendations from Ian and David had persuaded the
authorities to overlook the "youthful transgression" that had
caused him to leave the army in the first place.

The infant sleeping in the cradle by Juliet woke and began making discontented noises. Lady Sara said, "It sounds like the Earl of Ambridge wants to be cuddled."

As Juliet scooped up her flaxen-haired son, she said, "I hope this will appease him." She dropped a doting kiss on his tiny nose, then cradled him against her. "I have the alarming feeling that even though he has Ross's looks, he's inherited my temperament."

"A grave deficiency," Sara said, her eyes dancing. She fed a cake to her own small daughter, eighteen-month-old Maria, who had inherited her father's dark hair and striking green eyes, and her mother's sweet smile. "Speaking of earls, my father has been angling to get Mikahl an earldom. Papa doesn't approve of the fact that his only granddaughter is a commoner. The only way to fix that is to get the queen to make Mikahl an earl." She gave a smile of private amusement. "On the grounds that he's foreign royalty, which means he's worthy of a British title."

"What does Mikahl think about it?" Laura asked.

"He just laughs. I think he finds the idea vastly amusing."

Juliet leaned back, her son now smiling blissfully in her arms. "Ian is already in the House of Lords, and Ross will be when his father dies. Can you imagine what holy hell they'll raise if Mikahl joins them there?"

Sara gave a peal of laughter. "What a wonderful thought! I'll tell Papa to go ahead with his string pulling. Since the queen admires Mikahl, she should be amenable."

Maria gave a squeak of pleasure and tore down the patio steps. The three women looked after the child and saw that she was running to her father. The men had gone for a walk along the cliffs and now they were crossing the lawn to the patio, talking and laughing as their wives were doing.

When Maria reached her father, Mikahl swooped her up in the air, kissed her rosy cheek, then tucked her under his arm.

"What a splendid sight," Juliet said dreamily.

Wondering what her sister-in-law meant, Laura studied the approaching men. Ian made some comment and the other two laughed, Ross briefly putting his hand on his brother-in-law's shoulder. Laura exhaled with delight. "I see what you mean—it would be hard to find three more striking men anywhere."

"And so well matched," Sara murmured. "All the same height, but one dark, one blond, and one auburn, to make them more interesting."

"In purely abstract terms, I think Ross is probably most handsome," Laura said, attempting to be objective. It wasn't easy when her own husband was in view and he was surely the most attractive man in the world.

Sara's gaze went to Ian. "Perhaps, but there's something about a soldier that make female hearts flutter."

"What I would like to know," Juliet said thoughtfully, "is how a man like Mikahl, who looks exactly like Byron's dashing, dangerous Corsair, can at the same time look so completely natural with a giggling infant tucked under his arm."

They all laughed again. A minute later, the men reached the patio, each of them gravitating to his wife.

Laura reached up and caught Ian's hand. Softly she said, "Did I ever mention that the Brahmin priest said we were born to be together?"

Ian gave her a warm, intimate smile. "I could have told you that."